D1391900

The Court Martial
of Lord Lucan

JOHN HARRIS
The Court Martial of Lord Lucan

Severn House Publishers

This first world edition published 1987 by
SEVERN HOUSE PUBLISHERS LTD of
4 Brook Street, London W1Y 1AA

Copyright © 1987 by John Harris

British Library Cataloguing in Publication Data
Harris, John
The court martial of Lord Lucan.
I. Title
823'.914 [F]   PR6058.A6886/
ISBN 0–7278–1401–X

Printed and bound in Great Britain
at the University Printing House, Oxford

CONTENTS

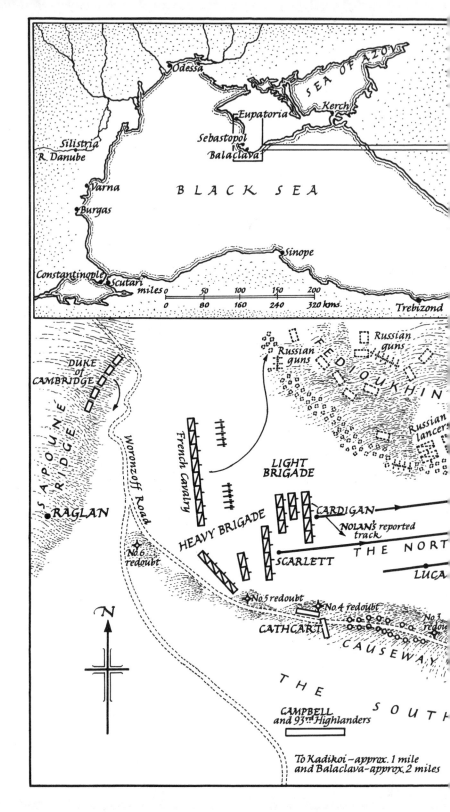

ODESSA
SEA OF AZOV
Kerch
Eupatoria
Sebastopol
Balaclava
Silistria
R. Danube
BLACK SEA
Varna
Burgas
Sinope
Constantinople Scutari
miles 0   50   100   150   200
0   80   160   240   320 kms.
Trebizond

DUKE of CAMBRIDGE
RUSSIAN guns
Russian guns
FEDIOUKHIN
SAPOUNE RIDGE
Woronzoff Road
French Cavalry
LIGHT BRIGADE
Russian lancers
RAGLAN
HEAVY BRIGADE
CARDIGAN
NOLAN'S reported track
THE NORT
SCARLETT
LUCA
No.6 redoubt
No.5 redoubt
No.4 redoubt
No.3 redou
N
CATHCART
CAUSEWAY
THE   SOUTH
CAMPBELL and 93rd Highlanders
To Kadikoi – approx. 1 mile
and Balaclava – approx. 2 miles

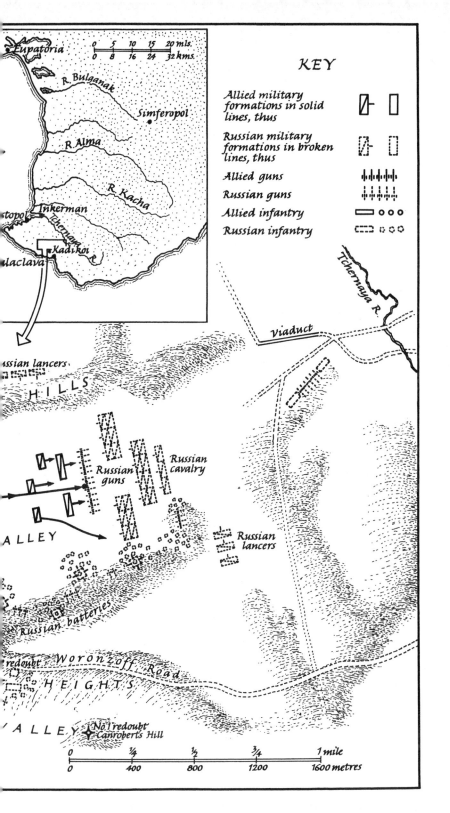

Eupatoria

R. Bulganak

Simferopol

R. Alma

R. Kacha

Inkerman

topol

Tchernaya

Kadikoi

laclava

0   5   10   15   20 mls.
0   8   16   24   32 kms.

KEY

Allied military
formations in solid
lines, thus

Russian military
formations in broken
lines, thus

Allied guns

Russian guns

Allied infantry

Russian infantry

Viaduct

Tchernaya R.

ssian lancers

H I L L S

Russian
guns

Russian
cavalry

Russian
lancers

A L L E Y

Russian batteries

redoubt   Woronzoff   Road

H E I G H T S

A L L E Y   No 1 redoubt
Canrobert's Hill

0   ¼   ½   ¾   1 mile
0   400   800   1200   1600 metres

CAST OF CHARACTERS
(fictitious characters marked with an asterisk)

The Court:

General Sir Edward Eyland (President)*
Lieutenant-General Sir Alexander Crowley*
Lieutenant-General Lord Fitzsimon*
Major-General Porter-Hobbs*
Major-General the Hon. Philip Hooe*
Colonel Rowntree*
Colonel Mortimer*
Colonel Lilley*
Colonel Woodley*
Lieutenant-Colonel Yapp*
Lieutant-Colonel Aitchison*
Lieutenant-Colonel Craufurd*
Lieutenant-Colonel Hayho*
Lieutenant-Colonel Jex*
Lieutenant-Colonel Minchin*
Mr Hector Gorvan, QC, Deputy Judge-Advocate*
Colonel Henry Harboursford, Prosecuting*
Captain George Thomas Jonas, shorthand writer*
Lord Lucan, Commander of the Cavalry Division in the
    Crimea, the accused
Mr Serjeant Souto, QC, advising Lord Lucan*
Thomas Archer, solicitor, instructing Souto*
Pizzey, clerk to Souto*

Sir Cordwell Hartop, QC, representing Lord Cardigan*

Sir Godfrey Goudge, QC, representing the family of the late Lord Raglan*

Mr Peter Quirk, QC, representing the family of the late Captain Nolan*

Mr Digby Valentine, solicitor, acting for the Nolan family*

Mr Archibald Babington, advising Quirk*

Witnesses for the Prosecution:

Major-General Sir Richard Airey, Quartermaster-General in the Crimea

Lord Cardigan, commanding the Light Brigade in the Crimea

Colonel the Hon. Somerset Calthorpe, nephew and aide to Lord Raglan

Alexander William Kinglake, historian

Colonel John Adye, aide to Lord Raglan

Major JA Ewart, aide to Lord Raglan

Sir Colin Campbell, commanding at Balaclava

Mrs Fanny Duberly, wife of Captain Duberly, 11th Hussars

Private John Arthur Lees, 17th Lancers

Witnesses for the Defence:

Colonel Edward Cooper Hodge, Commanding Officer, 4th Dragoon Guards

Lord Bingham, son of, and aide to, Lord Lucan

Lord William Paulet, Assistant Adjutant-General to Lord Lucan

Lord George Paget, Commanding Officer, 4th Light Dragoons

Colonel John Douglas, Commanding Officer, 11th Hussars

Troop Sergeant-Major Berryman, 17th Lancers

Captain Robert Portal, 4th Light Dragoons

Sergeant Albert Mitchell, 13th Light Dragoons

Captain John Brandling, Horse Artillery

Captain George Higginson, Grenadier Guards

xi

Captain William Morris, Acting Commanding Officer, 17th Lancers

William Howard Russell, of *The Times*

John Elijah Blunt, Consular Service, interpreter on Lord Lucan's staff

Henry Fitzhardinge Maxse, 13th Light Dragoons, aide to Lord Cardigan

Private G Badger, 17th Lancers

Private JW Wightman, 17th Lancers

Private William Pennington, 11th Hussars

Jack Orchard, actor*

Sergeant Robert Henderson, 12th Hussars

Mentioned in evidence:

Lord Raglan, Commander-in Chief, British Army in Crimea

Captain Louis Edward Nolan, 15th Hussars, aide to Major-General Airey

Sir John Burgoyne, Chief Engineer in Crimea

General Estcourt, Adjutant-General in Crimea

Sir George de Lacy Evans, commanding Second Division

Sir Richard England, commanding Third Division

Sir George Cathcart, commanding Fourth Division

Sir George Brown, commanding Light Division

Marshal St Arnaud, commander of the French in Crimea

General Canrobert, commander of the French on death of St Arnaud

Rustum Pasha, commander of the Turks at Sebastopol

Sir James Yorke Scarlett, commanding Heavy Brigade, Cavalry Division

JA (Tear 'Em) Roebuck, MP for Sheffield

Alfred Tennyson, Poet Laureate

Lord Aberdeen, Prime Minister during Crimean War

Duke of Newcastle, Secretary for War to Aberdeen

AUTHOR'S FOREWORD

The story of the disastrous charge of the Light Brigade at Balaclava in the Crim Tartary of Russia on 25 October 1854 is well known. Though the numbers of killed, wounded and missing were small compared with modern wars, they were enough for the light cavalry, which was always small in numbers, virtually no longer to exist. The charge took only twenty minutes from beginning to end and the army, many of whom had been able to watch from the heights surrounding the valley where the action took place, were appalled.

Lord Raglan, the Commander-in-Chief, rode down to the plain as the survivors returned and furiously accused Lord Cardigan, who had led the charge, with attacking a battery in front, contrary to all the usages of war and the customs of the service. Cardigan was untroubled and replied that he had received the order from his superior officer in front of the troops. In this he was absolutely correct, so the angry Raglan turned on Lord Lucan, commander of the Cavalry Division, who had launched the cavalry at the enemy, this time accusing him of losing the Light Brigade.

Lucan retorted by referring to the orders directing the cavalry's action which he had received from Raglan. Raglan replied that if he hadn't approved of the charge, he should not have ordered it.

Lucan's fury at the accusation startled the Commander-in-Chief who sent General Airey, his Quartermaster-General –

equivalent to a modern chief of staff – to talk him round. Airey suggested that in Lord Raglan's report on the battle no one would be blamed but, in fact, it by no means exonerated Lucan, and he wrote a letter home so that the British public should know the facts. It had, of course, to go through the proper channels – and Lucan was always a stickler for the proper channels. Having read the letter, Raglan three times sent Airey to suggest that it be withdrawn but Lord Lucan refused and the letter disappeared homewards – with Raglan's comments – on 18 December.

When it arrived, the government, already in trouble because of the mismanagement of the war, was looking for scapegoats. The middle classes in England didn't so much object to the aristocracy running the country, only that they should be fit to, and Raglan's habit of mentioning in his despatches no one but his generals and their staffs – most of whom were well-connected and many of whom bore titles – started the ball rolling.

On 23 January 1855 John Arthur ('Tear 'em') Roebuck, QC, the forceful Member of Parliament for the class-conscious Sheffield, demanded an enquiry. The country was eager for the heads of a few aristocratic officers and Lucan, by his letter, had virtually offered his own as the first. On 27 January he was recalled.

He arrived in England on the first day of March 1855, and at once sent his son, Lord Bingham, who was also his aide, to see Lord Hardinge, the Commander-in-Chief of the Army, to demand a court martial. To his surprise, it was refused. He appealed to the House of Lords and sent in another demand for a court martial. Again he was refused and in the end he never did get his court martial.

Supposing, however, that he had. This book makes that presumption.

I may have taken a few liberties with court martial procedure for the sake of the story but, with the exception of

xiv

one or two minor characters, all the people in the story existed and almost all the things they say in the book as evidence actually were said either orally or in print before, at the time of, or later than the events they refer to. I have tried not to take liberties with historical facts but if any reader should discover that some officer or ranker was elsewhere at the time he is claimed here to be giving evidence, or if some publication had not yet quite appeared when it is referred to, I can only crave indulgence and state that, while following the movements of soldiers round the world is possible, it was barely worthwhile under the circumstances. For the purpose of this book, which has to be fiction, anyway, they were all in England at the time when their presence was needed.

It is perhaps important to point out that, at this period in the history of the British Army, officers involved in courts martial had to conduct their own defence. Custom, however, allowed them to have legal advice, although it did not permit the lawyers to speak in court on behalf of their clients. As a result, although the prosecutor and the military defendant or prisoner were the only people allowed to act as advocates in the trial, the legal battle was really conducted by the lawyers who primed them with questions and objections, and sat beside them, always ready with the whispered word of advice or warning at dangerous moments.

It might be of help to the reader to explain that the mounted arm had developed into heavy and light cavalry and dragoons. Heavy cavalry, big men on big horses, often wearing armour, were used for shock action. Light cavalry, small men on fast horses, were employed mainly on reconnaissance, but, of course, each could do the other's job when necessary. By 1854 the difference had almost disappeared and Major Low, of the 4th Light Dragoons, was a man of fifteen stone, on a horse big enough to carry him. Dragoons were officially simply mounted infantry.

PART ONE

Chapter One

The wind that blew down Whitehall was bitingly cold. Above London's tilted housetops, the unbroken clouds scudded past like a fleet of galleons, grey-sailed and swift, torn to shreds by the wind that dragged away the smoke in horizontal lines from the crooked chimneys. There were not many people about and those who were leaned against the blast, the men holding on to their tall hats against the clutches of the gale, the women struggling with their vast skirts which acted like sails so that mashers waited in the doorways for a chance of a glimpse of lace pantaloons and pretty ankles.

Along the corridors of the Horse Guards, an officer, muffled against the draughts, his hands encased in grey woollen mittens, carried a file towards the office of the Commander-in-Chief. Tapping on the door, he pushed inside and headed for the fireplace. Three men were seated round the desk of the Commander-in-Chief, who looked up and gestured abruptly. 'Not now, Woollard,' he said quickly. 'Bring it back later.'

The officer's expression showed his distaste for having to climb all the stairs again, but he backed out, saying nothing, and headed back the way he had come. He was irritated, especially since the Commander-in-Chief, appointed only a few months before on the death of Lord Hardinge, was, in his opinion, no real commander-in-chief at all but just the Queen's cousin who had been given the post for no other

3

reason than that Queen Victoria enjoyed placing her near relations in positions of importance. Despite his rank, Woollard had leanings towards Equalism, and to him it seemed wrong that a man of only thirty-seven should hold the highest position in the army merely because he was a relative of the reigning monarch.

The Duke of Cambridge's sole experience of war, as Woollard well knew, was in the recent struggle with Russia in the Crimea when, despite his youth, he had been given command of the 1st (Guards) Division. It had been said, however, that at the Battle of the Alma, with orders to support the front line, he had had no idea when to act and had found himself at a loss on the approach to the river. Despite his academic know-how as a soldier and his ability to handle a division of five thousand men in line, he had shown little skill, while at Balaclava, when some fool had lost the Light Brigade, he had been slow to move when ordered to support the cavalry so that, despite what people argued, he could be said to in some way share the blame for the tragedy. At Inkerman he had once again misjudged the situation and had declined the proffered help of the French when it was badly needed, and when his horse had been killed under him had retired remarkably quickly from the field.

Reaching his office, Captain Woollard tossed the file down on his desk, sat down and picked up the copy of *The Times* that he kept in his drawer. For a while his eyes ran over the close-packed type but in the end he tossed that down also and allowed himself the luxury of a few more angry thoughts on the subject of the Duke of Cambridge.

Not noted for his aggressiveness during the war, the new Commander-in-Chief had even once suggested lifting the siege of Sebastopol, which was the whole point of the affair, and had chosen to disappear for home at the first sign of bad weather. With the newspapers filled with grotesque details of the Crimean scandals, criticism of his action had been inevitable. It was said that the Queen had been irritated by it, feeling that the only member of the Royal Family serving in Russia might at least have stayed with his men, and on a visit to Sheffield he had been greeted with cries of 'Who ran away from the Crimea?' Finally, when General Sir James Simpson, who had succeeded to the command of the army in the East after the death of its commander, Lord Raglan, had asked to be relieved, the Duke had been rejected as his successor on the grounds that 'he might fail in self-control in situations where the safety of the army might depend on coolness and self-possession'.

Woollard shifted restlessly in his chair. Yet, he thought sourly, this man, who had been rejected for command only eighteen months before, had now become chief administrator and commander of every unit in the British Isles and the British possessions overseas. To Woollard, it seemed monstrous.

Unaware of the dislike he engendered in those of his subordinates who were not toadies or place-seekers, the new Commander-in-Chief leaned forward over his desk. Opposite him, the three other men waited.

'Field-Marshal,' he said, 'what's your view?'

Field-Marshal Lord Templeton eyed his youthful superior with a look of condescension. Templeton had fought against Napoleon in the Peninsula and at Waterloo, and also in half a dozen minor wars in South Africa and New Zealand. His experience not only of army administration but also of war was immense.

'I am for court martial,' he said.

The Duke's head turned to look at the man next to Templeton. He was growing old and was hugging the fire which, because of the gusty wind, kept blowing puffs of smoke in his face.

'Tudor?'

'You know Lucan,' General Sir Owen Tudor said. 'He's a quick-tempered man and can't be relied on to keep his own counsel. He'll cause trouble.'

5

Templeton eyed Tudor with a faint expression of contempt. Tudor was big and fat and looked a little like Henry VIII. He was said, in fact, to be the descendant of one of Henry's bastards and the likeness was extraordinary, though Templeton often wondered whether Tudor deliberately cultivated the look to add weight to the rumour that he had royal blood. What Trollope had called 'lordolatry' was rife in Victoria's England so it was more than likely.

'Trouble's probably what we need,' he growled. 'Trouble might stir the army out of its sloth. We need change.'

'Change for the sake of change never works,' the Duke warned.

Templeton said nothing. He had a feeling that, though the Duke might be a good administrator, he was going to end up being a brake on everything. It might have been a good idea of the Queen to make him Commander-in-Chief because young ideas were needed, but now he was in office Templeton had a feeling he was going to take some unsticking and that he might still be there when he was old. The Duke of Wellington had clung to the office of Commander-in-Chief long after his days of usefulness had passed, sleeping most of the time and only half aware of what was going on, and look what a mess had resulted in the Crimea.

'Tudor's right,' the young man behind the desk was insisting. 'Lucan *is* a troublemaker, only a troublemaker would insist on a court martial.'

Templeton's eyebrows shot up. 'I would suggest, sir, that *that* was more the action of a man convinced of his own innocence.'

The Duke frowned. Templeton was known to be a believer in equality and to dislike the way commands and staff jobs were invariably given to wealthy or titled men, but he was being more difficult than had been expected. He turned to look at the man next to Tudor. General Sir Eustace Wykeham was as thin as a beanpole with a visage soured by a loveless marriage.

'Wykeham?'

Wykeham stirred himself. 'We all know Lucan,' he said. 'And you're quite right, of course. He *will* make trouble.'

'Dammit,' Templeton said, 'the man's been accused of a military mistake and he's not yet had a chance to answer the accusation. He should be allowed to appear before a court martial and, if he's found guilty of that mistake, his error should be made public. It would free the army from any suspicion of covering up for him. If he's found not guilty then he should be cleared of the charge.'

'Too much will be brought out.'

Unlike Wykeham, whose father was a viscount, Templeton's father had been no more than a country parson and he had dragged himself up by his own bootstraps so that, as a result, he had no regard for the snobbery that filled the army – even the country – and by which titled men gained all the plums. It was hard to explain the deference to the hereditary nobility which in recent years had become almost an epidemic as people endeavoured to claim relationship with well-placed families, but Templeton, having seen a few of them in action, had little time for it. Such young men considered their titles relieved them from any need to learn their job, and that, in Templeton's opinion, was one of the reasons for the disasters in Crimea where, but for the French, the British would have been flung neck and crop into the sea by the Russians, who if anything, were equally bad, if not worse.

'A little muck-raking,' he growled, 'might do a great deal of good.'

He knew he was not alone in his thoughts. There had been a considerable outcry in the press about the number of titled officers in high commands or on the staff (Lord Raglan, the Commander-in-Chief in the Crimea, had had five of his nephews among his aides!) and the fact that Lord Lucan had been titled had, without doubt, been one of the causes of his downfall. Templeton had never particularly liked Lucan but he was aware of the man's intelligence and was conscious of the fact that he had been plagued throughout his service in Russia by that idiot, his brother-in-law, Lord Cardigan, who wasn't fit to lead a sergeant's picket.

Wykeham was looking worried. 'We've already been through it all more than once,' he said gloomily. 'In the House of Lords, the McNeill-Tulloch report on conditions in the Crimea, and the Woodford Board to enquire into the findings of the report.'

Templeton frowned. The severe but balanced report by Sir John McNeill, a distinguished civil servant and medical man, and Colonel Alexander Tulloch had made it clear that the Commissariat Commissioner for the Crimea had suffered from administrative confusion, laziness, timidity, callousness and stupidity, with resulting shortages of food, clothing, shelter and animal fodder, and that the catastrophe of the winter had resulted in a complete breakdown in distribution even of what was available. The Enquiry Board of General Officers, which was said to have been concocted by the Horse Guards for no other reason but to rebut the findings of the report, had been composed of men who had never been near the Crimea and had exonerated both staff and regimental officers and finally pronounced, apparently, that nobody was to blame, something the general public, looking at the casualty lists, had found hard to swallow. They had called the sittings of the generals 'The White-washing Board'.

Templeton drew the attention of the others to this fact. 'Everybody said that was the only reason it had been put together,' he growled. 'To clear the army of blame. It didn't, of course, and a court martial such as has been suggested, properly conducted – and if I had my way, it *would* be properly conducted – would answer those suggestions for good and all. If the man's guilty, let him be seen to be guilty.'

Wykeham sighed. 'I dread such a thing,' he said. 'You

8

know what will happen. Lucan will quarrel with everybody. He has a foul temper and he and Cardigan will be at loggerheads at once, blaming each other for everything that went wrong. You'll remember what happened in the House when the matter was raised. Everything came to a halt as they argued with each other. The same thing happened with the Woodford Board. Those two have been used to tremendous wealth and nobody's ever said to them nay.'

The Duke looked up hopefully. 'Then you suggest there should be no court martial, Sir Eustace?'

Wykeham considered and sighed again. 'On the contrary,' he said. 'I think there should be.'

The Duke's face fell. He had expected the balance to be against a court martial. He didn't wish a court martial and he knew it was the Queen's wish that there should be no court martial. The army had come out of the Crimea without many laurels and it was the high command, not the regimental officers or the common soldiers, who had been blamed. He had no wish to see it all brought up again. He made another attempt to shelve the project.

'Aren't we making a lot out of nothing?' he said. 'Wasn't it all just the result of a quarrel between two brothers-in-law who couldn't stand each other. Everybody knows Cardigan has hated Lucan ever since Lucan married his sister and separated from her.'

'That's what everybody likes to think,' Templeton admitted. 'It's a good story and one the popular press has seized on. But it's not true. We all know they barely speak but it seems to me this quarrel of theirs had nothing whatsoever to do with the case.'

'There are many dissatisfied officers in the cavalry,' Wykeham said. 'I've spoken to a few. They consider that whereas Cardigan gained a great many honours by doing no more than he was told, and barely even that, Lucan, who after all had the courage to hold back the Heavy Brigade when it might also have been lost trying to get the Light

Brigade out of its mess, has gained nothing. Cardigan wasn't even in command. He merely led his men into action and you don't get honours for that, especially when, having arrived at the point of contact, you promptly turn round, head for home and leave them to it. His honours sprang entirely from the sentimentality of the British Public.'

'And that ass, Tennyson,' Templeton snapped. 'With his stupid poem.'

'Personally,' the Duke said slowly, 'I'm against a court martial. I feel it would do no good and it could do a lot of harm.'

'A man has been accused of one of the greatest military blunders the British army has ever suffered,' Templeton argued, indifferent to the fact that the Duke was the Queen's cousin and technically his superior officer. 'He should have the right to answer the charge. Not in the Lords, either, where the issue's political, and not in the Press where it's emotional, but in the proper surroundings, where he's judged not by idiots like that feller, Roebuck, but by other army officers who would understand. If I could, I would even direct it myself and I would instruct the officers sitting in judgement that there should be no favours – to anyone. Nobody should claim privileges, though Cardigan's bound to. This is 1857, and we must regard ourselves, *and* the army, as modern and forward-looking. The court martial should be set up and it should be set up quickly because too much time has already elapsed. And it should be fair and straightforward. If anything, it should lean towards severity, and the public should be present and the press should attend with all its appurtenances, so that it's *seen* to be fair. That is my opinion.'

'Why can't he bring a libel action against the Press?' the Duke asked fretfully. 'They're the ones who've been most vociferous against him? It would save a lot of trouble.'

'He probably prefers,' Templeton said dryly, 'to be judged by his fellow officers rather than by a jury in a civil court composed of builders, property developers and land-owners who know nothing about the subject. I know I would.'

The Duke frowned. 'How do we know they won't demand that everybody gives evidence?'

'It's to be hoped, sir,' Templeton rapped, 'that everybody who has anything to say *will* give evidence.'

'There's talk of trouble in India and, since the Crimean veterans are the only experienced troops we have, that they should be despatched there to strengthen the Indian Army.'

'The men involved can always be kept back.'

The Duke gave Templeton a sour look. He would very much have liked to have denied him his wish but he was not yet really settled into his seat as Commander-in-Chief. One of these days, he told himself, things would be different.

He cleared his throat. 'I was thinking of everybody,' he said pointedly.

Templeton frowned. 'Sir?'

The Duke flushed. 'Me,' he explained.

Templeton's face was expressionless. He didn't like the Duke very much and, like Captain Woollard, considered that he should never have been made Commander-in-Chief. He also guessed that he was afraid of the sort of baiting he'd received in Sheffield.

'Sir,' he said slowly, choosing his words, 'if you are called, then I think you should be willing.'

'To give evidence?'

'You are not accused of anything, sir.'

'It's not fitting that a member of the Royal Family should appear in the witness box in a court.'

'This would be a military court, sir, and you are a soldier and, without doubt, a witness of much that went on.'

'It can't be done, Templeton.'

Templeton sighed. 'As your Royal Highness pleases,' he said stiffly. 'I feel, however, that the presence of a royal duke among the witnesses would give the occasion a stamp of honesty, rectitude and fairness.'

'No.'

Templeton knew, like Wykeham, and indeed, like Tudor, that the Duke of Cambridge was nervous that someone might ask why he had left the field of Inkerman with a mere grazed arm when desperately wounded men had returned to the battle and led their men to the end. He wondered for a moment if it was worth trying to reach the Queen but he realised that she, too, would disagree. It was a pity, he thought, that the Royal Family could hold such important positions in a day and age when kings no longer led their troops into battle, available always to collect the honours but only too willing to shelve the responsibility when things went wrong.

The Duke was moving papers round on his desk. He had made it very clear he had no intention of being embroiled in any charges or counter-charges and was not going to lay himself open to accusations that he hadn't done his duty. Somebody was bound to make comments, he knew, and at the very least the public would be reminded of what had happened, while some of the more scurrilous newspapers might even be tempted to point out once more the date of his departure for home.

He shifted in his seat. Templeton was not bowing to his wishes and his reputation was high enough for him to be listened to, while Wykeham more than balanced Tudor. He saw that he was going to have to give way.

'Very well,' he said finally. 'Let it be arranged as soon as possible.'

Chapter Two

The chambers of Mr Serjeant Souto were decorated in green and white, quite different from the usual decorous dark brown that was deemed suitable for the rooms of men engaged in law. There were no books in evidence, not even a portrait of a judge, and the man sitting in the deep leather chair, his hands on his stick, began to wonder what he had taken on.

Nevertheless, he had heard that Souto was a good advocate and the note that had been sent round to his rooms seemed to indicate that Souto was more than willing to work with him when others more eminent had refused.

'I hear the prosecution's got Mr Hector Gorvan to advise 'em.' The little man in glasses sitting alongside him spoke quietly. 'He's good.'

'So's Souto, I'm told.'

The man in glasses shrugged. 'I'm not sure he always tries as hard as he should. I'd have advised Sir Murray Tuller. He's won most of his cases. Very highly thought of.'

'Not by me.'

The man in spectacles sighed. His client was showing all the edge of his rough tongue and he couldn't imagine him coming away from a case with the sympathy of the court.

'He'd have given them a rough passage,' he said.

'So will I, Archer. Have no fear of that,'

Thomas Archer, the solicitor, sighed again. His client

seemed to prefer the usual lordly unwillingness to indulge in conversation with individuals of lesser standing, but, after all, he had never been noted for an equable temper. Archer was all for favouring the aristocracy – it helped business – but he wasn't finding this member of the clan at all easy.

Still, he consoled himself, neither did many other people. The dispute over the Light Brigade had been going on ever since 11.20 a.m. on 25 October 1854 which was said to be the time the charge had ended and the men had straggled back to their position among the British army, decimated, destroyed and no longer of much use to their Commander-in-Chief. Accusatory pamphlets, the resource of people who could not command a hearing in any other way, had been issued with great asperity and replied to with bitterness. In January of the previous year, 1856, the report by Sir John McNeill and Colonel Tulloch had baldly attributed the destruction of the cavalry to the inefficiency, indifference and obstinacy of the Earl of Lucan and the Earl of Cardigan. There had been attacks in the Press and the two earls had rushed into print to defend themselves. In July the Chelsea Board of General Officers had handsomely exonerated them but the value of the finding had been nullified by the fact that nobody had believed it. Finally, one of the nephews of Lord Raglan, the Commander-in-Chief in the Crimea, the Hon Somerset Calthorpe, had published a book in which he had stated that after the charge Cardigan had not been present when he was wanted so that everybody had immediately jumped to the conclusion that this was meant to indicate he had not taken part in the charge at all. More pamphlets. More print. More letters to *The Times*. It seemed to have been going on for ever.

Archer had heard that the army was anxious to get the court martial moving, by which he felt they really meant 'over and done with', and for this he could hardly blame them. The continuing controversy was doing the army no good and the sooner it was over one way or the other the better.

He fiddled with his papers. Over two years had elapsed now and what had happened was history. Nobody was interested any longer, especially with trouble said to be brewing in India. Archer, who had never been out of England, was decidedly against India. He didn't understand it, didn't wish to understand it, and couldn't see why other people wished to understand it. In his view, and that of many Englishmen, India was a continent of dark-skinned natives all of whom were treacherous, dangerous, and given to unholy practices like suttee, whereby a widow burnt herself to death, and thuggee, which was the practice of strangling wayfarers with cords wrapped round their throats.

His mind came back to the task in hand. He had little hope for his client's success. Taking on the British Army was something he couldn't imagine ever succeeding. The British Army had been established a long time and would surely never take kindly to the idea of someone suggesting its leaders were less than honest, which, it seemed, was what his client intended to do. He rubbed his nose, wondering how much there was in it for him, because his client, reputed to be wealthy, in fact had had money troubles and was by no means blessed with a large income from his Irish estates.

He rubbed his nose and glanced at the other man who towered above him, tall, hook-nosed and bald. His eyes were dark and bright and he was reading *The Times*, Archer noticed, without the aid of spectacles – and at an age when it seemed to Archer positively indecent to have such good eyesight. His brows were drawn down over his eyes and one hand toyed with the dark whiskers on his cheek. There was no indication of any deterioration of health or vigour and one lean leg was crossed over the other, nonchalantly, as though he hadn't a care in the world, though Archer knew very well that he was a seething mass of anger. He could only assume that it was aristocratic good breeding that made him hide it, though on more than one occasion Archer himself had seen the towering rages of which he was capable.

'I suppose you've heard, my lord,' he said, 'that they've started assembling the witnesses. Even the rankers who were there.'

The other man nodded his approval. 'I'm glad they've got the rankers. They won't give a damn for title or position. It'll be their chance to say what they feel and they won't hesitate to say it.'

'Have you no fear, my lord, that some of them might be very much against you?'

'None at all.'

'You have a reputation for being a stickler for discipline.'

'No man ever needed to fear me if he was doing what he should.'

'I was surprised at Souto offering to take the case.'

'So was I. Damned surprised. Nothing to do with him, when all's said and done.'

'I still wish we'd gone for Tuller.'

'Dammit, Archer, stop going on about Tuller!' The black eyes glittered and the lean face flushed. 'The blasted man made it pretty clear in Brooks' that I find no favour in his eyes.'

'Nevertheless —'

'Archer, do you value the business I bring you?'

Archer wasn't so sure that he did. There wasn't a great deal of it and much of it was very acrimonious and lost him clients. On the other hand, the news that he had lost this one might well lose him still more.

'Of course, milord,' he said.

'Then, in the name of God, shut up about Tuller. Just hold your tongue and see what Souto has to say.'

During the pause that followed, Souto's door opened and a clerk, young, thin and intelligent-looking, appeared.

'My lord,' he said. 'Perhaps you'd like to come through now.'

Souto was a man of medium height, lean and almost as dark as his client.

16

'Lord Lucan,' he said, offering his hand. 'I'm glad you decided to see me.'

Lucan sat opposite his desk as he gestured at a chair. Archer, as became the lawyer in the case, chose a less comfortable chair, slightly to the rear of his client.

Souto sat down. His dark, narrow face bent over the papers on his desk and then he lifted his head and looked at Lucan. His manner was brisk and efficient.

'I'm glad you came, my lord,' he repeated, 'because my offer to act as adviser was somewhat forward and even bold.'

'Why?' Lucan asked in his brusque way.

'Why what, milord?'

'Why offer?'

Souto smiled. 'I have a young acquaintance who rode with Lord Cardigan into the Russian guns,' he said. 'Lieutenant Arthur Savage Morden, of the 8th Hussars.'

'Shewell's lot. Afraid I don't know him.'

'I would hardly expect a general of division to notice the existence of a mere cornet, which he was at the time. Nevertheless, he noticed you.'

'With generosity, I hope.'

Souto smiled. 'Not always,' he admitted. 'His letters came home and I read them all. He has two adoring elder sisters who undertook the task of copying them word for word and tracing any drawings he made, so they could be passed round the family and friends. Since mine is not a military family, as you can imagine, we were inclined to revere him rather more than he probably deserved. I would even hazard a guess that he was not always a good officer, though I suspect he has improved considerably since. He has learned a lot. In those days he was totally devoid of training. He could ride a horse but that was about all.'

'The fault of taking an officer into a regiment without first seeing to his fitness and then of neglecting it beyond teaching him how to behave in the mess.'

'I see, my Lord, that you're not unaware of what goes on.'

'I never have been.'

'Precisely. However,' Souto leaned back in his chair and, placing his hands together, rested his chin on the tips of his fingers, 'his letters from the moment he arrived in Bulgaria could hardly be said to favour you, my lord. He considered that you didn't know your job, that your orders were out-of-date, and that you interfered too much with your regiments.'

Lucan's face grew red but Souto remained unperturbed and lifted a hand to silence him as he was about to protest.

'Hear me out, my lord,' he said. 'Arthur Morden was just another young officer. A bit of a puppy, I suggest, considering himself important and perhaps even rather a braggart who thought he knew all there was to know about war. His experience at Balaclava seems to have changed him for the better. Knowing little about how to use a sword, he realised he was lucky to have escaped with his life and he has since made a point of learning. In the same way, he has also begun to study the martial arts and military history. I suggest he is better for it.'

Souto smiled. Lucan was watching him and Souto knew he was longing to tell him to get on with it, for God's sake. Souto was being deliberately long-winded, however, for reasons of his own, tormenting the other to see how long he could go before he exploded.

'Much of what young Morden wrote home,' he went on, 'was far from complimentary to your lordship. And after the battle, he wrote us a long account in which he stated quite clearly whom he considered to blame for the disaster to the Light Brigade. He then went on to recall criticisms he had heard of you on various occasions.'

'Who does he claim was to blame?'

'That, my lord, will come out in evidence. I shall not, of course, recommend calling him because he was not in a position to be much use as a witness. And that's a pity, because the Souto family would have enjoyed the opportunity for a little fame, and his parents and sisters would dearly have loved a seat in the court.'

'Go on, man, for God's sake,' Lucan snapped, his control breaking.

Souto didn't hurry. 'I might also add he had no great love for Lord Cardigan either. Or for the general officer commanding, and that in a way cancelled out his disapproval of you, my lord.'

'I'm obliged, I'm sure,' Lucan growled.

'When, however, he heard you had been recalled, he took the view that you had been shabbily treated.' Souto turned over a sheet of paper. '"I disliked Lucan,"' he read, '"but I consider him very badly treated. He is no favourite with us but we all sympathise with him and consider him badly used."'

'I'm gratified by his feelings.'

Souto smiled. 'He's interested in my daughter, Harriet,' he explained. 'She is a very pretty young woman.'

'Ha! I'm glad to hear Cupid's come to my aid. Is this why you offered to act as adviser?'

Souto gestured. 'Shall I say that when I learned you were having difficulties finding counsel who could agree with you, I remembered young Morden's letter and decided that, if a boy who came as near to death as is possible – he was three times wounded – could still consider his commanding-general had been badly used, then that commanding-general might be in need of a friend who knew the business of law.'

Lucan stiffened and his fingers tightened on his stick. 'You'll act as my adviser?' he asked.

Souto leaned forward. 'With the greatest pleasure, my lord. You will, of course, be acting as your own advocate at the trial —'

'I'm aware of army law.'

Souto refused to let himself be drawn. 'Only the prosecutor and yourself will be allowed to act as advocates, but, as I'm sure you're aware, the legal battle will really be conducted by Mr Hector Gorvan, who will be priming the prosecutor with questions, objections and, at dangerous moments, advice, and myself, who will be performing the same function on your behalf.'

Lucan sat back in his chair, satisfied. Souto's willingness to take the case seemed to hint at victory, suggesting as it did that he had been misjudged. Souto removed the satisfaction from his expression at once.

'There is one point we must consider, my lord.'

Lucan sat upright again.

'Public opinion. Your name has been too often in the papers as a result of the evictions on your estates in Ireland during the potato famine there.'

'That has nothing to do with this case.'

'The public will think so, my lord. It has a great gift for confusing issues.'

Lucan frowned. 'There were always too many useless and uneconomic plots. They could never support the families who worked them. I tried to unify them into one big holding. It was unfortunate that it happened just as the potato famine started.'

Souto gestured. 'You were undoubtedly right, sir, but it will nevertheless be held against you. There is one other thing, my lord.'

Lucan's head jerked round.

'You are not noted for the evenness of your temper.'

'Dammit —!'

Souto's hand was up again, silencing him. 'Indeed, you have a reputation for a quick temper, even for spectacular rages.'

'When I have occasion,' Lucan's voice rose.

'Nevertheless,' Souto smiled, quite unmoved, 'I would suggest that until the court martial starts you should practise control. You will need every scrap of sympathy you can get. It is very difficult to get away with accusing a senior officer, sir, as you intend to. The army will not like it. If it happened often the army would fall apart. Believe me, it will be in the army's interest to secure a verdict of guilty and they will be ardently supported by such men of experience as Lord Aberdeen, the Prime Minister at the time, and the Duke of Newcastle, who was his Secretary for War. The present Government will also not see things your way. No matter who is in office, they will consider that your plea of not guilty is an accusation of the politicians for their mismanagement of that unhappy campaign. A lot depends on calmness and I shall therefore have to refuse to take the case unless you can give me your word that you will control your tongue.'

'I shall tell the truth.'

'That's not what I asked. Hasty words are dangerous. Angry words are more dangerous still. I will need your promise that you will consider carefully everything before you speak. So far, sir, you have not done so. If I could advise a deep breath before answering any question that is put to you.'

Lucan's eyes blazed, then he paused and drew a deep breath. 'I will try,' he said.

Souto smiled. He had a feeling that, if he could be convinced, Lucan would do as he was told. A lot hung on the outcome and Souto had heard that Lucan had been picking up tips on how to conduct a court case by attending the committal proceedings of Dr Palmer, the Rugeley surgeon and racehorse owner who had been accused of poisoning a brother-sportsman.

'It wasn't too hard, was it?' he said. 'I have to warn you of this because I am quite prepared to throw up everything if things get out of hand. The press and the public are tired of the accusations and counter-accusations and will welcome an end to the case – especially if that end could come without bad temper. The circumstances of the war are well-known, of course.'

'Are they?' Lucan interrupted. 'I doubt if the circumstances surrounding any war are ever known until everybody who served in it is dead of old age.'

Souto considered the opinion, finding it more profound than he had expected.

21

'Let us say that the battles are known and Miss Florence Nightingale's work in the hospitals is known.'

Lucan snorted. 'I would suggest,' he snapped, 'that Miss Nightingale wasn't nearly so good as she made herself out to be.'

Souto had heard the rumour too, had even heard it substantiated that Miss Nightingale wasn't the gentle angel of mercy of the emotional pictures but a ruthless administrator who could just as efficiently have run a prison. But it didn't make any difference. In the eyes of the British public, she was a heroine and no one would ever believe she was flawed.

'Let us get on, my lord,' he chided gently. 'Let us return to the implications of quick temper.'

Lucan glared but Souto refused to be put off. 'Lord Cardigan will undoubtedly be called to give evidence and he, for one, is not noted for the lightness of his manner. The same applies to one or two others. It is my wish to present you as a reasonable man who does *not* make hasty decisions. I will therefore need your help in this matter.'

Lucan stiffened. 'I've promised to do my best,' he said.

'Then, perhaps, my lord, we can get down to business. Because there is a great deal to talk about. I have had information that the family of Captain Nolan, the aide who brought your orders, has every intention of defending him to the limit.'

'The man's dead. He was killed by almost the first shot.'

'Nevertheless, the family will not wish *him* accused of losing his head. I have been making enquiries about them. I have heard that his mother is of an aristocratic Italian family and that he came from an old military background. His father has been described as a distinguished Irish officer and a former British vice-consul in Milan. My clerk, Pizzey, is looking into it but it will take some overcoming. The suggestion of wealth, breeding, brains and military background will carry a lot of weight and will indicate that he knew what he was doing.'

'It didn't seem so to me.'

'That is something we must look into.'

'Now?'

'It will have more impact if we do it in court, my lord, and that involves both strategy and tactics.'

'Strategy? Tactics?'

'There are tactics and strategy in the law courts, my lord, just as there are on the battlefield. How one approaches a case, what line one should take, is the strategy. How one reacts to unexpected evidence is tactics. We must prepare our line and be ready with knowledge to counter anything unexpected. I can offer you my staff to handle the documents but we should also have someone else – someone who knows you intimately, how you think, where your papers are – to handle the more personal details and keep in touch with my clerk, Pizzey.'

'There is my son, Bingham.'

'He is capable, my lord?'

'All my family are capable.'

Souto could well believe it. 'Very well, then. Lord Bingham it shall be. Especially since there seems to be something more than mere interest in saving Captain Nolan's name. It soon became known, of course, round the Inns of Court that I had approached you and almost at once Pizzey, my clerk, received a visit from a gentleman by the name of Archibald Babington, who claims to be a cousin of Captain Nolan's. I gather he seemed to find it difficult to come to the point, and Pizzey got the distinct impression that money was being offered if I were prepared to co-operate.'

'Bad advice?'

'Something of the sort, I imagine, though nothing was said. However, it seems there *is* money available. Nolan's mother is still alive, of course, and she is very anxious to protect her dead son's reputation. The family also seems to be allied to influence and it seems that that "influence" has no wish to be associated with disaster.'

'Surely we have nothing to fear from this?'

'There is also Lord Cardigan.'

'That fool!'

Souto smiled. 'Your brother-in-law, my lord. He is noted for liking his own way. He also has no wish to be blamed. And, let's accept it, he has benefitted from the Charge more than you. He's been appointed Inspector-General of Cavalry and invited to Windsor. The fact that the Queen disapproves of his morals and preferred not to be present is by the way, and he appears to have the support of the Royal Family. He was also given a dinner at the Mansion House and he's been seen in Rotten Row on the horse he rode in the Charge. He also has enough money to be able to use it to make sure *he* is not blamed.'

Lucan was studying the other man now intently.

'There is one more thing, my lord.' Souto said. 'The Beaufort family.'

'The Beaufort family?'

'Yes, my lord. A very powerful family indeed. One the late Duke of Wellington never failed to support. Lord Raglan, the Commander-in-Chief in the Crimea, was the youngest of the Duke of Beaufort's children and he married a niece of the Duke of Wellington. He had power and influence behind him, which the family still wields.'

'Surely to God *they* wouldn't descend to the same levels as this fellow, Babington.'

'I'm sure they would not. But they will do their best, I'm convinced, to make certain the family doesn't come in for any kind of odium. We've all heard that Alexander William Kinglake, the historian, has been approached by Lady Raglan to produce a definitive history of the Crimean campaign. He was a great admirer of Lord Raglan and he, too, will not hurry to see him blamed. Now, suppose all these different and differing people came together – our friend Babington, Lord Cardigan and the Beaufort supporters, and there are plenty of them – it could be difficult.'

24

'The Beauforts would never enter into any conspiracy. Nor, damn him, would Cardigan!'

'I entirely agree, my lord. But there are hangers-on who will not be so honourable. And it has come to my notice that our friend, Archibald Babington, has already seen Lord Cardigan, not once but twice, my lord, which surely signifies something, and that he has also been seen around with one Denby Beaufort Spencer Valentine.'

'Who the devil's he?'

'A distant Beaufort cousin and a lawyer with chambers in Bankside. Not noted for his straightforwardness, I understand, but a man, I gather, who always endeavours to gain by his relationship with the family, and now a man who has undertaken to see that the family doesn't suffer in the coming court martial. The family has no wish to soil its fingers but no doubt it's not unwilling that Mr Valentine should do so on their behalf.'

'Good God!' Lucan seemed shaken.

'Exactly, my lord. However, now we have the facts and we can get down to business.'

Chapter Three

The court martial was scheduled for the first week in May 1857 and by the time it opened, the cool air of spring had changed to an unexpected gust of warm weather, though there was a breeze that stirred the last of the blossom and moved the fronds of the willows along the river near Hampton Court.

The trial had been arranged to take place in the Royal Hounslow Clubhouse near the Staines Road, the place where the officers from the Hounslow Barracks took their leisure. Plans had been drawn for a new clubhouse; a larger, better accommodation which was to contain rooms for reading, fencing, billiards, cards and smoking, where all the lively spirits of the army could gather to discuss politics, matters connected with the turf, and whether to visit the ladies some of them kept in little villas in the Bayswater or the St John's Wood areas a short cab drive away. Templeton had picked on Hounslow rather than Aldershot because it had long been connected with the cavalry and it was handy and, while he wished to keep a sharp eye on what was happening, he had no wish to travel far.

With the new loop line opened by the Windsor, Staines and South-Western Railway Company, running to Isleworth and Hounslow, a matter of fourteen miles with fifteen trains a day, taking a mere sixty minutes from Waterloo, it couldn't have been better. The frequency of the trains would allow interested civilians and the newspapermen from Fleet Street to view the proceedings and see for themselves that they were straightforward.

The Clubhouse had a ballroom – far from being as spacious as its users would have wished on the occasions when it was occupied for dancing – with smaller rooms leading off it that were normally used for dining or as retiring rooms for ladies. It was hardly large enough for what was wanted, but since it was the most commodious building in the area, it had been chosen to accommodate the large numbers of witnesses, lawyers, newspaper reporters and spectators, though if the judges should wish to debate a point in private the spectators, lawyers and press would have to retire to the draughty corridors while they discussed the matter.

The court consisted of General Sir Edward Eyland, two lieutenant-generals, two major-generals, four colonels and six lieutenant-colonels. Templeton's wish that the trial should be straightforward was being followed implicitly and with that number of judges it was considered there were too many for the junior officers to be influenced. If sides had to be taken, so be it, let them be taken.

General Sir Edward Eyland was a religious man who liked to run Bible classes for the soldiers under his command, was a member of the Total Abstinence movement, and married to a bishop's daughter. He also had a sense of humour and could be relied on to conduct the court martial with absolute impartiality. In theory, as president of the court, he could order anyone to shut up, stand up, sit down or leave the room, but he was well-versed in court-martial procedure and preferred to confine his activities to weighing evidence and attending to the military aspects of the trial and leave the conduct of the case to the Deputy Judge-Advocate, a civilian lawyer, whose duties were to ensure obedience to the rules, advise on points of law and sum up the evidence at the end so the court could deliver its verdict.

The two lieutenant-generals, Sir Alexander Crowley and Lord Fitzsimon, were considered to cancel each other out as far as influence was concerned. Templeton had selected them himself, knowing they were both outspoken and unafraid of saying what was in their minds and that they were also stubborn and would not give way under pressure. Yet he also knew them, like Eyland, to be fair and willing to see sense when it was presented to them. What the two major-generals, the four colonels and the six lieutenant-colonels thought was a matter entirely for them but, with Crowley and Fitzsimon to lead the way, he had a feeling that they would at least have the courage to say what they thought without fear of it damaging their prospects in the army.

Templeton had been watching carefully throughout all the preparations. In the last few days, an application had come from Mr Serjeant Souto suggesting that legal matters should be left to legal experts and that the custom of allowing military prisoners to have legal advice but not allowing their advisers to speak in court on their behalf should be set aside. 'It is,' Souto had suggested, 'a remnant of the old usage when all prisoners in criminal cases were denied the assistance of counsel and it was accepted that a man was considered guilty until proved innocent. Humanity and good sense have since conceded to prisoners the unfettered aid of professional legal men and I can conceive of no reason why the methods which have been found by experience to be the best adapted for the elucidation of truth in the case of Her Majesty's civilian subjects should not be equally applicable to prisoners before military tribunals.'

Templeton had not hesitated in his advice to the Duke of Cambridge. 'The application should be refused,' he said. 'Personally, I totally agree with him. It's a barbarous practice, but the present moment and this particular case is not the time to change it. We're seeking to put on a trial that will be seen to be straightforward, and any tinkering with the rules at this moment will inevitably be thought to have been done with the sole object of whitewashing the prisoner. There were too many accusations that the Woodford Board was a whitewashing affair. Let's be certain that they don't say it about this one. Justice must not only be done, it must also be seen to be done.'

A long table had been prepared for the members of the court, with the president sitting in the middle. It was covered with army blankets, and littered with papers, inkwells, pens, pencils and an array of books, among which were a Bible and several copies of *The Manual of Military Law* and *Queen's Regulations*. The duties of the members were virtually those of a jury, with Eyland as their foreman, while the duties of the judge were undertaken by the Deputy Judge-Advocate, in this case Mr Hector Gorvan, QC, whose place was at a table close to the president. He was a dark, saturnine man whom Templeton had chosen for his knowledge of court martials and who could be relied on to make sure there would be no arguments later that rules had been bent for the benefit of privilege. Two other tables at opposite sides of the room had been provided for the prosecuting officer and his advisers and for Lucan and his lawyers.

Between them was a chair for witnesses, and wooden barriers separated the central area of the room from the public, so that the court occupied the middle of the ballroom, with the public at either end of it. As the court opened, the spectators at one end consisted almost entirely of military men for whom no seats had been provided, noisy, restless and brilliant in their uniforms. The other end of the room, where seats had been provided, was solely for high-ranking officers whose interest was practical and for civilians, among whom were several women in bonnets and shawls, a fluttering little group whose eyes darted everywhere in search of gossip.

The Press had been given a table to themselves just in front of the high-ranking spectators, where they could hear clearly what was going on, and they were looking forward to revelations of scandal. They knew as well as anybody that when the troops had come home to reviews and presentations

29

of medals in Hyde Park, the discharge of maroons and set pieces of fireworks showing 'Pax,' 'Inkerman,' 'Sebastopol,' but never 'Balaclava,' and other patriotic slogans, there had been among them one or two which read 'In Mourning For A Dreadful Peace' and 'A War Disgracefully Conducted,' while among the houses of the poor there had been black flags, the slogans had been 'Starvation' and 'Misery,' and the rows of rushlights over the doors had been described as 'Watchlamps for the Dead'.

The Duke of Cambridge had jibbed at the presence of the Press because, when the court martial had been announced, he had immediately been, as he had expected, the target of their comments. 'Why should this young man,' the *Nottingham Journal* had asked, 'be raised to a position where he has the yea or nay of all things military. His experience is small and he was not noted for his devotion to duty in the Crimea.' The Sheffield newspapers had even brought up the old cry of 'Who ran away from the Crimea?'

Templeton, who had taken a firm grip on the proceedings, had refused to give way, however. 'If we are seen to be fair,' he said, 'we have nothing to fear from them,' and there they were, now, sharpening their pencils, opening their notepads and looking down their lists of witnesses and the counsel who would be taking part.

Shortly before eleven a.m., officers and men from the regiments who had taken part in the charge, newly home from the Crimea, were brought in. They were ordinary-looking men, despite the splendour of their uniforms, and to the spectators it was hard to accept that these mild-mannered men were the heroes who had ridden after Lord Cardigan down the ill-fated valley.

They were marshalled to their places by the court orderly, a troop sergeant-major of the Royals with a magnificent parade ground voice which produced an agonised expression on the faces of the civilian advisers every time he opened his mouth. As their names were called out, officers first, then sergeants, then troopers, they clicked to attention, answered and were marched out again. Their appearance had started a buzz of conversation round the court which continued until Lucan appeared, with his son, Lord Bingham, and his lawyers. They bowed to the President of the Court and sat down at the table that had been prepared for them.

'Where's Cardigan?' The words were quite distinct above the buzz of conversation, then someone noticed that the man who had led the Light Brigade down the valley had a chair to himself in the body of the court and that behind him were two legal advisers. He obviously intended to watch his own interests.

He was looking old these days, Souto noticed. There was grey in his whiskers and his eyes looked pouched and watery. He was said to be suffering badly from asthma and from the kidney ailment which had troubled him in the Crimea and which might well, like his failed marriage, be the cause of his notorious temper. Everyone knew the haughty manner which had led to him being removed from the command of the 15th Hussars in 1834. With his behaviour with women, his court cases, his duels and the sums of money he had spent to acquire his rank by purchase, his name was rarely out of the papers. Even the Queen's husband, the Prince Consort, who had become Colonel-in-Chief of the 11th Hussars, which Cardigan had eventually managed to acquire and which had escorted Albert on his arrival in England for his marriage, had decided it was not good for the Court to be associated with such a man and he had hurriedly given up the rank and title. To be fair to Cardigan, a lot of the talk, Souto knew, came from irresponsible newspapermen, but Cardigan had always relied, and still did rely, too much on the awe that sprang from wealth and no doubt brought the malice down on himself with his overbearing conduct.

As he was studying Cardigan, Lucan leaned towards him. 'They've got Harboursford to prosecute,' he whispered. 'He's considered to be one of the best brains in the army.'

31

Colonel Henry Harboursford was rising to his feet even as Lucan became silent. He wore the uniform of the Rifle Brigade and was impressive with the medals of fourteen years campaigning on his breast. They included the Kaffir Wars and the Crimea, their coloured ribbons catching the light, the metal discs clinking as he moved. As he shuffled his papers, the President of the Court, General Eyland, leaned forward.

'Is Captain Jonas present?' he asked.

An officer in the red coat of a regiment of the line rose to his feet. He was scholarly-looking and wore spectacles. In front of him was a row of pencils and a pile of notebooks.

'You are Captain George Thomas Jonas?'

'I am, sir.'

'You are, I believe, an expert in Mr Pitman's recently-invented shorthand and can therefore be expected to produce an accurate account of everything that is said in this court.'

'I can, sir.'

'You will show no fear or favour, but will put down everything that is said.'

'I will, sir.'

'Thank you.'

The proceedings began with Eyland taking the Bible and solemnly swearing to try the accused in accordance with the evidence before the court and not to disclose the verdict or the opinion of any member of the court. Lord Fitzsimon took the oath after him, followed by the other members of the court and then the shorthand writer. As they finished, Eyland nodded to Harboursford. 'Please proceed.'

Harboursford gave a little bow and lifted his papers. 'This court,' he said, 'has been convened largely on the wishes of the accused, Lieutenant-General the Earl of Lucan. Lord Lucan was the officer commanding the Cavalry Division in the Crimea, and thus at the Battle of Balaclava on 25 October 1854. Following his recall to this country in the spring of

1855, he requested a court martial to acquit him of the charges laid against him by his late Commander-in-Chief, the Lord Raglan, of having lost the Light Brigade in their magnificent, spectacular but entirely tragic action. Because of the war, the court martial could not be held until now.'

Harboursford paused, glanced at his papers, then straightened up and looked at Eyland. 'The charge, gentlemen,' he continued, 'is that, to the prejudice of good order and military discipline, he failed to take the proper precautions in the face of the enemy and that, against all the usages of war and the customs of the service, he ordered the Light Brigade to attack a battery of Russian guns in position to his front, when without the support of infantry or artillery. As you doubtless know, gentlemen, but will hear again, that attack led the Light Brigade down a mile-and-a-half-long valley towards the enemy guns. Behind those guns were ranged Russian infantry and a vast mass of Russian cavalry. On the Causeway Heights, the hills to the south overlooking the valley and well within range were the Odessa Battalions of infantry, and guns belonging to Boyanoff's Field Battery. These things, since the end of the war, we know. On the Fedioukhine Hills to the north, also within range, were more guns, more infantry and three squadrons of lancers. Lord Lucan, then, was in effect launching the Light Brigade, at that time numbering less than seven hundred men, against a fortified position and between two wings of an enemy army, together numbering thousands.'

'How do you answer the charge?' Eyland asked.

Lucan rose, stiffly, a tall figure in his general's dark frock coat. 'Not guilty, sir.' His voice was clear, brisk and unequivocal.

'I should point out, gentlemen,' Harboursford commented, 'that inevitably this charge, since the blame for the incident has been bandied about both in Parliament and in the Press, has led to accusations and counter-accusations concerning other men, two of them now dead, one of them still alive. Lord Cardigan, who actually led the Light Brigade into the fray, is here in the court. He is being advised by Sir Cordwell Hartop, QC. Other interests here being watched are those of the family of the late Lord Raglan, who died in 1855 while in command of the army in the Crimea. Their interests are naturally also being watched, in this case by Sir Godfrey Goudge, QC. There is yet one other family with interest in this case, that of the man who carried the message to Lord Lucan which brought about the launching of the Light Brigade – Captain Louis Edward Nolan. His mother is concerned for her son's honour and she is represented by Mr Peter Quirk, who is advised by Mr Archibald Babington, a member of the Nolan family.'

Eyland leaned forward, his mouth a tight line, his gingery eyebrows down. 'Before the business of this court commences,' he said slowly and clearly, 'it is my duty to remind everyone that this is nothing to do with the report put out by Sir John McNeill and Colonel Tulloch after their enquiry into the supplies of the Army in the Crimea. We are well aware what they decided about the cavalry, but let me say at once that it has nothing to do with us here.' Eyland paused. 'Nor, gentlemen, does this court have anything to do with the Board of General Officers which sat at Chelsea to examine the allegations contained in that report. I will therefore ask you to make no references to those two enquiries. There will also be no references to comments made at either of them or to their results. We will come to our own conclusions.'

Frowning, Eyland now turned to Cardigan's lawyers and the lawyers representing the Beaufort and Nolan families.

'I have also to remind you, gentlemen,' he went on, 'that while you are here representing the interests of your clients, *they* are not on trial. You may therefore advise them of their rights to object to anything you feel might be derogatory to their good name. But you do *not* have the right to question witnesses. Only one man, the accused, the Earl of Lucan, is on trial here. I wish you to remember that, and I trust you will not have cause to interrupt or interfere in any way. The charge does not concern your clients, except by default or implication, and I have no intention of permitting the court to develop a long argument about blame. Only one set of charges has been brought and I intend that those are the charges we shall hear.'

'Well,' Souto whispered to Lucan, 'that's put the opposition in its place. But have no doubt, they'll be working behind the scenes. I understand Babington had another meeting with Cardigan yesterday.'

Harboursford was speaking again. 'Your attention will first be drawn, gentlemen, to the situation that existed on that morning of 25 October 1854 —'

'Object,' Souto whispered.

Lucan frowned. 'On what grounds?'

'On the grounds that what took place started several months before. We *must* be allowed to refer to it.'

Lucan nodded. 'I object,' he said, jumping to his feet.

'On what grounds?' Eyland's brusque words echoed Lucan's own question.

'Because quite clearly what happened on the morning of 25 October was influenced by what had been happening ever since April of that year when the first British cavalry landed in the East.'

Eyland frowned. 'What possible bearing can those events have had on the morning of 25 October?'

'Tell him, a lot,' Souto whispered.

Lucan had no need to be directed what to say. He was clever, quick-witted and intelligent. 'A great deal, sir,' he said. 'Many people were influenced on 25 October by what had been happening for six months before.'

'Is this to be part of your defence?'

'It most certainly is, sir.'

'Very well. Colonel Harboursford, will you kindly re-phrase your statement?'

Harboursford gave a little bow. 'Let us say, sir, that the

court's attention will be drawn to the situation that existed on the morning of 25 October 1854, but also that you will be given a résumé of what had been happening before, from the first day British troops began to land on the shores of the Black Sea.'

Eyland looked at Lucan. 'Will that suffice, my lord?'

Lucan nodded his head in agreement and Eyland waved his hand at the prosecutor.

'You will be informed,' Harboursford went on, 'of the situation of the British army in the Crimea —'

Lucan interrupted again. 'With reference, sir, to the Battle of the Alma, the scouting of the cavalry in Bulgaria, and incidents leading up to 25 October. I require no more than references to these things, sir, so that I might bring them in if necessary as evidence.'

Lucan seemed to be enjoying himself but Eyland frowned. 'Let that be made clear, Colonel,' he said to Harboursford.

'Of course, sir. References will be made. Indeed, it was my intention to make the situation that existed quite clear. A map has been prepared which will be brought in at the proper time, which will show exactly where the different units of the British and the Russian armies were.'

'As well as the position of the commanding-general, I trust,' Lucan said.

Eyland was not the only one to frown this time and Souto decided he must make sure that Lucan, whose intelligence, he had already discovered, was mixed with arrogance and a supreme self-confidence, did not antagonise the court by overdoing it. He was already grasping the principles of his defence and he would need to be checked before he got out of hand.

'As well as the positions you mention, Lord Lucan,' Eyland agreed coldly. 'Now, please, the court would be grateful if you would allow the prosecutor to get on with his business without any more objections. I'm sure he will not forget.'

'It must be borne in mind,' Harboursford went on patiently, 'that we shall be seeing the battle as it developed and only in this way can we judge what happened. We will bring witnesses who knew exactly what was in the Commander-in-Chief's mind and witnesses to what went on when his message was received by the cavalry. The course of events will be made clear and it will be up to the court to decide where the blame lay for this now famous but still tragic event with its great and unnecessary loss of life.'

The judges were watching Harboursford closely, though the lieutenant-colonel on the end, a man by the name of Craufurd, in the uniform of the Scots Guards, was staring at Lucan, his face puzzled, as though wondering what sort of man he was examining. He was an intelligent-looking man with greying hair and a lean alert face.

'I think we must try to convince our friend on the right,' Souto whispered. 'He looks as though he might well be wondering how it came about and will be open to persuasion.'

Harboursford was speaking again, holding his papers in front of him to read from them. He seemed to have studied the behaviour of famous counsel and was rocking backwards and forwards on his heels as he spoke, easily and indifferently like an accomplished actor, as if he regarded this part of the business as unimportant and needed to retain his fire for what really mattered later.

'We need not go in depth,' he said, 'into the causes of the recent war. Let it suffice to say that Britain, the country of our dear Queen, and France, led by the Emperor Napoleon III, took the side of Turkey when in 1854 that country was threatened by Russia, which was clearly seeking to gain control of the Eastern Mediterranean, the Black Sea and the Turkish provinces in Eastern Europe. To this end, she invaded Turkish territory.'

He paused. 'The British army, one of the finest ever to leave these shores, was led by Lord Raglan as Commander-in-Chief, and consisted of six divisions, the First, the Second, the Third, the Fourth, the Light and the Cavalry Divisions. As you all know, a division is comprised of two or more brigades, and the Cavalry Division, with whom we are chiefly concerned, consisted of the Heavy Brigade, under Sir James Yorke Scarlett, and the Light Brigade, under the Earl of Cardigan. The Division as a whole was under the command of the accused, the Earl of Lucan.'

There was a little restless movement among the judges at the outlining of something they all knew but Eyland didn't question it, knowing it had been done especially for the Press and so that civilians reading the case over their breakfast, would understand how things were managed.

Again Harboursford referred to his notes. 'To give support to their eastern ally,' he went on, 'British troops began to land on the shores of the Black Sea as early as April 1854, though many of them had been in readiness in Malta much earlier than that. The intention was that they should be available to support our Turkish Allies against the Russians who had laid siege to Silistria on the Danube. To be nearer at hand, the troops were later moved to Varna some miles to the north. Lord Lucan joined his division there on 11 June. It was at Varna that the army began to suffer from the cholera which caused so many deaths. However, thanks to the assistance and advice of two young British officers, the Turks at Silistria fought well enough to oblige the Russians to raise the siege and a reconnaissance, led by Lord Cardigan with elements of the Light Brigade, was ordered to the Dobrudja area to find out whether they had withdrawn beyond the Danube. Lord Cardigan's report was that they had.'

'The damn fool came back with half his horses and men ruined,' Lucan murmured to Souto, who gestured to him to be quiet.

'To all intents and purposes,' Harboursford continued, 'the reasons for the troops being in the Middle East had now ceased to exist, but it was decided by the British government that Russia must never be allowed to cause trouble in the area again and, fearful of the Russian fleet at Sebastopol in the Crimea, which was aimed like a pistol at the head of Turkey at Constantinople, it was decided that the fortress must be reduced and the fleet destroyed. With this in mind, orders were issued to invade the Crimea.'

Souto looked about him. Everybody was listening intently, and most of them knew the story. Indeed, questions had been asked in Parliament because, once the army had been destroyed through neglect, it had suddenly occurred to everybody that the Crimean War had been one of the most pointless conflicts ever to be fought, and now that the allies had withdrawn from Sebastopol, the Russians would immediately build it up again. Souto had even heard it said that the decision to invade had been taken by Lord Aberdeen's Cabinet after a heavy dinner on a warm night when the diners were soporific after a lot of wine and were not thinking very seriously about what their decision might imply.

'On 12 September,' Harboursford continued, 'the allied troops landed at Eupatoria in the Crimea, a matter of fifty miles to the north of Sebastopol. Some, but not all, of the cavalry, was landed, and the army began its march south. There was a temporary check at the River Bulganak and a major check at the River Alma. But, as we all know, the gallantry of our soldiers carried both positions and the army advanced south to the coast, the British army taking over the port of Balaclava to support them while the French occupied the harbours of Kamiesch and Kazatch. So,' Harboursford waved his papers, 'the British and French and their Turkish allies, having taken up positions around Sebastopol, siege operations were put in hand and on 17 October the bombardment commenced.'

Harboursford was rattling his papers while he drew breath. 'On 24 October, rumours arrived that a Russian army which had gathered in the interior was on the move.

The cavalry and the Highland Brigade, under Sir Colin Campbell, were put on the alert and the following morning it fell to Lord Lucan, the commander of the Cavalry Division, and Sir Colin Campbell, who were on a tour of inspection with their staffs, to become aware that the Russian army of the interior was actually on its way.'

There was a long pause as everybody digested the information. As Harboursford became silent, a huge map was brought in and erected, where it could be seen by the whole court, and he now took up a billiard cue and began to indicate positions.

'A chain of redoubts had been erected along the Causeway Heights,' the pointer moved, 'a long line of low hills which carried the Woronzoff Road from Sebastopol to Baidar and separated the plain into two valleys, the North and the South. There were six of these redoubts and they were to guard against an attack against the British base, Balaclava, by a force approaching up the hidden North Valley. Three of the redoubts were armed with guns from HMS *Diamond* and four of them were manned by Turks. Numbers Five and Six were not manned and Number Six, due to the lack of time, was not even completed. What Lord Lucan and his staff saw on Canrobert's Hill, named after the French Commander-in-Chief, where the first redoubt had been built, was the signal that the enemy was approaching, and at that moment firing started from the redoubt. Lord George Paget, commanding the 4th Light Dragoons, hurried off to bring up the cavalry and horse artillery while a messenger was sent to inform Lord Raglan of the danger.

'Sir Colin Campbell then retired to where his Highlanders were drawn up on a small hill to the north of Balaclava, while Lord Lucan's horsemen found themselves under fire from Russian guns which were lobbing shells over the Causeway Heights from the North Valley. As the Russians captured Number One Redoubt and moved along the Causeway to capture Redoubts Number Two and Three, the cavalry found themselves in some danger and Lord Lucan moved his men towards the top of the South Valley. Meanwhile, infantry had been ordered down from the camps on the high ground round Sebastopol in an attempt to regain the lost redoubts. The first of four orders was now sent to the cavalry. It instructed them to move further under the protection of the allied guns on the Sapouné Ridge which surrounded Sebastopol and formed the western end of the plain.'

There was another long pause and the court was deathly silent, as though everybody was holding their breath.

'At this point,' Harboursford continued, 'Russian cavalry began to probe forward up the North Valley and four squadrons of them appeared over the Causeway Heights, heading towards Balaclava, which, if it had fallen, would have put the army in great peril because it was the only link between it and the sea. The Turks in the remaining redoubts immediately bolted in cowardly fashion towards the port and the Russian horsemen began to sweep down on the Highlanders.' Harboursford drew a deep breath. 'We have all heard of the magnificent stand of the Scots. Because of them, the four Russian squadrons were forced to halt and finally withdraw. As they did so, Lord Raglan sent a second order to the cavalry directing Lord Lucan to move the Heavy Brigade to the support of Sir Colin Campbell and the Turks in the remaining uncaptured redoubt. As the Heavy Brigade began to move towards Balaclava however, the main Russian cavalry force, up to now unseen from the South Valley, also appeared on the Causeway Heights. As they swept down towards Balaclava, they were met – again as we all know – by the British heavy cavalry in a charge as magnificent as anything on the day of Waterloo.'

Lucan was shifting restlessly in his seat and, seeing he was itching to interrupt, Souto laid his hand on his arm. 'Not now, my lord. Leave it to Lord Cardigan.'

'Flung into the attack solely on the initiative of their commander, Sir James Scarlett,' Harboursford's voice droned on, 'the Heavy Brigade, with some loss, drove the Russian cavalry back.' He paused. 'You may ask, gentlemen, where was the Light Brigade at this time? The Light Brigade, in fact, was positioned on the flank of the Russian host and it might have been expected that they would lend their weight to the Heavies. However, they remained where they were —'

'I object!' As Souto had expected, Cardigan was on his feet, bristling with anger.

'As one might imagine, my lord,' Eyland said gently. 'But now is not the time for objections – either by yourself or Lord Lucan. Colonel Harboursford is merely outlining his case and that not in great detail. He will be bringing witnesses, I suspect, to support his statement. That will be the time for you to object. We would therefore be grateful if you will wait.'

Cardigan sat down, muttering, a tall, handsome, pop-eyed figure.

'For whatever reason,' Harboursford continued, 'the light cavalry did not share in the Heavies' attack, and now the third of the orders to the cavalry was sent down to the plain by Lord Raglan who was watching everything that went on from his position on the Sapouné Ridge. His view was perfect and he could see the Russians retreating to the bottom of the valley to the north of the Causeway Heights, now known to posterity as the North Valley. His order read: *Cavalry to advance and take advantage of any opportunity to recover the Heights. They will be supported by the infantry, which have been ordered to advance on two fronts.* Lord Lucan, however, made no move beyond taking his men through a gap in the hills and halting them at the head of the North Valley facing towards the Russians.'

Again there was silence. Everyone knew they were reaching the climax of the drama now.

Harboursford continued. 'Some considerable time passed,' he went on, 'and, to Lord Raglan's bewilderment, the cavalry did not move. Twenty-five more minutes passed and Lord Lucan had still not moved. It was at this point that Lord Raglan lost his patience and sent a fourth, and more peremptory, order to the accused, who as commander of the cavalry, still seemed to be wondering what to do. This was the fourth order, the order that brought about the tragedy that followed. I will read it out, complete: *Lord Raglan wishes the cavalry to advance rapidly to the front – follow the enemy and try to prevent the enemy carrying away the guns. Troop Horse Artillery may accompany. French Cavalry is on your left. Immediate.* It was signed by Major-General Sir Richard Airey, the Quartermaster-General, on behalf of the Commander-in-Chief.'

For a long time, Harboursford remained silent, allowing the contents of the message to lay heavily over the court, then, like an actor who has paused to permit the effect of a dramatic sentence in a play to wash over the audience, he picked up his papers and continued.

'The message was handed to Captain Louis Edward Nolan, of the 15th Hussars, who was acting as a staff galloper, and was one of the finest horsemen in the army. Captain Nolan came from a old military family and as an experienced cavalry officer must have been well aware of what the Commander-in-Chief wished. As he swung his horse away, Lord Raglan ordered him to tell the cavalry to attack immediately.'

Harboursford cleared his throat and continued. 'It would have seemed to everybody that the order was clear. It followed the previous order instructing the cavalry to attack the Causeway Heights. It ought to have been immediately obvious to Lord Lucan what Lord Raglan wanted. Indeed, if only Lord Lucan had at some point reconnoitred the battlefield properly, he would have known *exactly* what was required. Instead, however, he launched the Light Brigade straight down the North Valley, a distance of a mile and a half – quite sufficient to wind any horse attempting it –

against a battery in position supported by infantry and cavalry, and between guns on the Causeway Heights to the south and on the Fedioukhine Hills to the north, which were also supported by infantry and cavalry. It should have been obvious that Lord Raglan could not have been contemplating such a disastrous course. Indeed, it should have been clear to the merest trooper, and, as we shall hear, many men immediately realised how slender were their chances of survival. Captain Nolan, who, you will remember, knew as an aide exactly what was in the mind of the Commander-in-Chief, realised at once that the cavalry was advancing in what was totally the wrong direction.'

Lucan's snort of disgust was echoed this time by one from Cardigan. Realising that for once in their lives they were in agreement, the two men exchanged startled glances. Harboursford had not noticed and went on with his speech.

'The Light Brigade,' he concluded, 'only six hundred and seventy-three men strong and devoid entirely of support of any kind, were allowed to advance to their destruction. One hundred and ninety-five of them rode back. Five hundred horses were lost. Why was this so? If Lord Lucan had only taken the trouble to find out what was expected of him, he would never have issued his fatal order. But was he at the time concerned with that family quarrel with Lord Cardigan, of which everyone knows? It seems very likely. And why did he not check with Captain Nolan, who knew the Commander-in-Chief's wishes? Because he was too angry with Captain Nolan's undoubted brashness on that occasion, too angry over Captain Nolan's oft-repeated criticisms.'

Harboursford paused before his final sentences. 'It is on this evidence,' he concluded, 'that you are asked to find Lord Lucan, the man who issued the unconsidered and fatal order, guilty of neglect and of hazarding his troops, against all the wishes of his commanding officer and all the usages of war.'

Chapter Four

With Harboursford's explanation of the case complete, everyone waited for his first witness.

He looked up. 'Sadly,' he went on, 'Lord Raglan is no longer with us to give his opinions as to his wishes. That noble figure was laid low by sorrow at the failure of his soldiers to succeed in the plans he had made for the attack on Sebastopol and, thus weakened, he was carried away in June 1855.' In addition to being brilliant, it seemed that Harboursford was also inclined to unctuousness. 'However,' he brightened up, 'we are fortunate enough to have with us today his Quartermaster-General, an equally distinguished and experienced soldier. Not only has he served his country well, but he has also travelled in one of her colonies, Canada, on the estates of a cousin where he built his own log cabin.'

'What in the name of God,' Lucan whispered to Souto, 'has a log cabin in Canada to do with a battle in Russia?'

Harboursford was continuing. 'He became military secretary to the Commander-in-Chief of the Army, the late Lord Hardinge, in 1852, and worked a great deal with Lord Raglan when he was Master-General of Ordnance. Indeed, it was Lord Raglan's wish to have him as his Quartermaster-General from the beginning but Lord de Ros was given that post instead and it was not until Lord de Ros fell ill that he succeeded to the position. It immediately became clear he was entirely fitted for the duties and he filled them admirably. I now call on General Airey to give his evidence.'

Airey was a tall man with side whiskers and a long nose that gave him the appearance of a bird. His manner was brisk and imperious, as if he were a man who enjoyed command. He had been criticised in the McNeill-Tulloch report for his lack of ability but he had been rescued by the Woodford Board and seemed now to feel he was blameless.

'General Airey,' Harboursford rose, smiling, almost as if he were greeting an old friend, 'since, unhappily, Lord Raglan is no longer with us, we are entirely dependent on you to learn what were his views.'

Airey nodded, as though accepting a grave responsibility.

'You are fifty-four years of age, General, and have been a soldier since you were eighteen.'

Airey nodded again. 'That's true.'

'In your capacity as Quartermaster-General to Lord Raglan you were often in contact with the officers commanding the various divisions in the Army of the Crimea: Sir George de Lacy Evans, of the Second Division, for instance; Sir George Brown, commanding the Light Division; Sir George Cathcart, commanding the Fourth Division. All of them, in fact.'

'I was.'

'As well as Lord Lucan, commanding the Cavalry Division.'

'That is so.'

'How did you find him?'

Airey frowned and hesitated. 'At headquarters,' he said eventually, 'he was considered difficult.'

'Difficult?'

'He often was.'

'In what way?'

'He continually questioned Lord Raglan's orders.'

'In any other way?'

Airey paused. 'There were complaints that his own orders were old-fashioned. He had been on half-pay for a long time and people complained that he was out of touch and had forgotten how to manoeuvre his regiments. It was felt at headquarters that, in view of the long period when he had been on half-pay, it might have been a good idea if he had taken on to his staff one of the experienced young officers from the Indian Army, who had had a great deal of cavalry experience in action. There were several of them available who offered their services. Sir James Scarlett acquired one for his staff in the person of Lieutenant Elliott, a grandson of the Earl of Minto, who happened to be in England when war broke out.'

Harboursford nodded. 'Let me cast your mind back to 25 October 1854, General. You recall that day?'

'With great clarity.'

'Perhaps you will tell us what you remember of it. From the beginning.'

Airey paused. 'I was awakened shortly after dawn by my servant,' he said, 'with the information that the Russians were on the move. Lord Raglan was already awake because a message had been sent to headquarters by Sir Colin Campbell and Lord Lucan to that effect. We immediately called for horses and rode to the Sapouné Ridge, which surrounds the port of Sebastopol, and overlooks the plain to the north of Balaclava. On the Causeway Heights, under Lord Raglan's instructions, redoubts had been built and were now manned by Turks.'

'Why Turks?'

'We were always short of men and it was considered that the Turks, never the best of soldiers, could at least manage the job of manning the redoubts. It was not expected that they would be called on to fight.'

'Exactly.' Harboursford spoke as if he were in complete agreement. 'Please continue.'

'I arrived on the edge of the Sapouné Ridge with Lord Raglan and most of his staff. It was quite clear what was happening. We could see every move the Russians made.

They had already pushed up a narrow bowl caused by a small spur projecting from the Causeway into the North Valley and the Turks' fire from the redoubts was being returned by the Russian guns. It was possible to see the round shot – like huge cricket balls – sailing over the Turks' position.'

'Where were the cavalry at this point?'

'In the South Valley just to the south of the redoubts. They were being troubled a little by the overs.'

'Overs, General?'

Everyone knew what 'overs' were but the question was for the benefit of the Press and Airey answered it politely. 'The round shot which didn't land on the Turkish position and continued in their flight to fall in the South Valley.'

'Then?'

'To avoid these the cavalry moved further up the South Valley but since, in Lord Raglan's opinion, they were still in some danger, he sent an order retiring them still further to the head of the valley, closer to the Sapouné Ridge.'

'Please continue.'

'It was then that Lord Raglan, who, of course, had a remarkably swift eye for what was happening, realised that the Russians were not aiming at Sebastopol, as he had first thought, but at Balaclava, and he ordered Lord Lucan to direct the Heavy Brigade to the assistance of Sir Colin Campbell's Highlanders, who were guarding the port.'

'Please continue.'

'A Russian probe with several squadrons of cavalry had now been joined by the main force of Russian cavalry and, by a fortunate chance, the Heavy Brigade found itself across their path. Sir James Scarlett immediately ordered a charge and the Russians were routed, returning over the Causeway and down the North Valley, some of them taking up a position behind a Russian battery stationed at the bottom, others on the Causeway, still others on the Fedioukhine Hills.'

'And then?'

'It was still possible to see everything that was happening and it became clear at once to Lord Raglan that the Russians in the captured redoubts would have to be removed. He sent down what has become known as the third order to Lord Lucan, ordering him to take advantage of any opportunity to recover the heights – that is, the Causeway Heights where the redoubts were situated.'

'Who wrote that message?'

'I wrote all messages. Lord Raglan, as you'll recall, lost an arm at Waterloo.'

'You knew exactly what he wished?'

'Exactly. He gave me his instructions and I put them on paper.'

'Please continue.'

'Infantry, of course, had long since been sent down to help in the recapture of the redoubts but for some reason, instead of preparing to accompany them, Lord Lucan did nothing. All he did was move his men into the North Valley where they faced towards the battery at the bottom. From where I stood, it was quite possible to see the Russian dispositions. It was estimated there were twenty-four thousand men, yet Lord Lucan —'

Harboursford held up his hand. 'One moment, General, please. You could see *everything*? All the Russians? The positions they were holding?'

'Quite clearly. It was even possible to recognise individual British Officers. I myself clearly saw Colonel Douglas of the 11th Hussars, and Captain Morris of the 17th.'

'What was Lord Raglan's opinion at this moment?'

'He couldn't understand why the cavalry made no move. The infantry which had been ordered down in support were on their way, and there seemed no reason why the cavalry should not be advancing on the captured redoubts. It seemed a simple matter from where I stood.'

'Please continue.'

'It was then seen that the Russians seemed to be making a move to remove the guns from the captured redoubts. Teams of horses with lassoo tackle were moving along the Causeway and, with the guns in danger of being lost, it was necessary to recapture them before they disappeared. Lord Raglan therefore ordered the cavalry to move quickly forward to this task before it was too late. "Inform them," he told me, "that they may take a troop of horse artillery with them and tell them French cavalry will support them on their left." He then sent off an aide to ask the French cavalry to be prepared to move forward, and turned to me and said "Mark the order *immediate*, Airey." This I did.'

'We have heard the message. Please read it again.'

Airey lifted a sheet of paper he held in his hand: '*Lord Raglan wishes the cavalry to advance rapidly to the front – follow the enemy and try to prevent the enemy carrying away the guns. Troop Horse Artillery may accompany. French Cavalry is on your left. Immediate.* It is followed by my signature.'

'Good. I see.' Harboursford made a great show of having understood. 'And then?'

'The most direct route to the valley was by a narrow track down the precipitous face of the Sapouné Ridge and it required a good horseman if the order was to arrive quickly. Captain Louis Nolan was at hand. He was one of the finest riders in the army and a brilliant and experienced soldier. Lord Raglan indicated that the order should be carried by him. Nolan was always eager and he leapt for his horse. Lord Raglan called after him, "Tell Lord Lucan the cavalry is to attack immediately."'

'That, in fact, ended your part in the affair? Until it was over.'

'Indeed.'

'You saw the Charge?'

'I did. The Light Brigade advanced steadily towards the Russian guns but, of course, it was on the wrong course –

down the valley instead of towards the redoubts on the Causeway Heights. Captain Nolan, seeing what was wrong, endeavoured to gallop across their front to turn them on to the right path, but unfortunately he was hit by a splinter from what was almost the first shell fired at them. He was killed before he could succeed in his task and the Light Brigade continued on its fatal course down the valley.'

'To its own destruction,' Harboursford concluded. 'Well, we need not here go into that. It has little bearing on what happened before, which is what we are seeking to elucidate. But tell us what happened afterwards.'

'We watched the Light Brigade disappear into the smoke. The Heavy Brigade which had moved forward in support turned back before they could give any help whatsoever. Then we saw the dismounted and wounded men returning. Mrs Duberly —'

'Who is Mrs Duberly?' Eyland asked. He knew perfectly well who Mrs Duberly was but he wished the court to hear.

'The wife of Captain Duberly, of the 11th Hussars, sir,' Harboursford said. 'She was an eye-witness of the whole campaign. She had arrived from Balaclava to watch the battle from the Heights.'

'Was that normal?' Eyland asked.

'There were several civilians with the army, sir. Even one or two ladies. Lord Raglan raised no objection.'

'I would have,' Eyland observed acidly. 'Go on.'

Airey coughed, a little put out by the comment. 'Mrs Duberly saw the men on foot returning,' he went on, 'and asked who the stragglers were. There were so few.'

Eyland looked at Harboursford. 'This is evidence as to what happened, Colonel?' he asked.

Harboursford gestured. 'It is an indication of how badly the Light Brigade had been cut up, sir.'

'I see.' Eyland nodded at Airey. 'Go on.'

'Eventually, Lord Raglan and his staff rode down from the Sapouné Ridge to the head of the valley where the Light

Brigade was trying to reassemble. They were, of course, much mixed up, and there were many wounded and dying. Injured horses were being shot and I saw Captain Morris of the 17th brought in. Lord Raglan was a man of a very sensitive spirit and he was, of course, distressed at the wounded and dying.'

Eyland leaned forward. 'What did he expect in a battle?' he remarked sharply.

Once more Airey looked a little disconcerted. 'He always felt great care for his men, sir,' he explained. 'He was also very angry that his orders had not been followed. He rode up to Lord Cardigan, who was sitting on his horse. His jacket was unfastened and his overalls were slit. Lord Raglan was gesticulating. Or perhaps I should say the stump of his arm that had been amputated in 1815 was moving.'

'What did he say?'

'He said, "What do you mean, sir, by attacking a battery in front, contrary to all the usages of war and the customs of the service?" Lord Cardigan replied, "My lord, I hope you will not blame me. I received the order to attack from my superior officer in front of the troops."'

'His superior officer being Lord Lucan?'

'Yes.'

'Did Lord Raglan then approach Lord Lucan?'

'He did. He said "You have lost the Light Brigade."'

'What did Lord Lucan reply?'

'He protested his innocence, of course. I don't recall the exact words. Farriers' pistols were going off all round us as injured horses were put out of their misery and there was a lot of shouting and a great deal of crying and moaning from the injured. But the following day – or it may have been the day after – Lord Lucan appeared at headquarters. He seemed to be very angry.'

'With damn good reason,' Lucan muttered.

'He had come to face the Commander-in-Chief over the accusation that he had lost the Light Brigade,' Airey said.

'He insisted that what the fourth order had said was not what Lord Raglan had meant, which of course was ridiculous. It should have been quite clear that the fourth order had to be read in conjuction with the third order and that the instruction to advance to the front was the instruction to advance as stated in the third order – to the Causeway Heights. In reply to Lord Lucan, Lord Raglan said that Lord Lucan, who was a lieutenant-general, should have exercised his discretion and, if he did not approve of the charge, should not have ordered it. There was some argument. Lord Lucan was very difficult.' Airey paused. 'Lord Raglan showed his appreciation of the men's efforts, of course, by going down to the Light Brigade camp on 27 October. The men ran out in their shirtsleeves to cheer him.'

'Did Lord Raglan inform the government of what had happened?'

'He wrote a personal letter to the Duke of Newcastle.'

'Saying what?'

'I forget exactly. But I remember he said the cavalry commander had made a "fatal mistake" and that the written order sent to him did not insist that he should attack at all hazards and contained no expressions that could bear that construction.'

'I thought,' Eyland looked puzzled, 'I thought Lord Raglan told Captain Nolan to inform Lord Lucan that the cavalry was to attack *at once*.'

'Yes, sir, he did.' Airey seemed uncertain suddenly. 'But *that* was a verbal instruction. Lord Raglan even sent me down to see Lord Lucan to try to get him into a better mood. I told Lord Lucan that he need not worry because Lord Raglan's report did not lay the blame on him.'

'But in his letter to the Duke of Newcastle, surely he did lay the blame on him?' Eyland was leaning forward, frowning.

'That was a *private* letter, sir.'

Eyland gave Airey a long stare, then nodded and sat back.

'Lord Raglan's despatch made it clear that what had happened had arisen from some misconception of the order to advance so that Lord Lucan considered he was bound to attack at all hazards. He was doing his best to make the blame as light as possible.'

Lord Fitzsimon whispered to Eyland then turned to address Airey. 'Did you consider Lord Lucan to blame?' he asked.

Airey stiffened. 'Of course, sir. Lord Raglan's orders were clear. Yet he didn't consider the men themselves had let him down. Indeed, he paid tribute to their conduct in a general order to the army four days later. It was then considered that the matter was over and done with and, of course, soon after that came the fight on Mount Inkerman and then we were heavily involved with the unhappy events of the winter. Lord Raglan was made a field-marshal for the victories of Alma, Inkerman and Balaclava.'

'Balaclava was considered a victory?' Eyland asked.

'The Russians were repulsed, sir,'

Eyland nodded.

'Lord Raglan was quite prepared to forget and forgive sir,' Airey said. 'But Lord Lucan worsened the situation by insisting on writing a letter home, so that the public in England, he said, should know what had happened. Lord Raglan was very distressed by its contents. Three times he sent me to ask him to withdraw it. But Lord Lucan refused and the letter was accordingly sent off on 18 December. On 27 January, the Duke of Newcastle wrote recalling Lord Lucan to England.'

Sir Alexander Crowley was whispering to Eyland now and, as Eyland gestured, it was Crowley who addressed Airey.

'As Quartermaster-General,' he said, 'you were witness to *all* the exchanges between Lord Lucan and the commander-in-chief?'

Airey shrugged modestly. 'Not all of them. Most of them.

'Am I right in assuming there had been trouble between them on many occasions?'

'I suppose there had,' Airey agreed. 'Lord Lucan was not noted for the calmness of his disposition,' Lucan's lips parted in a savage smile, as if he were amused by the description, 'and there were many occasions when he brought his complaints to Lord Raglan.'

'How did Lord Raglan react?'

'Lord Raglan was a man of gentle and sweet disposition. It was always his endeavour to calm Lord Lucan down and, of course, he always took into account that Lord Lucan had been on half-pay for many years —'

'How many?'

'Seventeen, to be exact.'

Chapter Five

The assembling of the court, the instructions to the lawyers, the introduction of the witnesses, had taken a lot of time and it was already growing dark as Harboursford sat down. It could be seen that Lucan was deep in conversation with Souto, and for a while, as the court waited, they continued to talk together.

Growing impatient, Eyland rapped on the bench in front of him.

'We would be glad if the accused would intimate whether he has any questions to put to the witness,' he said.

Lucan, arrogant, self-confident and supremely indifferent, ignored him for a few seconds longer, then he rose. 'I do have, sir.'

'Many?'

'Many, sir.'

Eyland looked about the courtroom. The gas lights had been lit, their yellow glow giving the faces below them a harsh strained look. Eyland conferred with the men on either side of him, who in their turn conferred with the men alongside them. Eventually heads nodded back and forth as messages were passed along the line to Eyland. 'In that case,' Eyland said, 'the court will rise and will gather again tomorrow morning.'

As he rose, everyone else rose, in a flurry of black gowns, wigs, and scarlet, blue and green tunics and gold braid. A murmur of voices came from the public section of the spectators as women rose, adjusted their hats and dresses and began to turn towards the doors.

As the court emptied, Souto looked at Lucan. 'We have a long way to go still, my lord.'

Lucan frowned. 'How do you think it looks?'

'So far, it's impossible to say. But so far also, nothing unexpected has turned up so we have nothing unexpected to fear.'

'Call General Airey.'

When the court commenced the following day, the temperature had increased considerably, so much so that the women in the public area carried sunshades and fans.

Airey headed for the witness's chair, confident in manner and certain that his reputation was unlikely to be touched. Harboursford crossed over and spoke quietly to him for a moment or two before returning to his table as Eyland and the other judges filed in, fifteen men hot and red-faced in brilliant uniforms that were ill-suited to the heat. They were men well used to making decisions and to Templeton, sitting at the back of the court, they seemed to be looking forward to the day's evidence.

By this time, Souto had managed to identify them. In addition to Eyland and the two lieutenant-generals, Crowley and Lord Fitzsimon, he could now recognise Major-General Porter-Hobbs and Major-General the Hon Philip Hooe, and was even beginning to sort out the colonels, Rowntree, Mortimer, Lilley and Woodley, and the lieutenant-colonels, Yapp, Aitchison, Craufurd, Hayho, Jex and Minchin. He had even separated them into Fors and Againsts. Eyland and the two lieutenant-generals, he had decided, were neutral and would make up their minds purely from the evidence. Porter-Hobbs, a red-faced pompous-looking man, he felt would come down on the side of the army whatever was said, but Hooe might well side with Lucan, if only

57

because he belonged to the same close company of the nobility. As for the colonels and lieutenant-colonels, he had decided that while Rowntree, Lilley, and Craufurd might be for Lucan, the others all might well be against.

Eyland was looking now at Lucan and nodding. 'You may begin your questioning, my lord,' he said.

Airey seemed to brace himself but he still looked supremely self-confident as Lucan rose, his hand clasping a set of papers on which questions had been written down for him by Souto in red ink.

He looked at Eyland. 'Before I start, sir,' he said, 'I should perhaps make a request of the court. I shall need to present the facts of the case in the right order. By that, sir, I mean *my* right order, not the right order of the prosecution. The order, in other words, that will allow my story to be properly told, in its proper context, and with proper stress on the salient facts as they affect *my* case.'

'That doesn't seem unreasonable, my lord,' Eyland said.

'It must be accepted also that much of my evidence will of necessity appear in the course of the court martial as I question witnesses, but naturally, I am open to explain things further when my turn comes to submit myself to cross-examination.'

Eyland nodded. 'I think we understand that, my lord.'

'However,' Lucan paused, 'it does seem possible that in my endeavours to present my side of the story I might need to recall witnesses.'

Eyland frowned.

'After they have given their evidence? That's most unusual.'

'But not unknown, sir, in the interests of justice.'

Eyland considered this. His brief was to see that justice was done, no matter how it affected the case.

'Will there be many?' he asked.

Lucan glanced at Souto. They had worked out just whose evidence would be likely to have the greatest effect if the witness was recalled. 'I trust not, sir,' he said. 'Perhaps none at all.'

'This is absolutely necessary?'

'In the interests of justice, sir, yes.'

Eyland considered it for a while, then conferred with the officers immediately to his left and right.

'Very well, my lord,' he said. 'In the interests of justice. But I would ask you to keep the numbers as small as possible.'

'I will endeavour to do so, sir.'

Lucan picked up his papers again and turned to the witness. 'Let us go back to the beginning, General Airey.' he said slowly. He faced the general squarely, his handsome features dark and angry, his black eyes glittering, an expression of contempt on his face.

'First of all, sir, yourself. We have been informed by the prosecutor that you are a distinguished and experienced soldier who has been in uniform since the age of eighteen and that you are now fifty-four years of age.'

Airey nodded. 'Yes.'

'What about the staff who worked with you? Were they good at their job?'

'Excellent. They were young but were hand-picked. Lord Raglan chose them himself as far as possible.

'I see. And were these among the people who considered me out of touch?'

'I fear they did.'

'Very well. Let us have a look at this question of my competence. You have informed the court that before the Crimea I had been on half-pay for seventeen years.'

'I believe that to be true.'

'But were you aware that I joined the army in the year after Waterloo and served continually from that moment until going on half-pay to attend to family business in 1837 – twenty-two years, in fact.'

'I *was* aware, my lord.'

'I won't trouble you with my reputation but I can say,

without boasting, that unlike many who acquire command, I did not sit back and enjoy myself. Are you aware that when I became colonel of the 17th Lancers I spent a great deal of my own money in an attempt to improve the regiment's efficiency?'

'I have heard so, sir.'

'Have you also heard that, in the long peace after Waterloo when there was little opportunity for active experience, I obtained leave in 1828 to join the Russian army as a volunteer against the Turks in Bulgaria, and fought at Varna, Widdin and Shumla, on the very ground, in fact, where the first engagements of the recent campaign were fought.'

'I have heard that, too, my lord.' Airey was trying hard to appear fair.

'Had you also heard that I commanded a cavalry division under the walls of Adrianople in 1829 and that when I returned to England I bore the Russian Order of St Anne, a good reputation as a soldier and a sound knowledge of both Russians and Turks? I will quote from a letter I brought back. It states that I was indifferent to discomfort and showed great physical courage. It says "Lord Bingham," as I was then, "never let slip an opportunity to be in the fighting." I also have here a copy of a note from the British Ambassador to Russia which states that my conduct was such as to draw the attention of the Tsar, who chided me for too frequently exposing myself to death.'

'I have heard that also.'

Lucan handed the sheets of paper to Eyland before continuing. 'I also brought back with me, sir, from a close acquaintance with the Cossacks, some useful ideas about the lance, and I might say that I probably knew more about the Russian army than anyone else of that day – or even of this, until the recent campaign in the Crimea. It is significant that I had a low opinion of their cavalry.' Lucan paused. 'Perhaps,' he went on, 'you did not know that when the recent war started, I offered my services at once, imagining that, since I knew the area where fighting was taking place and since I had fought with the Russians against the Turks, my experience might be of value to the Commander-in-Chief, whoever he was to be?'

'I was not aware of that fact.'

'It seemed to me,' Lucan went on, 'that to have my old enemies as allies and my old allies as enemies would be of great advantage. However, despite this, I was modest enough to suggest that I be given only a brigade of infantry. Were you aware of that?'

'No, sir, I wasn't.'

'As it happened, I was given the Cavalry Division. But that is old history now.' Lucan smiled. 'We have now heard my record of service – active service – before the recent war. Might I ask what *yours* was, sir?'

Airey was caught unawares. 'I served from the age of eighteen,' he said.

'Doing what, sir?'

'I was a colonel at the age of thirty-five.'

'By purchase, sir. I was a colonel at twenty-six, by the same method. It means little beyond the fact that you, like me, had sufficient money to ensure your promotion. What else, sir? Apart from building a log cabin in Canada. Before the recent campaign, had you ever seen active service?'

Airey had gone red. 'No' he said.

'And your duties from the age of thirty-five were entirely on the staff at the Horse Guards?'

'Yes.'

'Yet you presume to suggest that I didn't know my job.'

Airey started to interrupt but Lucan waved him to silence. Souto was watching his client with delighted pleasure. He had known Lucan was no fool but he had never expected him to learn a new trade so quickly. It looked as if, so long as he was fed with the right questions, he could safely handle them.

Lucan was speaking again. 'We have heard it said that

Lord Raglan died because he was heart-broken at the failure of his soldiers to make a success of the plans he had formulated.'

'That is so.'

'Because the men failed to succeed in carrying out his orders?'

'Exactly.'

'I trust those orders were clearer than the ones I was presented with at Balaclava,' Lucan snapped. 'In fact, Lord Raglan died of nothing so romantic as a broken heart but of the disease which killed so many – Crimean fever, or more plainly, cholera.' As Airey attempted to interrupt, he was once more waved to silence and Lucan continued. 'You became Quartermaster-General, we have heard, in succession to Lord de Ros, who had been sent home ill. What was the matter with Lord de Ros?'

Airey paused. 'He had sunstroke.'

'Sunstroke? Please be exact.'

'He had too much sun.'

'Why?'

Airey looked cautiously at Lucan. 'It was his habit to lie in the sun. He believed the sun had medical qualities when the body was exposed to it.'

'But he took too much.'

'Yes.'

Lucan nodded and said nothing. There was a long silence in which what he was implying became obvious. The staff that Airey was so proud of seemed to contain at least one strange character, and that character was the then Quartermaster-General, after the Commander-in-Chief one of the most important men in the army in the East. Heads turned and there was some whispering, and it was clear that more than one of the spectators was wondering if Lord de Ros's curious habits were perhaps the cause of so much going wrong in the Crimea. If he hadn't had the sense to make sure he didn't get too much sun, perhaps he hadn't had the sense to look after the army.

Lucan looked up. 'Lord Raglan,' he said. 'The Commander-in-Chief. What are we to know about him?'

'He was a great gentleman.'

'Was he indeed?'

'His concern was always for his soldiers.'

Lucan's eyes narrowed. 'Then why,' he snapped, 'did only four thousand of them die of wounds and sixteen thousand of them of disease? *That* doesn't seem to indicate concern.'

Airey looked furious and glanced at Eyland. 'Sir, I must object to this line of questioning.'

Eyland blinked. 'You raised the matter, General, with your comments on Lord Raglan.'

'Surely we're not here to libel a dead man?'

Eyland considered. He had been informed by Lord Templeton that he had to be entirely fair and that he was to allow nothing to slip out of sight that had to be brought out into daylight.

'Nobody wishes to libel anybody, sir,' he said. 'I'm sure the noble lord opposite you wishes only to extract the truth. Please answer his questions to the best of your ability.' He turned. 'On the other hand, perhaps the noble lord will note that the proper place for such remarks is at the end in your summing-up.'

Lucan, who was waiting patiently, bowed. 'Let me offer some figures, gentlemen. In one month three hundred and thirty men died in the hospitals from scurvy, dysentery, typhoid and other diseases, and during the worst of the winter the rate was worse. By Christmas 1854, eleven thousand men had been admitted to the hospitals rotten with disease but only about a hundred with war wounds. That total rose higher in January. Altogether sixteen thousand, three hundred died of diseases, while thirteen thousand were invalided. In contrast, only two thousand, six hundred and sixty were killed in action and one thousand, seven hundred and sixty died of wounds. In other words, it was disease that removed nearly half of the ninety-four thousand men who embarked for the east. How was it that Lord Raglan, in the words of the witness that paragon of virtue, that noble-minded man who cared so much for his troops, allowed this to happen?'

Airey could restrain himself no longer. 'He was unable to do anything about it!' he said angrily.

Lucan eyed him coldly. 'He had six months or more to become aware of the deficiences and have them put right, yet apparently he did nothing of the sort, and nothing *was* put right. You have heard of Earl Grey?'

Airey looked wary. 'Yes, I have,' he said. 'A very distinguished man.'

'Have you heard his comment on the failings in the Crimea? "It was the leadership," he claimed, "not the system. Raglan compared with Wellington. Wellington didn't hesitate to dismiss officers who failed in their duty, whereas Lord Raglan neither knew of the failings that emerged nor dismissed the men responsible when he *was* informed."' He looked again at Airey. 'You were offering *your* opinion on Lord Raglan —'

'Does the character of Lord Raglan have any bearing on what happened at Balaclava?' Lord Fitzsimon asked.

'It most certainly does, sir,' Lucan said.

As Fitzsimon subsided, Lucan turned to Airey. 'Lord Raglan?' he prompted.

Airey drew a deep defiant breath and glared at his tormentor. 'He was a man of retiring nature entirely without vices.' It was obvious he didn't hold the same opinion of Lucan. 'He was gentle and kind and always considerate to the people round him. He —'

'As a soldier, sir,' Lucan snapped.

Airey stopped dead. 'He had enormous experience, of course.'

'Where?'

'In the Peninsula and at Waterloo.'

'And since?'

'In the embassies of Paris, the Porte and St Petersburg. Then as military secretary to the Duke of Wellington.'

'In an office?'

'Yes.'

'For forty years. Longer off the battlefield than I was.'

'I don't see —'

'Never mind.' Lucan cut him short. 'Let us turn elsewhere. In the Light Brigade's action, apart from the soldiers themselves, there were four main actors, were there not? Myself, the Earl of Cardigan, Lord Raglan, the Commander-in-Chief, and Captain Nolan who carried the message. Perhaps five, sir, if we include yourself.'

Airey looked like a cat wondering which way to jump.

'Let us go back to the beginning,' Lucan said. 'The very beginning. Let us go back to the moment when the troops began to gather in the Middle East.'

Harboursford was on his feet. 'Sir,' he objected, 'has this really anything to do with the events of 25 October? It occurred six months before.'

Eyland looked at Lucan. 'Has it anything to do with the events of 25 October, my lord?'

'It has indeed, sir. It has a great deal to do with it.'

As Eyland waved, Lucan turned again to Airey. 'When Lord de Ros went home, you gave up command of a brigade in the Light Division and became Lord Raglan's Quartermaster-General?'

'That is so.'

'A position which, because of Lord Raglan's retiring nature, gave you more power than a divisional commander. You had been translated from a mere brigadier to someone who, because of Lord Raglan's dislike of show, to which you have already referred, was often mistaken for Lord Raglan's second-in-command.'

Airey looked modest. 'Lord Raglan had many things on his mind and left things to me,' he said.

'Doubtless,' Lucan snapped, 'he was writing some of the

ridiculous letters that were sent to the cavalry. One, I remember, requested them to keep out of the sun, take care of the horses and feed them well; another said he had meant to give orders to let officers share the rum ration but had forgotten.' Lucan turned to Eyland. 'It was a period, gentlemen,' he said, 'when too much discipline changed to too little. Shaving became optional, stocks were abandoned, jackets left open and officers appeared in mufti whenever possible. I felt it my duty to bring back some order to the cavalry, because, while two great powers, France and England, were showing only ineptitude, the Sick Man of Europe – Turkey – was carrying off all the laurels with its fighting defence of Silistria.'

Airey said nothing and Lucan continued briskly. 'Captain Nolan was on your staff. And had been before your translation to Quartermaster-General. Why? What qualities did he have to recommend him?'

'He was a brilliant officer and a brilliant trainer of horses. He had a great gift for languages. He wrote two books on the cavalry.'

'What else?'

'He came from an old army family and after service with the Austrian army was persuaded because of his skill and ability to return to England, I understand by high-ranking officers at the Horse Guards. His father was a distinguished Irish officer who was vice-consul in Milan where he married an Italian lady of high birth.'

'We seem to hear about this brilliant family from all corners. What else?'

'Captain Nolan had visited Russia and attended a review at which he saw Cossack and Circassian cavalry demonstrate their control of horse and weapon. The Duke of Cambridge thought him a most indefatigable man and an excellent riding master. He commanded the detachment of the 15th Hussars at the funeral of the Duke of Wellington. When Lord de Ros returned to England and I took his place I took

Captain Nolan with me, believing he would be a great asset with his knowledge of cavalry and of war. He was a very gallant officer.'

'The Duke of Wellington made a remark about gallant officers,' Lucan commented. ' "There is nothing on earth so stupid," he said, "as a gallant officer." He considered gallantry without skill was valueless and could result in the deaths of many men.'

'Captain Nolan was far from stupid. He was very experienced.'

Lucan didn't argue. 'I believe he had been given instructions to acquire remounts,' he said.

'That's correct.' Airey seemed to feel he was on safer ground. 'He was a great judge of horses. If anyone could provide good horses as remounts, he could.'

'How many did he acquire?'

'I don't know.'

Lucan held up a ledger. 'I do, sir,' he snapped. 'As commander of the cavalry it was my job so to do.' He turned to Eyland. 'Thirty-five, sir. He had been in the Middle East for some time but he had acquired no more than thirty-five.' He handed the ledger over to be perused.

'I understand he couldn't find them large enough,' Airey said.

'Very well. So why did he not buy baggage horses? The army was in desperate need of them and he could have bought them by the hundred. Why did he not do so?'

'He had no authority to do so.'

'Why not?'

'It was not in his orders. Other officers were looking for baggage horses.'

'Is this how the staff functioned? The horses were there, under his nose but, because he had no authority to buy them, they remained unbought and the army remained short of baggage animals throughout the campaign. Indeed, during the winter, cavalry chargers had to be used for the job, did they not?'

There was silence for a moment.

'Lord Cardigan,' Lucan continued. 'When did he join his troops?'

'He arrived at Scutari on 24 May.'

'Having come via Paris.'

Cardigan was on his feet. 'What is the noble lord implying?' he demanded loudly.

Lucan swung round and all the old hatred between the two men crackled like electricity. 'The noble lord is implying nothing,' he snapped back.

The dislike between the two brothers-in-law was well-known. The only things they had in common were their temper and their aristocratic arrogance and everybody was expecting sparks to fly before the day was out, but this time Cardigan subsided slowly, his eyes baleful and angry.

Lucan turned again to Airey. 'How soon afterwards was Lord Cardigan in contact with headquarters?' he asked.

'Very soon.'

'What about?'

'He complained that you were asking him to send brigade returns to you and he wished to send them direct to Lord Raglan.'

'But sending them to his immediate superior was surely normal enough, wasn't it? It's the normal direction of documents in a command. From the Brigadier-General, Lord Cardigan, to the Divisional Commander, myself, and from the Divisional Commander to the Commander-in-Chief, Lord Raglan.'

'He was under the opinion that he was *not* under your orders. He believed he had been given an independent command.'

'So I had,' Cardigan said out loud.

'Please be quiet, my lord,' Eyland snapped.

'I think —'

'Sir,' Eyland was not going to have any nonsense, '*I* am conducting this court. You will be allowed to speak at the right time *and if necessary*. For the time being, please be silent.'

Cardigan flushed, his face furious, and Lucan gave Eyland a glance of pure joy before turning again to Airey.

'Was it true?' he asked. '*Did* Lord Cardigan have an independent command?'

'Well —'

'Answer the question, sir!'

It was Airey's turn to flush. 'No,' he said. 'But he held that opinion.'

'How had he come by it?'

Airey shifted uncomfortably. 'I gather that when he was given command of the Light Brigade he objected to being under the orders of his brother-in-law with whom he was not on good terms – you, my lord.'

'That's true enough,' Lucan admitted. 'Then why did he get the impression that he held an independent command?'

Airey shrugged, gestured and hesitated, as if uncertain how to phrase his answer. 'I suspect, my lord, that Lord Cardigan's quick temper, being well-known, like your own, someone at the Horse Guards had recourse to a little deviousness in order to get rid of him without a scene.'

Cardigan glared at Airey but Lucan was well satisfied with the reply. So was Souto.

Lucan consulted his notes. 'Soon afterwards,' he said, 'the first detachments of the 8th Hussars, the Lancers and the horse artillery moved to Varna, did they not?'

'They did.'

'Under Lord Cardigan?'

'Yes. Lord Raglan had given him permission to move. He wrote requesting permission and Lord Raglan granted it.'

'Without either of them taking the trouble to inform the commander of the cavalry – me, sir. Why?'

Airey shrugged. 'I suspect Lord Raglan also wished to avoid trouble.'

'Indeed he did. Unfortunately, instead of avoiding it, he increased it.'

'I have this information only through Lord de Ros, of course,' Airey explained hastily. 'This was before I took over Lord de Ros's position.'

Lucan frowned and turned to Eyland. 'I am well aware that I was often disliked by the men under me,' he said. 'Because I objected to officers who grew moustachios in defiance of standing orders which existed for the very simple reason that a clean-shaved face is as necessary as a clean shirt. I was aware, too, of the inefficiency of the commissariat and said so, unfortunately much to my detriment at headquarters. I was also aware that, after I had stated quite correctly that the lady who has once been mentioned in this court, Mrs Duberly, had no right to be with the troops, Lord Cardigan gave her permission to continue and that she, too, had gone to Varna. Why does the chain of command exist, sir, if not to be used?'

By this time Souto was sitting back with his thumbs in the armholes of his gown. He seemed to be enjoying himself.

Lucan looked again at Airey. 'Are you aware what I wrote to Lord Raglan on 11 June? At that time, arrangements had been made for the Heavy Cavalry to go to Varna also and it seemed to me that the cavalry was not under my command but that of Lord Cardigan. Did you see the letter I wrote?'

'I did. Later. I gather Lord de Ros advised Lord Raglan that the cavalry commander should be with his command. I understand he persuaded your lordship to withdraw your letter of protest.'

'He did indeed. The first of many such withdrawals on behalf of Lord Raglan. Did it make any difference?'

'I gather not. I believe Lord Cardigan wrote to you insisting that his command *was* a separate and detached one and that he felt bound only to Lord Raglan.'

'What happened to that letter?'

'You passed it on to Lord Raglan.'

'Through the proper channels, as I was bound to. What happened?'

'General Estcourt, the adjutant-general, replied to you.'

'He did indeed. Are you aware what he said?'

Airey frowned. 'He pointed out that Lord Cardigan was suffering from misapprehensions and had been informed that you could make whatever demands you wished on him – whether for returns or anything else.' Airey paused. 'I believe things became more difficult later, on 20 June, because then Lord Cardigan was gazetted major-general, equal in rank to yourself.'

'Why was Lord Cardigan chosen to command the Light Brigade?'

'I assumed for much the same reason as yourself. He had travelled in Russia.'

'What about his background in England?'

'I knew he bought command of the 15th Hussars and that his behaviour resulted in the command being taken away from him, but that he was later allowed to buy command of the 11th.'

Cardigan was on his feet again to protest but Eyland waved him down. 'Does this have any bearing on the case, my lord?' he asked Lucan.

'It does, sir. A great deal.'

Eyland waved him on and Lucan turned again to Airey. 'Could not the then Commander-in-Chief, Lord Hill, halt this behaviour of Lord Cardigan's?'

'He tried. So did the Duke of Wellington. They never managed it.'

Lucan gestured. 'So, if the Great Duke and Lord Hill could not manage him, would it not have been difficult for a retiring man like Lord Raglan to do so?'

'Lord Raglan found it immensely difficult.'

'So did I,' Lucan snapped. 'Now, sir, do you recall the state of the regiments of cavalry when they arrived?'

Airey looked happier again. 'They were in excellent condition.'

Lucan's eyes gleamed. 'Were they, sir?' He turned to

Eyland. 'I will quote from the returns, sir. Too many of the horses went by sail and the voyage took eight weeks under appalling conditions, during which time the horses, which are always bad sailors, were never able to lie down or move about. On *Mary Anne*, in which the 13th Light Dragoons sailed – some of them, that is, because in all they had to use six different ships – the ballast broke loose and knocked over several animals. Twenty-six of the 17th Lancers' horses died. The Inniskillings' transport, *Europe*, caught fire, and they lost fifty-seven horses, the veterinary surgeon, twelve men, two women and all their equipment. On the *Deva*, in which the 4th Dragoon Guards sailed, the temperature in the commanding officer's cabin, which was the best in the ship, stood at 82 degrees. In the *War Cloud*, one hundred horses of the Heavy Brigade were packed into a space designed for fifty-six, and seventy-five died or had to be destroyed. More died in *Pride of the Ocean*, but the worst disaster occurred in *Wilson Kennedy*, carrying part of the Royals. They already had horses down in dozens when a deck collapsed, throwing the officers' chargers on to the troop horses below so that they all ended up with broken backs and legs among saddles, carbines and swords. They lost more horses on that occasion than at Waterloo. Altogether the Heavies lost two hundred and twenty-six horses in their passage to the Crimea, and the remainder when they arrived were in such a condition I could barely recognise them.'

Another sheet of paper was passed to the judges and Lucan faced Airey again. 'Were there any Irregular Horse in the Crimea?'

Airey was beginning to have a worn look. 'There were a few,' he said. 'They were Bashi-Bazouks. But when Marshal St Arnaud, who was the French Commander-in-Chief until his death in September 1854, ordered his army into the Dobrudja area of Bulgaria, cholera struck and his regiments were decimated. The First French Division lost six thousand men and the Irregulars, the Bashi-Bazouks, panicked and deserted. They were therefore disbanded and sent home.'

'Who were these Bashi-Bazouks? Please tell the court.'

'They were Kurds, Negroes, Arabs and Albanians and they were a barbarous lot.'

'Could they not have been reorganised under good leadership?'

'Lord Raglan disliked anything that was irregular.'

'Irregular or not, they would have been a great asset to the hard-pressed cavalry, of which there were far too few. Now, sir,' Lucan was leaning forward, his hands on the table, 'you people on the staff who were so quick to criticise the cavalry, did you know the conditions they suffered?'

'I knew it was not easy. It was not easy for anyone.'

'When the army reached its positions round Sebastopol, where did Lord Raglan live?'

'In a farmhouse.'

'With a roof and a fire. What about the staff?'

'They lived in the outhouses.'

'With roofs over their heads. Yet they didn't hesitate to deride my men who were living in the open, spending most nights on picket duty in deteriorating weather. For instance, were you aware that on the morning of 18 October, when fog covered the plain and there was nothing between the enemy and Sir Colin Campbell and his Highlanders at Balaclava but the cavalry, that the cavalry had been under arms for sixteen hours?'

'I was not.'

'As an officer remarked to me, "you can keep a cabman out all night and all he does is charge you double, whereas a cavalryman gets nothing but a cold." Were you aware how wearing these constant alarms were on the cavalry? Were you aware that Major Willett, commanding the 17th Lancers, died after such an alarm and such a chilling night? Did you know the horses were wretched, half-starved and lacking shelter, that many were lame and many had coats like sheep because there was never time to groom them?'

'I know now. I didn't know it at the time.'

'Because you never came near the cavalry, sir,' Lucan snapped. 'That is why. There was a lot of irresponsible gossip about the cavalry at headquarters at this time. What did you do to stop it?'

'It was not part of my duty.'

'Oh?' Lucan's eyebrows shot up. 'But this gossip began to reach other people as fact, did it not, so that the army began to believe the cavalry was useless? Let it be said immediately, however, that those soldiers who were so criticised behaved splendidly before, during and after Balaclava, as well-trained and well-disciplined units. Yet, from the beginning, both they and their mounts suffered from the cold and the lack of rest. Did you know they were *praying* for the arrival of the French cavalry to take a little of the load from them?'

'I heard so.'

'When orders were received in Bulgaria to prepare for the Crimea was it not found that there were many defects in equipment? Threadbare tents, rotten water-kegs, bad and unsuitable clothing?'

'That was the fault of the Home Government.'

'But didn't Lord Raglan inform the Home Government?'

'He did protest.'

'Vigorously?'

'He did not enjoy causing trouble.'

'Many men might be alive today had he done so.'

'When the weather turned cooler in the autumn twelve thousand greatcoats were requested.'

'Indeed they were! And nine thousand of them were still in store at Balaclava at the end of the winter, by which time many of the nine thousand men who might have worn them were dead.'

'He wrote letters,' Airey said doggedly.

Lucan's mouth twisted. 'I saw some of them. They have an old-maidish touch and were too often concerned with kindness and honour, and not often enough with the state of the army. Were you aware that dangerous sides were being taken against the cavalry?'

'No, I was not.'

'Did you not hear Fitz Maxse, Lord Cardigan's aide, say "Lord Cardigan is disgusted with having his command taken away from him?"'

'I did. Once.'

'Was it taken away?'

'Lord Raglan was trying to prevent Lord Cardigan behaving as a divisional commander, that is all.'

'Did he ever reprimand him?'

'He wrote letters.'

'More letters!'

'Lord Raglan did not enjoy giving orders. He preferred to make suggestions.'

'Which are splendid when the recipient is receptive, but useless when he is not. After the Battle of the Alma, there were many wounded, were there not? But were there bandages or splints, chloroform or morphia?'

'There was a shortage.'

'But did you – you, sir – not rebuke for being frivolous a number of officers at Varna who had pointed out these shortages?'

'No, sir.'

Lucan's eyes flashed. 'I was present, sir, when you did.'

Airey flushed. 'Well, I might have done,' he admitted.

'Does all this not show a great want of concern on Lord Raglan's part?'

'It should have been tackled from England.'

'I have said it before. I'll say it again. The army had had six months to prepare for these events. Why did not Lord Raglan *demand* these things?'

'He was aware that the Government did not wish unnecessary expense.'

'It is unnecessary expense to succour the wounded, to feed the hungry, to protect men against disease? At Khuton

Mackenzie did not Lord Raglan manoeuvre his army to a position beyond reach of the fleet, which was supposed to protect it?'

'It was the only way of getting round Sebastopol.'

'Why go round Sebastopol?' Lucan snapped. 'Why not attack it at once from the north? Did not General Cathcart say he could have walked into Sebastopol without trouble? Did not other officers say the place could have been taken without a battle and the war ended there and then? It was obvious the Russian army was demoralised after the Battle of the Alma. Surely that was the time to strike?'

'The French were being difficult. Lord Raglan was often wrung by the yoke of the alliance.'

'Was he? Or was it the French who were wrung instead? Things were left undone, were they not? And Lord Raglan did little to put them right.'

'It wasn't his job.'

'General Canrobert, who succeeded as leader of the French on the death of Marshal St Arnaud made it *his* job. When at the beginning of October he found that food stocks were down, he organised more and after that he kept a personal eye on the situation. Did Lord Raglan do that?'

'It was the job of members of the staff.'

'And they didn't do it, did they? It's been said that a bad commander can have a good staff but that no good commander can ever have a bad staff. This was certainly the case in the Crimea, was it not? When the troops disembarked in the Crimea, what did they have in the way of equipment?'

'What they could carry.'

'But, unlike the French, no tents so that they spent all the first night on the shore drenched by a downpour. Why?'

'Because of the problems of transport. However, within two days, carts, camels, and horses had been collected, together with waggonloads of poultry, corn, flour, and sheep. Much of it by the infantry.

'Why the infantry? Did Lord Raglan consider the cavalry badly handled?'

'He was worried about them.'

'On the day of Balaclava, where were you?' The questions were being fired at Airey like bullets.

'On the Sapouné Ridge,' he said.

'Where you could see everything. There were others there, were there not? Civilians, and the famous Mrs Duberly who should never have been in the Crimea.' Lucan paused. 'We've heard a lot of Lord Raglan's swift experienced eye. Did he not realise that the advancing Russian army was aiming for Balaclava?'

'Not at first.'

'He was about the only person who did not. What did he do?'

'He sent infantry down to support the cavalry.'

'Which infantry?'

'The First and Fourth Divisions under the Duke of Cambridge and General Cathcart.'

'Did they arrive?'

'Of course.'

'After the tragedy,' Lucan said, 'when I produced my copy of the order which had launched the Light Brigade, did you compare it with your copy?'

Airey looked like a baffled bull. 'We had no copy.'

Lucan said nothing but it was clear that he didn't think much of a staff which didn't keep copies of the orders it issued.

'General Airey, you got to know Lord Raglan well? Was he forward-thinking? Reactionary? What?'

'I suppose you would say he enjoyed good living but wasn't interested in the arts.'

'*Or* the sciences that are so changing the way of life in England?'

'I suppose that would be correct. He had a calm nobility.'

'An attitude that belongs to this bustling nineteenth century?'

'Perhaps not. But he knew his limitations and liked to model himself on the Duke of Wellington.'

'In what way?'

'He formed the same habit of understatement, the same dislike of military splendour, the same dislike of being cheered by the men.'

'The same attitude to nepotism?'

'I don't understand.'

'Isn't it a fact that he had five of his nephews on his staff?'

'Yes, I suppose that's true.'

'What were they like, these young men?'

'They were all very pleasant young men.'

'We are not interested in their pleasantness!' Lucan snapped. 'What about their ability? Had they been to staff college or did they believe, like so many, that going to staff college showed a certain amount of eccentricity?'

The Deputy Judge-Advocate, Hector Gorvan, leaned over to speak to General Eyland who nodded and addressed Lucan. 'I think we'll not pursue that line of questioning, my lord,' he said.

'Very well, sir. Put it another way. Was Lord Raglan a good chooser of men?'

'Yes, well —' Airey's hesitation was clear, then he lifted his head. 'Yes, he was.'

'So that he accepted such as Lord de Ros, who was noted for his eccentricities and good humour, but was entirely without experience and apparently not very interested in acquiring it. What about the Adjutant-General, General Estcourt?'

'He was very industrious and had a remarkably kind disposition.'

'But no experience in the job he was doing!'

'I think you've established your point, my lord,' Eyland said gently. 'Can we move on?'

Lucan bowed and turned again to Airey. 'On the day of Balaclava, when Lord Raglan issued his orders, it was your duty to put them on paper, was it not?'

'It was.'

78

'Let us look again at the third order: *Cavalry to advance and take advantage of any opportunity to recover the Heights. They will be supported by the infantry which have been ordered to advance on two fronts.* According to cavalry teachings, cavalry should always be supported by infantry and that message could mean that the infantry was about to attack and that the cavalry was to move forward with them when they arrived.'

'Oh, no, sir!'

'Oh, yes, sir!' Lucan snapped. 'At the very least it means that the cavalry ought to be able to expect the infantry to be somewhere nearby to offer the support that has been mentioned. But they weren't, were they? They were nowhere near the cavalry. And though the infantry might have known where the cavalry was, the cavalry certainly didn't know where *they* were.' Lucan glanced at his papers and looked again at Airey. 'It was Captain Nolan, was it not, who carried the fateful fourth order to the cavalry – a man who would be expected to know what was intended?'

'Of course.'

'Then, if he ordered me in the wrong direction, I could reasonably assume that he knew what he was talking about?'

'If he did, yes. I agree.'

'And, of course, you explained the order to him? Told him exactly what was intended?'

Airey looked disconcerted. '*I* did not.'

'Then we must assume Lord Raglan did. Is that so?'

'I don't know. I don't think so.'

'Why not?'

'Time was important. It was urgent to get the message away.'

'Even if the man carrying it did not understand it? Afterwards, after the charge, what happened then?'

'There was a truce to be arranged to collect the dead and wounded in the valley.'

'And Lord Raglan organised that?' Eyland asked.

Airey cleared his throat. 'Er – no. He had many other things on his mind. I believe Lord Lucan organised it.'

'Aren't you certain?'

'There were only thirty or forty wounded, of course. But the names of the captured were discovered and sent to headquarters to be sent home in the despatch.'

Lucan allowed the information to be digested before addressing his next question to Airey. 'Shortly afterwards, despite his accusation that I had lost the Light Brigade, did not Lord Raglan issue a general order to the army, paying great tribute to the brilliant conduct of the Cavalry Division?'

'Yes, he did. It was very generous.'

'And it drew attention to the fact, did it not, that they were under *my* command?'

'Yes, it did.'

'Odd, was it not, when he considered I had just lost the Light Brigade?' Lucan paused, then he looked up again at Airey. 'General Airey,' he asked, 'have you ever heard of Chillianwallah?'

'Of course.'

'Tell us about it.'

'Has this anything to do with the case?' Eyland demanded.

'I think it might have, sir.'

'Very well, answer the question.'

'It was in India,' Airey said. 'A cavalry battle when bad leadership almost brought about a defeat.'

'On the evening of 27 October, two days after Balaclava, you came to see me in my tent, did you not?'

'I did.'

'What were the conditions?'

'It was cold, with bitter winds. There was mud on the floor.'

'And at headquarters? There were fires, were there not?'

Eyland frowned. 'I think this has nothing to do with what we are examining, my lord, and we have already heard it once.'

Lucan shrugged. 'How did you find me?' he asked Airey.
'Very low in spirits.'

'I was indeed. I had been wounded and had lost one of the finest cavalry brigades ever to leave these shores. And among the destroyed regiments was my own old regiment. Do you recall your remark?'

'No.'

'I will quote it, sir. Under the circumstances it was re-markably light-hearted. You said. "It is nothing to Chillian-wallah." Was that the attitude at headquarters?' Lucan's fury was obvious. 'That the disaster could be brushed off lightly because there had been *worse* disasters?'

'I think, my lord,' Eyland observed quietly, 'that all this should be struck from the record.'

'Even the remark, sir? At least, at Balaclava there was no shame. The men were magnificent.'

Eyland paused. 'Very well, I think we might let it stand. And I hope you have not much more for us to hear.'

Lucan gestured. 'Not much, sir. I am almost finished.' He turned to Airey. 'You will remember I protested about Lord Raglan's accusations that I had lost the Light Brigade.'

'You insisted on writing a letter home.'

'That is so. And you came to my tent, did you not, and on behalf of Lord Raglan, requested me to withdraw it: yet another of the many letters I had been asked to withdraw lest they should cause trouble for him?'

'Lord Raglan thought it would not be in your best interests.'

'In view of what we now know, it wasn't in *his* best interests either, was it? Or *yours*, sir. You wrote the order. You wrote *all* the orders. And they were invariably obscure and unclear. Perhaps the less said about things, the better for *you*, too!'

Chapter Six

Airey seemed pleased to be allowed to go. He slipped quickly from the witness stand and headed for the door as if he were terrified of being called back. It was quite clear he had not enjoyed his cross-examination.

'That was very well done,' Souto murmured as Lucan sat down.

'I could have got more out of him,' Lucan growled.

'You need no more. You have your brother-in-law next, I understand. I beseech you, my lord, to watch your tongue. Don't let yourself be dragged into an argument with him.'

Lucan turned angrily. 'For God's sake, Souto, I spent the whole time in the Crimea trying my best *not* to get into an argument with him!'

'You were not face to face,' Souto said firmly. 'From my information the occasions when you *have* met face to face have not been graced by good humour.'

As Cardigan took the witness's chair, there was a certain amount of restless shuffling among the spectators because Cardigan was a notorious figure and everybody was interested to see how he would perform.

As he composed himself, Harboursford rose to his feet. 'Major-General the Earl of Cardigan?'

'Yes.' Cardigan was clearly in a bad temper and was obviously not intending to concede anything in the way of good manners for anybody he considered his social inferior.

82

'You are Her Majesty's Inspector-General of Cavalry.'

'Yes.'

The Woodford Board which had been able to concede that Lucan has 'used every exertion to meet the peculiar difficulties he had had to contend with,' had found it difficult to exonerate Cardigan of the accusation of indifference to the suffering of his men, but it seemed to have had little effect on his arrogance. Harboursford appeared to have had second thoughts about how to proceed with his case and since Lucan was harking back to the beginning, he seemed to feel it might be a good idea to forestall him by harking back first.

'Varna,' he offered.

'A damnable place,' Cardigan snapped.

Well, it was a start. 'In what way, my lord?' Harboursford asked.

'Blue sky. Constant thunderclouds. Storks. Eagles. Kites. Vultures. All going at the carcasses of dead animals which lay everywhere. Brilliant birds. In all the woods. Frogs going all night. Main street like a drain. Dead dogs. Rats. Stink beat anything I ever smelled.'

'What else, my lord?'

'Disease. Infantry were camping among the graves of Russians who died of disease in the war of 1828. The water from the wells came up green. Rats were colossal. Forage was rubbish. Little better than old bed-stuffing full of fleas. Heat was appalling. Dust everywhere. Lord Lucan being a damned nuisance with his field days and reviews. In most of which he clubbed the regiments. Still,' Cardigan paused, 'the men put on a good show.'

'What about horses, my lord?'

'Suffering. Except for those damned stallions of the Bashi-Bazouks which seemed to want to kick their way through everything. I was glad when Raglan had them disbanded and Scarlett added their commander to his staff.'

Harboursford seemed to have felt it wiser to let Cardigan

have his say. Now he got down to brass tacks. 'Let me take your mind back to 23 June,' he said. 'The day news came in that the siege of Silistria had been raised and the Russians had withdrawn. What happened?'

'The Turks wanted to know where they were.'

'So what happened?'

'Lord Raglan sent me off to make a reconnaissance along the banks of the Danube. I took a hundred and twenty-one men of the 8th Hussars and seventy-five of the 13th Light Bobs. Left the Lancers behind. Thought their lances might make 'em too easy to see.'

'Please continue.'

'Reached the Danube in four days. Russians already on the other side. Rode along the banks of the river and returned by way of Silistria and the old fortress of Shumla. Sent Lieutenant Bowen back with the information I'd gathered. Returned on 11 July. It was raining.'

'What had you discovered?'

Cardigan's eyebrows rose as if he felt he had already answered that question. 'That the Russians had gone and the country was deserted,' he said crisply. 'Lord Raglan congratulated me. Wrote that it was important. I covered three hundred and thirty-six miles in eighteen days.'

'What happened on your return?'

'We moved to Yeni-Bazaar, twenty-eight miles from Devna. Difficult march. Blinding sun. No water. Next day went on to Yasi-Tepe. Road littered with the carcasses of horses, bullocks, sheep and dogs. Midsummer by this time. Heat in the tents had reached one hundred and ten degrees.'

'You measured it, my lord?'

'I was told. Better there, though, than at Varna. Cholera had broken out in Varna. Epidemic. Men dying like flies. French were the worst off. Then the cavalry. Men cheerful and alert at noon, dead and buried by evening. Those who recovered were skeletons. Food damn bad, too.'

'You sampled it?'

'No. I had my own. But I was told. Salt pork. Dreadful stuff in that heat. Produced thirst. When the men couldn't get water, they went for water melons. And *they'd* been tainted. Brought on dysentery and cholera. Heat appalling. Lord Raglan had to let the stock fall into disuse. It was causing apoplexy. I was glad when orders came to head for the Crimea. So were most people. If only to get away from the cholera.'

'On what day was the Russian shore sighted?'

'12 September.' Cardigan was still as laconic as when he had started. 'Very exciting. Itching to do something, y'see. They put us ashore at Calamita Bay. No sign of the enemy.'

'None at all?'

'Well, an officer with a troop of Cossacks appeared on the hills. Wearing a dark green uniform and riding a bay. Fine horse. Saw him through my glasses. Sir George Brown nearly got himself captured. Short-sighted, y'see. Didn't notice the Russians. A party of the Royals saved him. They'd been stalking the Cossacks as the Cossacks were stalking George Brown. Fourteen thousand men were ashore by the afternoon.'

'Then?'

'It started to rain. Saw George Brown under a cart out of the downpour and Cambridge under a gun carriage. They put the cavalry ashore next day. I was sent into the interior to find carts and food.'

'And you found them?'

'Yes. Took two hundred and fifty men and two hundred and fifty of the Rifles. Travelled about thirty miles. Brought back a few carts. Found a few wells, but not many, and there was no means of hauling the water up. Streams and rivers all seemed to be brackish or salt. Horses wouldn't touch it. Did without water for thirty hours. We set off for Sebastopol the following morning.'

'A good march, my lord?'

'Bit hot.'

Field Marshal Lord Templeton in his seat near the judges saw the picture clearly. He had experienced it often enough. Great lozenges of colour as weary soldiers tramped along, bands playing, drums throbbing to give the step, banners flapping in the breeze over the stink of stale sweat and dirty bodies.

Cardigan was elaborating. 'Lots of men fell out,' he was saying. 'Heat stroke or cholera. Brilliant sight, though. Just after lunch we bumped into the Russians. Stream called the Bulganak. Saw their cavalry on rising ground beyond the stream. Light and Second Divisions were ordered up. I sent two troops across the river and followed with the rest. I had the 11th Hussars and the 13th Light Bobs with me and we were in front because we'd been the advance guard. 8th Hussars and 17th Lancers were on the flank under Lord Lucan between the army and the Russians. Other flank was guarded by the sea and the fleet.'

'Tell us what happened, my lord.' Harboursford seemed to be breathless with anticipation.

'Threw out a troop in skirmishing order and that was the position when Lord Lucan appeared and interfered.'

There was a rustle of anticipation. Lucan leaned forward but Souto laid a hand on his arm.

'Interfered, my lord?' Harboursford asked.

'He wanted to know what I was doing and told me I mustn't do it because the Russians had men behind the hills and the Brigade would be annihilated. It was no way to handle cavalry. I pointed out that perhaps I was to have no command at all and he answered that I had, but not at that moment.'

'There was a bit of firing, then that ass —' Cardigan paused and corrected himself, 'then General Airey arrived with an order to withdraw, I gave way, of course, not wishing to cause trouble. My men retired as quietly and as orderly as if at a field day on Hounslow Heath.'

'Let us continue,' Harboursford said. 'To the Alma. What did you see when you arrived at that position?'

'The Russian positions on the heights on the other side of the river. They were very strong.'

'We're not concerned with this battle a great deal, save to note that it was won by the gallantry of the British soldiers. Where were the cavalry during the engagement?'

'There was only the Light Brigade. The Heavies hadn't yet landed. We were on the left. Most of us in a melon field.'

'Doing what?'

'Nothing.' Cardigan looked furious. 'Nothing at all. We never did anything. We seemed to have been forgotten. Would have chased the Russians all the way to Sebastopol but no orders were given by my Lord Lucan. Just wasted time. Could have turned the retreat into a rout but all we did was take a few prisoners. Felt I had to protest. Pointed out that before leaving London I'd been assured that my command was an independent one. Ridiculous situation, especially when Lucan got the cavalry lost near Khuton Mackenzie on the march to Sebastopol.'

'Lost?'

'It was thickly wooded country,' Cardigan had thrown aside his taciturnity as he lambasted his brother-in-law. 'Lord Lucan was supported by a battalion of the Rifles and got himself lost so that Lord Raglan found himself in the van of the army and almost got himself taken prisoner. When eventually Lord Lucan appeared, I heard Lord Raglan accuse him of being late. "Lord Lucan, you're late," he said. Very angry. Didn't much like the cavalry, I'm afraid. When I went to call on him later, I caught the full force of his anger. Reminded him, of course, that I was no longer in command of the cavalry. Lucan's mistake did a lot of harm. Heard several people speak against him.'

Harboursford turned to the court. 'I do not propose to go into detail about the march towards Sebastopol, gentlemen,' he said. 'Merely to highlight one or two minor incidents en route.' Turning to Cardigan, he asked 'Do you remember the village of Duvankoi?'

Cardigan smiled. 'Certainly do. That was where Lord Lucan got me into difficulties again.'

'Please tell the court.'

Eyland leaned forward. 'I take it this has a bearing on the events of 25 October?'

'I am endeavouring to show, sir, the problems in the cavalry.'

'You seem to be endeavouring to show that Lord Lucan did not know his job.'

'Indeed, that is part of the prosecution, sir.' Harboursford swung back to Cardigan. 'Tell the court what happened, my lord.'

Cardigan gestured, still smiling faintly. 'He got the cavalry into a dangerous defile and in the end had to retreat along a road so narrow several of the baggage carts were upset. As I pointed out to Lord Paget, it seemed to be a habit of the cavalry commander. But, then, Lord Lucan was never trusted by Lord Raglan. Outside Sebastopol he sent a patrol along the side of one of the hills, which was considered very dangerous. Had woods on one side and a precipice on the other. Lord Raglan found great fault in him and ordered it to be discontinued.'

Harboursford permitted himself a slight smile. 'Let us proceed now to the events of 25 October.' He looked round the court. 'The port of Balaclava to the south of Sebastopol had been taken over and by this time the cavalry had all arrived. The Light Brigade had been joined by units of the Heavy Brigade and Lord Lucan's command was complete. Where was Lord Lucan's headquarters?'

'In a tent in the cavalry camp. Damned uncomfortable it was, too. Cavalry were on the plain near Balaclava. Camps had been set up for the infantry on the heights round Sebastopol and the siege had begun. But there had been a Russian army in the interior for a long time and it was feared they might attempt to capture Balaclava and cut us off from our supplies. Campbell was given the job of guarding the

place with the Highlanders. Only a brigadier-general, too.'
Cardigan sounded disgusted. 'Cavalry were down in the plain in support.'

'Were there skirmishes?'

'Now and then.'

'What about the day of 7 October.'

'Remember it well. Patrol of the 4th Dragoon Guards was surprised. Three wounded and taken prisoner. Lord Lucan led the cavalry and the horse artillery eastwards and waited on high ground overlooking the Tchernaya. Perfect opportunity to attack. Russians were below. But the trumpets didn't sound and, after a single gun shot, we returned to camp. Opportunity missed to inflict great damage. Lord Raglan very annoyed. I protested, of course. It was as a result of this affair that Lord Lucan got his nickname.'

'What nickname was that?'

Cardigan smiled. 'Lord Look-On. Lucan – Look-On. Everybody said that was all he did.'

Lucan shifted in his seat, his eyes glittering angrily but Souto had a hand on his arm.

'Following this,' Harboursford had turned to address the court again, 'as the court has been told, the bombardment of Sebastopol opened. There was another cavalry skirmish on 18 October which, like the others, came to nothing. The cavalry failed to attack. On 25 October, however, as we have heard, the Russian advance everyone had been expecting for so long commenced. We've heard how the Russian cavalry's first attack on Balaclava was repulsed by Sir Colin Campbell and his Highlanders and how the second attack was repulsed by the Heavy Brigade.'

Cardigan broke in. 'Perhaps I might interrupt here, sir.' he said, 'to set right the impression gained earlier that I failed to attack the Russian cavalry as they retreated.'

'Has this anything to do with the events that followed?' Eyland asked.

'Yes, it has,' Cardigan snapped. 'I've been accused of not

89

charging the Russian flank as they retreated. But I was placed in that position by Lord Lucan and told to guard it. He placed me there and told me not to move. Yet later he blamed me for not launching an attack against the retreating Russians. I —'

'Colonel Harboursford,' Eyland frowned. 'Is this discussion anything to do with the events that followed?'

'I consider sir —' Cardigan began, but Eyland stopped him.

'Please be quiet, my lord,' he snapped. 'As I've already said, *I* am conducting this court.'

Cardigan's mouth shut like a trap. He was not in the habit of being told what to do and clearly resented it.

Harboursford seemed at a loss. 'Well, sir —' he began.

'Is it, Colonel, or is it not?'

'I'm afraid not, sir.'

'Then please continue without it.'

Harboursford turned to the furious Cardigan. 'Let us turn immediately to the later events of the day, my lord,' he said cautiously. 'When Captain Nolan brought the order for the Light Brigade to advance to the enemy, where were you?'

'In the saddle in front of my brigade.' Cardigan directed an angry glance at Eyland but he answered the question briskly. 'We'd just been instructed by Lord Lucan to be prepared to move.'

'Why?'

'Understood we were waiting for the arrival of the infantry. They'd been ordered down from the camps to regain the redoubts on the Causeway Heights that the Turks had lost.'

'Please tell the court what happened.'

'Saw Nolan arrive. Handed the order to Lord Lucan.'

'Did you see it?'

'Not at that time. Lord Lucan seemed puzzled. Seemed to be a discussion going on.'

'An argument?'

'You might call it that.'

'Did Lord Lucan lose his temper?'

'He often lost his temper.'

'Did he on this occasion?'

'I suppose so.'

'Did he?' Eyland interrupted sharply. 'Did you hear him do so? Did you see him do so?'

'No.'

'Then have the goodness to say so, my lord.'

Cardigan flushed and Harboursford hurried to intervene. 'What happened then?'

'Lord Lucan rode across to me. I was in front of the 13th Lights. Showed me the message he'd received and ordered me to advance down the North Valley with the Light Brigade. I pointed out that we were attacking a battery in position, down a valley flanked by more guns. Considered it highly dangerous.'

'What did Lord Lucan say?'

'Seemed at a loss. He said "I know it, but Lord Raglan will have it. We have no choice but to obey." I argued no further. I was not, after all, in command of the cavalry. He told me to advance very steadily and keep the men well in hand.'

'You made a comment. What was it?'

'I said, "Here goes the last of the Brudenells."'

'Brudenell being your family name. Why did you say that?'

'I thought my last hour had come.'

'How was the brigade formed up?'

'The front line consisted of the 11th Hussars, the 17th Lancers and the 13th Light Dragoons. The second line consisted of the 9th Hussars and the 4th Light Bobs. The Divisional Commander informed me, however, that he wished the 11th Hussars to move back to form a line between the other two lines. I considered it a deliberate insult because the 11th were my old regiment and he knew I was anxious to see them lead the Brigade into action. Seemed to me then, and still does, a spiteful, malicious —'

'You have not been asked your opinion, Lord Cardigan.' Eyland seemed to be losing his patience.

Cardigan frowned and became silent.

'Please continue,' Harboursford said quickly.

'Rode across to George Paget, with the 4th Light Bobs, who was in command of the second line. Told him we were to make an attack to the front and that I expected his best support. I then galloped back to my brigade. Men who had been on other duties kept joining. There were also two Sardinian officers who wished to ride with us. There were six hundred and seventy-three of us.'

'Not many, my lord.'

'Been some difficulty when the war started of raising the division, and by 25 October sickness had reduced the numbers still further. Also one troop of the 11th acting as escort to Lord Raglan. Due to the problems of foraging, horses were not at their best. As I watched the squadrons forming, Captain Nolan approached me. Very excited he was. Even had the damned impudence to taunt me with the Light Brigade's failure to make anything of the Russians. I was very indignant, because I'd always been held back by the orders I'd received from Lord Lucan. Damned man had the nerve to suggest we might even be afraid. Didn't answer. Instead I moved to a position two horses length in front of my staff and five lengths in front of the right squadron of the 17th Lancers. Then I said "The Brigade will advance. First squadron of the 17th Lancers direct" and turned to my trumpeter, Britten, and ordered "Sound the advance."'

There was a long silence and Harboursford allowed it to continue as he moved papers about on the table in front of him. At last he looked up.

'Continue, if you please, your lordship.'

Cardigan drew a deep breath, clearly enjoying himself.

Whatever his morals, he was the hero of Balaclava. He had been first into the Russian guns and it had been acknowledged that he had led down the valley with distinction.

'It was as the brigade moved off,' he began, 'that Lord Lucan interfered again. The 11th hadn't moved so he sent an aide to tell them to fall back to form a second line. However, it caused no confusion.' Cardigan has clearly told the story many times before. 'As the walk changed to a trot, the brigade took up roughly one-fifth of the width of the valley and between the first and second line was a distance of 400 yards, with rather less between the second and the third, though I believe this decreased as we advanced, so that we ended up arriving practically in two lines as the pace of the third line advanced and they almost caught up with the second line. At that moment the firing started, and it was then that Nolan was killed.'

'How did it happen?'

'He had taken up a position with the 17th Lancers – I believe he was a friend of Morris, the commanding officer – and now the damned man rode forward.'

'Was he not trying to direct your brigade to its correct destination, to the redoubts on the Causeway Heights?'

'Probably.' The answer came grudgingly. 'Seemed to me to be trying to show me how to lead my brigade. It was my opinion that he —'

Harboursford held up his hand. His expression looked faintly irritated. 'Thank you, my lord. We understand that. What happened next?'

'A shell exploded between myself and Nolan. Next thing I saw was that he appeared to have turned tail and was bolting to the rear, apparently screaming like a woman.'

'He had, however, as we now know, been mortally wounded by a splinter of the shell and the screaming you thought you heard was the air escaping through his throat from his lungs. He fell from the saddle as he passed through the ranks of the 13th Light Dragoons. Is that not so?'

'So I heard later.' Cardigan seemed unmoved.

'Please go on.'

'Led the brigade down the valley, endeavouring to keep them steady and in their proper alignment. Had occasion to complain to one or two officers who pushed ahead. As the firing grew worse, of course, it grew more difficult to hold the horses back. Several times I called out that they must be steady. I'd already lost my trumpeter, who was mortally wounded soon after he sounded the Trot. The Gallop and the Charge were never sounded. As we reached the guns, they fired a last salvo. Horse shied. Flame from the explosion came very close. Chose a space between the guns and rode through it.'

'You were the first man into the guns?'

'I was. Remained beyond the guns for some time, narrowly escaping capture. Received a slight wound in the thigh, and a lance catching my pelisse almost dragged me from the saddle. In the end, I turned my horse and rode back through the guns and back up the valley with the survivors of my brigade.' Cardigan's face grew red. 'Valley was full of dead and dying men and horses! Nothing I could do! I'd lost my trumpeter, my orderly and my staff, but so as not to give the impression of too hasty a retreat, I rode back slowly, most of the time with my horse at a walk.'

'Despite the firing?' Harboursford said flatteringly. 'Despite the Russian lancers about the valley attacking the wounded and the survivors?'

'Yes, sir. Picked up Cornet Yates of the 11th and eventually reached the horse artillery.' Cardigan's face grew red again. 'And if anyone suggests I left the battle too soon, they're very wrong. The man they saw riding back early in the retreat was not me. It was Lieutenant Houghton of the 11th. Rode a horse similar to mine and wore the same uniform. Even looked a bit like me. Been wounded. Anyone who suggests that I never reached the guns —'

'Lord Cardigan!' Eyland looked up. '*Nobody* is questioning your courage. We're trying to get at the facts concerning this unhappy event. Pray stick to them.'

Cardigan scowled. 'Lots of cheers as we returned,' he said. 'Acknowledged them with my sword. When I reached my brigade, they were trying to form up and I had occasion to rebuke George Paget who was complaining that the Guards should have supported us. Of course they should, but it seemed to me more dignified not to make a fuss. Addressed the men. Told them it was no fault of mine. Somebody called out that they were ready to go again.'

'And the casualties, my lord?'

'Only one hundred and ninety-five men returned. The 17th Lancers could muster only thirty-seven troopers and the 13th Light Bobs only two officers and eight mounted men. My command had ceased to exist. When Lord Raglan appeared I pointed out to him that it was not my fault and that I had received the order to attack from my superior officer, Lord Lucan.' Cardigan glared across the court at his brother-in-law, clearly eager to make his point. He paused. 'Owing to illness, I was obliged to return home at the end of the year. Rewarded with the Inspectorship of Cavalry and invited to Windsor. Presented with a jewelled sword by the city of —'

Eyland sighed visibly. 'We're well aware of the honours that have come to you, my lord,' he said. 'As we're aware of the musical pieces and poems that have been written in your praise. They have little to do with what we are considering today, however.' He looked at Harboursford. 'Are there any more questions, Colonel?'

'No, sir.'

Eyland looked at Lucan. 'Lord Lucan?'

Lucan rose to his feet, his dark eyes angry and hostile as he stared at his brother-in-law. He was obviously intending to do battle.

'Yes, sir,' he said. 'There are indeed.'

'In that case,' Eyland said, 'I am going to close this session for today. Already we have heard a great deal and it is growing late. You will ask your questions tomorrow.'

Lucan was about to protest when Souto touched his arm. Lucan swallowed, took a deep breath, then he bowed.

'As the court decides, sir,' he said.

Chapter Seven

Souto was glad to head homewards. The crowded courtroom had been stuffy and he was tired. The case was already a *cause célèbre*. People were talking about it at London dinner parties and in the streets and it was occupying the attention of thousands on the home-going horse omnibuses. London seemed to have split into two camps. For the most part, opinion seemed to favour everyone but Lucan, and the newspapers, though unable to comment on the case, were similarly taking sides. 'It will be a discussion,' *The Times* announced pontifically, 'on the abilities or otherwise of the aristocracy. Are they entitled to command and, if they are, are they fit for it? Are there not others without titles just as able, just as capable of command as Lord Lucan and Lord Cardigan whose attitude seems to be to throw the blame on to a soldier who has the misfortune not to belong to that select body, Captain Nolan.'

The cab from Waterloo Station dropped him outside his house in Baker Street and Souto pushed open the door, glad to enter the bright interior. The colour was entirely his wife's idea, as was the colour in his chambers. Souto's wife appeared, smiling. She was wearing a bright blue dress that left her shoulders uncovered and he thanked God once more for her sense of colour. His chambers, he felt, were infinitely easier to work in than those of some of his contemporaries.

'How did the day go?' she asked.

Souto smiled. 'Better than I dreamed,' he said. 'Lucan's an imperious blighter, but he did well.'

'With your advice, no doubt.'

'He's known to have a good brain and, despite what people said of him at the time, he made a sound job of his farms in Ireland. In many ways it's a pity he wasn't at the War Office before the war instead of the Duke of Wellington. He'd have been better at the job than some who were and he certainly wouldn't have spent his time asleep like the Duke. He'd have made himself hated but he wouldn't have missed the things that were wrong; the army would have been properly supplied and equipped, and there'd never have been the uproar the Crimea caused.'

'If you win, you'll have him as a grateful client for life.'

Souto gave a rueful smile. 'I'm not sure I want him. Financially, he's not well off. From that point of view, I'd rather represent Cardigan. On the other hand,' his smile widened, 'I don't really think I could bear that. Lucan's bearable, though only just.'

His wife indicated the living room. 'Lieutenant Morden's here. To see Harriet. He'll be interested.'

Lieutenant Morden rose as Souto entered. He was a young man whose good looks were marred by the recently healed wounds he'd received to the head at Balaclava. 'How did the day go, sir?' he asked as they shook hands.

'Lucan did well.'

'Lucan's no fool,' Morden agreed. 'He knew what he was about in the Crimea. He never put a foot wrong, though it might have been better if he'd occasionally taken a chance. But he had to endure a great deal of vilification for not showing more initiative from people who didn't know the circumstances, including, I'm sorry to say, me.'

Souto accepted a drink from a footman. 'Did you really dislike him?'

Morden smiled. 'I detested him. So did everybody else. All he seemed to do was interfere. Tell the men to get their hair cut. Tell them to wash their clothes. Tell them to look to their mounts. We simply thought of him as an interfering old buffoon who'd forgotten everything he'd learned. Yet,' Morden paused, 'you know, sir, looking back, I think there was more to it than we realised. I noticed eventually that the men who had their hair cut and washed their shirts got no lice. The ones who looked after their horses were better mounted. It's true his orders were old-fashioned and it's true he hadn't served in the field since 1837, but there were a lot of others who'd been longer out of action, and *they* were never treated with the same contempt. I suspect it was his temper.' He paused again. 'And the fact that there were a few people on the staff who talked too much. How did he behave in court?'

'He was surprisingly restrained. Mind you,' Souto smiled, 'I threatened to withdraw if he weren't. And since he hadn't been able to get anyone else to advise him, perhaps he decided he needed me.'

'Will he win, Father?' Souto's daughter looked up.

Souto smiled. 'My dear Hettie, who knows?'

'What will happen if he's found guilty?'

This time Souto smiled. 'Well, you know what happened to Admiral Byng when he failed to relieve besieged Minorca. They accused him of roughly the same thing as Lucan, of not doing his duty as he should, court martialled him and shot him. "Pour encourager les autres." They won't shoot Lucan but it would mean disgrace. On the other hand, he might lose, and gain the sympathy of the public, in the same way that Cardigan might vindicate himself and lose it. It's one of those cases. However it turns out, I suspect nobody will win in the end.'

'Will the Duke of Cambridge give evidence?'

'I'd have liked to make him, but I understand he's declined.'

'Wasn't he a witness?'

'Certainly. He and Cathcart were ordered down to support the Light Brigade but he refuses to appear, and obviously Cathcart can't because he was killed at Inkerman.'

The court martial occupied them throughout dinner. Then, as Souto was sipping a brandy with his family, they heard the front door bell ring and soon afterwards the butler arrived to say that Souto was wanted.

'I'm not in to visitors, Warner.' Souto was faintly annoyed at the interruption.

'The gentleman says he thinks you ought to see him, sir,' the butler said. 'He insisted on giving his name. Mr Archibald Babington.'

For a moment Souto said nothing, then he put down his glass and rose and excused himself.

'Show him into the library, Warner,' he said. 'I'll see him there.'

His wife looked up. 'Who is it, dear? Someone to do with the court martial?'

Souto drew a deep breath. 'I suspect he has a great deal to do with the court martial,' he said.

Babington was a thin man with black hair and a large moustache that drooped about his mouth. His hair was long and wavy and he had the look of a gentleman; to Souto's shrewd assessing eyes, almost too much of a gentleman. While real gentlemen were often casual about their clothing, confident that what they wore was of the best quality and required no extra attention, Babington's looked as if he'd spent too long making sure it was exactly right.

Souto gestured to a chair by the fire. 'To what do I owe this visit?' he asked.

Babington smiled. 'The court martial, of course,' he said. 'What else?'

'How can I help you?'

'I'm anxious to know just how you intend to approach the subject of my second cousin, Louis Edward Nolan.'

Souto frowned. 'That's something that will come out at the right time,' he said sharply.

Babington smiled. 'I have evidence that may be of use to your client.'

'What sort of evidence, sir?'

'Letters.'

'What sort of letters?'

'Letters from my cousin, Captain Nolan, to his mother.'

'About what?'

'About Lord Lucan.'

'Suggesting what?'

'His unfitness for command. His neglect of his troops. His indifference to orders.'

Souto almost laughed in Babington's face. There was no one he could think of who would be less likely to be indifferent to orders than the pernickety, fussy Lucan. A man who had apparently kept every scrap of paper involved in his dispute over who was commanding the Light Brigade would never be indifferent. It appeared to Souto that Lucan had played the old soldier's game all along – instead of protesting about the orders he disagreed with, he had followed them to the letter and kept proof that he had. Souto was not an army man but he knew enough about it to know that the first rule with orders was obey them first and dispute them afterwards.

'I don't believe your letters will have much bearing on the case, sir,' he said.

Babington smiled. 'They come from General Bosquet for one; from General Scarlett; Sir George Brown; Colonel Beatson; General Bacon; Captain de Salis, who rode in the charge, Sir William Gordon and Colonel Shewell likewise; Captain Forrest, Henry Clifford, of the Rifles. Also, letters from Prince Radziwill, who was instrumental in saving Lord Cardigan's life when he was almost captured by the Prince's Cossacks, Mr Roger Fenton, the photographer, Lieutenant Elliott and Corporal Morley, who rode in the charge; Private Spring also. They are united in condemning Lord Lucan. I think you would be interested.'

Souto thought for a moment, then he smiled. 'Perhaps I can offer you a drink.'

'That would be most kind.' Babington looked like the sort of man who would accept a drink from anyone.

'One moment, I'll inform my butler. You must forgive me, the bell isn't working.'

Leaving Babington alone, Souto slipped from the room back to his family.

'Arthur,' he said quickly to Morden. 'Ask Warner to bring drinks to the library.'

'Why not use the bell?' his wife asked.

Souto held up his hand to silence her. 'Do as I say, Arthur,' he said. 'And tell him to send someone out to call a cab and have it standing near the house, just out of sight round the corner. Then have our coats, hats, scarves and sticks ready. We shall be leaving immediately my guest leaves.'

'But —'

Souto silenced his wife again. 'Just do as I say, Arthur.'

Returning to the library, Souto was followed almost immediately by the butler. As he handed a drink to Souto, he glanced up. 'I've sent the under-footman out, sir,' he whispered.

As the butler disappeared, Souto turned to Babington. 'The letters,' he said. 'I've been thinking about them. I shall need to read them carefully. Are you prepared to leave them with me?'

Babington smiled. 'Nothing doing,' he said. 'They don't go out of my possession. Things have been known to disappear.'

'I can hardly judge them without reading them. I shall need to spend time on them. Why are you offering them to me?'

Babington smiled again. 'I have an interest in my cousin's reputation,' he said. 'But I am also in need of money. I'm always in need of money, you might say. My aunt, my cousin's mother, is determined that his reputation shall not suffer in this enquiry and, judging by the way things are going, it might well. The army shoved all the blame on to poor old Louis because he carried the message. He told that

102

ass, Lucan, what to do, so they say it was his fault. It wasn't, you know.'

Souto said nothing and Babington continued.

'The army wanted a scapegoat, and because Louis was dead he was the one. But that's not good enough. Louis knew more about cavalry than any man living, certainly more than Lucan or that lunatic Cardigan. He wrote two books on it.'

'I've seen them. They're both very small.'

'But both very knowledgeable. He learned his tactics in India. He came home on the advice of senior officers here to help the army. The Duke of Cambridge was one, did you know? What he has to say in his letters will shake up that court if they're produced.'

'Are you suggesting they might *not* be produced?'

'They needn't be.'

'For a consideration?'

'Of course.'

Souto shook his head. 'It would be most unprofessional of me to hide them,' he said. 'It's the army's wish, as I've been told more than once, that this court martial must be conducted with the utmost impartiality, fairness and honesty. It would be something less than honest if letters concerning it were kept back.'

'They'd do your client a lot of no good,' Babington said.

'That's of little concern to me, sir. Naturally, I would like to see him win the case because I'm advising him and it's well known that, though an officer might appear to be conducting his own case, in fact he is following the instructions of a lawyer. It would add to my reputation if he won, but I should lose nothing if he lost – except his custom. My fee is guaranteed.'

'Perhaps my Lord Lucan would accept the letters.'

'He'd more than likely horsewhip you.'

'There's one other thing.' There was a sly look in Babington's eye. 'We have a witness of what happened on the field. At the time of the charge. Absolute proof that my cousin Louis attempted to change the direction of the cavalry.'

Souto's heart thumped. This was a new one. Nolan's actions were still the centre of a great controversy as people argued what he'd intended by his move at the beginning of the charge and he wondered whom Babington had found.

'He's a private in the 17th Lancers,' Babington said. 'He was in the first line and immediately behind Cardigan and my cousin Louis as they moved off. He heard my cousin shout to Cardigan to change direction.'

'Heard him?'

Babington smiled. 'Heard him. The man would disappear, of course, if necessary.'

'For money, naturally?'

'Of course.'

'I think, sir,' Souto said harshly, 'that you are a scoundrel.'

Babington smiled. 'That's often been said. But I have people behind me. The Beauforts, for instance.'

'I don't believe it.'

'Well, not the Beauforts exactly. But the Raglan family. In the person of Spencer Valentine. He's a lawyer. The family's as anxious as anyone else not to be saddled with the blame. My funds are being supplied by them. What do you say?'

Souto made a great show of considering the proposition. 'I shall need to think,' he said.

'You haven't much time.'

'I'm in court all day. I'll send my clerk along to take a look at the documents you mention. He'll be able to advise me. I take it that will be satisfactory.'

'Eminently.' Babington offered his card. 'That's my address.'

'Now, sir, I think you'd better leave.'

Babington shrugged. 'I'll finish my drink first,' he said.

* * *

104

As they left the room, Babington accepted his hat, coat and stick, and bowed to Souto. As the door was closing behind him, Souto turned to the butler. 'Let me know where he goes, Warner,' he said.

Lieutenant Morden, already cloaked and clutching his hat and stick, was waiting, Souto's clothing on his arm.

'Where are we going?' he asked.

'Out.'

Souto's wife tried to protest but he bent over her and kissed her cheek. 'Have no fear. With Arthur alongside me, we shall be all right.'

At the door, the butler turned. 'He's just picking up a cab, sir,' he said. 'Your cab is just round the corner out of sight.'

As they slipped out and found the waiting cab, Morden's curiosity appeared. 'What's happening?'

As they rounded the corner, they could see the other cab just moving off. 'We're following that cab,' Souto said. 'To wherever it goes. I'm interested to see, in fact, where it *does* go.'

The cab in front clip-clopped through dark streets, moving out of the bright lights of the West End towards the darker streets of Balham. Eventually, it turned into a wide space surrounded by walls of grimed yellow bricks. A sign announced it as Sick Heart Yard.

'I suspect we've arrived,' Souto said.

The darkness was thick now but they could hear the sound of a piano accompanying singing. It was just possible to see Babington's cab halted outside a public house and they read the sign, 'The Shades Vaults.'

As Babington entered the establishment, they followed, well muffled up and keeping their hats low over their eyes. Three steps down was a series of rooms of differing sizes, as though someone had knocked into one a group of old houses. There were three separate bars and three gigantic casks labelled Old Sam, Cream of the Highlands and Tip Top. The interior of the pub was full of smoke and poorly lit so that it was almost impossible to see across the room. As Babington sought out a table at the rear, Souto and Morden took another some distance away in the darkness of an alcove which gave them a good view of things. Because of its odd interior, the inn could accommodate all sorts of groups and still convey an illusion of privacy. At one end, a small party was carousing and dancing, with two buskers doing an act accompanied by a piano. There were railwaymen in another alcove, tradesmen, bargees, a few businessmen, a few stage door mashers, sweating men in ratcatchers' thigh boots with dogs and ferrets, a cripple on a trolley which he propelled with his hands among the spittoons on the saw-dusted floor, aproned salesmen, a bevy of whores, and one man sitting on his own with a carpet bag by his feet, who looked like a commercial traveller a long way from home looking for some fun.

A plump red-faced man was waiting for Babington. He wore good clothes but somehow still managed to look shabby. He carried a silver-topped cane and a pair of yellow wash-leather gloves.

'Nothing doing,' they heard Babington say. 'He was too fly. He probably won't play. We'll have to rely on Barney.'

He waved across the smoky room and they were joined by another man wearing a red neckcloth and a top hat with a dent in it. His face couldn't be seen in the shadows but he wore a shabby white waistcoat that seemed to be marked by the remains of his meals, and he had an air of flashy self-confidence about him. He accepted a drink and sat down at the table with the others.

'Know 'em, sir?' Morden asked.

'I know the fat fellow,' Souto said. 'It's Spencer Valentine. Claims to be acting for the Beaufort family, but if he is, I imagine what he's doing here is without their knowledge. He's a solicitor and his reputation's nothing to write home about. The man we followed is Archibald Babington, who claims to be a cousin of Captain Nolan.'

'And t'other?'

'I don't know him.'

They remained in the public house for an hour, sipping brandy and water and keeping an eye on the three men at the other table. It was impossible to hear what they said because their heads were close together and they were speaking quietly. Eventually, the solicitor, Valentine, finished his drink and rose.

'I'm off,' they heard him say.

Soon afterwards, Babington also left and the man they had called Barney disappeared to the back of the room among the smoke and shadows.

'What happens now?' Morden asked.

Souto frowned. 'I don't know,' he admitted. 'But I think I'll have a watch put on Valentine's chambers to see who turns up there. It might be interesting. At least we'll be prepared in case anything unexpected is produced at Hounslow.'

Chapter Eight

The following day's newspapers, of which Souto had bought a selection to read in the train, had it all down.

'Hounslow Court Martial.' The single column headline in the *Morning Post* jumped out at Souto at once. 'Balaclava Hero Gives Evidence. Lord Cardigan in Court.'

The evidence of Airey and Cardigan had been reported word for word, in small narrow print, column after column of it. Souto glanced over it. Nothing appeared to have been left out. Lucan's cross-examination of Airey had not been especially highlighted or cross-headed, however, and the details were lost in the mass of type, as though the editor did not consider it of much value. There was also a leader which was an unctuous airing of opinion. The paper considered that the presentation of the facts of the case was totally unnecessary, since they had already been outlined in pamphlets, in the House of Lords, in the McNeill–Tulloch report and by what it once again called 'The Whitewashing Board'. 'It is impossible to decide,' it said, 'what else could be observed about this tragic affair. All it can do is outline the inefficiency of the cavalry command and the fact that many men lost their lives quite unnecessarily.'

Lucan had also read the papers and his face was angry as he greeted Souto. 'They're already giving their verdict,' he snapped.

'Opinions,' Souto said equably. 'It's up to us to change

them. Perhaps by tomorrow they'll be singing a different song.'

'They've not even noticed what an ass Airey seemed.'

'Airey's not important.'

'He wrote the damned orders.'

'Let's see what they think of my Lord Cardigan. If you handle him as you handled Airey, they may be giving him a different title tomorrow from "Hero of Balaclava."''

Lucan's eyes flashed and Souto decided to reiterate his warning. 'I do beg you, my lord, to be careful. Ask no questions if you don't know what the answer should be. That's the first precept of cross-examination.'

'I'd like to roast him,' Lucan frowned. 'In hell if possible. He caused me more trouble than any other man, even including that old woman, Raglan.'

'Then I implore you to handle him as you handled Airey. Don't bungle it. Stick to your brief, watch your questions, and if you're in any doubt, remember I'm right there at your side. If I feel you're heading along dangerous pathways, I shall touch your sleeve. Bear that in mind, my lord. It is important.'

There was a stir as they appeared. The place was ablaze with colour from the uniforms that crammed the room. In addition, everybody was hopeful of seeing a great deal of spirit this day. Everybody knew of the dislike the two brothers-in-law had for each other. It had been common knowledge in the army for a long time and even the newspapers had taken it up. The old story that the conflict between them had been the cause of the disaster to the Light Brigade had been dragged up again and there was a thrill of anticipation because everybody expected fireworks.

Lucan rose slowly. Cardigan eyed him arrogantly, but with a barely hidden wariness.

'Let us go back to the beginning,' Lucan said, his voice harsh and grating. 'Since everybody else seems to be starting at the beginning, we will too. Scutari. When did you arrive there, my lord?'

'24 May,' Cardigan barked.

'How did you arrive?'

'Travelled via Paris.'

'Where you were invited to the Tuileries?'

'Yes.' Cardigan snapped the word.

'Wouldn't it have been better if you had gone as fast as you could to your command?'

Eyland looked up sharply. 'Lord Lucan,' he snapped. 'Like many other people, I am fully aware of the feelings that exist between yourself and Lord Cardigan, and I have to warn you that this court will not tolerate any bickering between you. I was a spectator at the Woodford Board and I saw the unseemly arguments that took place. I will not have them here. Let that be understood.'

About to attack, Lucan grew red. Then he glanced at Souto, drew a deep breath and nodded. 'I will endeavour to remember, sir,' he said.

He turned to Cardigan. 'You have spoken many times,' he said, 'of the difficult position you were placed in by my orders right from the beginning. However, is it not true that I went out of my way to remember that we were soldiers on active service as well as related by marriage?'

Cardigan sniffed. 'Didn't notice it. Seemed to me that —'

'Lord Cardigan.' Eyland's voice was sharp. 'I have had occasion to warn you already. What I have said to Lord Lucan applies equally to you. We are not seeking your opinions. We are seeking facts. Confine yourself to them.'

Lucan waited for his brother-in-law to compose himself before continuing. 'Did I not meet you at Scutari and invite you to dinner?'

'Yes,' Cardigan's agreement was grudging.

'Did it not pass off well, as our first meeting had?'

Cardigan frowned. 'Food was dreadful,' he said.

Lucan frowned back, but he visibly drew another deep breath.

'When the 8th Hussars, the 17th Lancers and the horse

artillery moved to Varna, did you request permission to accompany them?'

'Of course I did. Been led to believe I held an independent command.'

Eyland seemed about to interrupt, then he changed his mind and Lucan continued.

'And you departed,' he said, 'without informing me, your Divisional Commander?'

'Thought I had an independent command,' Cardigan reiterated. 'Assumed Lord Raglan would inform you.'

'Are you aware that he did not and that I was left completely in the dark as to what was happening?'

'I was not aware.'

'Were you *never* aware?'

'I learned at Varna.'

'Didn't you think it strange?'

'I believed I had an independent command.'

'Would it not in any case have been merely good manners to inform me?'

'Didn't seem necessary. Thought I had an independent command.' The words came like a litany.

'Did you know that my first intimation of your departure was a note from Lord de Ros asking me to make arrangements for you?'

'I wasn't privy to what Lord de Ros did.'

'Nevertheless, did I not write you a letter, mild in tone, saying that the service could not be carried on as it should be, if a subordinate officer were allowed to pass over his immediate responsible superior, the Divisional Commander, to communicate directly with the General Commander-in-Chief or his staff?'

'I don't recall.'

'I do, sir,' Lucan snapped. 'I have a copy of that letter here because I took care to keep copies of everything that passed between us.' His voice had grown harsher and more peremptory. 'Did I not say "I write privately, as I wish this

111

letter to be of the most friendly nature?" Did I not continue that I hoped that the arrangements I had made for your embarkation were, as I intended them to be, as agreeable and convenient as they could be?'

Cardigan looked sullen. 'I don't recall.'

Lucan stared at his brother-in-law with dislike, then held up the letter for Eyland to see. 'A copy of that letter is here, sir, and I offer it to the court.' He turned again to Cardigan. 'Despite the mild tone of the letter, despite the attempts I was making, in the face of our old emnity, to behave like a couple of senior officers on active service, into whose duties private dislikes should not be allowed to enter – despite this attempt at friendliness, did you apologise, comment on my letter, or ever thank me for the arrangements I had made?'

Cardigan frowned. 'I don't recall.'

Lucan sighed, annoyed at Cardigan's dourness. 'You were now at Varna,' he said. 'How many horses were lost in the landing?'

'I don't recall.'

Lucan held up a slip of paper. 'I have the returns, sir,' he said. 'Seventeen were injured in being put ashore. On top of those which had suffered severely from the voyage out from England. Why was this?'

'I don't recall.'

'Was it because the arrangements had been hurriedly made and were quite inadequate?'

'No, sir,' Cardigan's voice rose. 'If I am to be accused —'

'Lord Cardigan!' Eyland's voice rose too.

'He is accusing me —'

'He is not accusing you, my lord. He is asking a question. If you have a satisfactory answer, that is what we want.'

'It's over two years ago.' Cardigan's voice was indignant. 'I don't remember everything. All I remember is that the place was damned unhealthy, both for men and beasts. I had established my headquarters in a house near a stream and was occupied in sending patrols to the north.'

112

'British cavalry patrols?' Lucan asked.

'No, sir,' Cardigan snapped. 'Turkish, accompanied by British officers. But occasionally British cavalry.'

'To whom you made it clear you would be disappointed if they found no Cossacks?'

'Lord Lucan, you are putting leading questions.' Eyland's words were accompanied by a touch on the arm from Souto and Lucan drew a deep breath.

Cardigan scowled as Lucan went on relentlessly. 'How many copies of your report did you forward to divisional headquarters?'

'I don't recall.'

'I do, sir,' Lucan snapped. 'None. Why was this?'

'The heat was terrific.'

'It was terrific for everybody. On 11 June, did I not write to you insisting on returns and reports?'

'Yes.'

'Did you send them?'

'I expect so.'

'I can assure you, sir, you did not. It was because of this that I complained to Lord Raglan that the cavalry division seemed to be under your command while I was left behind at Scutari without troops and without duties. I was therefore hurriedly ordered to Varna and foolishly persuaded to withdraw my complaint. I arrived at Varna on 15 June. It was then that I finally received a reply to my letter demanding returns and reports. Do you recall what you wrote?'

'No, sir, I do not.'

'Let me remind you.' Lucan produced another of his everlasting sheets of paper and began to read. 'You said you considered that your command was a separate one and that you did not feel bound to anyone but Lord Raglan, to whom it was your intention of submitting an appeal. Do you remember that?'

'I considered my command an independent one.'

'So you have repeatedly told us. From then on, did I ever give you a direct order until the day of Balaclava?'

'You did not.'

'Were you aware that this was because your letter had made me decide that if there was to be no trouble between us it could only be by *never* giving an order personally but only through an aide.'

'I can't read other people's minds.'

Lucan seemed to be enjoying himself. 'Were you, after that date, informed by the Adjutant-General that your beliefs about your command were entirely misconceived, and that you should understand that I could call for whatever returns I felt necessary and take what steps I wished to look into the efficiency of my command.'

'I don't recall.'

'You seem to recall very little.'

Cardigan turned to Eyland. 'I must protest, sir —' he began, then as Eyland lifted his head, frowning, he became silent, his face red.

'Were you aware,' Lucan moved on remorselessly, 'that I was requesting at this time permission to join my command, which by now had moved to Devna?'

'How can I know such things?'

'Of course,' Lucan said sarcastically. 'You cannot. But let me assure you, *I* did. I was told, however, that I should remain in Varna to inspect further detachments of cavalry which were due to arrive. I have now, as I had then, my own suspicions about the reasons for that refusal. I suspect it was so that you, sir, could continue to act independently and thus cause no trouble to Lord Raglan. In fact, at that moment a large proportion of my cavalry was about to leave Devna and disappear into the blue, was it not?'

'I don't know what you mean?'

'The siege of Silistria had been raised and you had been ordered by Lord Raglan, again without my being informed, to reconnoitre the banks of the Danube. You were given written orders. Do you recall them?'

'I've already given evidence on this matter. I was to discover if the Russians had withdrawn. I did discover that fact.'

'Did not your orders also say that if you found water and foraging difficult you were to use only a small portion of your force?'

'I believe they did.'

'Was I aware of these instructions?'

'You seemed to be unaware.'

'Did I not invite you to breakfast with me that morning in an attempt to keep the peace between us?'

'We had breakfast together,' Cardigan conceded.

'And at that time you already had Lord Raglan's order in your possession?'

'Yes.'

'But you did not see fit to inform me?'

'I thought my command was independent.'

'You had just been informed by the adjutant-general that it was *not*. How many men did you take?'

'Almost two hundred.'

'You consider that a *small* portion of your force.'

'Water and foraging were not difficult.'

'Were they not? Did you take food with you?'

'Only the minimum.'

'Tents?'

'No.'

'Were the horses fit for such a long journey at the pace you set?'

'Of course.'

'They had only recently come from the transports after many weeks *en voyage*. Did their saddles fit well?'

'Of course.'

'I have a report here, sir.' Lucan held up a sheet of paper. 'It is from the commanding officer of the 13th. It states that, because of their leanness, their saddles no longer fitted. He also complains that, since no baggage carts or tents were taken, they were absurdly overloaded with extra equipment and rations.'

Cardigan glowered, saying nothing.

'You returned on 11 June?'

'Yes. It was raining.'

'How did the men arrive?'

'In excellent fashion.'

Lucan held up a book. 'I have here,' he said, 'a recently published book. It is by Mrs Duberly, wife of the paymaster of the 11th Hussars. We have already heard of her.'

Souto was sitting back, enjoying himself, and wondering why Lucan had never gone in for law. His showing in Parliament on the occasion of his protest had been much admired, though his appearance at the McNeill–Tulloch Enquiry had been marred by bitter exchanges with Cardigan and refusals to answer questions. Under control, he seemed to know exactly what to do.

Lucan was still holding the book in the air. 'Mrs Duberly saw the patrol return. She says so here. She says it was a pitiful sight. Do you call that in good spirits and condition?'

Cardigan didn't answer.

Lucan was now holding up another book. 'I have here a copy of a book called *The War Up To The Death of Lord Raglan*. It was written by Mr William Howard Russell, the correspondent of *The Times* newspaper. He also has something to say about your patrol. He suggests that it effected very little service, that you had been more than once lost and on one occasion allowed your exhausted men to bivouac in full view of a Russian battery across the river, which, fortunately for them, did not fire. Were you aware that your patrol became known in the cavalry as the Soreback Patrol?'

Cardigan scowled. 'I never heard the expression.'

'Naturally not. But I have the returns. Not, I might add, supplied by yourself. Five of your horses dropped dead, and seventy-five were dying when you returned, almost a hundred lost out of two hundred at a time when it was necessary to conserve their strength. Of the remainder, most were judged to be totally unfit for anything but light work

116

because of a foot disease they had picked up through too much fast trotting on hard roads.'

'That's a damned lie!'

'It's in the report of the veterinary surgeon who examined them.'

As the paper went to the judges Lucan held up another sheet. 'I have here a report from a French officer. He says he met you as you returned. You had all your men mounted. He was surprised, because when he had first seen them your men were leading their horses and carrying the saddles because of their sore backs. He said you appeared to have difficulty in getting the men to put the saddles on at all. He thought it was all a little showing-off.'

'The French never did tell the truth,' Cardigan snapped. 'Lord Raglan wrote to me to say I had done all that he required of me.'

'He was not made aware of the number of horses that had returned sick, and was therefore not aware that the cavalry was seriously incommoded by the loss of so many horses at a time when Captain Nolan, who was seeking remounts, was finding it extremely difficult to buy them.' Another piece of paper appeared. 'I have here an order issued by myself. It is dated 11 June – the day your patrol returned. It states that no horses were to be destroyed except in the case of broken leg, glanders or farcy, which, as the court will know, are highly contagious diseases introduced into the division by the Royal Dragoons, which had picked them up en route from England.' Lucan held up yet another sheet of paper. 'This is another order, sir. It indicates a route up-country to a new camp and it states that it has been selected for its easiness in the hope of reducing fatalities. Why would these orders have been issued save for the fact that the two hundred horses you had taken on your patrol were no longer of use as cavalry mounts?'

Cardigan glared as Lucan shrugged and passed the papers to the officers on the long table.

'There were several incidents, were there not, when your men narrowly escaped capture?'

'Never.'

Lucan held up Mrs Duberly's book. 'According to Mrs Duberly, you felt for neither man nor horse.'

'Mrs Duberly is a woman. She doesn't understand.'

'On the contrary, sir, she is a brilliant horsewoman. I often wished she were not in the Crimea and, indeed, she had no right to be there because I had given strict orders that she was not to be there, orders, which incidentally, you countermanded —'

'Lord Lucan!' Eyland's sharp words halted Lucan.

Lucan stopped dead. 'Very well, sir,' he managed stiffly. 'I'll not refer to that. However, Mrs Duberly is well-known for her ability to care for horses, and it's for this reason that I produce her book – the document I hold in my hand – and offer it as evidence.'

Eyland sighed. He knew Lucan as pernickety and careful and had heard that, finding things difficult in the Crimea, he had taken the precaution of preserving every single scrap of writing that had come into his possession. It had probably been a wise precaution but he felt that before the end of the case they were going to be snowed under by Lucan's documents.

He gestured and Lucan turned to Cardigan again, probing remorselessly. 'Is it not a fact,' he asked, 'that many of your men were brought in on carts because they had collapsed from exhaustion on this successful patrol of yours?'

'They were not exhausted!' Cardigan almost snarled the words. 'I took care. Though I was a major-general, I could feel for my men.'

'Did they take their clothes off during the days you were on patrol?'

'We were in the face of the enemy.'

'Did they take them off?'

'No.'

'Where did they sleep?'

'On the ground.'

'You shared their hardships, of course?'

'Of course.'

'How did *you* sleep, my lord?

Cardigan's face went red. 'I had a spring sofa bed.'

'In the open? Under the stars?'

'I had a tent.'

'But your men did not?'

'I had duties that demanded I should be alert. It was necessary to sleep and remain in good health.'

'But not your men. Did you allow them to carry cloaks?'

'Of course.'

Lucan held up a sheet of paper. 'According to this report by Lieutenant Percy Smith of the 13th, you did not. Did you remain in good health throughout?'

'I thought I bore it well.'

'Then why did Lord Raglan's letter of congratulation to you end with the hope that your fatigue would not prove injurious to your health?'

Cardigan glowered. 'How did you get that letter?'

'I have a copy. It came to me from a member of Lord Raglan's staff. It was one of the few occasions when a copy of anything was kept at headquarters.'

'They wouldn't let *you* see Lord Raglan's letters!'

'I saw this one. I got the impression that the officer in question had no love for you, sir, and not much admiration for Lord Raglan either. Doubtless he was not a relation.'

'It gives a wrong impression. It was merely a kind thought. I was not exhausted.'

'Then why did you inform me you would be unable to attend to your duties for some days due to exhaustion?'

'I said no such thing.'

Lucan said nothing. He merely picked up a sheet of paper and passed it to the judges. Eyland accepted it with a raised eyebrow. 'I have to congratulate you, my lord,' he said, 'on your efficiency in keeping all these small pieces of paper.'

'It is a habit of mine, sir.' Lucan turned to Cardigan again. 'Soon after your return, did you not move with your brigade to Yeni-Bazaar, twenty-eight miles from Devna?'

'Cholera had broken out in Varna.'

'Indeed it had. But did you or Lord Raglan bother to inform me where you had disappeared to?'

'There was much to do. And it was very hot. When a well was found, there was such a rush for it, Captain Lockwood's horse almost fell in.'

'This well. It was near your tent. Did you not slap a sentry on it so that the men couldn't use it?'

Cardigan looked daggers. 'There was a fear that the water was tainted with the germs of cholera.'

'And when Mrs Duberly selected a spot for her tent in the shade of a clump of trees, did you not insist on her moving it so you could place yours there instead?'

Cardigan's glare was basilisk. 'She was taking up room and water that the troops required. And she shouldn't have been there.'

'Then she shouldn't have been in the Crimea either, should she? But you appealed to Lord Raglan to allow her to go and when he refused, you did not stop her, did you?'

There was a long silence in court as Cardigan sat and seethed. He was unable to reply and there was considerable movement among the bonnets and shawls with the rumours that the reason had been because Mrs Duberly, despite her earlier detestation of Lord Cardigan, had suddenly become very friendly with him.

Lucan was addressing the court. 'I will not dwell on the period of the cholera epidemic, save to say that it caused considerable casualties in the cavalry camp. As Lord Cardigan has already stated, men fit and well at noon could be dead by evening. It was worst in the French camps. In one night six hundred men died. I myself saw hands and feet sticking from the soil where men had been hurriedly buried and bodies floated in the sea, defying all efforts to sink them.'

'Are you offering this as evidence, my lord?' Eyland asked.

'I am trying merely to give a picture of the conditions, sir. The fact that the army was shabby and listless had little to do with the cavalry really, but affairs among them were so bad that the 5th Dragoon Guards, which had suffered severely, were attached to the 4th Dragoon Guards, with the result that the commanding officer of the 4th, Colonel Hodge, became known as the colonel of the 9th.'

There was a murmur of laughter in the court. Eyland let it go. It seemed a good opportunity to release some of the tension engendered by the exchanges between Cardigan and Lucan.

'Let us go now,' Lucan said, 'to the Crimea.' He looked at Cardigan. 'Am I not right in saying that the orders issued from Lord Raglan's headquarters were that only one horse was to be allowed for each officer on the understanding that others would follow and more would be available when the army landed in the Crimea?'

Cardigan considered the question, saw nothing offensive to him in it, and answered briskly. 'You are right.'

'But, unfortunately, due to the fact that the depot formed for those that remained behind was so badly organised by the staff and the commissariat, most of them starved to death.'

Again Cardigan had to agree.

'Despite the fact that by this time I had been gazetted lieutenant-general, is it not a fact that you were instructed to take the cavalry to the Crimea while I was to remain in Varna?'

'Lord Raglan wished to give me back my independence of action.'

'You had never had an independence, sir! Are you aware what resulted?'

'I know you wrote to Lord Raglan.'

'I did indeed.' Lucan passed a letter to the judges. 'That is what I wrote, gentlemen. You will see that I protested that, since I was supposed to be Lord Raglan's official adviser on cavalry, I could not understand what use I could possibly be to him in the Crimea if I were to be left at the other side of the Black Sea. I pointed out that this state of affairs had already happened too often and that Lord Cardigan was still not sending me the returns he had been ordered to send, that he appeared to have repudiated my authority altogether and that he had left me ignorant of my men's positions, their duties, efficiency and discipline.'

'You have made that very plain, my lord,' Eyland said dryly.

Lucan turned again to Cardigan. 'Before the troops were embarked, did I inspect your brigade?'

'You did.'

Lucan passed up another sheet. 'That is my report, sir.'

Eyland frowned, accepted the report and read it aloud. 'The men are not cleanly in their appearance or in their persons,' he said. 'Their clothes are unnecessarily dirty and stained, their arms are not as clean as they ought to be, their belts, leathers and appointments, both of man and horse, are rusty and dirty. It would appear as if the object were that every soldier on service should appear as unsoldierlike, slovenly and dirty as possible.' Eyland seemed to find Lucan's efficiency as tedious as Cardigan's inefficiency.

'I had not been well since the patrol to the Dobrudja,' Cardigan interrupted.

Lucan pounced at once. 'You have just told us you were *not* ill!'

'Gentlemen!' Eyland's voice rapped sharply across the clatter of voices. He paused and glanced at the report. 'I notice, my lord, that you also complain of the depot being dirty and full of deserted chargers and baggage animals.'

'That was my duty, sir.' Lucan turned to Cardigan again. 'En route for the Crimea, did you not take it on yourself to issue an order for a court martial? For what reason does not matter here, since you had no such right and were so informed by me, along with a reminder that I would require embarkation returns on landing.'

Cardigan scowled. 'Lord Raglan had informed me in the most distinct terms before leaving Varna that you would not interfere or deprive me of the Light Brigade.'

'Of course I would not, sir,' Lucan snapped. 'I was merely trying to stop you usurping command of the *division*. Nevertheless, you replied informing me of that belief, which you have just passed on to the court. When I did not bother to reply, did you not send another, more aggressive, letter to the *Simla*, in which I was travelling, stating that it was impossible to carry out your duties until your position in the expedition was made clear?'

'I don't recall.' Cardigan was once more taking refuge in a failing memory.

'Let me remind you.' There was nothing wrong with Lucan's memory and he self-righteously offered a sheet of paper to the judges. 'That is a copy of my reply. It states: "To circulate a memorandum that disembarkation returns should be required on landing, a memorandum which has been circulated to all senior officers, is not an irregularity, nor is it disrespectful or any encroachment on your authority." It states also that I much regret that you should entertain what I considered a misconception and points out that, while I knew my own position, I also knew and respected yours, and that your position as a brigade commander would not differ from that held by any other brigadier, of whom there were so many in the six divisions of the army.'

Eyland listened impatiently to the harsh driving voice. He was clearly growing bored with this dispute. 'I think, my lord,' he said slowly, 'that you have made your point. We accept that Lord Cardigan was labouring under a misconception about his command and that you, while endeavouring to retain your temper, had no intention of permitting him to overstep the mark. We would prefer to move on a little, if we may.'

Lucan stiffened and then bowed. 'Very well, sir. I will do my best.' He bent to confer with Souto, then rose and faced Cardigan again.

'On landing on the shore of Crimea,' he said, 'were you reminded that, due to the small numbers of cavalry available, it was the duty of the Light Brigade for the time being to remain on the defence and not to engage the enemy without authority?'

'Of course I remember that. I had been ordered into the interior to capture carts and food for the army.'

'How many men did you take?'

'Two hundred and fifty cavalrymen and two hundred and fifty Riflemen.'

'What happened?'

'I saw no enemy and brought in a number of carts.'

Lucan passed over another of his interminable sheets of paper. 'An indignant report, gentlemen, from the commanding officer of the Rifles,' he explained. 'You will notice that he complains that Lord Cardigan had not noticed that men on foot do not travel as fast as men on horses, even when the horses are ridden at a walk. You will notice also that he points out that most of the few carts that were brought in were used not to carry food back to the army but to carry the exhausted men of the Rifles.' Another sheet of paper was passed across the table. 'That is my report to Lord Raglan on the suffering of the horses which were without water for thirty hours.' Yet another paper. 'That is a report from the Spahis, the French cavalry, who, it seems, did rather better, and brought in flocks of sheep and cattle and a long string of country carts and camels heavily laden with grain.'

'What are you trying to show, my lord?' Eyland asked. 'I take it this has some bearing on the later events.'

'It does indeed, sir. As I shall show.'

'Very well. Proceed.'

Lucan glanced at Souto and drew a deep breath. 'I'll not dwell on the flank march, save to say that for some reason best known to themselves the staff considered it wise to march right round Sebastopol and sit down to a siege instead of attacking it immediately from the north and thus finishing the war at once.'

He paused. 'I will also not dwell on the deaths from cholera and heatstroke that the march occasioned. Let us go instead to the skirmish at the Bulganak. I do not dispute the evidence Lord Cardigan has already given. He did exactly as he says he did. He prepared to attack, and I have to admit that from his position what he did was correct. But from where I was, it was not. I was higher than he was on the slopes and had seen more Russians beyond the few cavalry patrols which were facing his lordship. So, moreover, had Lord Raglan, and that was the reason for my refusing Lord Cardigan permission to attack and the reason why General Airey arrived while we were discussing it – I might even say, arguing about it – and made it clear that Lord Raglan did *not* wish an attack. A few shots were exchanged and the cavalry retired.'

Again a pause. 'I will also not dispute Lord Cardigan's evidence of the Alma. The cavalry were on the left of the line and in a melon field. Indeed, the soldiers were reaching down with their lances and sabres and lifting the melons, which they ate to quench their thirst. When the battle had finished, however, we had the position of two thousand British soldiers left unsupported in the captured Great Redoubt, with a large Russian column and nearly four thousand Russian cavalry close at hand. It was my wish to go to their help but the only orders I had received that morning were strict instructions not to move until told to do so. They left no room whatsoever for personal decisions. In the end, I did move my men to the river on my own initiative but when I tried to move them further forward in support, I received an instruction ordering the recall. It caused me considerable anger but there was no doubt about what it meant.'

'I take it that this will appear in evidence?' Eyland asked.

'It will, sir. For the moment I wish only to show the direction of events. I had no other course but to turn loose the prisoners we had taken and gallop back to support the guns. Lord Raglan had forgotten that I had once commanded a Russian cavalry division and that my opinion of them was not high. As they showed at Balaclava they possessed no dash and, despite our fagged horses, we could have driven them from the field of the Alma and started a rout.'

Eyland moved restlessly. 'Let us leave that for the time being, my lord, and proceed.'

Lucan gave a little bow. 'There were other things that bothered me,' he said, turning to Cardigan. 'Did you not, at this totally inopportune moment, send, via me, to the Commander-in-Chief, a letter containing all your old complaints about me and reiterating that the Light Brigade should be independent of my orders?'

Cardigan scowled. 'I wrote no such letter.'

Lucan passed over the inevitable piece of paper. 'That is a copy, gentlemen. I sent it to headquarters with a note.'

'Expressing your views, no doubt, sir?' Eyland said.

'Of course,' Lucan agreed. 'I pointed out that I had continually gone out of my way to be helpful, friendly and pacific. Three days later,' he continued, 'long after the Russians had had time to reorganise, the allies moved after them.'

'I take it,' Eyland said, 'that you are now indicating the confusion at headquarters.'

'It has great bearing on what happened afterwards. Much has been made by the prosecution of the fact that the cavalry under my command got lost on the way to Khuton Mackenzie. I will not now go into that fact except to say I brought the cavalry back to their proper position at once.'

Lucan had now turned to Cardigan. 'What was the position of the army at this time, sir?'

'We were advancing on Sebastopol,' Cardigan said, 'and were just emerging from a stretch of forest when we stumbled on the Russians retreating on Sebastopol from the Alma. They ran like hares.'

'And you, sir. What did you do?'

'Set off with the 17th Lancers down the hill after them.'

'So far ahead, in fact, one of your aides warned that you were in danger of capture, and you had to be recalled after one of your sergeants had been made a prisoner. Is that not so?'

'I don't recall.' Cardigan said.

'*I* recall that you immediately made it clear to Lord Raglan that you had not been in command during the time the cavalry had been lost.'

'Gentlemen!' Eyland warned sharply.

Lucan acknowledged the rebuke. 'Let us come to 7 October. The day you said the Russians moved forward and the cavalry took up a position from which they might have attacked but did not.'

Cardigan sniffed. 'I remember it well.'

'Where were you?'

'With the cavalry.'

'Then you will be aware, my lord, that on this occasion I was much criticised by the rest of the army and, in particular by Captain Nolan. Yet,' once again a sheet of paper, 'a letter arrived at my headquarters from Lord Raglan, praising my forebearance in refraining from attack.' Lucan looked at Eyland. 'It points out, sir, as you will notice, Lord Raglan's concern that, due to the shortage of cavalry, he was anxious that we should not get involved in unnecessary fights in the plain, that his most active concern was the siege of Sebastopol, and that he wished that I should do nothing to draw any troops from that object. You will see even that my request for an additional troop of artillery and a few infantry is turned down on the same grounds of his concern with the siege.' Lucan turned to Cardigan. 'You have stated that it was on this day that I acquired a nickname?'

'Look-on. Yes.'

'Because, despite Lord Raglan's wishes, I did not attack.'

'I knew nothing of Lord Raglan's wishes.'

'Of course not. Nor, I think, were you aware of what I discovered later – that sixteen squadrons of cavalry and up to two thousand infantry were laying in wait for any advance on our part. Were you aware of that?'

Cardigan frowned. 'I was not.'

'Why not?'

'I don't recall why not?'

Lucan passed up one of his slips of paper. 'Returns, sir,' he said. 'It shows that Lord Cardigan was *not* with the cavalry, but was off duty sick and did not return until the 8th.'

Eyland looked at Cardigan. 'Is that so, my lord?'

Cardigan flushed. 'I could have sworn I was there.'

'But you were not, were you?'

'No.'

'Then you could have known nothing of what happened or of the opportunities offered, could you?' Lucan snapped.

'I was told.'

'Who by?'

'Captain Nolan. He was there.'

Lucan nodded. 'I will come to Captain Nolan later,' he said ominously. 'It's my belief that it was Captain Nolan who thought of the name Look-On.' He paused and Souto recognised the gleam of malice in his eye. 'Since we're on the subject, my lord, did you not acquire a nickname yourself?'

Cardigan frowned. 'Not to my knowledge.'

'Never mind. Let us proceed to the morning of 25 October. When I, together with Sir Colin Campbell and Lord George Paget, were busy turning out the cavalry after becoming aware of the Russian advance on Balaclava. Where were you, my lord?'

128

'I was asleep.'

'I did not ask in what condition. I asked where.'

'Aboard my yacht.'

There was a long pause. Lucan had even learned the art of letting things sink in.

'Where?'

'In Balaclava harbour.'

'A luxurious yacht, in fact, complete with a wine cellar and a French chef, which took up valuable space in an already choked harbour that ships bringing supplies, munitions and reinforcements might have used. Did Lord Raglan suggest, or request, or order, that it should be removed?'

Cardigan sniffed. 'It was a private yacht. He didn't consider it part of his duty.'

'A great pity. Was that yacht not the cause of *your* nickname, the Noble Yachtsman?'

'Let us not descend into personalities, gentlemen,' Eyland warned.

'No sir,' Lucan said. 'I have nothing more to say on the subject.'

But the point had been made. Cardigan had lived in comfort on his private yacht while other senior officers had lived in tents on the Russian uplands, and when he had been wanted, he was not there.

'I merely wished, sir,' Lucan explained, 'to indicate one of the reasons for the attitude of the rest of the army to the cavalry.'

Privately, Eyland thought that the rest of the army had good cause. As an infantryman, he had often considered the cavalry a lot of overdressed poseurs, but he pushed the thought from his mind and tried to keep it neutral.

'Let us come to the morning of 25 October,' Lucan said. He indicated the map which had been placed where everybody could see it. 'That is the situation, and I have to ask the court to note the spur of land which projects into the North Valley from the Causeway Heights. It lay across the Light

Brigade's path and brought the enemy guns and riflemen within close range. So close, in fact, the fire was murderous.' He paused, 'I have no wish to denigrate the actions of Lord Cardigan on that tragic morning, so I will not question him save on a few small points.' He looked at Cardigan. 'The army was quick to notice that the defence of Balaclava was given not to me, a lieutenant-general, but to Sir Colin Campbell, a mere brigadier. Is that so?'

Cardigan frowned. 'I heard so.'

'In fact, it made little difference and, since Sir Colin and I were on good terms, we consulted regularly and he made various suggestions at the opening of the battle which I was more than happy to accept. Did you know that?'

'I was not privy to your thoughts.'

Lucan smiled. 'But when the command was announced, complaints were made about Sir Colin's junior rank, weren't they?' he said. 'Despite Sir Colin's forty years of experience in battle.'

Cardigan shifted uneasily. 'I don't know.'

'You don't, sir?' Lucan gave a hawk-like smile. 'Was it not you who made them? Harping on the old theme of an independent command. Did you not ask how *he* had got one when you had not?'

Eyland's head jerked up. 'That will be enough of that, Lord Lucan,' he snapped. 'I have already intimated that the court has had quite enough on that subject.'

Lucan bowed. He had made the point and everyone was aware of it.

He turned to the judges. 'It was becoming clear by this time, gentlemen,' he said, 'that the army was going to have to spend the turn of the year on the uplands of the Crimea. There were already difficulties which grew eventually into the crisis of the winter when the army all but sank into the ground. I'll not question Lord Cardigan on the letters that passed between us on the subject of him living on his yacht in Balaclava harbour so that the time of orderlies had to be wasted in the transference of messages —'

'I trust you will not, sir.'

Lucan had once again slipped in evidence. By this time Souto was almost wondering if he couldn't somehow use him in his chambers.

Lucan was shuffling his papers.

'Lord Cardigan,' he said, 'since you were asleep on your yacht when the battle commenced, you were not there when the Light Brigade was drawn up to the south of Number One Redoubt at the time it was under fire from the Russian guns.'

'No!' Cardigan snapped.

'It was at a time when horses were being knocked over and when Cornet Goad of the 13th was so badly injured he had to leave the field.'

Cardigan scowled. 'I arrived as soon as possible.'

'Of course. Let us continue. To the point when the cavalry was withdrawn on Sir Colin Campbell's advice to a spot clear of the cavalry camps but protecting them and in a position where it could attack in flank any attempt on Balaclava. Were you aware of Lord Raglan's order withdrawing us still further?'

'I'm aware that the order came to move back.'

'Let us go to the Heavies' charge. You had been placed in position. Do you remember my words?'

'I do not.'

'Were they not to the effect that you had been placed there by Lord Raglan himself for the defence of the position? You were to attack anything and everything that came within reach but you were to be careful of columns or squares of infantry.'

'I remember only that I was adjured to remain exactly where I was placed. There was no mention of attacking.'

Lucan shrugged. 'I will not argue. After the Heavies' attack, did not Captain Morris, commanding the Lancers, ask if you were not going to attack the retreating Russians?'

'No.'

'Did he not say it was your positive duty to follow up the advantages created by the Heavies?'

'No.'

'Did he not beg to be allowed some sort of pursuit? Did he not ask to be allowed to charge them with the 17th?'

'No.'

'Did he not finally turn to his officers and say "Gentlemen, you are witness to my request?"'

Cardigan's head was down and he answered doggedly. 'He made no such request.'

'Did you not hear him say, sir, "My God, what a chance we are losing"?'

'No.'

'You did not consider it part of your duty to attack?'

'I had been placed where I was to guard the position.'

'What did the position consist of?'

Cardigan looked surprised.

'Was it not merely a space of open ground of little value?'

'It was part of the plain.'

'Then why guard *that* part? Why was it different from the rest?'

'I had been given my orders.'

'Did not my aide, Lord Bingham, appear with a message ordering the Light Brigade to sweep round the retiring Russians' right flank and pick up stragglers? And did he not point out that I was extremely disappointed at not having had the support of the Light Brigade in the Heavies' action and that when the Divisional Commander was attacking in front it was your duty to support him with a flank attack?'

'I remember no such message.'

Lucan shrugged again, as if he were growing tired of his obdurate brother-in-law. 'Nevertheless,' he ended wearily, 'is it not a fact that a few men of the Light Brigade, unable to sit still and see an opportunity go by which might have swept the Russians clean off the field and won the day if it had been taken, sneak away and join the Heavies for their charge?' He paused. 'Let us come now to that splendid but unnecessary action of the Light Brigade. I remember afterwards that I was so impressed by the way it was conducted that in my despatch I paid high tribute to the cavalry and especially to General Scarlett and yourself. Is that not so?'

'You were kind enough to refer to the attack as "very brilliant and daring," and that I had led it in the most gallant and intrepid manner.'

'I did indeed, and very rightly. But why did you not halt when you saw the casualties being inflicted on your brigade? Were you not told to advance steadily? Why did you not try to interpret that order as something other than a command to proceed to the martyrdom of your brigade? Did you never turn to see what was happening to it?'

Cardigan glared at the implied criticism. 'I was concerned with leading well.'

'Which is something we must concede you did with great courage. But if you had seen what was happening would you still have proceeded?'

'I was given the order to advance.'

Lucan grimaced. 'One more point we must get clear. It has been stated that the Light Brigade was entirely unsupported. Where were the Heavies?'

Cardigan hesitated. 'I did not see the Heavies.'

'Were you not aware that the Heavy Brigade advanced down the valleys close behind the Light Brigade to give them every support they could?'

'I was facing front.'

'Did you not hear?'

'I heard they were halted before they reached the guns.'

Lucan turned to Eyland. 'They were halted, sir, because, having seen that the Light Brigade was doomed, I had no intention of losing the Heavies too. If they had continued, Lord Raglan would have had no cavalry left at all. None whatsoever. So I halted them.'

There was a long pause because this was a point most people had not been aware of.

After a while Eyland looked up. 'You have more questions to put to the witness, Lord Lucan?' he asked.

Lucan frowned, as if he were deeply concerned. 'No, sir,' he said briskly. 'I have not.'

Chapter Nine

The questioning had gone on all morning and as they recessed for lunch, it occurred to Souto that, with a little help from himself, Lucan had made a remarkably good job of his cross-examination. He had not only contrived to show that he was not as inept as he had been painted but also how difficult a subordinate Cardigan had been.

A lot of the evidence had been slipped in outside the rules of procedure and had been overruled by Eyland, but that was something all advocates did. It was one of the tricks of the trade to say something, withdraw it, then pause, leaving it hanging in the air for everyone to think about, disallowed by court rules but said nevertheless and hard to forget. But he had produced nothing yet which could absolve him from blame. He had received orders from Lord Raglan and had sent the Light Brigade down the valley on the wrong course and against the wrong guns. Nothing so far had emerged to explain that and Souto couldn't for the life of him see the court believing a straightforward explanation unless they knew what had happened before.

The newsboys were shouting their wares as Souto and Archer, the solicitor, made their way to the crowded dining room of the Pestle and Mortar Inn, across Hounslow Heath. It was an hotel with a good menu popular with the officers from the barracks and, like many of the legal men involved in the court martial, Souto had arranged a table daily for himself and his guests.

Souto liked to eat well and the fare at the Pestle and Mortar suited him perfectly. Not deigning to discuss the afternoon, Lucan had declined his invitation to join him and had gone off on his own, doubtless to some other establishment. Still, Souto thought equably, he was well known to be indifferent to food and comfort and, while other senior officers in the Crimea had gone to tremendous lengths to ease their conditions, he had lived not unhappily in a muddy-floored tent.

For the benefit of its diners, the Pestle and Mortar kept one of its staff outside the court, with a hired cab who was said to be in contact with the court orderly, and the minute there was any sign of the court rising for lunch, he leapt into the cab and galloped across the heath to the hotel with the news, so that everything was ready when the first of the diners arrived. As Souto and Archer seated themselves, two pots of beer were placed in front of them. Souto liked his beer; his wife said it was his country background showing.

'How do you feel it's going?' Archer asked.

'I had expected a riot,' Souto admitted. 'And angry words between Lucan and his brother-in-law. But he holds his temper remarkably well.'

'Are we going to pull it off, do you think?'

Souto smiled. 'He's scored heavily with Cardigan. I wager the newspapers will temper their views on the Hero of Balaclava a little tomorrow.'

'Who's next?'

'That's up to Harboursford,' Souto said. 'But I heard it was to be Somerset Calthorpe.'

'Raglan's nephew and a member of his staff. He'll not give away points in favour of Lucan.'

Colonel Calthorpe was a tall man with long whiskers and a casual manner that hid a quick intelligence. He also had the self-confidence of wealth and position and the assurance that he belonged to a great family.

'Colonel the Honourable Somerset Calthorpe,' Harbours-ford said, letting the name hang in the air as if hoping to gain some advantage from the weight of it. 'We will not trouble you concerning the events leading up to 25 October 1854, because you were not involved. On that morning, however, you took up a position, I believe, with Lord Raglan on the Sapouné Ridge, looking down on to the plain of Balaclava. Our interest is with the North Valley where the action with which we are concerned took place.'

Calthorpe nodded and waited.

'When you arrived at the position stated, what was the situation in the valley below?'

Calthorpe considered. 'The Turks had been driven from Canrobert's Hill, where the Number One Redoubt was situated. Fleeing from the Redoubt, they were being cut down by the Cossacks who were pursuing them towards Balaclava. Shortly afterwards, the Turks in Number Two Redoubt also fled and shortly after that, those in Numbers Three and Four. An attempt to support them by a battery of horse artillery had come to nothing and the battery had been badly hit and its commander, Captain Maude, desperately wounded. Several horses were down and a troop of the Light Brigade was occupied in trying to drive away the Cossacks pursuing the Turks.'

'Did Lord Raglan make any comment?'

'None that I remember. He took in the situation at once, of course. It was possible to see everything that happened. Russian infantry and artillery were pushing in ever-increasing numbers along the Causeway Heights and several squadrons of their cavalry were trotting unopposed up the North Valley. They had also firmly established themselves on the Fedioukhine Hills to the north of the North Valley.'

Harboursford looked at the map and nodded. 'Thank you. That makes everything plain, I think. What about the British cavalry? Where were they?'

'They were moving about the South Valley but were

coming under the fire of Russian riflemen in the captured redoubts and had got themselves in the line of fire of Sir Colin Campbell's guns outside Balaclava. They were therefore moved further up the valley to a position on the south slopes of the Causeway Heights just beyond the Fourth Redoubt.'

'Did they move in proper order?'

'They carried out the movement by alternate regiments in precise and careful formation so that their rear and flank were always secure. They were also protected by Maude's battery, Maude had been carried away, of course, but fresh ammunition had arrived.'

'You could see all this quite clearly?'

'Oh, perfectly.' Calthorpe smiled, unbiased and friendly. 'It was a little like being in a box at the theatre. There had been a mist but it had gone by this time and the day was brilliant. I could even see a patch of blue sea at Balaclava. There were heavy clouds on the hills but they made the hills stand out more clearly and the sun was sparkling on the Russian bayonets. I could also see the Highlanders in their kilts and feather bonnets and it was possible even to hear the clink of bits and rattle of sabres and the yells of the Turks and the shouting of orders. I identified Lord George Paget, Captain Jenyns, and Major Low.'

'Was Lord Raglan worried?'

'He was concerned that the advance in the plain was a feint to draw troops away from Sebastopol.'

'What was his view of the cavalry?'

'He thought they might let him down. By going too far or too fast. That sort of thing.'

'When he looked on the cavalry down in the plain, what did he do?'

'He sent Captain Wetherall down with an order for them to move closer to the Sapouné Ridge where they could come under the guns of General Bosquet and the French on the escarpment.'

'Do you know what Lord Lucan's reaction was?' Eyland asked. 'We cannot ask Captain Wetherall as he is not in the country.'

'Well,' Calthorpe shrugged, 'Wetherall told me that Lord Lucan was in a proper tear. Those were his words. He was furious at having to move to what he considered a worse position and insisted on Wetherall remaining with him until the order was carried out. However, the order *was* obeyed, the regiments moving as before. Half of the Light Brigade halted facing the redoubts, the other half facing the Causeway at a gap in the Heights leading from the South to the North Valleys. The French were firing over their heads. It was then we saw the mass of Russian cavalry moving up the North Valley. They had artillery and infantry with them and were moving round the spur that projected across the valley. It was clear they were intending to turn to the south out of sight of Balaclava and throw their weight against the British base. Lord Raglan sent an order for eight squadrons of the Heavies to support the Highlanders and the Turks, and to guard the village of Kadikoi and the cavalry camp. The first probing attack by the Russians, four squadrons of hussars and dragoons, was already moving to the south.'

'I see. Thank you for making the position so clear. Please continue.'

'We then saw the four Russian squadrons advance on the Highlanders but before they got within reach of them they were driven back by volley fire and by Sir Colin Campbell's artillery. They wheeled to their left and galloped off towards Canrobert's Hill, leaving a few riderless horses and dead and wounded behind them. It was at this time that the Heavies were moving towards Balaclava and, as they went, the main mass of the Russian cavalry happened to cross the ridge to their left. The Heavies were perfectly placed to attack and the Russians were driven back over the Causeway to the bottom of the North Valley, where they began to unlimber a 12-gun battery.'

'What did Lord Raglan decide?'

'He had already sent the First and Fourth Divisions, under the Duke of Cambridge and Sir George Cathcart, down to support the cavalry in driving the Russians off the Causeway Heights and, with the retreat of the Russian cavalry, he saw that the Russians on the Causeway Heights had become unsupported and that a little pressure would cause them to retreat. He therefore sent the order to Lord Lucan which instructed him to advance to recover the Causeway Heights.'

'What happened?'

'The cavalry moved through the gap in the Heights between Number Six Redoubt and the Sapouné Ridge and into the North Valley and waited there. It must have been over half an hour.'

'And Lord Raglan?'

'He became very concerned. It was then he prepared the fourth order. General Airey wrote and signed it and, as I was the next aide for duty, he placed it in my hand. Lord Raglan, however, insisted on Captain Nolan, who was called forward. He snatched the order from my hand and went down to the valley.' Calthorpe paused. 'I saw him killed.'

Harboursford gestured. 'Thank you, Colonel Calthorpe. That will be all.'

Lucan rose slowly to his feet. 'Colonel Calthorpe,' he began, 'you were at Varna?'

'I was. And I didn't enjoy it. Fleas plagued us, and there were immense rats that gambolled about all night like cats.'

Lucan glanced at his papers then looked back to Calthorpe. 'We won't go into the problems I suffered as the result of my clashes with Lord Cardigan,' he said.

'I'm glad to hear it, my lord,' Eyland commented dryly.

Lucan gave him a sour glance and turned again to Calthorpe. 'However,' he said, 'I must ask you what was Lord Raglan's view of the patrol led by Lord Cardigan into the Dobrudja.'

Calthorpe considered, clearly trying to give an honest

answer. 'He was worried. Captain Nolan's efforts to find remounts had not proved successful and, now, he learned the cavalry had lost almost two hundred horses —'

'How many?'

'Two hundred.'

Lucan made no comment but he let the number be thoroughly absorbed. Eventually he nodded. 'Please continue. He was concerned that it might well happen again?'

'He felt Lord Cardigan might overdo something and overstrain his horses.'

'I must protest, sir!' Cardigan was on his feet.

'My lord,' Eyland said, 'you have had your turn. It's now the turn of someone else. Please answer, Colonel.'

Calthorpe didn't hesitate. 'Yes,' he said. 'I think he did feel that.'

'Did Lord Raglan have favourites?' Lucan asked.

Calthorpe smiled. 'I suppose he favoured his nephews, of which I was one. He was often kind to me.'

'How about Lord Cardigan?'

'He always received him graciously. I got the impression they were friends and, despite the wrong impression Lord Cardigan had that he held an independent command, that Lord Raglan felt he had to do his best to help him.'

'But after the Dobrudja Patrol?'

'He seemed to try to avoid him.'

'As if he felt that Lord Cardigan's view of his independent command was going to cause difficulties?'

Both Cardigan and Harboursford were on their feet.

'I must protest,' Harboursford said. 'This is assumption.'

'How else can we discover what Lord Raglan thought?' Lucan snapped.

Cardigan's words had almost drowned the protest. 'I cannot sit here and hear my name slandered!' he roared.

Eyland conferred with the Deputy Judge-Advocate before giving his view. 'This is a court, my lord,' he told Cardigan, 'and it therefore has a number of privileges. What is said here cannot be considered slander. It is evidence. Nevertheless,' as Cardigan sat down, muttering to his counsel, Eyland turned to Harboursford and Lucan, 'we cannot accept this witness's views of what Lord Raglan thought unless there are clearer indications in the form of some comment.'

Lucan nodded, his expression showing that, despite the warning, he knew that the court had heard.

'Did Lord Raglan ever say anything on the subject?' he asked.

'Not to me, sir. But General Airey did.'

'What?'

'He said "The Commander-in-Chief is worried. Lord Cardigan must be restrained or we shall have no horses left."'

'This was General Airey's view. Did you never hear Lord Raglan's view yourself?'

'Not directly, sir.'

'Why not?' Lucan's eyes gleamed as he changed direction.

Calthorpe made a gesture with his shoulders. 'Members of the staff, on taking up their appointments, were told "Never trouble Lord Raglan more than necessary with details, listen carefully to his remarks, try to anticipate his wishes, and at all times make as light as possible of difficulties."'

'So the policy of the staff was not to trouble Lord Raglan with anything unpleasant? A strange position, don't you think, for a Commander-in-Chief to be kept in the dark about the army's problems?'

'Lord Raglan was not —'

As Calthorpe stopped, Lucan nudged him on. 'Was not what?'

'Was not a young man, sir.'

'Perhaps it would have been better if he had been.'

Eyland looked up. 'Please confine yourself to questions, my lord,' he said.

Lucan gave him a little bow, aware again that the remark had sunk in.

'Let us move to the Crimea. You crossed the Black Sea with the main army?'

'I did, sir. It was very bad. The cholera had got among us and the French lost over a thousand men on the short voyage. The bodies were thrown overboard but they weren't properly weighted and rose to the surface and bobbed in the swell. It was almost possible to follow the route by the line of floating corpses. Yet when we landed the French were better off than we were. They had small tents. We had nothing and had to endure a downpour with no shelter whatsoever. The confusion was terrible.'

At the back of the court, Templeton smiled. His instinct had been right. He was learning more about the war than he'd ever learned from Raglan's reports or from the disclosures of the McNeill–Tulloch Enquiry.

Lucan was still probing. 'Let us consider this day of the landing in the Crimea. That day when Lord Cardigan led a heavy patrol into the interior to round up carts and food. What was the view at headquarters of the result of that affair?'

Again Cardigan was on his feet but Eyland waved him to be seated. Calthorpe answered quietly.

'General Airey decided in future to use officers of his own department to collect supplies. Captain Nolan brought in eighty Russian waggons laden with flour – *without* a cavalry escort.'

'Did Lord Raglan say anything?'

'I heard him say that Lord Cardigan had not shown much efficiency and that in future the foraging had better be left to the infantry.'

Lucan nodded. 'Let us go to the skirmish at the Bulganak. Where were you as Lord Cardigan moved his horsemen down to the river?'

'Near Lord Raglan on high ground. It was possible to see a whole mass of Russians just beyond the rise and Lord Raglan told General Airey that he did not wish to bring on a general engagement so soon. General Airey moved forward to make his views known, and the cavalry retired. They showed great steadiness and Lord Raglan was pleased about this and in a despatch to the army drew attention to the Light Brigade's behaviour and to Lord Cardigan in particular for having kept his men under perfect control.'

'On the day of the Alma, when the battle was almost over, where were you?'

'Again at Lord Raglan's side.'

'Did he say anything regarding the cavalry?'

'He was concerned that they would attack and be destroyed among the mass of Russians. General Estcourt was sent to say that under no circumstances were they to attack the fleeing enemy. "Let them know," Lord Raglan said, "that no advance is to be made without artillery support and that their duty is only to escort guns which are moving forward to where they can fire on the Russians."' Calthorpe paused. '"Mind," he said to General Estcourt, "the cavalry are *not* to attack." He laid great stress on this. Then, however, he saw the cavalry were taking prisoners and he sent a second order instructing them to return to their duty of escorting the guns. When they continued to take prisoners, he sent a third order. It was quite peremptory.'

'You are sure about that?'

'I carried it, sir. I was instructed to make Lord Raglan's orders very clear. They were to return to the guns.'

'Do you recall my reaction?' Lucan asked.

'You were very angry, sir. But the army depended for its safety on the cavalry and against the thousands of Russian horsemen we had only a few hundred because, at that time, the Heavies had not yet arrived, and I think Lord Raglan was afraid that Lord Cardigan might be —' Calthorpe glanced at Cardigan, 'that he might be over-eager.'

Cardigan half-rose, saw Eyland looking at him, and sat down again. Lucan seemed delighted with the response. Calthorpe continued cheerfully. 'Lord Raglan commented that a mere nine hundred men on tired horses, desperate for water and forage, would have been opposing almost four thousand untouched Russians with well-fed mounts.'

'Were you aware of the ill-feeling these orders roused?'

Calthorpe smiled. 'It was a matter of some humour that in the returns for the killed and wounded at the Alma, under the heading of "Cavalry" would come the entry "One horse, wounded."'

'Whose fault was that, would you say, sir?' Lucan snapped. 'Do you remember me calling on General Estcourt?'

'I do, sir. You said you wished Lord Raglan would allow you to act on your own initiative, as otherwise many opportunities would be lost.'

'After the battle, why was no move made against the retreating Russians?'

'Because the French claimed they were not ready, nothing was done.'

'Did Lord Raglan get on well with the French?'

'He was often very dissatisfied with them. But he was also still worried about his cavalry, and considered he hadn't enough to take chances. When the Scots Greys arrived, it was his wish to show them on their conspicuous horses so that the Russians would think we had more than we had.'

'Did the Russians so think?'

'A prisoner we took merely thought we had mounted the Guards. The red tunics and bearskins, y'see.'

'I have heard it said that Lord Raglan thought the cavalry was being wretchedly handled. Is that so?'

'I never heard *him* say so. His chief concern was that he had too few of them and therefore daren't risk them.'

'We will not go into the question of why the allies sat down to the long and protracted siege of Sebastopol. That's not important to what we're studying here today. But when the allies took up their position I think there was considerable gossip about the cavalry, was there not?'

Calthorpe smiled. 'There was a lot of irresponsible talk among some of the junior staff officers.'

'Were they encouraged by anyone?'

'Captain Nolan did not think the cavalry was being active enough.'

'Did you know Captain Nolan well?'

'Indeed. I admired his books, though I thought his ideas were somewhat extravagant.'

'Why did he think the cavalry was not active enough?'

'He always said that cavalry should attack at once. I think he was inclined to be over-bold.'

'I object, sir,' Harboursford said. 'This is opinion, and dangerous opinion.'

'I agree,' Eyland said, turning to the shorthand writer. 'You will strike that out, Mr Jonas.'

As Jonas rose and bowed, Lucan turned again to Calthorpe.

'Was Captain Nolan aware of the restrictions Lord Raglan had placed on the cavalry?'

'If he was, it made no difference. He never hesitated to say what he felt. With respect, sir, you were called the cautious ass, and Lord Cardigan the dangerous ass.'

Cardigan's face went red but for once he made no attempt to interrupt. Lucan smiled. 'These young men of the staff who discussed the cavalry so ardently were sleeping in their beds at night, of course?' he asked.

'Most nights, yes, sir.'

'Are you aware that this shortage of numbers you have referred to resulted in the cavalry being overworked and constantly being alerted by alarms that the Russians were coming?'

'I have since heard so.'

'There were many skirmishes, were there not?'

'I understand so.'

'Then why did the British public know so little about them? Why did they imagine – and, I might say, still do – that the cavalry were doing nothing except preening themselves? The infantry were often mentioned in Lord Raglan's despatches for their work in the trenches, but never the

146

cavalry, whose work was just as important. Why was the part they played ignored?'

Calthorpe looked faintly uncomfortable. He looked at Cardigan. 'I think, sir, it was because Lord Cardigan was constantly late for stand-to —'

Cardigan immediately half-rose and was just as quickly waved down by Eyland. 'Not now, sir! The witness will continue.'

Calthorpe gave a little bow. 'And it was done to avoid unnecessary publicity of the fact,' he ended.

Lucan seized on the comment gleefully. 'Why did Lord Raglan allow such privileges?' he asked. 'When the French general, Bazaine, spent the night with his wife, General Forey, his superior officer, reported him to General Canrobert for deserting his post.'

Calthorpe made no attempt to answer what was intended, anyway, as a rhetorical question.

'Let us continue,' Lucan went on. 'On 7 October, after the skirmish when the cavalry were withdrawn instead of attacking the Russians in the plain, we have been told that Lord Raglan was very annoyed by what had happened. Is that so?'

'No, sir.' Calthorpe lifted his head and made no bones about his answer. 'Both he and General Bosquet praised you for the work you were doing. Lord Raglan was by no means anxious to become involved in a fight to the east. The only thing in his mind was the prosecution of the siege of Sebastopol. I have to say, sir, there was a strange attitude to you. You were considered to be a bully with a violent temper and everyone was against you. Yet both General Cathcart and General Pennefather had the same reputation, but in their case no one seemed to mind.'

'Could this have been caused by all the gossip you have referred to?'

'There seemed to be a clique at headquarters against you.'

'Led by whom?'

Calthorpe paused. 'Captain Nolan,' he said. 'I heard him

suggest that the reason Sir Colin Campbell, who was only a brigadier, had been given the command at Balaclava instead of yourself was because Lord Raglan didn't trust you. But I never heard Lord Raglan say such a thing. I suspect it was gossip.'

'Let us go back to the morning of 25 October, the day of the Russian attack. Was it expected?'

'Not that day, sir.'

'You were on the staff of Lord Raglan and therefore can be assumed to have a shrewd idea of what was going on in his mind. You have also given a clear description of the battle as it was seen from the Sapouné Ridge. Did Lord Raglan or any of his staff go down to the plain?'

'Not until after the battle, sir.'

'Lord Raglan was a disciple of the Duke of Wellington, was he not?'

'He was, sir.'

'So much so that he habitually referred to his enemy in the Crimea as "The French," when in fact the French had become allies?'

Calthorpe smiled. 'I'm afraid that is so.'

'He knew the Duke's sayings?'

'Oh, certainly.'

'Was one of them that his cavalry had a habit of galloping at everything, and then galloping back as fast as they galloped at the enemy?' Lucan asked.

'I believe so.'

'Was another that they never thought of manoeuvring before the enemy? So little, in fact, one would think they could not manoeuvre at all.'

'I think that is the case.'

'That they never kept a reserve?'

'Yes.'

'Could these comments have influenced Lord Raglan's attitude to his cavalry?'

'They could have.' Calthorpe sounded hesitant.

'He liked to follow the Duke's example?'

'Yes, sir.'

'Did this attitude apply to guns?'

'Guns?' Calthorpe queried.

'Like the Duke, did he consider losing guns to be a disaster?'

'I believe he might have, sir.'

'And just before he issued his fourth order to the cavalry, the order which set them off on their attack, did not someone draw attention to the fact that teams of artillery horses with lassoo tackle could be seen moving along the Causeway towards the redoubts where the naval guns supplied to the Turks still remained?'

'Yes, sir, I remember that.'

'So that they appeared to be in danger of being captured? Contrary to the precepts of the Duke of Wellington? Did not someone cry out "By Jove, they are taking away the guns!"?' Lucan asked.

'Yes, sir, someone did.' Calthorpe agreed.

'And Lord Raglan's fourth order which said "Try to prevent enemy carrying away the guns?" – could the reason for it be different from what we have heard? We have been told that Lord Raglan believed the Russians on the Causeway Heights had become isolated and unsupported and that they would retreat on the application of a little pressure. Could it not be true to say simply that he was more concerned with the possible capture of his guns.'

Calthorpe paused, frowning. 'It is possible, sir.'

'What was the significant phrase in the funeral ode of the Duke of Wellington? "Nor ever lost a gun." Lord Raglan was a disciple of the Duke and the French general, Canrobert, was standing alongside him on the Ridge. Could that phrase have been ringing in his ears and was he beginning to wonder what Canrobert might think?'

Calthorpe frowned. 'That is also possible, sir, I must admit.'

'So that the swift instinct for battle we have heard so much about might not, in fact, have existed at all. It certainly did not appear at the Alma. Or at Inkerman. On both occasions, for most of the time he was not to be seen by his troops. No more questions, sir.'

There was silence.

Chapter Ten

The press had suddenly begun to follow the case with great interest, and the following morning's *Post, Telegraph* and *Times* were all giving it considerable space. The headlines were to the point. '*Lord Cardigan's Evidence. Difficulties in the Cavalry.*'

The day was well advanced and surprisingly hot for the time of year by the time Souto headed for the station, and the public life of the poor was already visible in the streets. Sellers of sheet music were out, and women offering trays of fruit, spices, ribbons, magazines, toffees, and fourpenny rabbits dripping blood. A few women, aproned but not bonneted, were heading for the soup kitchens. The cab horse's hooves were dulled as it crossed a patch of straw and dung spread over the road in front of the house where someone sick lay in bed, then a three-horse omnibus lumbered past, shaking the foundations, all the straw in the world unable to kill the clatter.

The first witness of the day for the prosecution was Alexander William Kinglake, the writer, and as the name was called out, Lucan turned to Souto alongside him.

'Surely,' he snapped, 'we don't have to listen to the meanderings of a scribbler. He's not a soldier.'

Souto shrugged as he arranged his papers. 'We wish to call Russell of *The Times*,' he reminded. 'If we object to Kinglake they'll object to Russell.'

Kinglake was an intelligent-looking sturdy man, his dark clothes sombre among the brilliant uniforms around him. He seemed to be awaiting Harboursford's questions with eagerness.

'You are a writer, Mr Kinglake?' Harboursford asked.

'I am, sir,'

'Of some distinction, I believe. You are an historian and have travelled extensively in the east and have written a book on your experiences.'

Kinglake smiled. 'Yes,' he said.

'You were also in Algeria in 1845 where you accompanied the flying column of General St Arnaud, later to become a marshal and the first commander of the French in the Crimea.'

'That is correct.'

'And you have offered to come here without pressure to give evidence?'

'I have. I might say I insisted. Because of my admiration for the late Lord Raglan. It seems to me his name has been taken in vain with respect to the recent campaign in Russia and it is my wish to see justice done to the name of a man who, alas, is no longer here to defend himself.' Kinglake's manner was just a little self-satisfied.

'What are you working on now?'

'At the moment, I am engaged on preliminary studies with a view to writing a history of the Crimea up to the death of Lord Raglan. Earlier this year, Lady Raglan placed in my hands the whole mass of the papers which her husband had with him at the time of his death and made a request that I would consider writing such a history. She made no demands but it seemed to me that a lot of false impressions had been formed, so, having been in the Crimea myself and seen so much, I decided to do that very thing.'

'An admirable sentiment.'

'At the moment, of course, I have only studied the papers and have written little. But Lady Raglan, with a singleness of purpose and strength of will which reminded me of her relative, the Duke of Wellington, promised not to be impatient and not to allow anyone else to be so.'

'And these papers?'

'There are not only all the military reports which were addressed to the commander of the army, Lord Raglan, by the generals and other officers serving under him, but also his official and private correspondence with sovereigns and their ambassadors,' here Kinglake allowed himself a small satisfied smile, 'with ministers, generals, admirals, the French, the Turks and the Sardinians who were our allies, with public men and official functionaries of all sorts and conditions, with adventurers, men propounding wild schemes, and dear and faithful friends —' Kinglake paused again, still smiling, 'even with a humble writer, myself.'

'And doubtless,' Lucan muttered, 'with the great Lord God Almighty himself.'

Kinglake's diatribe was still continuing unchecked by Harboursford. 'There is a completeness in this body of authentic records,' he was saying, 'which enables me to tread with confidence to my task. So methodical was Lord Raglan that all this mass of authentic matter lies in perfect order, including the strategic plans of the much-contriving leader of the French, Louis Napoleon, still carrying the hosannas which aid the ingenuity of the Tuileries. Because of what was placed in my hands, I have since taken care to converse or correspond with statesmen, admirals and generals with a view to expanding my knowledge of what happened.'

There was a restless movement among the members of the court, as if they had heard enough of Kinglake's self-conceit, and Harboursford hurried to get to the evidence.

'Let us refer to the war,' he said. 'You were with the army from the moment it landed in the Crimea, were you not?'

'I was.'

'And were present on the day of the Alma?'

153

'I was.'

'You saw all that happened?'

Led by Harboursford, Kinglake described the battle, the brilliant sun, the flying banners, the rolling clouds of smoke, and the long lines of red jackets moving slowly up the hill. With a writer's skill, he conjured up a picture which left the court in no doubt about the splendour of the scene. He then went on to describe the dead and wounded, the men left in rows with their heads knocked off by flying cannon balls, or propped against wrecked limbers or broken walls, staring in bewilderment at the spot where their legs had been not long before. He was clearly enjoying his reputation and his mastery of words.

Harboursford allowed him to finish before he got down to the details of the friendship with Lord Raglan that had led to his admiration.

'I had a fractious pony,' Kinglake said, 'and someone drew Lord Raglan's attention to me and the fact that I was the well-known writer.' His smile was a little smug. 'When it finally threw me, he very kindly took the trouble to enquire how I was and invited me to dine with him after the battle. I was captivated by his charm and gentlemanliness.'

'You have heard of the incident near Khuton Mackenzie when the vanguard of the British army moving through the woods bumped into the Russian column escaping from the Alma?'

'I have. Because of the cavalry's absence, Lord Raglan was the first to stumble on them, of course. But he sat on his horse, unmoving. The Russians were held motionless, awed by his demeanour, until help was rushed forward and the Russians were driven away.'

'Did you see the charge of the light cavalry?'

Kinglake didn't answer the question directly. 'I understand it was caused by Lord Raglan's quick spirit deciding that the Russian troops on the Causeway Heights had become cut off from their friends and that there was an opportunity to recover the redoubts.'

Nudged by Souto, Lucan jumped to his feet at once. 'This is not evidence, gentlemen. We might just as well hear the opinion of the British Ambassador who was at the other side of the Black Sea. The witness can have no idea what Lord Raglan thought.

'I was informed,' Kinglake said.

Eyland conferred with the Deputy Judge-Advocate and shook his head. 'That is not enough,' he said. 'I have to agree with the accused.' He gestured at the shorthand writer. 'Strike that out, please.'

Harboursford acknowledged the ruling with a bow and turned again to Kinglake. 'Very well,' he said. 'However, I believe you *do* have sound evidence about Captain Nolan's attitude when he took to Lord Lucan the Commander-in-Chief's fourth message that launched the Light Brigade's action at Balaclava.'

'That is so.' Kinglake was in no doubt. 'The gesture down the valley, which appeared to indicate a course, was in fact no more than a taunt. It was brought about by his anger at the way the cavalry had been handled, and was not a direction at all.'

Eyland looked hard at Lucan as if expecting him to protest but he was deep in a whispered conversation with Souto.

Harboursford continued. 'You have, in fact, direct information to this effect, important information which explains Captain Nolan's intentions when he rode across the front of the brigade just before his death? You have a diagram, I believe?'

'That is correct.'

'How do you come to have this information?'

'When word got around that I was planning a history of the campaign I naturally received many letters and one which came was from an officer who claimed to be in a position to see exactly what happened. He saw Nolan riding alongside Captain Morris of the 17th Lancers. But, then, clearly realising that his gesture to Lord Lucan had been

155

misunderstood, Captain Nolan rode across the front of the brigade in an attempt to turn them on to their correct course, towards the Causeway Heights.' Kinglake offered a sheet of paper to Harboursford. 'That, sir, is a copy of the diagram that was sent to me.'

Harboursford passed the diagram which appeared to consist of two diverging arrows to the judges. 'You will see, gentlemen, that it indicates the course of the brigade and the course of Captain Nolan as he endeavoured to turn them.'

'The diagram makes it quite clear,' Kinglake offered. 'Captain Nolan had realised that his gesture had been misunderstood and was making an attempt to retrieve the situation by directing the brigade towards the Causeway Heights. There is no question about what he was intending to do.'

'None at all?' Eyland asked.

'None, sir.'

Eyland's eyebrows rose and he glanced at Lucan. Lucan said nothing but as Harboursford resumed his seat, he rose quickly. There was a sardonic smile on his face.

'Alexander William Kinglake,' he said slowly. 'Writer. Historian. A barrister also, I believe.'

Kinglake smiled. 'I am. But I have never practised.' His expression seemed to suggest that working as a barrister was beneath him.

'Because you are a wealthy man?'

'That is so.'

'And why were you in the Crimea?'

'To see what happened.'

'As a journalist?'

'Oh, no!' There was a hint of contempt in Kinglake's tones. 'I paid all my own expenses.'

'It must have been very difficult for a gentleman not connected in any way with the war to get around.' Lucan was all smiles and Kinglake smiled back.

'Not at all,' he said. 'I obtained a horse and servants from Lord Raglan and the right to draw rations from the commissariat.' He sounded proud to have been accorded such privileges.

'In spite of being only a civilian there to see the war?'

'Yes.'

'Was this because you knew Lord Raglan?'

'I met him while out with the Duke of Beaufort's hounds.'

'And again in the Crimea?'

'At the Alma. As I've said, my pony was very ill-behaved. Lord Raglan very kindly sent his groom over to tighten its girth.'

'Privileged treatment, wouldn't you say?'

'I suppose so.'

'As the result of this, you spent the whole day with him and dined with him that night after the battle?'

'I was proud to do so.'

'While you were dining with Lord Raglan, other men were helping with the wounded.'

'I helped, too. I gave water.'

'The Judge-Advocate worked among them until midnight,' Lucan snapped.

'I helped the following day also.'

'By which time,' Lucan commented brusquely, 'many were dead. Mr Kinglake, in your history, will your comments on the personalities in the Crimea, with particular reference to Lord Raglan, be entirely without bias?'

'Oh, yes, entirely. I am always careful not to let my personal feelings intrude.'

'But a moment ago,' Lucan looked puzzled, 'you made a comment on the Emperor of the French, Napoleon III, to whom, I noticed, you gave the somewhat derogatory title of "Louis Napoleon." You said – I will quote – "the strategic plans of the much-contriving leader of the French, Louis Napoleon, still carrying the hosannas which aid the ingenuity of the Tuileries."'

Kinglake smiled. 'Louis Napoleon is different from other men.'

Lucan's eyebrows lifted. 'Don't you have a very high regard for him?'

'In my opinion he is an ingenuous but still a contriving man. He became the President of France by a coup d'état – by fraud – and Emperor in the same manner. Marshal St Arnaud, his first commander in the Crimea, was one of his henchmen, more of an adventurer than a soldier, and he cared nothing for decencies. Lord Raglan turned scarlet with shame and anger at the way his troops behaved.'

'It's a pity he didn't turn scarlet with shame and anger at what was happening to his own troops!' Lucan's comment jarred but he managed to smile at Kinglake. The smile he received in return had suddenly become wary. 'You have written articles about what you saw in the Crimea. These, I understand, are to be incorporated into this history you have undertaken to write.'

'That is so. Some of it is already written.'

'Can you tell the court what you have written about myself?'

'Yes. I wish to be fair. I have written that you saw like a hawk and that your energy was that of a much younger man. That you were lithe and slender and still possessed of a tearing energy. I also stated that your intellectual abilities were of a very high order.'

'That was kind of you. Have you ever seen the diary of the late Captain Nolan?'

'It is in my possession.'

'What does it have to say about the cavalry at the Alma?'

'It showed a clear belief, based apparently upon somewhat strange processes of reasoning, that the commander of the cavalry, that is yourself, sir, was the man on whom the blame for not following up the Russian retreat at the Alma should rest.'

'You have told us how you were helped by Lord Raglan, you dined with him. What impression did you form of him?'

'I formed the impression that I was in the presence of a saint.'

'Saints are not known for their skill on battlefields. We are discussing his capacities as a soldier.'

'His skill as a soldier?' Kinglake hesitated. 'It seemed consummate to me. He saw everything clearly. His instinct for battle was extraordinary.'

'Was it indeed? What was his sight like?'

'I believe he was shortsighted.'

'What about Sir George Brown, de Lacy Evans, Sir Richard England, Sir George Cathcart, Sir John Burgoyne, all of whom held responsible positions? They were all veterans of the Napoleonic Wars and all well over sixty. Were they shortsighted too?'

'I believe they were, sir.'

'They could see no further than the ends of their noses,' Lucan snapped. 'But you *did* notice that I could.'

'That is correct.'

'What about you? Are you shortsighted?'

'I am a little, I have to admit.'

'Then how did you manage to see so much? Or is what you are about to report in your history merely from the words of other people?' There was a short pause. 'You have stated your admiration for Lord Raglan.'

'His concern was always for his men, for their care, their comfort. After the Alma, he was distressed by the condition of the wounded.'

'Have you already written your views on the action of the Light Brigade?'

'Some of them.'

'What have you written about Lord Cardigan and *his* ability?'

Kinglake flushed. 'I have written that a bishop or a doctor of divinity would probably have been more competent to seize the right moment for a cavalry charge.'

Cardigan's face went purple.

'You have not ridden in a cavalry charge?' Lucan asked.

'No.'

159

'You have not been under heavy fire?'

'No.'

'In fact, you can have no conception of the skill or courage of Lord Cardigan, who, despite our differences, I must admit led the charge down the valley with all the steadiness I expected of him. However,' Lucan paused and referred to his papers, 'let us look more deeply into what has been said. You have referred to Captain Nolan's gesture to me as he pointed down the valley. You have suggested it was a gesture of contempt, a taunt.'

'That is my conception. In any case, the difference between the course the Light Brigade took and the course they should have taken was only a matter of thirty degrees. It was a mistake that could easily have been made.' Kinglake seemed nervous suddenly and almost as if he were trying to placate the man who was questioning him. Lucan didn't respond.

'Did you see this gesture?'

'I was told. I have said so.'

'Who by?'

'The officer who was present, who sent me the diagram.'

'We have not yet heard his name, sir.'

'I don't have it. I don't recall it.'

'Isn't it on the letter he sent you containing the diagram you have produced?'

'I no longer have the letter. It seems to have been mislaid.'

'A great deal of evidence brought by the people who accuse me seems to have been mislaid,' Lucan snapped. 'Do you recall where this officer – whose name we do not have, whose letter has been lost – was when he saw what caused him to draw the diagram for you?'

Kinglake frowned. 'I don't know. Perhaps he didn't tell me in exact terms. But I well recall that he said he was in a position to see.'

Lucan said nothing, allowing the court to absorb the fact that Kinglake's important information about Nolan's inten-

160

tions was a little less exact than he had claimed. Kinglake waited, the self-satisfied look gone suddenly.

Lucan looked up. 'Let us talk about Lord Raglan,' he said. 'This military genius who understood things so clearly. You were with him, you say, during the Battle of the Alma?'

'I was.' Kinglake's head came up proudly.

'Where was he?'

'With the troops.'

'Of course. But where? Do you remember accompanying him when he moved forward during the battle? He moved from the position he held in rear of his troops, did he not?'

'Yes, he did. He was eager to see what was happening. He led his staff – I was with them – down a small gulley and then on to rising ground, finally ending up on a knoll from which it was possible to see the whole Russian position. He had a quick grasp of an extraordinary opportunity, of course, a tremendous instinct for an advantage, and he immediately called for guns to be sent up.'

'Where was this knoll?'

'Well in advance of the army.'

Lucan's sardonic look had returned. 'Outside,' he said, 'is an officer of the Royal Artillery who served at the Alma with the Second Division under Sir George de Lacy Evans, who seemed to be the only general officer that day who realised it was wiser to assault the Russian position with artillery instead of a wall of flesh and blood and had been collecting guns from anyone who would lend them to help him in his assault. When Lord Raglan's message came for guns, he sent two and the officer now waiting outside led them forward. He is prepared, sir, to give evidence that the knoll selected by Lord Raglan for his view of the Russian position was in fact *behind the Russian lines*.'

There was a profound silence. Kinglake looked disconcerted and Lucan went on quickly. 'Did this tremendous instinct of his, this quick grasp, inform him that it was an advantage to be completely out of touch with his army –

something he seemed to manage also at the fight on Mount Inkerman – and in this case in danger of being captured? That would have been an extraordinary occurrence, would it not? The Commander-in-Chief and all his staff taken prisoner in the first major engagement of the war. Together, I might add, with *you*, sir. Would you have continued to regard Lord Raglan as noble-minded had you ended up a Russian captive for a matter of two years like so many other men who found themselves victims to this quick instinct for battle that you have described?'

Harboursford was on his feet. 'I have to object, gentlemen. Lord Raglan cannot defend himself.'

'I will agree,' Eyland said. But he was studying Lucan with some interest.

Lucan turned again to Kinglake. 'You arrived in the Crimea just before the Alma?'

Kinglake was looking nervous suddenly. 'That is so,' he said.

'Since you know so much about how Lord Raglan's mind functioned, can you tell us why it was he caused the Light Brigade to advance?'

Lucan paused, waiting for Harboursford to object that this was supposition. But Harboursford, sensing that it might be to his advantage, said nothing and Lucan smiled.

'I notice, gentlemen,' he commented, 'that we have no objections to witnesses informing us of what Lord Raglan thought on *this* occasion.' He looked at Kinglake. 'Please answer.'

Kinglake gestured. 'It was because he perceived that the Russians might be driven off the Causeway Heights.'

'Did he discuss the matter with you?'

'Well, no. Of course not.'

'Then how do you know?'

'It was obvious.'

'It did not seem obvious to me waiting in the valley with the men who were shortly going to die. Where were you at the time? What was your position? On the Heights? In the plain? At Balaclava? From what angle did you see the battle?'

Kinglake frowned. 'I didn't see the battle.'

'You didn't see it?' Lucan sounded surprised.

'I had been taken ill. I was aboard ship on my way home.'

'Indeed you were!' Lucan's voice was suddenly harsh. 'Like many others. But unlike them *you* were accorded special privileges. Is it not true that the packet boat in which you travelled, which incidentally was carrying despatches, was stopped alongside Admiral Dundas's flagship, *Britannia*, so that you – you, sir, a civilian – could go aboard to say farewell to the wardroom?'

Kinglake didn't answer.

'I can't imagine that happening for a junior officer, not even for a *wounded* junior officer.' Lucan paused before addressing the witness again. 'You mentioned – very airily, I might add – that there was only a difference of some thirty degrees between the course the cavalry took and the course it should have taken. Thirty degrees, sir, is a great deal in a direction and can make all the difference when in one case it means pointing to the top of a ridge and in the other to sending six hundred and seventy-three men down a valley to face death.'

Kinglake was looking decidedly uncomfortable now. Souto watched him carefully. He knew him to be a man for all seasons. He belonged to the same upper classes and was unlikely to desert them. Certainly when Florence Nightingale had requested his assistance in bringing to light the deficiencies in the Crimea, he had refused to take her side because he was too shrewd to break the links he had forged with the War Office and the official world of Clubland to become a propagandist for a crusading female, though doubtless, when he came to write his history he would make eloquent obeisance to her.

Lucan's eyes glittered. 'This history of yours, Mr Kinglake. You have said you were given Lord Raglan's papers.'

163

'I was approached by Lady Raglan.'

'To save Lord Raglan's reputation?'

'No, sir,' Kinglake snapped. 'To describe what happened.'

'Will it refer to the sufferings of his soldiers?'

'That was not Lord Raglan's fault. He was always bitterly hurt by the allegations that he saw nothing of his men and remained ignorant of their hardships.'

'How do you know? Did he tell you?'

'He informed Lady Raglan in his letters, extracts from which I am privileged to have in my possession. He tried to show himself in the camps.'

'But never more than once a week and not then if the weather was bad.'

Kinglake was frowning. 'He was a man of profound compassion. He could not have known of the conditions. He was a kind man.'

'The army didn't want kind old gentlemen,' Lucan snapped. 'It wanted a young, iron-fisted dynamic cad.'

And Lucan, Souto thought, might well have fitted the bill.

'Did he ever shout, threaten, storm or abuse?'

'He never raised his voice.'

'More's the pity. At the end of January 1855, the army was only eleven thousand strong, with twenty-three thousand sick and wounded. Are you aware that General Canrobert said "The English seem not to take much interest." And that the French Emperor told the British Ambassador in Paris that the British had an "old woman" for commander-in-chief?'

'I don't believe it.'

Lucan's face was grim. 'The British Ambassador is in London at this moment,' he pointed out, 'and has offered to speak if necessary. Do you wish me to call him?' He paused. 'Let us think of this history of yours. It will be entirely unbiased?'

Kinglake looked indignant. 'Of course!'

Lucan stared at him. 'The Emperor Napoleon III,' he

said. 'You have referred in various writings of yours to his "crooked science," to his "ability to deceive," that he "knew how to strangle a nation in the night-time." In this very court you have described him as a "contriver" and "a fraud." Would you say *that* was without the bias you claim to wish to avoid?'

'No. All that is true.'

'You didn't like him?'

'No.'

Lucan's eyes gleamed. 'Do you remember a lady by the name of Lizzie Howard, otherwise called Elizabeth Howard, Harryet or Herriot?'

Kinglake flushed. Everyone in London society knew he had admired the lady. 'Yes,' he muttered.

'You were once very interested in her, were you not?'

Eyland leaned forward. 'Is this anything to do with what we are studying, my lord?'

Lucan's eyes narrowed. 'I think it is, sir. It refers to the value of this witness's evidence.'

'Very well. Let the question be answered.'

Kinglake was still flushed. 'Yes,' he said. 'I was.'

'Very interested?'

'Yes.'

'But unfortunately, along came this same Napoleon and, by means of his "crooked science", his "contriving", his "ability in the night-time," he took her from you, did he not, so that she remained at his side in what might be called very intimate circumstances until his marriage, when she retired into the French nobility as a countess?'

Kinglake's face was livid. 'Yes.'

'Perhaps the glamour and magnetism attaching to the person of a man who could make himself an emperor was greater than that attaching to a barrister.'

'I protest,' Harboursford was on his feet. 'This is infamous!'

Eyland frowned. 'I think you must withdraw all this, Lord Lucan. It has nothing to do with the case.'

165

'I suggest, sir, it has a lot. It indicates that this witness's bias *for* Lord Raglan might well be as strong as his bias *against* Napoleon. In his various comments on the Emperor Napoleon III – and I have been careful to read them – there is not one that is not bitter. In his comments on Lord Raglan there is not one that is not adulatory, even fawning, crouching to a great family. In the Crimea he contributed nothing to the army's efforts, yet, despite this, he received every help from the Commander-in-Chief while, as I shall show, other men, such as the correspondent for *The Times*, who were doing a job for their country, were virtually ignored. Is there little wonder he is biased?'

'Nevertheless, my lord,' Eyland insisted, 'I think you must withdraw it.'

'Very well, sir. I withdraw my suggestions of Mr Kinglake's bias.'

Souto smiled to himself. Lucan's sharp brain was picking up the tricks at great speed. He was silent now, allowing his allegation to be absorbed by the court. It had been withdrawn but it would inevitably influence. Kinglake, he had shown, could well have been swayed by kindness or unkindness and, though there was no proof that he had been, it left a shadow of doubt in the mind. Lucan was undoubtedly clever, he saw, but he was also beginning to see that underneath the cleverness there was also a great deal of cruelty. He had virtually demolished Kinglake, and the author was looking considerably less self-satisfied.

Lucan looked at Eyland. 'I have withdrawn my comments on the witness's bias, gentlemen, but I take it my observations on his presence in the Crimea are to be allowed to stand because they are true. I have been wondering why he is here, in fact. He has given us no evidence of any value, offered nothing but hearsay. He did not see the Light Brigade's ride yet he insisted – those were his words – on being here and on producing a useless diagram for which we have no corroboration whatsoever. We don't know the name of the

166

officer who sent it or where he was standing when he saw what he claims to have seen. How are we to know that diagram is not a figment of Mr Kinglake's imagination, another example of his bias towards Lord Raglan —'

'Lord Lucan!' Eyland leaned forward.

Lucan stopped dead and bowed. 'Whichever way we regard his evidence, sir,' he said, 'I think for a barrister he should be ashamed of himself.'

Eyland made no comment. Instead he asked a question. 'Do you wish the evidence to be struck from the record, my lord? Is that what you are asking?'

'No, sir.' Lucan's voice was acid with contempt. 'Let it stand! Let it be seen for what it is worth! He was nothing more than a civilian in the Crimea, there for his own satisfaction to see the war. There were many like him: the troops had an expression of contempt for them. "Travelling gentlemen", they were called; hangers-on of military campaigns, extracting a vicarious pleasure from the killing —'

Harboursford was on his feet again. 'This is insulting, gentlemen!'

'Why else was he there?' Lucan snapped. 'Not to admire the scenery, surely? There is no pleasure in battle for soldiers. It is the civilians who complain about a disgraceful peace, never the soldiers, who are only too glad to have survived. This witness gave nothing, yet he expected privileges —'

Harboursford's voice rose over Lucan's. 'I *insist* this is insulting, gentlemen.'

Lucan rounded on him angrily. 'How else do I describe him, sir? He was not a soldier. He was there as a spectator. What else is that but a hanger-on. We had too many in the Crimea and they did nothing but get in the way.'

Eyland conferred with the Deputy Judge-Advocate, then looked up at Harboursford. 'I think you asked for it, Colonel,' he said. 'You introduced the witness.'

Lucan turned again to Kinglake. 'Let us have it clear, sir,' he said. 'In what capacity *were* you in the Crimea? Please tell us.'

'I was there as a spectator, sir, as you suggest.' Kinglake's face was crimson.

'Neither a soldier, nor a camp follower. Not someone who was there to help with the wounded or feed the sick. Not someone who would carry messages or make a point of going into the thick of a fight. A mere spectator.'

'Lord Raglan did not object.'

'Lord Raglan did not object to many things he should have objected to.' Lucan's comment was biting. 'You have heard of Miss Florence Nightingale?'

'Of course. Who hasn't?'

'Do you know what she has said of you? I'll read it out. "He has no judicial mind, not much feeling, not much conscience – and takes a superficial view of the whole thing. But his history will be as clever as everything he writes and everybody will read it and be deceived. He is a good counsel but he strikes me as a very bad historian." You have heard that?'

Kinglake went red with anger. 'No, sir, I haven't, and I must protest —'

'You are not here to protest, sir,' Lucan snapped. 'It is quite ridiculous for a civilian with no knowledge of war to suggest I did not behave as I should have done. Just as it is ridiculous to suggest that cavalry were capable of recapturing the redoubts without the assistance of infantry. It seemed to me obvious that I was to wait for the infantry but there was no sign of infantry. Your value to this court is the same as your value to the army in the Crimea and I'll waste no more time on you. I think you are a prater, a valueless mass of misconception, and I suspect your history will be the same.'

Chapter Eleven

There was dead silence as the shaken Kinglake vanished, his face red from Lucan's withering contempt. He had entered the court, full of his own importance, the man people talked about, the man who proposed to write the definitive history of the Crimean campaign; he left it utterly devastated.

As Lucan sat down, Souto leaned over. 'I think you demolished him completely.'

Lucan gave an angry grunt. 'I have no time for civilians who go to war as spectators. War is a bad business at the best of times and should have no place in the activities of people who are not involved, no matter who they are.'

'Not even newspapermen?'

'Newspapermen are different.'

'Especially,' Souto murmured, 'when they are on our side.'

As the court rose Souto was handed a message to call in at his office when the day's session ended. The message said it was important and Souto hoped it would be, because the court had sat late and he was tired. He was also a little depressed; the ghost of Lord Raglan, with his saintly features, his rectitude, his reactionary attitudes, brooded over everything that was said and Lucan was leaving no stone unturned to make sure the court was well aware of it. To save his own reputation, he felt no qualms about destroying another man's. While Souto felt he could hardly blame him under the circumstances, it illustrated the streak of ruthlessness in Lucan.

Because of the increasing heat, Souto rode back to London with the windows of his compartment open and reached Waterloo feeling dusty and soiled with the smuts that had whirled inside. Taking a cab to his chambers, he found his clerk, Pizzey, dozing in the armchair in his office. The clerk leapt to his feet in confusion as the door opened, his thin face strained and tired.

'Sir, I must apologise,' he said. 'I was worn out. I took the liberty, sir. I felt sure you wouldn't mind, especially in view of the fact that I was out late last night about our business.'

'Of course not, Pizzey. I quite understand. What have you learned?'

'Well, sir. I've learned something of Captain Nolan's background.'

'Didn't we know it already?'

'I'm not sure we did, sir. However, we do now. I have acquired birth certificates and depositions from the family lawyer. It is now all quite clear.'

'What about the letters, Pizzey, that Babington produced? Have you seen them?'

'I have, sir. They look bad. They're full of accusations.'

'Are they genuine?'

'That I can't say yet, sir. But I have taken the opportunity to despatch letters to all the senders. I discovered their addresses and have sent them off already. Marked urgent. I have even sent a messenger across the Channel with one for General Bosquet, who happens to be in Paris at the moment. I expect him back tomorrow with a reply. The others should arrive shortly. I just hope they are in time.'

'Pizzey, you're a gem. Why did you request me to see you?'

Pizzey drew a deep breath. 'The man, Babington, and the solicitor, Spencer Valentine, sir. They seem to see a great deal of each other.'

'That's not really abnormal, is it? Spencer Valentine's supposed to be watching the case for the Beauforts and

170

Babington's watching it for the Nolan family. They both oppose us.'

'Mr Valentine, sir, has been suspected in the past of somewhat dubious activities along the fringes of the law.'

'So I'd heard. Have you gathered proof?'

'No, sir. Nor am I likely to, I suspect. But friends of mine who run the offices of other solicitors in Bankside, where Mr Spencer has his office, know a lot about him. It's largely hearsay, of course, but it has been said he was involved in some of the unhappy business of missing army supplies in 1854, sir.'

'That's interesting and worth noting, but not a lot of use.'

'No, sir. However, Mr Babington, sir, is very much in debt.'

'That's also interesting but, again, not of great value at Hounslow. What I'm interested in is what they're up to, because they're certainly up to something.'

Pizzey smiled. 'I acquired another friend of mine to watch Mr Valentine's chambers. He's an ex-policeman and knows how to go about these things. He noticed that Mr Babington – he established his identity satisfactorily – visits him, as I've said, from time to time. As also does a younger man by the name of Barnaby O'Halloran.'

'The man "Barney" we saw in the Shades Vaults?'

'I imagine so, sir. I have an interested party in Mr Valentine's office.'

Souto's eyebrows rose. 'A Trojan Horse? Are you paying him, Pizzey?'

Pizzey smiled. 'I buy him liquid refreshment, sir! It appears to be very important to him and he finds it hard to raise enough money to satisfy his requirements. I sometimes also buy him a pasty in the Globe eating house, sir, together with drink with his meal, and a small libation beforehand in the bar. He seems satisfied. I think he'll learn Mr Barnaby O'Halloran's part in the affair eventually. He listens hard, I gather, to everything that goes on.'

Souto laughed and slapped his shoulder. 'Well done, Pizzey,' he said. 'I think you deserve a strong brandy and soda to fortify you for your journey home.' He moved to a cupboard. 'In fact, Pizzey. I think you had better take the bottle home with you and share it with Mrs Pizzey. It can be replaced tomorrow.'

When Pizzey had gone, Souto sat for a while at his desk, deep in thought. What was Babington up to? They were doing quite well at Hounslow but still so far nothing had been produced to prove that Lucan had not lost his head on the field of Balaclava and destroyed his command by a stupid mistake.

And the advantage always lay with the prosecution so that it wouldn't require much to convince the judges he had so lost his temper he had ignored Nolan's advice or had been in such a fury that he had not even listened to it. Lucan's tempers were well-known throughout the army and though he was doing remarkably well to hold himself in check during the trial, Souto had no doubt that the officers sitting in judgement were as aware as he was that Lucan was making a supreme effort and that he might well, in a moment of greater strain elsewhere, have exploded and ignored instructions. All those slices of paper – Exhibit 1 to Exhibit whatever it now was, in the region of 20-odd, Souto suspected – didn't mean a thing. All they showed was a painstaking man who made a point of covering his own rear. It added nothing to what had happened to the Light Brigade.

Souto slept badly that night. The case was beginning to get on his nerves a little because he was working with a man whom, though he had to admit he was clever, had an abrasive character which he found wearing. Lucan was not a likeable man and it brought up the question of which was better: an indifferent leader who was able to work with people, or a competent man blazing with energy who aroused nothing but resentment. It was clear that, until his removal from his command, Lucan had found few friends in the army, while Raglan, despite his acknowledged inability to deal with many of the stresses of campaigning, was a man who had roused nothing but admiration, even love, from those who knew him.

Souto rose feeling irritable and breakfasted alone, his wife keeping quiet as she saw he was deep in thought. The journey to the station in the butter-yellow sunshine was slow and the cab was constantly held up by the crowding carts and omnibuses. There was a market on the route, stalls improvised on cart tilts; pigeons, canaries and rabbits being sold among the cats' meat, chipped china, artificial jewellery and the hucksters shouting their cure-alls in the raucous voices all market traders seemed to develop.

Lucan also seemed in a bad temper and in no mood to talk, so Souto made no attempt to converse. Even Harboursford, after the poor showing of Kinglake, seemed unhappy, too, and Souto could only put it down to the discomfort of the heat.

The first witness was a tall soldierly figure who waited quietly as Harboursford gathered his papers. Finally Harboursford turned to him.

'Colonel John Adye?' he said. 'You have been called, Colonel Adye, because of your position – at the time as a captain – on the general staff, and because you were close to events. While you were at headquarters, you must have heard evidence of the Commander-in-Chief's views on the cavalry.'

Adye nodded. 'Yes, sir. I did. He was very worried about them. He considered the Dobrudja patrol had done a great deal of harm in reducing the numbers of cavalry horses available and I heard him say to General Airey, "One more like that and we shall have no cavalry left."'

'Did he say anything about Lord Cardigan's patrol into the hinterland to find food and carts?'

'Yes, I was present. He said, "I shall have to keep a tight hold on the cavalry, Airey, or we shall lose the lot."'

General Crowley leaned forward. 'Who was he criticising?' he asked.

'In my opinion, Lord Cardigan, sir. But it also seemed to include Lord Lucan for permitting it.'

Lucan rose as Harboursford sat down. 'Did you know a man called George Palmer Evelyn?'

'I did, sir. He was a TG – a travelling gentleman and an ex-officer. He was a friend of Captain Nolan's. I saw them together on several occasions. After the vanguard of the army ran into the Russian column near Khuton Mackenzie I saw him trying to set fire to one of the Russian waggons by applying his cigar to the hay it contained.'

'Were you aware of the gossip at headquarters?'

'I was, sir. Only too aware. It seemed to revolve chiefly around Captain Nolan. He and Evelyn were always chattering and laughing.'

Lucan leaned forward. 'What about?'

'The cavalry. Evelyn showed me his diary. It contained a sentence I remember well: "Our cavalry are the most inefficient in Europe." Another sentence said that the commander of the cavalry, yourself, sir, had given much dissatisfaction at headquarters.'

'Why was that?'

'As far as I could make out, because you continually complained about the conditions your men had to live under.'

'Would you consider that a cause for dissatisfaction?'

Adye was wary. 'I don't know, sir. I didn't know the Commander-in-Chief's mind.'

Lucan gave a snort of triumph. 'At last we have someone who *doesn't* know what the Commander-in-Chief was thinking,' he said. 'Who was involved in all this gossip?'

'Chiefly the junior staff, sir.'

'Why did they dislike me?'

'Because you criticised them.'

'Are you aware that among the fighting troops they were not very popular themselves. I'll quote from letters I have

174

received: "that nest of noodles;" "the greatest set of muffs possible;" "a parcel of lazy, idle, swearing fellows."'

Adye managed a smile. 'I have heard some of those, sir.'

'Would you say they were true?'

'I trust not of me, sir. But I believe they could be applied to some.'

'Captain Nolan. He was a handsome man, was he not?'

'Yes, he was.'

'Who liked to dress well?'

'He seemed to.'

'And while the rest of the army grew more tired, hungry, ragged and dirty, did not these members of the staff who were so critical of the cavalry continue to appear in snowy linen and gaudy lace.'

'Some did, sir.'

'"Handsome cavaliers" is the expression I have. Nolan was always among them, was he not?'

'I think he was, sir.'

'How did he seem to you at this time?'

'Handsome, vehement, restless, sir. He was always raging on about the cavalry and about yourself, sir.'

'Did he behave like a responsible staff officer?'

'He was always easily excited. I think the successes he had had went to his head a little. He shouted to me one day "Isn't this fun? I think it's the most glorious life a man can lead."'

'What was he referring to?'

'Being on active service.'

'It probably was to him. Unlike many of my soldiers, he slept in his bed at night. These successes you refer to: what were they?'

Adye hesitated. 'I know of none in particular but I often heard of them.'

'From whom?'

Adye frowned. 'I suppose they would be from Nolan's friends.'

'Why did he so dislike me?'

'He wished to see put into practise the theories he had written in his books. He blamed it on you that they were not. He felt that, while the infantry did the work, the cavalry were being mollycoddled like a lot of invalids.'

'Why was he so keen on the cavalry being in action?'

'He believed that Englishmen, with their love of fox hunting, were natural horsemen. I suspect also he wanted a little glory.'

'For himself?'

'For the cavalry, and I suppose, through them for himself, since he had written books on them.'

'Was he aware that regimental colonels, more careful of the lives of their men, disliked young officers of the staff who didn't hesitate to rush to the front and urge them on?'

'I don't think he was concerned with caution, sir. It was his view that the cavalry could accomplish miracles if they were only allowed to attack with vigour and speed.'

'Did you ever hear his attitude to uniforms and horse furniture?'

'Yes, sir. He did not approve of the lance or of the fripperies that had entered uniform, any more than he did the shabraques, sheepskins and other appendages which dangled round horse and rider. He considered them to be useless encumbrances which only added weight to the horse.'

'Did you see him at the time of Balaclava? On his horse?'

'Often.'

'What did he have on his horse?'

'A tiger skin.'

'He didn't like a shabraque, which is made of cloth, but he was happy to have a tiger skin, which is heavy and hot. Why?'

Adye smiled. 'I suspect he was trying to cut a dash, sir.'

Lucan nodded. 'I think he was too,' he said. 'Thank you, that is all.'

*   *   *

'Call Sir Colin Campbell.'

Campbell was a small man with a head full of tight ringlets, and a face that was lined with years of service. Harboursford got him to admit at once, in a broad Scots accent, that he had foretold that the cavalry would be involved in a disaster.

'You even had cause to berate them at the Bulganak, I believe,' he said.

'Aye.' Campbell nodded. 'My men were drinking fra' the stream after the march when the cavalry appeared alongside and stirred up the mud wi' their great hooves.'

'And again at the Alma?'

'They moved so close on the left o' my Highlanders they got in the way.'

'I believe you had little time for cavalry officers because they liked to fall out from their regiment and go to the front and then give their opinion on things they knew nothing about.'

'Some of them – not all – talked a lot of nonsense. But so did the staff and some infantry officers. They liked tae go on all the time aboot attack, attack, attack, but I wasna' there tae fight a battle or gain a victory. I was there tae defend Balaclava and I wasna' goin' to be tempted oot o' a strong position by jeers.'

Harboursford seemed to scent that his questions were leading into dangerous waters. As he sat down, Lucan rose. He nodded to Campbell and the grizzled face cracked in what might have been a smile.

'Sir Colin,' Lucan began. 'Good morning. You and I got to know each other well, did we not?'

'Aye, that we did.'

'How did we get on?'

'Well.'

'Even when you were in command of Balaclava instead of me?'

Campbell's shoulders moved. 'There wasna' any trouble. We worked together.'

'We'll say nothing about your comments on the cavalry at the Bulganak or the Alma because what you say is fair comment. But these young officers who were quick to jeer: do you remember how I dealt with them?'

Campbell nodded. 'I mind one who took himself off patrol to watch the first bombardment of Sebastopol. He found himself in verra hot water.'

'How did *you* regard the staff?'

'They didnae' like me and I didnae' like them. I minded they would bring a disaster the way they went on aboot the cavalry.'

Under guidance, Campbell described how he had been with Lucan and the members of their staffs at dawn on 25 October when the first indications had come that the Russians were advancing, and, in his thick accent, went on to tell how the cavalry, unsupported, had had to manoeuvre about the plain, trying to look threatening while keeping out of danger.

'When they came within range of the Russian riflemen and in the line of fire o' ma guns,' he said. 'I advised their withdrawal up the South Valley.'

They had no wish to break off the action, he said, but the position they took up was a sound one because it protected the cavalry camp, supported his Highlanders, and allowed them, if necessary, to attack in flank any attempt by the Russians to swing down towards Balaclava. It was while they waited there that the first order arrived from the Sapouné Ridge, telling them to withdraw under the guns on the escarpment.

'Yon was a bad position,' Campbell growled. ''Twas too far away to impose a threat tae a Russian flank, it gave no support to ma men, and it abandoned the cavalry camp to the Russians who were swarming across the South Valley.'

Harboursford climbed to his feet. 'Sir,' he said to Eyland. 'Must we detract our attention from the main events by a summary of this trivial business?'

'Trivial?' Campbell's face was purple. 'Ye call it trivial, sir, that ma Highlanders stopped the Russians dead! I told them they had tae be prepared to die where they stood and they never moved. They were lying in the long grass just behind the crest of a hill and the Russians never kenned they were there until they stood up. They stopped 'em in their tracks.'

'What happened then?' Lucan asked gently.

'You came down from the Causeway, sir, and brought the warning that the Russian cavalry was approaching. The Heavies, who were just movin' down the valley, were in a perfect position tae stop them.'

'One last question, Sir Colin. The French occupied the bases of Kamiesch and Kazatch while the British occupied the port of Balaclava. What was the difference between those bases?'

Campbell frowned. 'Apart fra' a few Spahis, the French had no cavalry and 'twas felt it would be better for the British tae be on the outer perimeter o' the allied defence system because the British cavalry, though small in numbers, was greater by far than the French contribution and could protect the flanks fra' any Russian army lurking in the interior. So Kamiesch an' Kazatch lay securely within the protection o' the French army. Balaclava was exposed an' was protected only by ma men and by the cavalry who had to do all the patrollin' towards the East from where we expected the Russian army.'

'And from where it eventually came?'

'Aye.'

Harboursford now began to call a string of witnesses to show the events leading up to the Light Brigade's charge. Major Ewart, a strongly-made officer who had been on Raglan's staff, next took the witness's chair.

'There has been a lot of doubt cast,' Harboursford said, 'on the presence of the First and Fourth Infantry Divisions in the plain on the day of the battle. I have heard it suggested that the action of the Light Brigade was caused by their absence. Yet, you, I believe, were actually sent by Lord Raglan to order them to the plain.'

'Yes, sir,' Ewart agreed. 'I was.'

'And they did, in fact, reach the plain before the cavalry's action?'

'Yes, sir, they did but —'.

Harboursford drove on. 'The Fourth Division had actually reached the Causeway Heights and were waiting there?'

'That is correct, sir.'

'Thank you.'

As Harboursford sat down, Lucan rose. There was a dangerous gleam in his eye.

'Your job, sir,' he said, 'was to persuade Sir George Cathcart to take his Fourth Division down to the plain, was it not?'

Ewart stiffened. 'Yes, sir, it was.'

'Did you understand why?'

'I assumed they were to be part of some move Lord Raglan had planned.'

'But you were not certain?'

'I assumed it was to be the recapture of the redoubts.'

'Were you told just how this was to be done?'

Ewart looked puzzled. 'No, sir. I was told to bring on the infantry, which, I knew, were to be used with the cavalry, but I wasn't sure just how. I assumed that further orders would be issued.'

'When you arrived in the presence of Sir George Cathcart, what was he doing?'

'He was just sitting down to breakfast.'

'Did he rise and prepare his men to march off as requested?'

'No, sir. He did not. Sir George was often difficult. He held a dormant commission to take over command of the army in the event of Lord Raglan's death in action and, while none of us knew this, I think it made him a little impatient with Lord Raglan's methods. He often questioned orders and on this occasion, he said it was quite impossible to move to the plain. I told him my orders were quite positive but again he refused. His men, he said, had just come from the trenches. He offered me breakfast but I was very worried and when he again refused, I began to ride back to Lord Raglan. Then I decided I must insist and at last he gave way. But it was already late.'

'Did you accompany Sir George to the Causeway?'

'I did.'

'What did he say when he arrived?'

'When he saw Canrobert's Hill which was the farthest distant of the redoubts, he was aghast and once again very critical. He said "It's impossible that there can be one as far away as that." He was convinced there must be some mistake about his orders and, because of that, continued to wait near the Fourth Redoubt where he was protected from fire by the rising ground.'

'So that although both the First and Fourth Divisions had come down from the Heights, they were not in action.'

'That's so, sir.'

'In fact, had either of them received any further orders since leaving the camps on the Chersonese Hills?'

'I believe not, sir.'

'So they weren't even certain what they were supposed to do?'

'I can't speak for the Duke of Cambridge, sir, but that was certainly the case with Sir George Cathcart.'

'What was the time, sir, and the position?'

'It was eleven o'clock, sir, and three and a half hours since the Turks had been driven off Canrobert's Hill.'

'Did you see the charge?'

'It was impossible from where we were.'

'So,' Lucan seized on the point, 'if it were impossible for you to see the cavalry, it would also be impossible for the cavalry to see you on the Causeway Heights.'

'I suppose so, sir. I had no knowledge of what was happening until Captain Brandling of the Horse Artillery appeared with his battery. "There's a bad business over there," he said and pointed to the North Valley. "They have sent the Light Brigade into the heart of the enemy's position." Soon after that Lord Cardigan appeared. He had a tear in his overalls where a lance had gone through. He joked they would no longer keep the cold out, but I could see he was very distressed. He said he had lost the Light Brigade. From where we had been waiting, we had no idea of what had been happening, though, of course, we had heard a great deal of gunfire. Not knowing what he was talking about, we could only stare at him.'

'It was one of the features of the position, was it not, that some people – those on the escarpment for instance – could see everything that was happening in both valleys, while those below all too often saw surprisingly little?'

Ewart agreed and went on to describe how he had found the body of Nolan and, nearby, his friend, Captain Morris, of the 17th Lancers, with terrible wounds to the head. A little further on was a Heavy with his jaw smashed. When asked his regiment, he could only point to his buttons which indicated the 5th Dragoon Guards. Riding back to Number Four Redoubt, now reoccupied by the Turks, Ewart persuaded them, he said, to help him lift Nolan, Morris and the dragoon but when the Russian fire began to fall near them, they dropped their charges and bolted. Nearby, he said, Sir William Gordon, of the 17th Lancers, was being treated for the five sabre wounds he had received to the head. He had managed to reach safety only by lying across his horse's neck and trying to keep the blood from his eyes. His horse, shot through the shoulders, had crashed down even as he was lifted from the saddle.

'Did you know Captain Nolan well?' Lucan asked.

'Tolerably so, sir.'

'What was his view on cavalry?'

'He thought cavalry capable of breaking through anything – guns, squares, whatever faced them, scattering them so they could be destroyed piecemeal. Despite the improved tactics of the infantry, he felt improved cavalry tactics had more than made up for them, and that to charge was to conquer.'

'Would you say he was a cavalry fanatic?'

'I think I would, sir.'

'What was his view of the Irregulars in Turkish pay?'

'He thought they could never resist a Russian attack.'

'Did this influence Lord Raglan in his decision not to employ them?'

'Probably, sir.'

Lucan paused. 'What was Lord Raglan's attitude to Lord Cardigan?'

'They were good friends.'

'And his attitude to me?'

'Not good, sir.'

'To Sir Colin Campbell?'

'Not good.'

'Sir George de Lacy Evans?'

'Not good.'

'Why was this? Sir Colin Campbell was a man of great experience, as was Sir George de Lacy Evans. They had seen much of war. Should not their advice have been welcome?'

'Lord Raglan did not get on with them.'

'Why not?'

'They did not fit in.'

'Because they were rougher than the smooth young men with whom he chose to surround himself? Because they were not aristocratic like the five nephews he had on his staff? Was he not a man who had favourites and had no time for anybody else?'

'I must protest,' Harboursford said and Eyland nodded his agreement. Lucan did not argue but turned again to the witness.

'There had been trouble in the 5th Dragoon Guards, had there not? Before reaching the Crimea.'

'There had. The commanding officer had behaved very foolishly and caused much resentment. For some reason he felt his men would mutiny and attack him and he slipped away and left for home.'

'Was Lord Raglan aware of this state of affairs?'

'No, sir. It was kept from him. We had no wish to trouble him with unnecessary worries.'

'Unnecessary worries? A mutiny in his army? General Scarlett, who intervened, Sir George Brown, the Duke of Cambridge, myself – we were all aware of it. But the Commander-in-Chief did *not* know. Were the staff aware that at this time things were so bad with the army that my aide, Captain Beauchamp Walker, was so reduced he bought a pair of trousers at the sale of a dead man's clothing to mend his own with, that his coat was ready to fall to pieces, that officers of the Guards wore holed shoes and shirts that were in rags and were eating salt pork without complaint.'

'I heard so, sir.'

'Was anything done to help?'

'Lord Raglan tried.'

'With polite letters to the Government? A little ill-temper might have gone a great deal further.'

'We have heard a lot in this strain, my lord,' Eyland said. 'What are you endeavouring to show?'

'That the command at the top was not competent, sir,' Lucan snapped. 'This is the basis of my defence.'

Chapter Twelve

The prosecution's next witness was Mrs Fanny Duberly. She was already well known because of her book on her experiences in the Crimea, and was well known in the counties for her skill as a rider and her knowledge of horses.

She was a dainty, fair-haired attractive woman in a bonnet and gown who smiled readily, clearly had a great deal of brisk commonsense, and seemed totally impervious to the heat. Souto had heard a lot about her, not all to her credit, but on one thing everybody was agreed: in the Crimea, she had never shown fear and had always been in the tumult of bombardment or on the field of carnage. She was said to have taken a house in the area for the duration of the trial and to be daily exercising her horses on Hounslow Heath where the cavalry from the barracks performed their manoeuvres.

As she appeared, everybody in the court sat up for a better view of her, particularly the women because there were stories that, while her husband had been busy on the uplands round Sebastopol, she had been having an affair with Lord Cardigan on his yacht in Balaclava Harbour.

Treating her with great gallantry, Harboursford extracted from her the information that she had happened to see the Light Brigade's action.

'My husband sent a messenger with a horse,' she said. 'He

said the Battle of Balaclava was about to begin and warned me to lose no time and not wait for breakfast.'

'You went?'

Mrs Duberly smiled. 'I did not wish to miss a battle,' she said. 'But as I rode up, I found myself surrounded by Turks who had fled from the redoubts. They had kits on their shoulders and arms full of bedding, kettles and plunder. They blocked the road and a commissariat officer I met advised me to get among my own people as quickly as possible. "Ride fast," he said, "or you may not arrive alive."'

'What did he mean?'

'He may have meant I was in danger from the Russians or it may have been the Turks? I have no idea. However, I rode as fast as I could because the situation was looking serious by that time. I arrived on the Ridge just in time to see the cavalry take up its position near the Fourth Redoubt.'

She had taken her place with the crowd of onlookers surrounding Lord Raglan and had quite clearly seen the Light Brigade form up and move down the valley. The valley had filled with gunfire and their return had been in ones and twos and small groups emerging from the smoke.

'All formation had been lost,' she said. 'I couldn't make out what was happening. "What can those skirmishers be doing?" I asked. Then I realised what I was seeing. "Good God," I said, "It is the Light Brigade."'

Lucan rose slowly.

'While you waited on the Sapouné Ridge for the battle to develop, Mrs Duberly,' he asked, 'what were the staff doing?'

'They were sipping sherry and eating sandwiches, as I recall.'

'Like a picnic?'

'Yes.'

'More like a field day, in fact, than a war?'

'I suppose so.'

'You are a civilian and a woman. Let us therefore confine

ourselves to the things you know about. You accompanied the army to the east because your husband was a paymaster with the 11th Hussars, and of course, you wished to be with him. Very well. You remember Lord Cardigan's Dobrudja patrol?'

'Yes.'

'What did it produce to your knowledge?'

'Not much in the way of information. But it produced nosegays for me.'

'You saw the patrol return?'

'Yes. The men were plodding in on foot, carrying their saddles and driving and goading the wretched, wretched horses, some of which could hardly stir.'

'You know horses?'

'I certainly do. These had been grossly ill-used.'

Heads craned forward, looking for Cardigan's expected protest. But he was not in court. After the first two days he had lost interest and was leaving his lawyer to look after his affairs. Souto also knew that, while his wife was suffering from an incurable disease, he was busily paying court to a lady by the name of de Horsey who was young enough to be his daughter. Half London knew he was itching to marry Miss de Horsey who was said to be good-looking in a Spanish style, something she was obviously well aware of because she liked to dance Spanish dances wearing Spanish costume.

By this time, Mrs Duberly was describing how the men of the Light Brigade had received the orders to proceed to the Crimea, not with cheers but in the gloomy silence of men with sickness and death uppermost in their minds.

'They had suffered dreadfully from the cholera,' she explained. 'Far worse than the infantry.'

'How was Lord Cardigan?' Lucan asked.

'He was unwell, but when Captain Wetherall came from headquarters with the news that he would be in command of the cavalry, he recovered quickly.'

'Wetherall brought news that *he would be in command*?' Lucan stressed the words.

'Yes.'

'From headquarters.'

'Indeed.'

'In fact, he wasn't, was he?'

'I believe not.'

'You smuggled yourself aboard a ship, did you not?'

Mrs Duberly smiled. 'You did not see me because I was dressed as a camp follower and you were looking for a lady. And, of course, there was still a great deal of cholera and many sick to occupy the attention. Captain Longmore, who helped me aboard the *Himalaya*, was dying within an hour or two.'

'When you reached the Crimea, did you notice the reactions of the soldiers?'

'Most officers were aware that it might well mean death and they were silent and thoughtful. But Lord Cardigan was very excited and impatient. He ordered my husband ashore when he was sick. I told him to ignore the order.'

'How did you get on with Lord Cardigan?'

There was a sudden silence in the court as if they were expecting some sort of salacious confession, and the bonnets and shawls started to flutter in the public section. But Mrs Duberly showed no sign of being disconcerted.

'Very well,' she said.

'Yet, in your book you say "he neither feels for man nor horse" and on another occasion "I hope that Cardigan, whom all abhor, will get his head in such a jolly bag he will never get it out again." On yet another, when he made you move your tent so his own could take its place in the shade by the stream, you say, "I wish a great damned wind would come and blow down those damn trees on his damned old head."'

There was another silence as if Mrs Duberly might be expected to burst into tears. Instead she gave a tinkling laugh. 'In fact,' she said cheerfully, 'the spring overflowed during the night and flooded his tent.'

'These seem strange sentiments for someone who later managed to dine with His Lordship on his yacht at Balaclava.'

Again, to the disappointment of the women in the court, Mrs Duberly shrugged it off. 'He was kind to me,' she said. 'He lent me a horse,' and Souto decided the rumours he had heard about her sprang entirely from Cardigan's well-known inability to ignore a pretty face.

Lucan changed course. 'While in Balaclava did you hear gossip about the cavalry?'

'Oh, yes, from the young officers on the staff.'

'Did you believe it?'

Mrs Duberly's head came up. 'Certainly not,' she said. 'My husband is a cavalryman.'

'Call John Lees.'

The man who came forward was dressed in shabby civilian clothes. He limped and his face was badly scarred, a red stitched-up weal stretching from the left eye down to the right side of his mouth beneath the heavy beard he wore. Despite the scar, there was a flashy look about him and a curious confidence. He wore the Crimean medal, what people called 'a half-crown and a pennyworth of ugly ribbon.'

Harboursford looked at his papers. 'This witness, gentlemen, was a private in the 17th Lancers and rode in the charge but, because of the wounds he suffered on that occasion, he has since been discharged.'

There was a murmur of sympathy as Harboursford began his questioning.

'John Lees,' he said. 'Lately a private in the army.'

The man in the witness box stiffened. '841 Private Lees, sir. 17th Lancers, and proud of it, too. My name's on the rolls of the regiment for anybody to see.'

'But you are no longer with the regiment?'

'No, sir. Discharged unfit for service.'

'Why?'

'Well, the charge, sir, see. It left me with a lame leg and a face like I'd been struck by lightning.'

189

'You were wounded?'

'I was taken prisoner, sir. At first they thought I was dead, because my horse had gone down. But I was picked up on the field afterwards and taken to the Russian camp.'

'What was your position when the charge started?'

'Right-'and squadron, sir. End of the rank. Which brought me just about behind Lord Cardigan, because we was on the left of the first line. The 13th Light Bobs was on our right.'

'Tell the court what happened.'

The witness frowned. 'I don't remember much, sir. We was riding forward and the pace had quickened a bit when there was a bang and I was 'it in the leg. Then soon afterwards my 'orse went down and that was that. When I come to, the Russians was trying to tie me 'ands. I tried to fight 'em and one of 'em 'it me across the face with his sword and gev me this.' His hand went to the scar. 'And a nice sight it is, too,' he added bitterly. 'And not much of a pension to go with it. It leaves me short of money.'

There was a murmur of sympathy but Souto guessed it wouldn't lead to much. As with all wars, the men who had suffered in the Crimea had been quickly forgotten. The Guards had returned home to a scanty meal of ham and lettuce with a half bottle of stout, while some of the line regiments had settled for a mere pie and pea supper. Apart from the Crimean crocuses which had been brought home and planted in gardens, and the popular pianoforte piece, *Alma*, little else had been produced to recall a campaign which everyone was now agreed had been characterised by indifference, ineptitude and inanity.

'Finally,' the witness was still speaking, 'they led me down the valley. There were a few others what 'ad been taken prisoner.'

'Because of your position, you were well placed to see everything that happened at the beginning of the charge?'

'That I was, sir.'

'You could hear Lord Cardigan's orders?'

'Very plain, sir. 'E 'ad a very strong clear voice. I heard him tell Captain Morris to hold his men steady, sir.'

'You could see Captain Nolan?'

'Right in front of me, sir.'

'When the movement forward started, what happened?'

'Captain Nolan tried to stop it.'

'Stop it? How?'

'Well, he tried to turn it, didn't 'e?'

'In which direction?'

'To the right, sir. Towards the 'ills.'

'Which hills?'

'The Causeway 'Eights, sir.'

Glances were exchanged about the court and two of the men sitting at the long table began to whisper together. This appeared to be proof of what Harboursford had been maintaining all along and what Lucan had constantly denied – that Nolan was very clear about where the Light Brigade should have gone and was endeavouring to turn it. It seemed to indicate at once that Nolan had *not* misunderstood his orders and that it was Lucan on whom the blame should be laid for the misunderstanding.

Harboursford allowed a long pause for everyone to digest the information, then he turned again to the witness.

'What exactly happened?'

''E yanked at his reins, sir, didn't 'e, clapped in the spurs and began to ride forward. 'Ard as he could. Across the front of the Brigade.'

'What else was he doing?'

'He was pointing. With his sword, sir.'

'Where to?'

'The right, sir. The Causeway 'Eights.'

'Did he say anything?'

'He said a lot, sir, at the top of his voice.'

'What did he say?'

''E was shouting, sir. 'E was shouting "To the right. On to the 'ills. The guns on the 'ills." Something of that sort. I don't remember exactly, being more concerned with keeping my 'orse in check. She was trying to run away with me, see, sir. But I 'eard what 'e said all right.'

Harboursford glanced at Lucan. 'You're quite sure of this?' he asked. 'He pointed to the Causeway Heights and shouted "To the right. On to the hills. The guns on the hills."'

'Quite sure, sir.'

Harboursford turned to Eyland. 'That is all, sir.'

Souto was frowning as he left the court with Lucan. 'The man, Lees, did a lot of damage, my lord.'

Lucan made no comment, nodded his goodbye without a word, and disappeared to the indifferent eating house where he took his meals. Lieutenant Morden was waiting for Souto.

'You seem in a low mood, Arthur,' Souto said as they took a schooner of sherry each.

'I am, sir. I hope you will not be.'

'Oh?' Souto looked surprised. 'Why?'

'Your daughter, sir. Harriet. She has informed me this morning that she entertains for me the same sentiments that I entertain for her.'

Souto smiled. 'Then why are you so low in spirits?'

'I still have to ask you for her hand, sir.'

'Consider it asked. Have you told my wife?'

'Yes, sir.'

'What did she say?'

'She kissed me, sir, and was kind enough to say she was pleased.'

'So why should *I* not be pleased?'

'Are you, sir.'

'Of course I am. I'm delighted for Harriet and for you. I'm also pleased for my wife and myself, that we have a hero in the family. When do you plan to marry?'

'I first must attend to my finances, sir.'

'Harriet is not without means and there is a house in

Richmond which belonged to her grandfather and which I'm sure you could use. It isn't big but it ought to suffice.'

Morden was blushing with pleasure and Souto reached across the table and slapped his arm. 'Under the circumstances, Arthur,' he said, 'I think we should have another schooner of sherry. Not champagne or I shall fall asleep with my head on my brief, but let us not allow the occasion to pass without a small celebration.'

Souto was in a warm glow of pleasure when the court reopened. The witness, Lees, was already in position and Lucan was glaring at him.

His first question was harsh and aggressive. 'Who produced this witness?' he demanded.

'I did, sir,' Harboursford said.

'Where from?'

'From the ranks of the 17th Lancers, my lord, as we have heard. Mr Valentine, solicitor for Lord Raglan's family, found him. He was turned up by Mr Archibald Babington, a cousin of the late Captain Nolan, who felt we would wish to have his evidence. It appears to be important.'

For some time Lucan stared at the witness as if he wished him dead. He was silent for so long that Eyland leaned towards him.

'Lord Lucan, do you wish to cross-examine this witness?'

Lucan whispered to Souto, then rose and faced the witness.

'841, John Lees,' he said. 'How old are you?'

'Thirty-six, sir, and nowadays feeling fifty-six.'

'You were in the 17th Lancers. My old regiment. Known as Bingham's Dandies, weren't they?'

The witness looked startled then he nodded quickly. 'That's right, sir. They was.'

'Very smart regiment. Always rode dark-coloured horses, didn't they? Blacks and browns chiefly.'

'That's right, sir.'

'What was yours?'

'Black mare, sir. Very 'andsome animal.'

'Who was your officer?'

'Well, er, Captain Morris, sir.'

'Your troop officer.'

Lee paused. 'I don't rightly remember, sir.'

'And your right-hand man?'

'I don't remember that neither, sir. I reckon this welt across the phiz did me a lot of no good, y'see. Upset the old brainbox a bit.'

Lucan managed a smile. It looked like a snarl. 'Well, I'm pleased to meet you, 841 John Lees. Your regiment did well that day.'

'Thank you, sir.'

Lucan paused and Eyland leaned forward, looking surprised. 'Do you not wish to cross-examine the witness further?'

Lucan smiled. 'Not at the moment, sir. But I might wish to, later, when I present my case.'

'Is it necessary, my lord?'

'It is very necessary, sir.'

'Very well. Let it be so.'

As the bearded man left the court, Souto watched him carefully with narrowed eyes, then he turned and leaned towards Archer, the solicitor.

'I think we should have that man watched, Archer,' he said. 'Get in touch with my clerk, Pizzey, and tell him to find out where he goes and whom he talks to. He'll know what to do.'

The prosecution's final piece of evidence was a sheaf of papers, copies of the messages which had been sent from the Sapouné Ridge to the cavalry and ending with the fourth order which had sent them down the North Valley. Lucan didn't dispute the evidence, but he made Harboursford read the order aloud.

'*Lord Raglan wishes the cavalry to advance rapidly to the front – follow the enemy and try to prevent the enemy carry-*

ing away the guns. Troop Horse Artillery may accompany. French cavalry is on your left. Immediate.' Harboursford looked up. 'It is signed *R. Airey.'*

'You wish to ask questions, my lord?' Eyland asked.

'No, sir. But I would like the court to bear in mind several words. "Rapidly." The cavalry to advance rapidly. "To the front." To the front gentlemen. And "immediate." Immediate, which indicates at once, and does not suggest that there was time to delay. I beg you, gentlemen, to bear these words in mind.'

As he sat down, Eyland leaned forward. 'Is that all, my lord?'

'It is, sir.'

'In that case, sir,' Harboursford said, 'the prosecution closes.'

PART TWO

Chapter One

Lucan opened slowly, taking his time to sort his papers.

'Don't disclose too much of what you intend,' Souto advised quietly. 'Let's keep them guessing.'

Watching Lucan, it occurred to Field-Marshal Lord Templeton that if he had not been plagued in the Crimea by Cardigan and commanded by an old woman like Raglan he might have done well. He would never have been popular, it was clear, but popularity had never needed to be one of the assets of a successful leader.

He was explaining his situation carefully but without a lot of detail. 'My position in the army of the east was never easy,' he was saying. 'That was not because I was out-of-date and old-fashioned, as has been suggested, because I have always been quick to learn. And no one could claim I neglected my command. I was always concerned for my men. As for those orders that have been said to club the regiments on parade in Bulgaria, how important were they? The troops put them right, because the other ranks have always had a gift for dragging their leaders out of the messes of their own making – as many a junior officer has good reason to know. The army is largely run by the NCOs and in an emergency *they* always get it right, something which is proved by the fact that whenever the cavalry were involved in large or small engagements with the enemy, they always behaved with skill and efficiency. And, contrary to Lord Raglan's belief, they had learned a lot since Waterloo – but caution, gentlemen, not Captain Nolan's ideas of speed and dash.' He paused. 'As for me, I believed mere bravery was not enough. I believed in example and shared the hardships of my men. There were others, however, who disappeared homewards as soon as the winter arrived and spent the next months stumping the country, basking in a popularity that scandalised the army in the Crimea.'

Lord Templeton smiled. He knew Lucan was thinking of Cardigan but the Duke of Cambridge was coming in for a lot of implied criticism too and was unlikely to forget it and he was already unhappy about the suggestions of dilatoriness on the day of Balaclava. 'They said I was late,' he had growled. They had indeed and now it was being said again that he had gone home in a hurry as conditions had deteriorated.

Lucan was still speaking. 'At the time I was sent home,' he continued, 'Balaclava was one big pigsty. It had been a pretty village, full of honeysuckle and clematis, but now the stench of misery and despair hung over it like a miasma. Piles of amputated arms and legs, the sleeves and trousers still on them, could be seen through the water into which they had been thrown, and corpses rose from the mud to float on the scummy surface and became entangled with ships' ropes and anchor chains. The sick were suffering from malnutrition and we all know the conditions in the hospitals at Scutari before Miss Florence Nightingale arrived. My colonels were reduced to sorting through sacks of rotting vegetables to find food, the cavalry had become quite useless and the horses were dying of starvation, cold and wet. My final humiliation was when I had to tell my men they had to give up five hundred animals a day to carry provisions from Balaclava to keep the infantry alive. The fine cavalry that Lord Raglan – he of the all-seeing eye and swift intellect – had been so eager to preserve had been destroyed by his own neglect. His letters home gave little idea of the condition of the army, and his despatches were gentlemanly examples of the bluff that enables commanders to bury the relics of their own ineptitude. Up to the end of the year all that was said was that the ground was "in a lamentable state", yet by 16 December there was a dead or dying horse every ten yards on the road to Balaclava. But, while the staff, most of them Lord Raglan's own nominees and most of them without any military education, were sitting in their warm billets unaware of what was happening, I could, and did, produce a formidable list of what constituted a private soldier's day. Nobody back home noticed this.'

Lucan paused to allow his words to sink in. 'By then,' he went on, 'the cavalry were calling themselves the Butcher Boys because of their job of carrying provisions, and they were angry as they saw their horses die, not by this time because there was no hay but because the feed bags had rotted in the wet and thousands of new ones lay unused under other supplies at the bottom of the ships' holds in Balaclava. As a result the corn that was obtained had to be placed on the mud and the horses were so wretched they didn't even try to eat it.'

'We are discussing the Battle of Balaclava, sir?' Harboursford enquired. 'Did these things which happened later have anything to do with it?'

'They have very much to do with it, sir,' Lucan snapped, 'in that they indicate the situation which existed throughout the campaign. There were many complaints about me. That I freely admit. But where are those men who made the complaints now? They have not appeared as witnesses for the prosecution. Why not? Because their views have changed or, if they have not, unlike others, they have been able to understand the difference between an unpopular driving leader and an incompetent fool who could lose his command by carelessness. I have had letters from them,' a sheaf of papers was handed to the judges, 'some of them even apologising for what they once thought of me. And they all say how wrong it was to accuse me of losing the Light Brigade when the fault lay elsewhere. But there was dissension in the Army of the East and it was not of my making.' Everyone knew whom he meant and eyes turned to where Cardigan's lawyer sat. 'As for Captain Nolan, many people at home have rushed to his defence with praise and there has been a great attempt to make him a martyr. But let me remind you, gentlemen, none of these people who are now so vociferous were there in the Crimea. None of them knew of the frustrations the cavalry suffered, not only from the caution of the Commander-in-Chief but also from the jeers of such men on the staff as this famous Captain Nolan.

'It is my contention that the Light Brigade's charge was brought about by this same Captain Nolan's intolerance and by his dislike of senior officers. But let me also say that *he* was only the bearer of the message and the real responsibility was never *his*. A commander's message should be clear and leave no doubt in the mind of the officer to whom it is addressed. The messages I received were *not* clear and for that the blame lay with Lord Raglan, who should have made sure they were clear, or with General Airey, who wrote them, and in his haste was not careful enough. I had no option but to send the cavalry forward because I did not know that there might not have been some other emergency that demanded the sacrifice of the cavalry, the role cavalry has always been called on to perform on a battlefield. Both I and Lord Cardigan have been blamed for not exercising our discretion, but the assumption that we possessed any arose only *after* the event. There was certainly no opportunity to show any *before* and it always seemed to me that we had *none*.'

Lucan's first witness was Colonel Edward Cooper Hodge of the 4th Dragoon Guards, a minute man who had been coxswain of the Eton boat as a boy. He had a gloomy face and a depressed manner, as if he found life hard to handle.

'I was aware of the difficulties between Lord Cardigan and Lord Lucan,' he said, addressing Eyland. 'I knew they did not speak and how this would answer on service I could not think. I was also having difficulties with horses. I had had to get rid of fifty-three young and unreliable mounts and a few older, overweight men, and when I was instructed to provide two hundred and fifty horses and two hundred and ninety-five men for the campaign I had no idea where I might find them. In the end, the horses came from the King's Dragoon Guards and in return I gave twenty of my young ones. I felt ashamed because they were as great a set of brutes as I ever saw.'

Hodge frowned. 'I was not relishing campaigning and did not expect much comfort or happiness from it. No more did I look forward to a march to the East across France, as was at first advocated, because it would be hot and there would be too much cheap brandy and the horses would be knocked up. Fortunately, in the end we went by ship.'

'What kind?' Lucan asked. 'Steam transport.'

'Sailing ship. It seemed slow and I knew little about transporting horses over long distances. But I bought a book on the subject and we managed. I was very seasick.'

'What did you find when you arrived in Varna?'

'A land shimmering with heat. There was an arid shore covered by men and horses. The staff's organisation was pathetic.' The complaints came one after the other. 'Tents were crowded because there were not sufficient, saddles had to be kept in the open air because headquarters had provided nowhere for them, no transport had been provided by the commissariat, and only a regulation number of pack animals was allowed.'

'And the horses off the ships?'

'They were mad with joy. Freedom, after being cooped up for weeks. Kicking. Biting. Not fit for service, though, and not likely to be for a long time. My job was to get them into shape. Dreadful place. Beautiful spot rotten with disease.

Glad to move to Varna. The temperature at the coast was ninety in the shade and the horses suffered dreadfully because there was a freezing dew at night and they were tethered in the boiling sun all day with a plague of insects to drive them mad. We covered their eyes with bandages of rags and mats but a lot of 'em already had bad eyes through the glare and were coughing from the dust.'

'How were the relations between you and me, sir?' Lucan asked.

'I found no difficulty,' Hodge said indifferently. 'And later I found you were most kind. I had heard of you as a man of violent temper, but when a native boat came ashore bringing rum and I seized its cargo wishing to flog the crew, you contented yourself with spilling the contents and letting the men go.'

'Perhaps I was more aware of the hostility of the natives towards the army and thought it wiser. Do you remember Lord de Ros returning to England and his place being taken by General Airey?'

'I had not much time for Airey,' Hodge sniffed. 'He seemed conceited to me, but at least he had energy, something that was desperately needed because there was a great lack of it at headquarters.'

Lord Fitzsimon spoke to Eyland, then leaned forward. 'Did you hear comments on Lord Lucan?' he asked.

'Often, sir. Chiefly from my second-in-command, Major Forrest.'

'Did you believe them?'

Hodge gestured disapprovingly. 'Forrest is an amusing man of much wit who enjoys scandalising people. However, he was also not noted for the amount of work he did. Mind, it was always difficult. When Varna caught fire, I was turned out with my men to patrol the place against looters. It was most uncomfortable with the ash, the smoke, the dust, and the shortage of water. It was believed to have been started by the natives and I felt George Paget was right when he said the French had the best idea when they shot them.'

'You remember the departure for the Crimea?' Lucan asked.

'I never agreed with it,' Hodge's small face was gloomy. 'I felt the government were crouching to *The Times*, which was eager for a war. After the siege of Silistria was raised, the war seemed to me to be over. I thought we'd go home. However, I was glad to leave Varna. The dust was so bad the ink in my inkwell was like mud and we had dreadful problems with watering horses. I was worried, though, because the men did not have winter clothing and the flannels they had brought from England were already worn out. I decided a fortnight in wet weather and mud would finish us all off and that if we were to depend on a stormy sea for our supplies we were going to find it hard. I was right too. Before Balaclava, we were wearing everything we could get our hands on.'

Hodge was followed by Lucan's son, Lord Bingham, a young man with his father's dark good looks but none of his aggressiveness. He described how a Turkish spy, sent by Rustum Pasha, the Turkish commander at Balaclava, had come in on 24 October, the night before the battle.

'He was examined by Lord Lucan and Sir Colin Campbell,' he said, 'and it was decided that the information he brought about an impending attack was serious enough to inform Lord Raglan. A letter was written and I carried it to headquarters.'

'What was Lord Raglan's reaction?' Lucan asked.

'He did not like spies. He was a great believer in honour and had a detestation of anything he considered underhand.'

'This is assumption, gentlemen,' Harboursford said.

'No, sir.' Bingham's answer was quiet. 'This is how I constantly found it.'

'Please say exactly what happened when you saw Lord Raglan,' Eyland said.

Bingham gave a little bow. 'He seemed very much aware that General Cathcart had been angry after an earlier false alarm which had caused his men to lose sleep and did not wish to upset him. He seemed, in fact, a little in awe of General Cathcart?'

'So what did he do?'

'Nothing, sir. He gave no other acknowledgement of the letter except to say "Very well." I got the impression that he thought the attack we were expecting was a mere feint to hide an attack on our lines from Sebastopol.'

'Was that *your* view?'

'No, sir. It was the view of everyone down in the plain that the attack we had been expecting for so long was now hanging over us. Especially when Engineers heard Russian bands playing loudly in the villages by the river.'

Following the battle, Bingham concluded, he had gone down the North Valley to try to bring in the body of his cousin, Captain Charteris, but the valley had been covered by fire and he had had to leave the body, only bringing back Charteris's watch and sword and a few other things.

Lord Bingham was followed by Lord William Paulet, Lucan's Assistant Adjutant-General, who had come under criticism from some officers at headquarters because he had served all his life in the infantry.

'It was said, sir,' he pointed out, 'that I was ill-fitted for the job. But, of course, it was also said that Major MacMahon, the Assistant Quartermaster-General, had never served anywhere but on the staff, that Captain Beauchamp Walker had a lot to learn, and that Lord Bingham was not efficient enough for his post.'

'Where did this gossip come from?' Lucan asked.

'I attributed a great deal of it to Captain Nolan.'

'Where were you during the charge of the Light Brigade?'

'Just behind you, sir.'

'And where was that? Please explain.'

'You had arranged the Light Brigade in three lines, sir, and had formed up the Heavy Brigade in a similar formation some distance behind.'

'Why was that? Do you know?'

'It was very clear, sir. Your idea was to reduce the size of the target being offered to the Russians, and also so that the attack would not be one single shock, but a series of shocks.'

'Please tell the court what happened.'

'As we followed the Light Brigade down the valley the fire was very heavy and horses and men were going down. It was clear the Lights were having difficulties in holding their horses and the steady advance had become a gallop, though purely because of the firing on the horses, not because of any lack of control.'

'What about the Heavies?'

'We were still moving forward at a solid trot, sir, and we were being left behind. In an attempt to hold the connection between the two brigades, you rode further and further ahead of the Heavies and your staff followed you. As the Light Brigade entered the smoke at the end of the valley, you were well in front of General Scarlett, somewhere about opposite the fourth redoubt. But it was becoming clear that the Heavy Brigade were also in danger of being destroyed because the Russian guns had the range to an inch by this time and we were coming under the withering cross-fire that had decimated the Lights.'

'Were there casualties?'

'Indeed, sir. The Heavies suffered more casualties at that time than during their own charge. The batteries were cutting us up terribly. The Royals had lost twenty-one men, killed, wounded or dismounted, and Colonel Yorke was disabled with a shattered leg. I saw seven or eight horses of the Greys knocked over by a single shell. I also saw other horses blown off their feet and riderless horses galloping away or trying to rejoin the line. Captain Charteris was killed near me, and I had the cover cut from my cap and my horse wounded by grape.'

'What happened then?'

'It was a difficult position. I heard you say "They have

sacrificed the Light Brigade. They shall not have the Heavy if I can help it.'''

'What did that mean, do you think?'

'I assumed it was because you considered that the Lights had been sent into the attack by some unfortunate order and that the Heavies were in danger of going the same way and that you intended to hold them back.'

'And then?'

'Your trumpeter, Joy, sounded the Halt and we were ordered to retire. I admit I was not sorry. There was some confusion at first because General Scarlett, who was well ahead of his men, didn't realise what was happening and ordered his trumpeter to stop the rearward movement that had started. Eventually, however, we were halted once more and faced about towards the bottom of the valley. As though on parade, sir. Finally we were moved back again out, of range but still far enough forward to make the journey back a little easier for what was left of the Light Brigade.'

After lunch Lucan called Lord George Paget, a sturdy, fair-haired, good-looking man who was the son of Wellington's cavalry commander at Waterloo, a man brisk and confident in his background.

'You were colonel of the 4th Light Dragoons at Balaclava and rode in the charge in command of the second line,' Lucan said.

'That's correct, sir,' Paget replied.

'How did you regard your regiment joining the cavalry division?'

'With some trepidation, sir. I knew that Lord Cardigan and yourself were not on speaking terms and I could not see it being of much help. I'd also just married, and as my father, the Marquess of Anglesey, had just died I'd sent in my papers, intending to retire. I'd only stayed in the army to please him. But when the war broke out I thought people might get the wrong impression about me and felt obliged to withdraw them. I had a good regiment, however. Known as Paget's Irregular Horse, from the loose drill it had got used to in Afghanistan under my predecessor.'

'Let us go to your arrival at Varna. What was your first duty?'

'To face you, sir.'

'You didn't relish it?'

In his reply, Paget made no bones about his doubts, especially when he found that some officers – most of them unworthy men, he added – were complaining of Lucan's inability to handle cavalry, that he was out of date and had forgotten the correct orders. It was his job as senior colonel and second-in-command of the Light Brigade to present the complants and he had had great fears of getting between Lucan and Cardigan. To his surprise Lucan had proved considerate and forebearing. 'In fact,' Paget turned to Eyland, 'to the end of the campaign I never had an angry word with him. Of course, I occasionally caught the rough edge of his tongue, but I noticed he was as hard on himself as on everyone else.'

For the march south to Sebastopol, his regiment, the 4th Light Dragoons, had brought up the rear. 'The French,' he said, 'were full of unpleasant remarks.'

'What about?' Lucan asked.

'Our staff, our uniforms, our equipment, our tents. Everything. Lord Raglan was considered old and old-fashioned. Our job was chiefly to pick up the sick and the dying but there were so many we found it difficult to avoid riding over them.'

'At the Alma, did you come into action?'

'No, sir. Though we were occasionally under a hot fire from the Russian guns.'

He considered the quality of the staff work very poor and after the battle, when he thought there was a wonderful opportunity for a pursuit and had even begged Lord Lucan to let him move forward, he had been informed that he should do nothing.

'Lord Cardigan and Captain Nolan were furious,' he told the court. 'I was furious, too, but I learned later the Divisional Commander had been forbidden to pursue the enemy. Personally I felt the Russians had had such a dressing they would never come into the open again. Colonel Windham, who was with me, agreed. He said that if the Russians had been pursued, the campaign might have been ended there and then.'

'After the battle,' Lucan asked, 'did Lord Raglan make a remark to you about keeping the cavalry under tight control?'

'Yes, sir. My father, of course, was an old friend of his because both had been at Waterloo with the Duke of Wellington and when I saw Lord Raglan dining in the open after the battle he invited me to join him. He was very dissatisfied with the French. He seemed to be *obsessed*, in fact, with his dissatisfaction with them. "They were," he said, "always too-tooing on their trumpets." I asked if the cavalry could not be permitted to do more, but he shook his head and said that his object had been to shut them up, to keep them in a bandbox, because there were so few of them.'

'As you followed the army towards Sebastopol, did you find it difficult to obtain forage for your horses and food for yourself?'

'Yes, sir. We passed through the litter of the wrecked Russian waggon trains near Khuton Mackenzie and when I discovered an abandoned packhorse with its baggage twisted beneath it, I was delighted, because it happened to be my own and I was hungry. My horse was so weak by that time it stumbled with every step and five others died of exhaustion. We were so short of food I was hoarding a few onions, half a loaf of bread and a ration of salt pork. I tried to load up the horses with hay from a deserted farmhouse but I had to leave it behind because we were ordered to join the Third Division under General Cathcart.'

Major-General Porter-Hobbs leaned forward. 'Did *you* hear the gossip concerning the cavalry?' he asked.

'Yes, sir. It annoyed me. I thought the Divisional General a man of considerable ability and even enjoyed having someone over us who worked so hard for our behalf. I also enjoyed serving under General Cathcart, but not Lord Cardigan. Lord Lucan was the surprise, however. I had heard he was a tyrant but we always adjusted our differences in a workmanlike way. It was difficult to get fodder, of course, and I was always planning forays down to the dangerous area of the River Tchernaya, because the horses were almost done for. However, there was no time – there never was time because we knew the Russians were planning a move against Balaclava to cut us off from our ships. The constant alarms were wearing everyone out, by this time, of course, but I considered it was better to have five hundred of them than one surprise, and the allegations of missed opportunities were entirely unjust.'

Paget paused and there was silence. To the public, the cavalry's role had been only to charge the enemy and no one had thought of the endless monotony and danger of patrols.

'The picket duties in the cold were the poorest fun I ever came across,' Paget went on, 'and the people on the staff who handed out the nicknames didn't have to do them. Personally I found no fault in Lord Lucan's dispositions and Sir Colin Campbell took the same view.'

'What about the relationship between Lord Lucan and Lord Cardigan?' Porter-Hobbs asked.

'Always difficult, sir. There was one flare-up when Lord Lucan refused to allow anyone, not even Lord Cardigan, to have forage for their horses before the men guarding the outer perimeter. It was a stand I admired enormously. By this time, I was certain that the talk that was going on was going to cause a catastrophe of some sort because everyone was against the cavalry and Lord Lucan in particular. Sir Colin Campbell was also prophesying disaster, because he was afraid we might do something silly just to show the staff we weren't useless. We were in a very difficult position.

When mounted, our place was outside the army but, dismounted, we were helpless and our camp should have been inside. Yet our camp was virtually in the front line and we were constantly at work, patrolling. Personally, I regarded alarms philosophically but every one had to be looked into and every time everything had to be packed and, as they all too often came at mealtimes, the men often went hungry.'

'As the days grew colder what happened?' Lucan asked.

'Forage became increasingly difficult and even when we picked some up we often had to leave it behind because of an alarm. I decided that the staff thought we rode a peculiar breed of animal that didn't need food.'

'Did Lord Lucan help?' Eyland asked.

'Lord Lucan always had the welfare of his men at heart, and I grew very angry that the nickname "Look-ons" should be given to the cavalry as a whole and didn't enjoy the allegations from certain staff officers who slept in their beds at night that we weren't doing our job properly.'

'You remember Lord Cardigan's illness?'

'Yes.' Paget smiled. 'We welcomed it. Whenever he appeared he was very awkward. I had made up my mind never to answer him back and I took everything he flung at me so that I got by, but it was more difficult for others. When he was ill, we considered it a relief. But living on his yacht was very inconvenient and very time-consuming when we wished to contact him. As second-in-command, I regularly took the parade because he wasn't present, and every night – and, sir, they were often very cold – we were outside the lines on outpost duty and both men and horses were weary.'

'Let us go to 25 October,' Lucan said. 'You were with me when the alarm was given.'

'Yes, we saw the flags on Canrobert's Hill that meant the Russians were advancing and we saw the Turks overrun by the Russians in the redoubts.' Paget turned to Eyland. 'It was very humiliating, sir, and we had to wait a long time under the Russian fire. A cannon ball went through my horse's legs and a splinter of a shell struck my stirrup. Lord Lucan moved us to a place of greater safety but this order was countermanded soon afterwards by an order from headquarters which moved us so far back as to make us useless as support for the troops guarding Balaclava. The retreat across the plain was one of the most painful ordeals it is possible to conceive. Our defences were falling one by one and not a soul seemed to be coming down from the main camp to give us support.'

'Where were you,' Lucan asked, 'during the charge of the Heavy Brigade?'

'By a gap in the Causeway Heights that led from the South to the North valley.'

'Did you see the Heavies' charge?'

'No, sir. The first line of the Light Brigade was kept mounted but the second was allowed to dismount. I was not aware of the action building up in front until I sauntered about fifty yards to my right. The mounted regiments could see everything. We could see nothing.'

'Why was this?'

'It was one of the oddities of the ground. From some places you could see everything. From others you could see nothing.'

'You could see nothing?' Lucan stressed.

'That is so, sir. It was very strange terrain.'

'Let us come to the Light Brigade's action,' Lucan said. 'Where were you when the message arrived?'

'We were eating biscuits and hard-boiled eggs and drinking rum. I had just lit a cigar when I realised action was imminent and I wondered whether to get rid of it. I decided in the end it would do no harm to keep it and, in fact, it lasted me to the guns.'

'What happened then?'

'There was some discussion over the order – I was too far away to hear – then Lord Cardigan rode over to me to tell me to take command of the second line and that he expected my best support. By this time all sorts of people were arriving, determined not to miss the action – men who'd been with the commissariat or acting as butchers in Balaclava. They arrived with their equipment thrown on over the white canvas smocks they wore.'

'You led the second line to the guns and back?'

'Yes, sir, I did. The discipline never failed. It was a disciplined attack all the way down the valley. I was so concerned with my alignment, in fact, that I forgot to draw my sword until I was reminded by my orderly.'

'Did you see the first line enter the guns?'

'Yes, sir. Lord Cardigan's horse shied violently at the last discharge of the guns, then they were into them hot. But that last discharge had almost finished them. Men and horses crashed down until there were hardly any left. When we arrived we were having to avoid unhorsed men struggling to reach safety. When they lost their riders, the horses behaved as they'd been taught and tried to force their way back into the ranks. With a man in the saddle they showed no fear, but the riderless animals kept ranging themselves alongside me to make a line until my overalls were red with their blood. Once I was in the middle of seven of them and they almost unhorsed me. I had to use my sword to drive them away.'

'Please continue.'

'When we reached the bottom of the valley the confusion and the smoke were such that I never saw the guns until was among them. I had lost my second-in-command by then as well as my trumpeter and my orderly. I saw Lieutenant Hunt trying to unhook the traces of the guns so the Russians should not drag them away and I shouted to him to mount at once. I was told I accounted for one Russian but I have no memory of it. We then broke through and joined up with the 11th. I was looking for Lord Cardigan who had asked me to support him but there was no sign of him. We needed orders. We had been told, we thought, to capture the guns and there we had them captured but, without infantry, we

214

had no hope of holding them. I didn't know what to do but I remembered my father's advice about keeping control of cavalry when in difficulties, something he learned, sir, at Waterloo. I ordered them to face front.'

'Go on.'

'The numbers were small now but the men behaved well and I ordered threes about and we rallied and turned back up the valley. As we did so, the Russian lancers edged forward but our people, little more than a rabble by this time, simply put their heads down and brushed past them. If the Russians had shown anything like common courage, like English ladies, someone said, we should never have escaped. As we finally made it back to our lines, Lord Cardigan appeared.'

Paget paused, frowning, 'Shewell was leading the survivors of the 8th Hussars in, with a few others who had joined them, and hearing the cheer that greeted them, Lord Cardigan took up a position in front to lead them in. But the moment his back was turned, I saw some of the men behind him shake their heads and make signs of disgust. They had seen him down the valley and were aware of how soon he had set off back.

'I was very angry. I had lost every one of my trumpeters and two out of three sergeant-majors, and I thought the 13th and the 17th were no more, while the second line were not much better. Lord Cardigan had demanded my best support and I had expected him to see us out of trouble. But he had simply ridden back, indifferent to our fate. As if he didn't know what to do.' Paget looked at Eyland. 'In fact, sir, I later considered it my duty to write an official complaint. I told him that we had the Russian guns and carriages taken but received no support. He admonished me. When we reached our lines someone, who perhaps thought the same as I did, called out "Hello, Lord Cardigan, weren't you there?"'

Paget paused for a moment, frowning as if the memory

were an unhappy one. 'By this time,' he went on, 'I was feeling very low. Wounded men were crawling in to safety or bringing in their friends. Surgeons were amputating limbs and sewing up the awful sabre cuts which some of the men had received. Reaction had also set in and the men were shocked and excited and a few were noisy because they'd been given rum on empty stomachs. They'd had nothing to eat that day.'

Paget paused again and the court hung on to his description of the scene. 'But every man who made his way back was cheered,' he went on. 'Wounded horses were standing about, wretched, exhausted, bleeding, and wanting comfort, but all that could be done was to put them out of their misery. One came in, I remember, with a broken hind leg swinging round and round in a dreadful fashion. Just behind it was a wounded grey with one of the Chasseurs d'Afrique, covered with blood, lying across its neck, trying to find a surgeon to attend to two other wounded men. A man came creeping up the slope on his belly and a sailor wearing a dragoon's helmet brought him in. Eventually, as the day ended and darkness came, the women who had accompanied the regiments went out and began bringing in the bodies of their husbands and washing them and wrapping them in blankets or unwanted greatcoats for burial. It was horrible because there seemed to be blood everywhere, with amputated limbs and discarded bits of uniform.'

Paget drew a deep breath. 'Then I heard that Lord Raglan was blaming Lord Lucan for losing the Light Brigade. I was exhausted, I had a voice like an old crow from all the shouting I had done over the guns, and I felt very bitter after all the sneering against the cavalry that we were being blamed for something that was not our fault. I noticed Lord Cardigan did not blame Lord Lucan, though, of course, he did not allow himself to be blamed either. I was further embittered when Lord Raglan visited the camp two days later. I longed for him to say he was pleased with us. Just to say "My boys, you have done well." Something like that. We were in low spirits, we had lost many friends, yet he gave no indication that he was pleased. I couldn't see why he had bothered to come at all. He never got on with Lord Lucan.'

'Why do you say that?' Eyland asked.

'Lord Lucan had many foes at headquarters. Some he had made himself, but that should not have been held against him for Balaclava. Even his insistence that his camp was in a dangerously exposed position was ignored.'

'Was it ever moved?'

'Yes, it was, sir.'

'Who moved it?'

'Lord Raglan. But not until *I* made representations. I carried some weight as the son of his old comrade from Waterloo and then it was done at once. Lord Raglan was a man who had favourites but Lord Lucan was not one of them. I never came across a worse-treated man. After the charge, there was strong feeling for him in the cavalry, which was odd, because before they had often disliked him for his fussy ways.'

'Go on, sir.'

'I also thought it very wrong of Lord Raglan to choose Captain Nolan to carry the order that sent us against the guns. He was headstrong and quite unconciliatory, and his constant disparagement of the cavalry made him totally ill-suited for the carrying of so important a message. Lord Lucan was very upset. He had had to obey the order, he told me. "A man might just as well put a bullet through his head as disobey an order," were his words. There were tears in his eyes and I couldn't find it in me to disagree with him.'

Chapter Two

During Harboursford's cross-examination of Paget, Souto had become aware of his clerk, Pizzey, at his side. He turned and Pizzey smiled, his face shining with moisture as if he'd been hurrying.

'Sir,' he said. 'I think I have something that will interest you.'

'Let me see it.'

'Not here, sir,' Pizzey said.

'I can't leave the court.'

'It isn't necessary, sir. But, if you would perhaps meet me this evening, I'd be glad to show you.'

'What is it, Pizzey?'

'I'd rather leave it for you to see, sir.'

Souto stared at his clerk. Pizzey he knew, was an astute young man well versed in law who had often been a tremendous asset in digging out information. Souto trusted him implicitly.

'Very well,' he said. 'Where?'

'The Shades Vaults, sir.'

'Good God, why there?'

'You will see, sir. I gather you have been there once.'

'Yes, I have. What are we going to see?'

'What you will see, sir.'

'May I bring a companion? A young man, I know. Lieutenant Morden.'

'A good idea, sir. And might I suggest a stout walking stick and your least noticeable clothes? It is not a very salubrious district.'

'As I well know,' Souto smiled. 'Very well, Pizzey. We're in your hands. I hope it's worth it. Will you see that a message is delivered to my home for Lieutenant Morden. I suspect he'll be there. If he isn't I'm sure my daughter will know where he is.'

Pizzey smiled, nodded and vanished.

The evidence of Lord George Paget had been straightforward and largely non-controversial, and Harboursford obviously considered it did not advance the case for the defence. He didn't cross-examine at length and Lucan now introduced several soldiers who had ridden in the charge. Though their evidence did not add a lot, it was effective because they had endured the Russian guns, which was something most of Harboursford's witnesses had not done. Harboursford made little attempt to question them, clearly deciding their descriptions of what they had seen, while dramatic, had little to do with his case, yet he leaned forward like everyone else to hear more clearly, because their evidence was powerful stuff.

Souto was equally fascinated. As a civilian he had often tried to imagine what it would be like to be under fire and have to question your own courage.

The witnesses were quiet men for the most part, proud to have taken part in the Light Brigade's charge, but none of them was self-important or boastful.

Colonel John Douglas, an extraordinarily handsome man in the brilliant uniform of the 11th Hussars, of which he had taken command on Cardigan's appointment as brigadier, described the journey to the east and the cholera at Varna, where, because there were so many deaths, he had dispensed with the playing of funeral music. He commented that at the Bulganak, when they had retired, he had seen no sense in exposing his men unnecessarily to fire and had led them off at the trot, only to be reprimanded by Lord Cardigan for retiring too quickly.

'What was the weather like in the Crimea?' Lucan asked.

'By the time of the charge,' Douglas said, 'the nights were sharp enough to kill off the weaker horses and foraging was becoming extremely hazardous. I myself was wearing a fur coat captured from the Russian baggage train in September.'

'Did you expect the attack on 25 October?'

'I was so sure of it I had been warning my men that when it came they were not to cut but to use the point of their swords.'

'But at headquarters they were surprised when it came?'

Douglas's eyebrows lifted. 'I can't imagine why,' he said. 'Everybody in the plain knew it was on its way.'

As the 11th Hussars began to move into the charge, he continued, an aide arrived from Lord Lucan warning him to drop behind the first line. It seemed very sensible because it would make a third line. During the charge their position on the left caused them to outflank the guns down the valley and they tried to trap a group of Russians at the entrance to a small gulley but eventually came to an abrupt halt facing a great mass of Cossacks and other cavalry.

'I felt it was the whole Russian army,' Douglas said. 'I shouted to the men to retire. By this time we were only seventy strong but we began to move back in good order. As the Russians trotted forward I checked the retreat and we fronted to face them. I was all for another charge but as we moved forward they wheeled and galloped away. We were under fire still but, since the Russians were retiring, I thought that with adequate support we might yet drive them from the field. Then I saw a body of Lancers and shouted for my men to rally on them, thinking they were the 17th, but Cornet Palmer shouted that the lance pennants and headgear were not those of the 17th, and we decided we hadn't long to live.'

*   *   *

Troop Sergeant Major Berryman of the 17th, riding a wounded horse, was run through the leg by a Cossack lance. Sergeant John Penn tried to help, he said, and speared a gunner then, as he'd seen native troops do in India, he left his lance in the body and rode with his sword at a Russian officer whom he decapitated. By this time Berryman's horse had stopped dead at the guns and he dismounted to find out what had happened.

'While I was wondering whether to shoot it,' he said, 'Captain Webb rode through the smoke in a daze of agony with a shattered shin and asked what he should do. I advised him to stick to his mount and caught hold of a riderless horse to assist him. As I swung into the saddle, though, it was hit in the chest and the two of us crashed to the ground.'

He had later recovered consciousness to find Captain Webb, halted, unable to ride with the pain of his shattered leg. He was lifting him from the saddle when Sergeant Farrell of the 17th and Private Malone of the 13th appeared, followed by Private James Lamb, also of the 13th, whose horse had been brought down.

'We none of us had water bottles so we took a chance and Lamb went back down the valley, searching among the bodies until he found a half-full calabash on the saddle of a dead horse. We all drank, then Farrell and I carried the captain up the valley while Lamb went with Malone to help another wounded man.'

Captain Robert Portal, a slightly-built man in the uniform of the 4th Light Dragoons, was a man whose opinion of Lucan had changed as the weeks had gone by. He made no bones about his opinion on the management of the cavalry, however.

'It was not good,' he admitted. 'At Varna we seemed to do nothing but bury our comrades. I sometimes thought we were commanded by a pack of old women but I later realised the fault came from general headquarters.'

Major-General Hooe leaned across the judges' table.

'What about the situation outside Balaclava in the days before the attack when there were constant alarms?' he asked.

'The Russians were clearly trying to draw us,' Portal said, 'and it wasn't difficult to exhaust us. Whenever there was an alarm we had to run out, even though the threat might be small, because it was impossible to tell whether or not it might be an advance guard of the Russian army we knew to be outside Sebastopol. The horses were in dreadful condition.'

'We have heard of a patrol along the side of one of the hills,' Hooe said. 'A route with a precipice on one side and a dense wood on the other? Do you remember it?'

'I do. It was much gossiped about. Major Forrest said it was so dangerous Lord Raglan had ordered it to be discontinued and had found great fault in Lord Lucan for sending the patrol out at the same hour every day. But when I protested about it, Lord Lucan told me he had *always* considered it dangerous and quite improper for cavalry unless accompanied by infantry, but that Lord Raglan had insisted on it. In fact, he protested so much at headquarters, the next time I went out we were accompanied by the French.'

In a quiet voice, Portal claimed he would never forget the charge. 'I don't think cavalry was ever before or will ever be again exposed to such a fearful fire,' he said. 'The number of wounds indicated how bad it was. Some men were wounded ten, eleven, even thirteen times. It was worse coming back than advancing as by that time both riders and horses were exhausted. My own horse was killed by a splinter just as I reached what I thought was safety. It was the maddest and most extraordinary order ever given to cavalry. Yet I saw little sympathy for us from headquarters afterwards and within a very short time our horses were dying on their feet and our clothes were in patches and begrimed with mud. Some men even had no boots and wore hay tied round their feet. Lord Lucan endeavoured to organise stables but unfortunately they were badly sited and the horses died. Five weeks after the charge our horses were so useless they could only be used to carry supplies.'

Eyland looked up. 'Lord Lucan, this is nothing to do with the responsibility for the charge,' he said.

'It has a lot to do, sir, with the attitude of headquarters, and with the way the cavalry were treated,' Lucan pointed out. 'While they were dying on their feet, they could see the smoke issuing from the chimneys of the buildings where the staff were housed.'

Albert Mitchell, a sergeant in the 13th Light Dragoons, was a strong-looking man with a face lined with humour. Lucan started by asking him about the horses Nolan had produced for the cavalry from his search in the Middle East.

'How did you regard them, sir?'

Mitchell sniffed. 'They were the worst I ever saw, sir. They were wild, untameable and small, and they were always fighting together and breaking loose.'

'You had to handle them?' Eyland asked.

'I was there when they arrived, sir.' Mitchell's face split in a grin. 'The best joke, o' course, though, was that they were picketed near Lord Lucan's tent and the noise they made prevented him from sleeping. He expressed himself strongly on the quality of Captain Nolan's purchases, sir, believe me.'

There was some laughter and when it had died, Lucan turned again to Mitchell. 'You rode in the charge?'

'Yes, sir. I was spattered by the brains of Corporal Aubrey Smith, who was hit in the face by a round shot. His horse continued trying to close in as it was trained to do, jostling the others and causing a lot of confusion. In the guns, I saw a man ride past, and called to him to help but he was stone dead and was just held in the saddle by his rider's muscles. The Russian gunners were diving under their guns and running for their lives, then a shell hit my horse, carrying away its shoulder and part of its chest. As I went sprawling, another shell exploded and only the fact that I was on the ground saved my life.'

He had been trapped with one leg under the saddle, and as the 4th came up he shouted to them to be careful of him. He had managed to drag himself free but bullets were picking off the dismounted men and someone shouted to him to get down behind his dead horse, but he had thought it safer to get out of the battery.

'Lord Cardigan passed me as I went back,' he said. 'But he was on a horse and I was on foot and very tired because I'd been up since four a.m. and had had no food since the night before. I tried to catch more than one horse but they were all frightened. Then I saw the Greys who were waiting for us up the slope start to retire from the shellfire, and saw Cossacks coming and fell in with an unhorsed Grey who'd been blinded. I bandaged his head and led him off the field.'

Listening to the stories one after the other, Souto could only agree with Eyland that they had little to do with the responsibility for the charge but they were holding the court spellbound and somehow seemed to help Lucan's case, especially as nobody, either Eyland, nor Harboursford, nor the Deputy Judge-Advocate, made any move to stop them. Eventually, however, Gorvan decided they had had enough.

'I think, my lord,' Eyland said after Gorvan had leaned over and whispered to him, 'that we are wandering off the subject. You promised we would learn something about whose was the responsibility for the charge.'

'I think you will see that I am arriving there, sir,' Lucan said. 'May we call Captain John Brandling of the Horse Artillery?'

'For what purpose, sir?'

'Because, sir, I have been accused by my denigrators of not bothering to reconnoitre the ground before launching the Light Brigade. Captain Brandling will show that I did.'

Brandling, a hawk-nosed man with a cavalryman's gait, did exactly that.

He had seen Lord Lucan with his staff just before the Heavies' charge riding up on to the Causeway to find out where the Russians intended to strike. He had seen him there until the four Russian squadrons broke away from the main body in the North Valley at the beginning of the battle and began to cross the Causeway, followed more slowly by the main mass of the Russians.

'He found it too dangerous to remain there,' Brandling explained, 'and came hurtling down the slope with the warning that the Russians were advancing.'

He had also been present when Captain Nolan had arrived with the message that had launched the Light Brigade.

'Was there an argument?' Eyland asked.

'No, sir.'

'A loss of temper?'

'I would call it a discussion. If anyone was angry it was Captain Nolan.'

The soldiers had given their evidence quietly and in a way that clearly impressed the court. Harboursford was frowning as Lucan sat down and seemed to be wondering how to launch his final cross-examination. As it happened, Eyland looked at his watch and rose.

'I think, Colonel,' he said, 'that, owing to the lateness of the hour, we will leave your cross-examination until tomorrow.'

Harboursford bowed and it was Souto's opinion that he was glad of the opportunity to do a little thinking.

Lucan rose, said a brisk goodbye to Souto and vanished, Souto stared after him. Despite his admiration for Lucan's ability, he had still not got under the man's skin and had still not managed to form any warm feelings for him.

When he reached home, Morden was waiting for him. He was dressed in a lightweight suit and a soft collar. In the hall was his cloak, a stout walking stick and a hard melon-shaped bowler hat.

'What's on, sir?' he asked at once.

'I have no idea,' Souto admitted. 'It's some stunt thought up by Pizzey, my clerk. I gather it's important.'

They ate a hurried meal of cold beef and pickles, then a cab was called and they set off for the rendezvous with the clerk.

The weather had suddenly become even warmer. The night was windless and the still air allowed the smoke from countless kitchen fires to hang low in a grey haze over the white-painted façades of the houses of the wealthy. As they crossed the Thames, the heat seemed to increase the stink of the river and they crawled past carts and drays acrid with the smell of the stable, rattling through the narrow streets of Pimlico and over the setts towards Balham. Other cabs, with top-hatted men and befeathered women secretive behind half-drawn blinds, rolled past bucketing three-horse omnibuses, dodging the drunks picking their way through the piles of horse-droppings.

As they reached the crammed houses of the poorer areas, blackened with dirt and smoke, the shops had a pinched look – steamy windows of hot pieshops, eel shops, tripe shops, all with their freshly-lit flaring gas jets giving an orange glow. With the heat, everybody seemed to be in the street, and a great many people were still at work, women trying to sell lavender, sweating coalmen in leather hats making late deliveries, fishwives trying to empty their baskets of bloaters, matchsellers, muffinmen, and once on a corner under a lamp post a hurdy-gurdy surrounded by a group of dancing children. They began to see warehouses with little cranes to the upper floors, offices where penurious clerks still worked over their ledgers with their quill pens as they totted up the amounts and costs of tea, cotton, spices, wool, coal, iron, wines, spirits and precious stones. Outside some of the shops were piles of second-hand furniture, bedding, pots and pans, stacked as often as not under the three-ball symbol of a pawnbroker. Here and there in a doorway a girl wearing only a chemise called out to them as the cab passed. This was a district of insanitary houses smelling of drains, the breeding grounds for disease which surrounded pockets and hillocks of trodden earth where rat-infested rubbish heaps lurked. Scraps of black crêpe commemorating the end of the war they were debating at Hounslow still hung crookedly from an occasional house and on one wall, now beginning to fade, was the indignant message in whitewash. '2 Ded. Victims of a shamefull war.' The campaign in the Crimea had not been popular. After an initial euphoria, Russell's despatches had shown that the war was not only disastrous but also pointless and it had lost popularity. When the Government had sought to raise reinforcements, all the shillings, beer and meat pies offered by the recruiting sergeants had managed to produce no more than immature youths who had promptly died when faced with the rigours of the Russian uplands.

Sick Heart Yard looked the same as ever but it was early and the Shades Vaults were not busy. It was still smoky from the afternoon drinking, however, and heavy with the heat. Pizzey led them to a table and produced brandy and soda water.

'It's a warm night, sir,' he said. 'Brandy and soda will cool us down.'

'What have you found, Pizzey?' Souto asked.

'Take your drink, sir,' the clerk said. 'Then we'll go and see. We're going to the theatre. Pester's Theatre in Memorial Road.'

Souto's eyebrows shot up. 'The theatre, for God's sake? Pizzey, what are you up to? I hope this isn't a joke.'

'No joke, sir, as I'm sure you'll agree.'

'I'm not a theatregoer.'

'You are tonight, sir. You'll enjoy the experience.'

Souto wasn't so sure. The theatre generally was suffering from hard times and actors came and went with melancholy regularity, like the infant prodigies who also appeared, one of whom had once caused the House of Commons to suspend its sitting so that the Members could see his interpretation of *Hamlet*.

'I won't ask why,' he said slowly, 'because you've obviously got something up your sleeve. What are we to see? *Julius Caesar*? *King Richard III*?'

'Nothing so grand, sir.'

'Melodrama?'

'Of course, sir.'

Souto didn't fancy melodrama. The acting lacked subtlety and the parts showed all the Gothic influence which seemed to have arrived in England from Germany with the Queen's husband, Prince Albert.

Mr William Pester's Theatre was a small hall of shabby demeanour. Its paintwork and gilt were peeling and there was a seedy run-down look about it. The placards outside the doors indicated a programme interspersed by songs, hornpipes and recitations. Melodrama always had pride of place in the cheap theatres but sometimes a comedy might be played as a curtain raiser or as an afterpiece for the half-price customers who had missed the main event. Tonight there were to be two melodramas, *The Corsair's Revenge* and *Her Father's Face*, and there was already a queue outside for the cheap seats.

'Which one have we come to see, Pizzey?'

'Both of them, sir. I don't think you need bother with the song by Master Mars or the hornpipe by Miss White but I would be glad if you would pay full attention to the plays, sir.'

'Are you a keen theatregoer, Pizzey?'

'Oh, indeed, sir. But I'm not alone in my interest. I've discovered one of your witnesses, ex-Private Pennington, formerly of the 11th Hussars, is a great follower of the thespian arts.'

As they took their seats, Pizzey passed over a programme. 'It's repertory, sir,' he said. 'Mr Thomas Rowan's Players.

228

Not one of the best companies, sir, but very hard-working. Two representations every week, each comprising two plays. You might also profit from a visit to Taylor's Theatre, sir. They're playing *The Charge of the Light Brigade* there, complete with Miss Florence Nightingale saving the dying at Scutari. Very topical.'

Souto laughed and looked round the small theatre. There were no boxes at Pester's, just a sloping floor, rising slowly from where there had once been the orchestra pit but now housed only a piano. It was divided into three parts, the pennies, the tuppennies and the fourpennies. Though the fourpennies were the best seats in the house, they still left a lot to be desired and were singularly uncomfortable and probably full of fleas.

They were filled with what would probably be considered the affluent of the district, small tradesmen for the most part enjoying a night out on eels or whelks, then a drink or two and finishing with the theatre. Below them, stifling in the cheaper seats, were people who might well have been costers, shabbily-dressed young men and women clinging to each other's arms. The smell of warm bodies was strong, and within two seats there was a man who, judging by the faint whiffs that came their way, was clearly a fishmonger.

The Corsair's Revenge, put on with a great deal of thumping from the piano, flashing red and green lights and a lot of smoke which drifted out into the auditorium and smelled of wet coke, concerned a Cornish pirate chief who was really the local squire driven from his possessions by a wicked uncle. It concerned the love of a village girl – all purity and swooning, played by a lady who looked neither a villager nor a girl, nor even very pure – who was forced to marry the villain to save her lover. It ended, as expected, after a lot of cheering and booing, with the heavily bearded, evil-visaged villain dead on the stage and the heroine in the corsair's arms as he was restored to his property. The audience loved it and, to his surprise, so did Souto and he and Morden found themselves clapping enthusiastically.

'I must come here more often, Pizzey,' Souto said, dabbing at his perspiring face with his handkerchief.

'I'm glad you enjoyed it, sir. Strong passions and vigorou action are the essence of melodrama. Did you notice any thing, sir?'

Souto turned. 'Should I have?'

'Did you not notice the villain, sir – the man with the beard?'

'I couldn't see much under all the make-up.'

'Never mind, sir. Watch harder during the next one. *He Father's Face*. You get a better view and he stands still for bit. You might be surprised.'

Souto frowned. 'Come on, Pizzey, what are you up to?'

Pizzey looked prim. 'Sir, it isn't my job to convince you. I is up to you to make up your own mind.'

The song by Master Mars was a sea shanty and Maste Mars looked less of a master than a mister while Miss Whit turned out to be a thin woman of uncertain age and agilit but the audience loved her, beating time to the piano as sh cavorted with a hot red face round the stage.

'Now, sir,' Pizzey said. 'Do take notice this time.'

The second play was a new melodrama, a spine-chillin presentation which was thoroughly enjoyed by the audience A comic maid fed faggots to the heroine's baby and ther were references to local streets, policemen, buildings, alde men, even a salacious reference to Lord Palmerston anything that might raise the laughs that were striven for as variation from the high drama. It concerned a girl whos village was terrified by something called the Monster Menen which killed the inhabitants and sucked their blood

The play brought an enthusiastic response from the aud ence with cheers, jeers, shouts of abuse and wild clappin when the hero, the over-plump effeminate young man who ha been the Corsair in the previous play, did his stuff. Once agai Souto thoroughly enjoyed it, enough in fact to forget wh they were there until Pizzey reminded him during the interva

'The second act, sir,' he said. 'This is the confrontation scene. Just keep your eyes open and watch the window. You'll probably have noticed the man who appeared in a wide black hat and a high-collared cloak, with a red muffler up over his face. He was the villain in *The Corsair's Revenge* and you'll be seeing him again in this act.'

'I thought he'd just been killed off.'

'He has, sir. But it's not finished yet, sir. Not by any manner of means. They like ghosts and apparitions. Gauze on the stage to make mist, an ascending wire for the soul going to Heaven in the death scene. Makes the actors feel sick, I'm told, and gives them an ethereal appearance.'

The play pursued its creepy course, with displays of histrionics that would have been laughed off the West End stage but went down remarkably well in Balham where the audience hissed, booed and cheered. In the second act, the heroine, banished from home, was warned she was being watched.

'By whom?' she cried.

'By the one who always watches you.' The voice came from the wings. 'The one who knows and protects you. Your dead father.'

'A few minutes more, sir, before the end,' Pizzey whispered. 'Watch the window.'

The act proceeded along its melodramatic way until the hollow voice of doom came once more, this time from a window set in the backcloth. Clutching her bosom, the heroine spun round, looking for the source. The hero gave a hoarse cry.

'Now, sir,' Pizzey whispered.

'It's the face!' the hero screamed. 'Her father's face!'

There was a puff of smoke beyond the window, then from the smoke appeared a deathly pale face, topped by a wide black hat. Lit by a blue light, it remained in the window for no more than a few seconds, but it was long enough to give the heroine time to faint into the arms of the hero before it was gone. The smoke cleared, and the hero, clutching the unconscious girl, was left staring, horror-stricken at the empty window. As he did so, the moth-eaten red velvet curtain, one of its heavy gold tassels missing, swept down.

'You saw, sir?' Pizzey asked.

Souto stared at him. 'I saw,' he said. 'Indeed I saw. And very interesting, too. I give you full marks, Pizzey, for your discovery. I think it will pay us to have a word with your friend from the 11th Hussars, ex-Private Pennington.'

Chapter Three

The extraordinary heat had now become stifling. Though every window in the courtroom was open, the windless air seemed thick and hard to breathe. The number of people in the public area of the room had been drastically reduced and in particular there were far less women. Those there were fluttered fans and held small bags of aromatic herbs to their noses.

It was not the time of the year for cholera but the warm air drifting up from the Continent was more than enough to worry people with the memories of the great epidemics of the 1830s and 1840s still in their minds. The more recent one had not disappeared until 1855, and had spread to the army, virulent enough, as they had heard in court, to kill enormous numbers of the men serving in the East. It was, it was felt, about time for another period of pestilence and the early and unanticipated heat was enough to cause alarm. People disliked being in crowds in warm weather and those who could bolted for the safety of the countryside. As a result, only the most interested had braved the possibility of germs and the smut-laden train journey with open windows from Waterloo.

When Lucan arrived, Souto related his discovery to him as the court reassembled.

'You saw him?' Lucan asked.

'With my own eyes.'

'He must be watched. We'll need him.'

'I'll attend to it, my lord. Indeed, I *have* attended to it. My clerk, Pizzey, is an excellent man for cloak and dagger work. He has a number of very capable acquaintances who go in for this sort of thing.'

As the day opened, Lucan changed tactics.

'Let us now, sir,' he said, addressing Eyland, 'concentrate on this vexed business of the responsibility for the charge. You have heard the stories of the men who were there and what led up to it, but let us now try to decide what brought it all about? I would like to call Captain George Higginson of the Grenadier Guards.'

Higginson was a tall, handsome man, upright and confident in his bearing. Most of the men in the court had heard of him because in Varna he was reported to have forced one of the native vendors of raki, the local drink, to swallow a pint of his own poisonous spirit so that he had passed out cold, and he was also credited with having saved the lives of many of his men when the cholera epidemic was at its height by giving them bottled Bass.

'I believe you bumped into Captain Nolan just before the Light Brigade's action,' Lucan asked.

'Yes, sir. I did. I was moving down with the First Division to the plain. Captain Nolan had just carried a message of congratulation to General Scarlett for the success of the Heavies' charge.'

'How did he seem?'

'He seemed in the stress of some great excitement. As if he had somehow lost control of himself.'

'Did you understand why?' Eyland asked.

'From his words it seemed very clear to me. He was a light horseman himself and always talked of the Heavy Brigade as heavy men on heavy horses too slow to be of value. He thought that light cavalry was the answer, men with sharp swords moving at speed, and he was furious that the Light Brigade had not joined the Heavies' charge. He was full of life and said he was determined somehow to make Lord Lucan do something with the cavalry.'

'Because I had not already done so?' Lucan asked.

Higginson shrugged. 'He did not consider the Heavies' charge of great moment.'

'What was your view of Lord Raglan, Higginson?'

Higginson looked at Eyland who waved his hand. 'You had better answer,' he said dryly. 'Everyone else has given his opinion.'

'I considered him a poor general, sir. When the army suffered in the winter he and his staff kept themselves warm in a stone-built building while the rest of us lived in tents in the snow. One officer I spoke to who carried a message there said how glad he was of the warmth and comfort he found. Yet nothing was ever done for us and I personally felt that the staff just didn't know or care what was happening and, because they kept Lord Raglan from worrying, neither did he. There was great bitterness over his despatches even. The list of men who were created Companions of the Order of the Bath amazed me. Lord Raglan mentioned no one but his generals and their staffs, most of them well connected. While junior officers and NCOs who had done magnificently in the fighting and whose names had been brought forward by their divisional commanders were all ignored, Lord Raglan's five nephews all received rapid promotion. The story went about after Inkerman when Lord Raglan was made a field marshal that he was also to be made the Duke of Inkerman.' Higginson gave a little smile. 'I suspect, however, that this was merely sarcastic. But, Captain Sterling, Brigade-Major to the Highlanders, was very bitter at the awards. "If only I had a bit of interest," he said. "Or was Lord Tom Trumpeter!" He meant that had he had influence, he too might have got a CB or promotion. Windham, of General Cathcart's staff, said when Lord Raglan was made a field-marshal that he hoped he would use his baton to flog matters on a little faster, and Henry Clifford of the Rifles said Raglan had more to thank the army for than it had him. He had just seen the sick taken down to the ships in appalling conditions. He said "Field-Marshal" must sit heavy on Lord R's shoulders.'

Higginson was followed by Captain Morris of the 17th Lancers. He was a short sturdy man whose stature had given him his nickname, the Pocket Hercules. He looked pale and ill, however, and there were still livid pink scars on his temple and behind his ears from the wounds he'd received.

'I have been accused of being rusty in my knowledge of warfare,' Lucan began, 'and it was often pointed out that General Scarlett, whose experience of war was small, was not too proud to have two Indian Army officers to advise him. Did I have any such experts to advise me?'

Morris looked surprised. 'Myself, I suppose, sir,' he said.

There was a murmur round the court. Morris, it was already known, had taken part in three campaigns and charged with cavalry on four occasions, including the Battle of Aliwal in 1846 with the 16th Lancers. He had changed to the 17th Lancers and, on returning to England, had passed with distinction through the Senior Department of the Royal Military College at Sandhurst, one of the very few men in the Crimea who had.

Harboursford stood up. 'Are you telling us that Captain Morris was *not* with the 17th Lancers in the charge? I thought he commanded them.'

'He did, sir,' Lucan snapped. 'But he was on my staff until the night before the battle, when he took over the regiment on the death of the commanding officer from cholera. It is every officer's wish to command his own regiment and he was next in seniority and clearly I couldn't refuse him.'

'I took over,' Morris explained, 'at such short notice that I was still wearing a frock coat and the gold peaked cap of a staff officer. I had been ill with cholera and really in no condition for active duty because I had only recently rejoined. I was barely known by some of the men I commanded.'

'You had been worried about duties in the plain?' Lucan asked.

'Yes, my lord, I was so worried about the hazardous nature of them that I had written a letter to my wife which I gave to Captain Nolan, who was a friend of mine, to be sent to her in the event of my death. He gave me one for his mother to be sent under the same circumstances.'

Morris carried on to say that during the Heavies' charge, when the Russian cavalry had been halted, he had implored Cardigan to allow him to attack them in flank.

'I told him it was our positive duty to follow up the Heavies' charge with a flank attack,' he said, 'but he refused to allow it. I pleaded again with him but again he refused and I returned to the 17th, pointing out to the officers that they were a witness to my request – in case it should be said that I had not known my duty. We lost a tremendous chance at that point to drive the Russians off the field.'

'Were you there when Captain Nolan brought the message to the light cavalry?' asked Lucan.

'I was with the 17th. Because he was a friend, as he passed I asked him what was going to happen and if we were going to charge. He replied "You will see." That's all. "You will see."'

'What did he do as the Light Brigade prepared to go into action?'

'He took up a position on my right. I was in front of the 17th's left squadron. He was clearly determined not to miss the opportunity.'

'For what?'

'For glory, I suspect.' And Morris grimaced.

'As the brigade moved forward, what happened?'

'He put spurs to his horse and began to gallop ahead of the brigade which was advancing steadily as it had been ordered to.'

'How did he look?'

'He seemed to me to be smiling. He seemed, in fact, to be wearing a *triumphant* smile. I decided the excitement and enthusiasm had gone to his head and, aware of the distance we had to cover, I called out to him "That won't do, Nolan," I said. "We've a long way to go and must be steady."'

'A long way?' Eyland asked. 'The Causeway Heights were on your right and close by.'

'It never occurred to me that that was our direction, sir. The only enemy I could see properly was down the valley and that was where I thought we were intended to go. It was my impression also that that was where Nolan intended us to go.'

'Did he return to his position?'

'No, he did not, sir. He was killed a moment later.'

'And you, sir?'

'I rode behind Lord Cardigan. He kept telling me to keep the 17th steady because we were setting the pace and the course of the attack. We passed through the guns and about twenty of us, all that seemed to be left, found ourselves facing a solid mass of Russian horse. I warned the men to remember everything I had told them and to keep together, and we flung ourselves at them. I ran the commander through the body with my sword but, as he fell from the saddle, I couldn't withdraw it and, with it tied to my wrist by the sword knot, I was brought to a halt, leaning from the saddle as his men swept past. As I struggled to free myself, I received a cut above the ear which carried away a piece of bone and was then knocked unconscious by another blow which struck the acorn of my cap. It penetrated the acorn and went into my skull. As I came round I found my sword had somehow been wrenched free but I had hardly pulled myself upright when I was surrounded by Cossacks. My temple was pierced by a lance point which lifted the loose piece of bone. I was in great pain and, convinced I was dying, I surrendered.'

'Please continue.'

'Nearby was Lieutenant Chadwick. His horse was so starved and so weak with loss of blood from wounds that, on arriving at the battery, he could not make it move an inch further. He defended himself but a lance point took him in the neck and lifted him from the saddle. Cornet Wombwell was also taken prisoner, his horse shot from under him. I was hardly able to see for blood but I told him to look out and catch a riderless horse. At that very moment, several came past and Wombwell dodged the Russian lances, grabbed one and got away. I also ran into the thick smoke and caught a riderless horse, but I was too weak with loss of blood to pull myself into the saddle and I was dragged along until I fell unconscious again.'

There was a total hush in the court room. Somewhere at the back someone coughed and it sounded like an explosion in the silence.

'The next thing I remember,' Morris went on quietly, 'I was stumbling up the valley. A Cossack approached and I headed into the drifting smoke again. As another loose horse passed, I caught it and this time managed to mount it, but just as I turned it up the valley, it was killed by a crossfire and pinned me to the ground as it fell. Once again I lost consciousness.'

There was another silence as Morris drew breath and went on.

'As I recovered, I worked my leg free from the dead horse and set off on foot up the valley as fast as I could manage. On the way, I was caught up by Trumpet-Major Smith of the 11th, who made some comment. I hardly heard him. Then I saw Nolan's body, blackened, burned and covered with blood, and, remembering he had been the first to fall, I decided I was finally safe and collapsed alongside him. I was found there by Surgeon Mouat and Sergeant-Major Wooden of the 17th, who carried me in. I remember calling out "The Lord have mercy on my soul" in my agony. The letter Nolan had written to his mother was found in my pocket and set on one side and the letter I had given to Nolan was found on his body and, in error, believing me dead, was sent to my wife.'

'And now, Captain Morris? I trust you are recovered?'

Morris gestured. 'I am more valuable than I was before,' he smiled. 'I have a silver plate let into my skull.'

Lucan nodded. 'Your friend, Nolan. You must have waited alongside him for the brigade to start moving. Did he ever indicate to you what was in his mind?'

Morris shook his head. 'We talked for a minute or two but he never gave me the impression that we were to charge any guns but the ones we did. *I* certainly expected to charge the guns down the valley because I could see no others.'

'And your impression of Nolan before the charge and of where he was leading you?'

'I believed, as I have always believed, that he was spurring ahead, excited and enthusiastic, to charge the guns down the valley. My call, "We have a long way to go," would not have been correct if we were intended to attack the Causeway Heights. He sat alongside me as we waited to attack, and he never once suggested that we should be going anywhere but where we were clearly preparing to go – down the valley.'

'Could he not have changed his mind about the direction?'

'He could. But I still believe he thought we were intended to go down the valley. Either he had misunderstood Lord Raglan or he had not heard him properly, because it certainly seemed to be his view that we were to attack *down* the valley not *across* it. I felt his movement forward was merely because he didn't agree with the steady pace set by Lord Cardigan – who, sir, led throughout like a gentleman and a soldier.'

Lucan paused. 'Captain Morris,' he went on. 'You served at Aliwal. What happened on that day?'

'The Lancers captured the guns. They charged the Sikh artillery, passed through the guns and destroyed a square of infantry behind. As the Sikhs broke and fled we charged again.'

'That was a famous victory.'

'It was, sir. I am proud to have been there.'

'And Captain Nolan? Was he also proud to be there?'

Morris looked puzzled. 'He was *not* there, my lord.'

'Nor at the Battle of Sobraon, another splendid victory for the cavalry in which you rode?'

'No, sir.'

Lucan seemed puzzled but Souto knew it was feigned. 'But doubtless,' he said, 'being in India as he was, though he took no part in these splendid victories, he would hear much talk of them?'

Morris nodded. 'He must have.'

'Of how British cavalry, properly handled and moving at speed had routed the enemy.'

'Yes, sir.'

'Thank you. That is all.'

Chapter Four

William Howard Russell, of *The Times*, Lucan's next witness, was a familiar figure to the soldiers in the court who had served in the Crimea. His short, sturdy figure had then been clad in a mixture of military and civilian clothes, and his face had been graced by a beard. Now he was dressed as a civilian and wore only a moustache and whiskers.

There was a lot of movement among the civilians and those soldiers who had not served in Russia to get a glimpse of this famous figure whose despatches had exposed the criminal negligence of the government of the day, had set Florence Nightingale on her way east to clear up the mess in the hospitals and had eventually brought about the defeat of the government, and a measure of improvement and even change in the army.

Harboursford was on his feet at once, however, objecting, and Russell had to wait by the witness's chair for the argument to finish.

'This man,' Harboursford was saying, 'is not a soldier and knows nothing about what was going on.'

Lucan rose, his eyes glittering with anger. 'God help us,' he said, 'we have had to endure Mr Kinglake. His comments on Lord Raglan were that he was a saint. Surely to Heaven, Mr Russell, who at least has a true journalist's attitude to what he sees, rather than that of a mealy-mouthed admirer, is to be accepted?'

'I think that is quite a point, Colonel Harboursford,' Eyland said. 'We must accept Mr Russell as we have accepted Mr Kinglake.'

As the war correspondent sat down, Lucan addressed Eyland. 'I would like now, sir, to introduce an exhibit to the court.'

'Another?' Eyland sounded weary. There was already a large pile of Lucan's books and slips of paper on the desk in front of the members of the court.

'Another, sir,' Lucan insisted. 'A plan of the field of Balaclava.'

Eyland frowned and indicated the map that was hanging up for everyone to see. 'We already have one,' he said.

'That is a map, sir,' Lucan said. 'I wish to introduce a plan. With elevations. We have heard much about the clarity of the view from where Lord Raglan stood. Should we not ask ourselves *why* it was so clear?'

'Is it absolutely necessary?'

'For the clarification of the court, sir, yes.'

'Let it be brought in.' Eyland was beginning to grow a little tired of Lucan's tactics.

Lucan's plan was brought in, a large sheet of white drawing card with a thick single line drawn on it in red. It started at the top left hand corner, dropped steeply to the bottom, travelled about half the distance across the card, rose in a small pimple, then fell again and continued in a flat line to the opposite side.

'Is that it?' Eyland said.

'It is, sir.'

'All of it?'

'All that's needed, sir. The high point at the left of the line is the spot on the Sapouné Ridge where Lord Raglan applied that swift eagle eye of his to what was happening below him.'

'Please let us refrain from unpleasant remarks, my lord.'

Lucan's eyes crinkled but he gave a little bow. He had obviously heartily detested Raglan. 'That point, sir,' he

243

explained, 'was high above the plain. The low flat stretches are the North and South Valleys where the cavalry actions took place. The hump in the middle represents the Causeway Heights, considerably lower as you can see, gentlemen, than the Sapouné Ridge where Lord Raglan stood, so that everything that happened there was visible from the higher point; but higher by a long way from the valleys, where the cavalry were operating and from where nothing could be seen of what was happening there.' He turned to Russell. 'You observe that plan, sir?'

'I do.'

'Lord Raglan's position was some five hundred feet above the plain, was it not?'

'I think that was about it.'

'And four hundred and fifty feet above the Causeway Heights?'

'That's so.'

'So what was the relation to the Causeway Heights of the men in the plain?'

'They were about fifty feet below them.'

'If you were fifty feet below an object, do you imagine you could see what was happening up there?'

'No, I could not.'

'But if you were four hundred and fifty feet above?'

'I would see everything.'

'Thank you. Now, sir, you were sent by *The Times* to the seat of war as a correspondent.'

'A *war* correspondent. The first in history.' Russell was proud of his distinction and answered briskly in a voice that retained a trace of his Irish background. 'I reported the collapse of the army nursing system and the agonies of the soldiers.'

'And, though such things had always happened, this time your newspaper brought it to the people at home over their breakfast tables.'

'I'm proud to say that is so. The fundamental difficulty, I found, was the subordination of the medical officers to their military colleagues and their inability to make decisions for sanitation and comfort, while, in addition, the military officers retained the ablest and most intelligent men for the fighting so that only the ne'er-do-wells and walking sick were available for —'

Lucan held up his hand to stop Russell's torrent of words.

'Thank you, Mr Russell. We are aware that typhus, cholera, dysentery, battles and lost supply ships overwhelmed the system and that men died in their hundreds. You had certain views about the cavalry, I believe?'

Russell cleared his throat, obviously determined to be straightforward. 'I thought the government had made a monstrous choice in its commanders,' he said and Lucan was taken aback for a moment. 'Because it was well-known that both yourself and Lord Cardigan had quick tempers and were already at loggerheads. I could see nothing but trouble ensuing. And neither could anyone else I spoke to.'

Lucan frowned but pressed on. 'You were aware of the difficulties existing in the cavalry?'

'Even at Varna. It was my view that if Lord Raglan had been anything like a commander-in-chief, he ought to have realised it was ridiculous to expect you and Lord Cardigan to work together. In view of Lord Cardigan's behaviour, he ought to have been removed from command. Having accepted you as commander of his cavalry, he ought to have backed you up.'

Harboursford was on his feet again. 'This is purely an opinion, gentlemen. Moreover, not the opinion of a soldier.'

'I think you had better withdraw it, Lord Lucan.'

Lucan nodded. 'Very well, sir.' He turned to Russell again. 'You saw me often, I believe, as I went about my duties.'

'That is so. No officer was more vigilant or more careful of his command. Indeed, I was of the opinion that your constant appeals to headquarters on the subject of the care of baggage animals, the composition of the squadrons, the picketing of horses, their shoeing and marking and heel-ropes, the carriage of ammunition, the dress of officers, the packing of valises, reports, et cetera, were something of a headache to headquarters.'

'Hm.' Lucan had got rather more than he had expected but at least he had the answer he wanted. 'You saw the condition of the army at Scutari and Varna?'

'I did. The Guards had become so weak they had to divide the march from Aladyn where they were encamped, to Varna – a mere ten miles – into two parts. Colonel Hodge of the 4th Dragoon Guards buried twenty-three of his men and it was becoming difficult to find a spot for a grave which had not already been dug over. On one occasion I saw empty carts waiting and asked the French NCO in charge what they were for. He replied "Pour les morts". By 19 August it was possible to see whisps of straw sticking from the sand and beneath them a dead face. Corpses hidden under the stones that were lifted from the sea to make a jetty, floated free upright in the water, their feet shotted to make them sink.'

'Let us go to the skirmish at the Bulganak. You were close to where the action was taking place?'

'I was well up to the front with the artillery. I saw the Russians come over the hills in three great blocks and the British skirmishers look round anxiously for the horse artillery.' Russell was addressing Eyland now and was talking of Lucan as if he were not there. 'Lord Cardigan was clearly eager to try his strength but then I saw more dark columns beyond the first and I heard Lord Lucan order Lord Cardigan to gather in his skirmishers. The horse artillery moved up and then General Airey arrived with orders for the cavalry to withdraw. Lord Cardigan wanted to be at them, and it took both General Airey and Lord Lucan to restrain him.'

'Was Captain Nolan there?' Lucan asked.

'Yes.'

'Why? Did his duty carry him there?'

'No. He was simply eager to be able to say he had been under fire. He never had been before.'

'I thought Captain Nolan was considered to be an expert.'

'It was largely theory. But it didn't stop him behaving as if he *were* an expert. He went forward to the skirmishers, clearly pleased to be there. He later said to me that he had enjoyed being under fire.'

'Was he under heavy fire?'

'Not really. A few bullets flying around. But he seemed to need to be seen. He liked to draw attention to himself. I heard him say "Those Russians are damned bad shots." Very loudly.'

'Was he a good officer?'

'He was brave and intelligent, but he was very impulsive. He was itching to see the cavalry in action. He had written a lot about them and wanted to see his theories put into effect.'

'These theories. do you know what they were?'

'He considered light cavalry could achieve wonders by their speed. He believed they could capture batteries because they could overwhelm them before they could defend themselves. He thought they could break squares and pointed out that it had happened at Aliwal in India. At the Bulganak he seemed to wish to see the four squadrons which had advanced flung pell-mell against the Russians. Instead, they were withdrawn and only a few shots were fired. The cavalry behaved well. They could not have been more solid or immoveable, though I'm sure no one enjoyed watching the round shot bounding past. I didn't.'

'Did you hear the comments as they withdrew?'

'I heard one of the infantry say "Silly peacock bastards, serve them right."'

'Why did he say that?'

'There was enmity between the two arms and it was often felt that the cavalry was all show and no action. The infantry resented the cavalry being withdrawn.'

'What did *you* feel?'

'Gentlemen,' Harboursford protested again, 'this witness is not an army officer.'

'Nevertheless,' Lucan snapped, 'he surely has some knowledge after being in the Crimea of whether troops behave well or ill.'

'I think it must stand, Colonel,' Eyland said.

Russell shrugged. 'I have often been a critic of the army, gentlemen,' he admitted. 'But I considered the affair very well managed and that the cavalry had done splendidly.'

'Did the cavalrymen think so?'

'Those I spoke to were disappointed. They had not seen the Russians behind the hills and felt they were being withdrawn like whipped dogs to the kennels. Especially when the Russians jeered at them as they went.'

'How about Lord Cardigan?'

'He was clearly angry. Not only with Lord Lucan but also with the 11th Hussars, his old regiment, because they had not retired as slowly as the others.'

'Let us move to the day of the Alma. Did you see Captain Nolan on this day?'

'He was to have carried Lord Raglan's message to set the infantry in motion but his horse was shot dead and the message was taken on by one of Sir de Lacy Evans' staff.'

'You watched the battle?' Lucan asked.

'I did, sir. And I considered it singularly misconceived. It seemed only a bulldog rush at the Russian throat and I felt that in his years as Military Secretary in London Lord Raglan had lost the faculty for handling large bodies of men. There seemed a great want of generalship. One officer said to me that the only orders he received the whole day were "March" and "Halt".'

'Must we have more of Lord Raglan?' Eyland asked.

'It will not hurt Lord Raglan if I am proved to be innocent of the charge made against me,' Lucan argued. 'It will hurt me, however, if I am not so proved, because of a refusal to discuss a man who is dead and can't be harmed.'

Eyland nodded. 'You make your point, my lord,' he agreed.

'Thank you, sir. Mr Russell, let us deal with the behaviour of the cavalry at the Alma. They were not involved in the action. What did Captain Nolan feel about that?'

'He said to me, "There were one thousand British cavalry looking on at a beaten army retreating with its guns, standards and colours, with a wretched horde of Cossacks and cowards who never struck a blow ready to turn tail at the first trumpet within ten minutes' gallop of them." He considered it disgraceful, infamous. He said, "It is enough to drive one mad."'

'You heard this?'

'I did.'

'Said to whom?'

'To officers of the cavalry. I heard him – as did the correspondent of *The Morning Post* – using observations not made for the tongue of an aide-de-camp.'

'Who was he blaming for this failure to follow up the Russians? Lord Raglan?'

'Oh, no, sir. Yourself.'

'Did he continue in this way?'

'Often. Long after we had reached Sebastopol. I often heard him speak disparagingly of you. Of course, by this time he had heard of Lord Raglan's wish to keep the cavalry in a bandbox and I heard him say "Did anyone ever hear of cavalry in a bandbox doing *anything*?" The heat never cooled down.'

'Did he ever accompany the cavalry on its patrols?'

'Not to my knowledge. It seemed to me most of the time that he was resentful that he could not persuade anyone to use cavalry as he felt it should be used – in a swift bold stroke. It had got around somehow that he had done well at the Alma and that it was entirely due to his suggestions that the cavalry had kept at bay the vast mass of the Russian horsemen.'

'Was that so?'

'Not to my knowledge.'

'Where did this story come from? Nolan himself?'

'From his friend, George Evelyn. I often heard Evelyn saying things, but, of course, they may have been put into his head by Nolan. I don't know.'

'What was *your* view of the Russian cavalry?'

'I did not consider them very good.'

'Did you ever hear my opinion?'

'You once told me that they were as bad as could be, though the Cossacks worried you.'

'By this time you had noticed a lot wrong with the army, I believe? Things of which everybody is now aware.'

'I wrote home about them.'

'Were you ever assisted by the staff at headquarters?'

'Never. When I arrived I asked for tents and rations, as had been arranged for me at home. I found, however, that I was looked on not as the representative of a responsible and prestigious newspaper, but as an interloper. It seemed I had no right to be there and Lord Raglan's Military Secretary told me flatly that the request could not be granted. Yet Mr Kinglake, who was there in an unofficial capacity and was not an accredited correspondent but was with the army merely as a travelling gentleman, was given every facility by Lord Raglan because he was well connected.'

'Did you speak with Lord Raglan?'

'He treated me as if I didn't exist. He never spoke to me at all and seemed to regard me merely as a camp follower.'

'Did this make you bitter?'

Russell smiled. 'It's happened before. It's a habit of the aristocracy towards tradesmen.'

'Did it affect your writing?'

'I told the truth.'

'*The Times* had a name for Lord Raglan, did it not?'

'Yes, sir. We called him "The Invisible Commander". We pointed out that he had scarcely been seen since Inkerman. I think he brought the army to ruin. People didn't like what I said, but I was convinced that he was too old, too gentle in manner, too indifferent or too unaware of the sufferings of his men to lead an army through any arduous task. I stated in my despatches how the army had suffered from mismanagement and much of the blame was laid on the Commissary. But Lord Raglan must have been aware from the beginning what was wrong, and yet it was never put right.'

'Once again, we're not asking this witness for his opinion of the Commander-in-Chief,' Harboursford said, jumping to his feet.

'*I* am,' Lucan snapped back.

'Let him state what he saw or heard, not what he thinks.'

'I based my opinion on what I saw and heard,' Russell said briskly.

Harboursford glared at Russell but Lucan seemed delighted and Eyland made no move to have the remarks struck from the report.

Turning to Russell again, Lucan shuffled his papers. 'You saw the building of the redoubts on the Causeway Heights, those redoubts that were to cause so much trouble?'

'I did. Wretched molehills, I thought them. Mere sketches with a spade. They seemed to invite attack, especially as they had been placed so far ahead of the army.'

'Let us go on to the evening before Balaclava. Where were you?'

'I was at the cavalry camp.'

'Were you there when a Turkish spy arrived?'

'I was. Lord Bingham was sent up to headquarters with the information he brought.'

'What was the feeling in the cavalry camp?'

'Everyone felt that the attack they had been expecting for so long was about to fall on them. I was told that the Russians in the valley were very strong and were "all over the place."'

'Did you see Captain Nolan?'

251

'As I set off back to headquarters to find out what was to be done, he joined me.'

'What did he say?' Eyland asked.

'A great deal, sir. He was loud in his contempt for Sir Colin Campbell's anxiety about Balaclava and very critical of the information which had been taken to headquarters by Lord Bingham. All the way back he kept letting out at Lord Lucan and Lord Cardigan.'

'Did you take any notice of him?'

'Not really, sir. By then he had been complaining so long that no one did. When we arrived, the officers who were sharing my tent merely laughed when I told them what he had said. "He's an inveterate croaker," one of them commented – I can't recall which – "I wish he was in Jericho with his cavalry." I said nothing, because Nolan had lent me his cavalry cloak and I was glad of it. It was cold and wet and pouring with rain. He said, "I shall not want it tonight." As it happened, he never wanted it again.'

'Did you see Captain Nolan the following day as the Light Brigade began its attack?'

'Yes. He was with the 17th Lancers. It was quite easy to identify him.'

'What did he do?'

'He rode forward.'

'Urging them to change their direction, across their front, pointing to the Causeway Heights?'

'That was not how it seemed to me. I got the impression he was trying to urge them to the greater speed he had always believed in.'

'Did you read the *Morning Chronicle*'s report on the battle?'

'I did.'

'I'll quote it. "By an imbecile command . . . the flower of the British army were . . . led to butchery. . . . Never was more wilful murder committed than in ordering an advance to such . . . certain destruction. The popular voice has united in subscribing this great calamity to Captain Nolan." Is that what it said?'

'As far as I can remember.'

'Did it also refer to my own reputation for prudence?'

'It did.'

'Did it also continue as follows: "On the day of the Alma, when the complete rout of the enemy and perhaps the fate of Sebastopol hung on a dashing cavalry pursuit, then our own force was deemed insufficient. But now, in a miserable skirmish, this very force was despatched against formidable batteries, a cavalry twice superior in number, and an unknown force of infantry."'

'As far as I recall, that *is* what it said.'

Harboursford was on his feet again. 'The opinion of a newspaperman,' he said.

'Nevertheless,' Eyland observed, 'an experienced one. It will stand.'

Lucan gestured at Russell. 'Last year, following the enquiry into the McNeill–Tulloch report and the suggestion that it existed merely to whitewash the army, did you write something further?'

'I did. I wrote that you had as little to do with the bungle at Balaclava as I had. I felt that justice had not been done to a rugged, violent and ardent officer who had left himself no friends – and had bought none – and whose recall was a very high-handed exercise of authority to cover with a false appearance of vigour the weakness of those who had made him a victim of their own shortcomings.'

'Perhaps you'd explain that,' Eyland said.

'You are asking my opinion, sir?' Russell queried.

'I am asking for an explanation.'

'It can only be an opinion, sir, and, if I am to be regarded merely as a newspaperman without knowledge of army matters, then I prefer not to give it because it would be worthless. If I am to be asked my opinion of how it happened, then I will give that opinion and be happy to do so.'

'Please give it, sir. I'll be the judge of it.'

'I knew Lord Lucan had never been popular. I knew he

253

never let up on the cavalry and always insisted on the very best that could be got. I know he punished officers who failed to provide themselves with spyglasses and compasses and other things he considered necessary. I also know that he was constantly railing at the people at headquarters for what he considered their failings. As a result he was not popular there, and this as much as anything brought about his downfall. I felt, as I feel now, that Lord Raglan and his staff were incompetent. At one time I saw men dying on the beach without any medical assistance within sight of headquarters. Lord Raglan was never able to grasp the fearful conditions exterminating his army. And he wasn't the only one. *The Times* raised £30,000 for comforts for the troops, but the British Ambassador to the Porte could only suggest that it should be used to build a Protestant church. *No one knew what was happening.* Or, if they did, then they didn't care.'

'Surely we don't need to hear this, sir?' Harboursford asked.

'I do,' Eyland said quietly. 'Please go on, Mr Russell.'

'Thank you, sir. I considered that one of the finest armies ever to leave these shores was sacrificed to mismanagement and I could only blame lethargy and indifference. It was all this, I considered, coupled with Lord Lucan's angry charges at headquarters that caused him to be recalled.'

'This is the opinion of a civilian, sir.' Harboursford tried again.

Russell sighed and half-turned away. Eyland held up his hand.

'I will decide that, Colonel,' he said. 'I asked for Mr Russell's opinion and I appreciate it.'

Harboursford rose slowly and began his cross-examination. 'Mr Russell,' he said, 'is it not true that the Russian commanders said that they didn't need spies so long as the correspondent of *The Times* was in the camp?'

'I've heard it said,' Russell agreed. 'What was I supposed to do? Ignore everything?'

'Mr Russell, was this your first assignment of this type abroad? And after the Crimea did not your career take a turn for the better so that you have become internationally famous?'

'That's correct.'

'We have heard a lot about the despatches you sent home. Could it be that they were not exact in every detail?'

Lucan jumped to his feet. 'Sir, there is no suggestion whatsoever that Mr Russell distorted the truth.'

'Nevertheless,' Harboursford snapped, 'it is true that he has been accused of writing accounts which are not accurate and that he has caused offence in some regiments by accusing them of not facing their tasks courageously. Is that not so, Mr Russell?'

Russell seemed superbly unmoved. 'Of course I did. In most cases the fault was due to bad leadership. Where the officers were good, the regiments behaved well. Where the officers were indifferent, so were the regiments.'

Harboursford thought for a moment then continued slowly, speaking to the court. 'We have to remember, gentlemen, that this was the witness's first foreign assignment. Would he not be anxious to make a good job of it? He was young and eager. In his eagerness did he paint pinks red and blues purple? Did greys become harsh black and white?'

'This seems a reasonable argument,' Eyland said.

Harboursford turned back to Russell. 'What do you say to all this, Mr Russell?'

A stubborn expression appeared on Russell's face. 'I saw what I considered were a lot of wrongs,' he said. 'And I felt it was important that the country should be made aware of them. It was certainly not my intention to gain fame. I was concerned only with telling of what I saw.'

Harboursford tried Lucan's trick with Kinglake. 'Because

you were angry that Lord Raglan had spurned you, perhaps?' he asked.

'No, sir,' Russell snapped. 'Because an army was dying on its feet.'

Chapter Five

As they waited for the next witness, Souto was startled to see Pizzey appear alongside him.

'Our man's disappeared, sir,' he whispered.

'What?' Souto looked round.

'I went to the theatre where they were due to rehearse a new spectacle for next week. *The Squire's Daughter*, it's called. They were unable to proceed because our friend, who was to take the villain's part again, had not turned up. They'd checked at his digs but he wasn't there and they were trying to decide who should take his place.'

'Go on.'

'I went to his digs, too, and learned he was visited there last night by a gentleman and promptly started packing his belongings.'

'Who was the gentleman?'

'That I haven't been able to discover. The landlady is very shortsighted and she was unable to give me a description. However, our friend had just left with a small carpet bag, saying he had to catch a train. She doesn't expect to see him back.'

'Do we have any idea where he went?'

'I have suspicions, sir. I am making enquiries.'

'He must be found, Pizzey.'

'I shall do my best, sir.'

'It's important, as I'm sure you know. You mustn't fail us. Where's he gone, do you think?'

'Only one place he would go, sir. The Continent.'

'Can he afford it?'

'It would pay the people who employed him to make sure he could.'

'Can he be halted?'

'I don't know, sir. I'd better get on the way at once. In the meantime, however, I'll telegraph the terminus and get the railway police in action.'

When Souto looked up again, Russell had vanished, to be followed by a sturdy and intelligent-looking young man, his face browned by the sun.

'You are John Elijah Blunt?' Lucan asked. 'A member of the Consular Service, born in Turkey, with service behind you in that country, and an expert in the Turkish language?'

'Yes, sir.'

'What was your part in the recent campaign in the Crimea?'

'I was taken on to your staff, sir, as interpreter. You suggested that since the Turks were our allies it might be a good idea to have someone who could speak the language and that I might even enjoy the experience.' Blunt smiled. 'Those were your words, sir. I did *not* enjoy the experience.'

There was some laughter but it died quickly.

'Were there any other Turkish experts in the Crimea? On the staffs of other officers? On the staff of Lord Raglan, for instance?'

'Not to my knowledge, sir. A few could speak the language a little but as far as I know we – you and I sir, and Sir Colin Campbell, for whom I also acted at times – were the only people communicating easily with them in their own language. The Turkish leader, Rustum Pasha, was always very pleased.'

'Why didn't Lord Raglan employ someone like you?'

Blunt shrugged. 'He didn't approve of the Turks, sir. He considered them inferior as soldiers and as men.'

'How would you say I behaved to my staff? Well? Or ill?'

Blunt smiled. 'You were inclined to overrate your ability

to get through work, sir, and we often had to remind you of the time. When at Varna you went to dine at the Embassy, the fare for the caïque was placed in a paper in one pocket marked "Boat", and the money for the hire of a horse up the hill in the other marked "Pony".'

Lucan listened to the laughter expressionlessly. Blunt seemed to enjoy pulling his leg.

'What about the Division?' Lucan asked.

'Though you were largely indifferent to your own comfort – and I might add, sir, to ours, too – you never forgot your soldiers and their mounts. You also took care to insure the horses of your staff – something we were to bless you for eventually – and you were always engaged in trying to improve conditions for the men.'

'At the Alma. Did you see Captain Nolan?'

'He was very anxious to be seen.'

'You remember the affair near Khuton Mackenzie when the cavalry became lost?'

'I do, sir.'

'In fact, who lost them. Me?'

'Oh, no, sir.' Blunt smiled. 'The staff officer sent by headquarters to act as guide – Captain Wetherall. He had a poor map and didn't know where he was. *He* lost them.'

'Did you later hear comments on the subject?'

'When I visited headquarters there was no mention of Wetherall. Just things like "The cavalry are at it again."'

'We know who said it, too, don't we, Blunt?'

'Yes, sir. It was Captain Nolan.'

'Did he say anything else?'

'He spoke disparagingly of you, sir. He could not have known the true facts.'

'Others did. Why didn't Nolan?'

'Perhaps he had closed his mind to them, sir. Captain Nolan was hot-tempered. He had strong views on how cavalry should be handled and didn't hesitate to criticise anyone who handled them differently. I think it had become

259

something of an obsession and he could see no good in anyone who didn't agree with him. He was very forceful and, I think, very biased.'

'How did the cavalry get on with the Turks?'

'Excellently, sir. Yourself and Sir Colin Campbell appeared to be the only people who did. Most people disparaged them and called them "dogs". Many of these people had not been under fire, of course, but, despite the Turks' excellent showing on the Danube, they called them "cowardly curs".'

'What was your view of the Turks?'

'Probably biased, sir,' Blunt admitted, 'as I had lived among them. But, in fact, though they were badly equipped they were capable and commanded at Sebastopol by an able intelligent man, Rustum Pasha. With the Highland Brigade and the cavalry division, they had the task of defending Balaclava.'

'Who was placed in command there?'

'Sir Colin Campbell.'

'Did anyone complain?'

'Yes, sir.'

'Me?'

'No, sir.' Blunt smiled. 'Lord Cardigan. He wanted to know why Sir Colin Campbell had an independent command when he had not.'

'What about the work in the plain?'

'It was always difficult, sir. The cavalry had to be constantly on the alert. However, you insisted that they should always be ready for action. Your view was "Better safe than sorry". It didn't stop the gossip, though. I often heard Captain Nolan complaining.'

'We have heard that headquarters were not expecting the attack of 25 October. *Were* you?'

'Oh, certainly, sir. Everybody in the plain was.'

'Let us go to the battle. Did you see the Turks?'

'Yes, sir. They fought well. You yourself commented on

their courage. They were holding off the advance of the Russians alone but the redoubts were very lightly built and when eventually guns were brought to bear and when no help was sent, they finally had to retreat. As the Heavies moved forward, I was sent to tell the survivors to form up behind the Highlanders to the north of Balaclava. They were thirsty, exhausted and angry. They had lost many men and couldn't understand why no troops had been sent to their support. When I rode back to you, sir, the situation had become serious.'

'I really must object.' Harboursford was beginning to sound desperate. 'This man is not a soldier and we have heard from too many of them.'

'He was a soldier at the time, sir,' Eyland pointed out quietly. 'Let him continue.'

Blunt bowed. 'Two of the six redoubts had now fallen to the Russians,' he said, 'and Sir Colin Campbell, who had never been happy about them being placed so far forward, began to be worried about Balaclava. Maude's battery was out of action and Captain Maude had been carried off the field in a blanket badly wounded. Lieutenant Dashwood took over the battery but had two horses killed under him at once. After twelve horses had been lost he ordered the battery to retire. By this time the Turks in Number Three Redoubt were also retreating and a troop of horse was sent to drive away the Russians who were following them, while I was sent forward again to order these men also to move towards Balaclava.'

'By whom were you sent?' Lucan asked.

'By you, sir.'

'The Heavies' charge: who ordered it?'

'You, sir. But it seemed to me that, though the Greys heard your order and obeyed it, the Inniskillings and the 5th took their orders from General Scarlett. However, there was no confusion as both orders directed the same thing.'

'You saw the Light Brigade's action?'

'As I returned from one of my errands they were pre-paring to move off. I had been chased by a Cossack who had struck at me but missed and mortally wounded my horse. A Russian horse had been brought up for me but I didn't like the look of it. It looked too strong and unmanageable. But I was waiting beside you when Captain Nolan brought the fourth order.'

'Was there a discussion?' Eyland enquired.

'There was.'

'An argument?'

'It didn't seem so, sir, to me. Lord Lucan indicated the pointlessness of advancing against guns with cavalry but Captain Nolan said very sharply and very clearly, "Lord Raglan's orders were that the cavalry should attack im-mediately."'

'What was the reply?'

'"Attack, sir! Attack what? What guns?" Those were Lord Lucan's words.'

'Why, do you think, that question was asked?'

'From where we were, it was impossible to see any guns at all except those at the bottom of the valley.'

'What about the guns on the redoubts?' Lord Fitzsimon asked. 'The naval guns in the redoubts which had been captured.'

'It was impossble to see them.'

'Lord Raglan saw them.'

'Lord Raglan was high above them, sir.'

'Could *you* see any guns, Blunt?'

'Only the guns down the valley, sir.'

'But not the guns on the Causeway Heights?'

'From where we were at that moment, I could not even see the redoubts.'

'What happened?'

'Captain Nolan threw out his arm towards the bottom o the North Valley and said, "There, my lord, is your enemy There are your guns."'

'He said that?' Eyland asked. 'You're sure?'

'I heard him, sir. I'm very sure.'

'What did he mean. Are you sure he wasn't merely taunting Lord Lucan?'

'I was not a professional soldier, sir, but I had already learned that an aide is expected to know his commander's wishes. I assumed from his manner and his words that it was Lord Raglan's wish for us to attack the guns down the valley. Indeed, it was my belief that I would have to accompany the attack and I wasn't looking forward to it. But I saw no alternative and I was just taking up my position when Lord Lucan stopped me and told me I was not to take part. I have to admit I was very relieved.'

Eyland gestured to Lucan who took up the questioning. 'Did I give you anything?' he asked.

'You gave me the fourth order and told me to take care of it.'

'Did you read it?'

'Yes, sir.'

'There was a reference in it to preventing the enemy carrying away the guns, was there not?'

'Yes, sir.'

'Did you read the third order?'

'Yes, sir.'

'Was there any reference in that to guns?'

'None whatsoever, sir.'

'Would you have assumed that the two orders should be read together, as we have been told they should have been?'

Blunt smiled. 'Certanly not, sir. They seemed entirely unconnected.'

Lucan paused. 'Why do you think I gave you the fourth order and told you to take care of it?'

Blunt grinned broadly. 'With respect, sir, you were a precise, careful, even fussy man and, like me, you seemed to be certain that the Light Brigade was heading for destruction. But you knew that orders should not be questioned in the middle of a battle because, as I supposed at the time, there might have been a good reason for what Lord Raglan had ordered. The only thing you could do was obey the order and question it afterwards. That is why you told me to take good care of the message, so that if the action turned out as you clearly expected it to, you could not later be accused of misinterpreting it. There had been several occasions before when there had been difficulties and you had always kept the orders you received as proof of what you had been ordered to do.'

'Indeed, he did,' Eyland said dryly. 'Pray continue.'

'It was my opinion, sir, that the Commander-in-Chief, for reasons of his own, was being forced to sacrifice the cavalry, perhaps to protect some other point of the field, but that Lord Lucan was sufficiently worried to feel that perhaps there might be a mistake and that if his actions were later questioned he would need proof of the order. As Lord Lucan moved away, sir, Captain Charteris, his nephew, who had often been kind to me in my inexperience, asked to borrow a handkerchief. I told him mine was not very clean but he replied that it would suit his purpose and, drawing his sword, he twisted the handkerchief into a loop round the hilt and his wrist to strengthen his grip. "This will do," he said. Then he added, "But I doubt if I shall ever return it to you."'

'You mean he believed that he was riding to his death?' Eyland asked.

'Yes, sir.' Blunt paused. 'He did not return, sir. I never saw him again.'

'What happened to you?'

'I watched the beginning of the charge from the slopes, then the Russian horse I had been given became restive at the gunfire and the trumpet calls so I decided to return to the cavalry camp. Unfortunately, the horse ran away with me and I could see myself being carried into the Russian lines. However, as it reached Number Five Redoubt where Rustum

Pasha had placed five hundred men after the Heavies' charge, it fell. A Turkish soldier who ran to help me was killed by a shell. The horse galloped across the valley to the Fedioukhine Hills on the other side. I remained in the redoubt, sheltering from the shellfire.'

'This shellfire?' Lucan asked. 'Where was it coming from?'

'From the Fedioukhine Hills on the other side of the valley. Many of the Turks had been killed by it.'

Lucan affected bewilderment. 'But we have heard that the Russians on the Causeway Heights were considered by Lord Raglan to be isolated and unsupported.'

'It didn't seem that way to me, sir,' Blunt said briskly. 'Not with those guns dropping shells on us. Rustum Pasha was very bitter that the information from his spy about an attack, which he had sent to Lord Raglan, had not been acted upon and that many of his men had been lost. After the charge, as I returned I was once more without a horse, and I passed the body of Captain Nolan. The face was burned black and the body was covered with blood.' Blunt turned to Eyland. 'The Duke of Cambridge was nearby, sir. He was saying "Poor Nolan." Having seen what had happened to the Light Brigade, my view was very different. I eventually found Lord Lucan on his cot with his leg stretched out having a wound in it dressed. He was not concerned with the hurt, though, and said it was not serious but he intimated that he would want two or three copies of the Commander-in-Chief's order.'

'You still have this order?' Eyland asked.

'I retained a copy for myself, sir. I have it here.'

'What was your opinion of it?'

'It bewildered me, sir. I could see no other meaning, especially after Captain Nolan pointed down the valley, but that we were intended to attack the battery there. I could see no guns on the Heights, sir, and the message said "to the front," which meant down the Valley. The guns on the heights were to our right.'

Chapter Six

It was already dusk as Souto's clerk, Pizzey, reached London Bridge Station. The platform was crowded, the faces of would-be passengers pale and strained-looking in the poor light. People were saying goodbye under the shadows of the engines that kept sneezing their showers of smuts over everyone – women embracing their menfolk, a few soldiers under a sergeant heading for the coast, people exchanging bread, poloney and black pudding, their voices, excited at the prospect of a train ride, complaining, boastful, or just plain drunken, echoing together under the high vaulted glass and iron of the roof.

The engine had got up steam and was puffing grey spurts of white vapour into the vast blackened arch of the station. The lamplighters with their tall poles were pushing through the crowd now and one by one the gas flames shot up and threw long strips of flickering light over the crowds. An unearthly glow spread over the platform and the faces looked yellow in the pools of light from the globes and the spade-shaped jets that sprouted from the soot-blackened walls. They looked inhuman, saffron-coloured, distorted, skull-like and menacing, while the poles of the lamplighters looked like pikes and the walking sticks lifted by travellers to call porters seemed like swords. From the driver's window, a sweat-streaked visage peered through the yellow-brown fumes the engine vomited, the planes and angles of the cheeks reflecting the glint of the firebox.

Pizzey found a seat in a compartment crowded with people; a woman with three children, an old man in a shovel hat, a travelling salesman, and a young man who was drunk, in a deep sleep, and, much to the delight of the children, now snoring on the shoulder of the embarrassed salesman. Leaning from the window, Pizzey could see the dark paint and bass of the engine's boiler. Ahead of him were the yellow and brown first-class carriages, behind him the low-sided waggons of the third-class, open to the weather. As he withdrew his head, the train jerked with a clank of buffers. The sleeping man woke up with a snort and stared around him as if surprised to find himself where he was. The salesman edged away and the woman with the children sniffed contemptuously.

As the train pulled out of the station, a gust of smoke entered the compartment and Pizzey smiled round at the others and hoisted the window into place. He had a long way to go so he settled his hat over his eyes and tried to sleep. But he managed no more than a doze.

Eventually, he woke, bathed in perspiration, coming to life as they passed through a tunnel. Someone had opened the window and the carriage was full of sulphurous yellow fumes like fog. The oil lamps in the compartment were too poor to enable him to read the newspaper in his pocket so he decided to sit it out and stared blankly in front of him until they reached their destination.

As the train pulled in, Pizzey caught the smell of salt sea breezes and heard the banshee crying of seagulls. The wind was whipping the smoke over the chimney pots and there were fleeting white shapes against a dark sky as the seabirds were swept along on the wind.

A policeman and an inspector of the railway police were waiting by the barrier as he approached it. They seemed to guess who he was and stepped forward to meet him.

'You found him?' he asked.

'Not on the train, sir,' the inspector said. 'But we knew where he'd be going, especially after we received your message. We called a cab at once and off we went. And there he was. He'd taken breakfast in the town, sir, and was just about to hop the twig.'

'Where is he now?'

'In custody, sir. Will you be wanting to talk to him?'

I'll be wanting more than that,' Pizzey said. 'I'll be wanting him to return with me. Under escort.'

Young Blunt had given his evidence quietly and in a way that clearly impressed the court. Now, the following day, Harboursford endeavoured to shake him on several points, particularly on the argument between Lucan and Nolan. But he refused to be budged. He was definite and very clear and made no attempt to embroider his evidence, and in the end Harboursford gave it up as a bad job.

They were clearly getting down to the nub of the matter now and Lucan's next witness was Henry Fitzhardinge Berkeley Maxse of the 13th Light Dragoons, who, from his arrival in the East to the day of Balaclava, had been an aide to Lord Cardigan. As Lucan rose to cross-examine him, Souto leaned forward.

'We've found our man, my lord,' he whispered. 'I've arranged for him to be brought back at once. He should be here at any moment.'

'How did you perform that miracle?'

'A policeman, my lord. Or an ex-policeman. One of the acquaintances of my clerk, Pizzey. He is able to call on a variety of helpers.'

Lucan gave a grim smile and turned to the job in hand, rising to face Maxse, who started off by stating quite firmly that in all the disputes between Lucan and Cardigan that had bedevilled the cavalry, he had very firmly taken the side of Cardigan.

Cardigan, who had appeared in the court for the first time in two days, and was sitting in full uniform, listened carefully, nodding as Maxse made his point.

'I felt he had had his command taken away from him,' Maxse said to Eyland. 'That, of course, was because we had been given to understand it was an independent command and had nothing to do with Lord Lucan. I later learned this was not so.'

Cardigan gave him a sour look and slumped down in his chair, at once disinterested again.

'On the day of the charge,' Lucan asked, 'where were you?'

'I had been sick but, like everyone else scenting action, I insisted on being on duty.'

'You were hurt in the charge?'

'I was hit on the foot by a splinter of shell or a spent round shot and was in great pain for much of it. In the smoke by the battery, I was trying to make out what was happening when the first line swept down. I saw the Lancers appear and shouted to one of them. "For God's sake," I said, "don't ride me down."'

'And then?'

'I directed them to rally on Lord Cardigan. But everyone was scattered and it was very difficult. I then made my way back up the valley, faint with pain and clinging to my horse's neck and only able to use my left stirrup. I had cut at two Russians as we had passed through the guns and one of them had pointed a pistol at me. As I rode back I was terrified he would pot me and dragged out an old pistol belonging to my brother. But he wasn't waiting for me and instead I pointed it at a Russian cavalryman who chased me. It misfired.'

'Please describe the retreat.'

'Men were still crouching over their dying chargers, others were staggering along, dragging injured mounts. Captain de Salis of the 8th was leading his horse with a wounded private in the saddle. All formation had been lost, the pace was terribly slow and there was more than a mile of ground to cover. Men carried friends on their backs or helped them to limp along, while all the time the Russians kept swooping down to cut off isolated men, to take prisoners or spear the wounded. Men were running, hopping and crawling to safety. Horses with shattered legs were struggling to rise, then rolling back on their trapped riders.'

'When the charge began,' Lucan said, 'you were close to Lord Cardigan as he took up his position in front of his brigade?'

'I was. He was two horses lengths in front and five lengths in front of the right squadron of the 17th Lancers. Behind him were George Wombwell, myself, and Captain Lockwood.'

'You were therefore in a position to see what happened when the charge began?'

'Indeed.'

'And close enough to see everything that Captain Nolan, the aide who brought the message, did.'

'Yes. He took up a position close to Captain Morris of the Lancers, who was a friend of his.'

'What happened as the brigade began to advance?'

'I heard Captain Morris, who was just behind me, shout out to Nolan that we had a long way to go.'

'Why did he shout that?'

'Nolan had put spurs to his horse and was beginning to gallop ahead. He caught me up and passed me. It was then that Morris shouted.'

'Did Nolan look back?'

'No, sir.'

'Did he spur across the front of the brigade from left to right, waving his sword and shouting words that were probably indistinguishable but seemed to indicate that he had decided his gesture down the valley had brought about a disaster and was trying to put it right by turning the brigade towards the Causeway Heights?'

Maxse's expression was cold. 'That was not my impression,' he said firmly. 'To me he seemed to be riding straight down the valley, as if he were trying to encourage us to go faster. Having heard him on more than one occasion expound his theories of speed, that was inevitably what I thought he was doing.'

'So he was *not* attempting to turn the brigade to the right?'

'Never, sir.' Maxse's words were brisk and very definite.

'It's been said by Mr Alexander William Kinglake, who is engaged on a history of the campaign, that that is what he was doing. He claims to have a witness. Is that what *you* saw?'

'Definitely not, sir. If he says that, he's wrong. I was in a better position to see than anyone else, wherever they were, and I have no recollection whatsoever of Captain Nolan's divergence to the right of the advance – either by deed or gesture – until he was hit. He was killed close to me and to suggest he was trying to turn the brigade is as absurd as to suggest he was wanting to charge any other guns but those we did. Only death saved him from a court martial.'

'Go on.'

'One of the first shells from the Fedioukhine Hills exploded close to him and as the smoke cleared I saw that his chest had been sliced open. The sword dropped from his hand, though his arm remained high in the air, and with his legs still holding him in the saddle, the horse wheeled about and began to gallop back towards the advancing brigade. There was a weird cry coming from his throat. It was not a living cry. He had been riding straight down the valley until the shell exploded near him and he was already a dead man when the horse swerved.'

'Are you sure of this?' Eyland asked.

'I was riding a stallion, sir,' Maxse said, 'and it was rather fractious and I was having difficulty controlling it. Nolan's horse passed so close it shied and the two animals almost collided. After that, we were into it hot. The fire was smashing down men and horses like a sickle through grass.'

271

'And Lord Cardigan?'

'He was moving in fine style. I swear he rode down the valley more or less in a state of phantasmagoria and never saw or thought of anything but doing his duty properly as a leader. He went magnificently. Then we were into the battery. It was a ridiculous business. It was totally unnecessary. I have heard the story about Nolan trying to direct us to the Causeway Heights before and I have always considered it utter nonsense. Nolan was intending to charge no other guns than the ones we did charge. I believed they were the ones we were to charge, so did Lord Cardigan and so did everyone else. Though none of us could understand why, unless we were being sacrificed to save some part of the field we couldn't see. To suggest Nolan was trying to turn us is absurd.'

As Maxse disappeared, a private of the 17th Lancers called Badger appeared to confirm his story. He had been wounded in the charge and knocked unconscious as his horse was brought down.

'When I came round,' he said, 'I saw Captain Oldham lying nearby. He called me across and told me to take his personal treasures, but as I reached him he was hit by another bullet and fell back dead, still clutching the watch and purse he was holding out.'

Seeing Cossacks approaching, he had caught the stirrup of a loose horse of the 13th but, unable to run with his wound, had had to let go. As the Russians halted by the body of Oldham, however, he had escaped and was almost the last man to stumble into the British lines, his uniform soaked with blood from the wound in his side.

'You were in the first line?'

'Right behind Lord Cardigan, sir.'

He had seen Nolan's move to the right but he would not agree that it was an attempt to turn the brigade.

'He was riding straight ahead, sir,' he insisted, 'until he

was hit, then, as he clutched his chest, his horse swung to the right. I was nearly knocked over by him so I saw everything that happened.'

As with Maxse, Harboursford endeavoured to shake his story but Badger, a small man with a thin frame, refused to be put off.

'That's what I saw,' he insisted.

He was followed by a slim handsome young man also in the blue uniform and white plastron of the 17th Lancers. Upright, clutching his black lance cap to his side, he said his name was Wightman and that he had ridden in the charge when he was wounded several times and finally taken prisoner. His speech was far from rough and he gave the impression of intelligence and ability.

The Brigade, he said, had advanced in good style, though a few people had kept pushing forward.

'I believe they thought it best to go at speed,' he pointed out, 'and get it over and done with.'

'Or because they felt it was the best way to make an attack?' Lucan asked.

'I don't think anyone felt there was *any way* we could make an attack, sir. We all knew we were doomed and we just wanted to get out of the hail of bullets and shells. But Lord Cardigan held us back. I had heard you order him to advance steadily and that's what he did. He kept shouting "Steady, steady, 17th Lancers." Only the fact that the shells burst too high saved us from complete annihilation. But Lord Cardigan never budged. He sat on his horse tall as a steeple. I heard someone say, "By God, he's a wooden man." And he seemed like one, because he never looked back.'

Listening to the praise, Cardigan, for the first time, looked as if he were interested and he sat up, his face almost benign as Wightman talked.

'By that time,' Wightman was saying, 'I'd been hit twice

and my horse had three wounds in the neck. I was told to fall out but I thought that in a minute or two we'd be into the enemy and decided to stay where I was. I drove my spurs home and it was then that I saw Sergeant Talbot's head carried off by a round shot, though he stayed upright in the saddle, headless, the lance still under his arm, for another thirty yards.'

'As we reached the battery,' Wightman continued, 'my horse gave a gigantic leap into the air but I never knew or saw what it cleared. Then I saw Private Melrose smashed down. He was a good man. Very clever, sir. He was well-educated and used to give Shakespeare recitals to us from time to time. He'd noticed it was the anniversary of Agincourt and I heard him shout – in a sort of ecstasy of patriotism and excitement, I suppose – "What man here would ask another man of England?" Then down he went. I also saw Captain Oldham, who was riding a fractious horse and was just a bit ahead of me, go down, too. A shell blew off the horse's hind legs and knocked over several others and they all went down in a tangled heap. Captain Oldham jumped up unhurt, his sword and pistol in his hands, ready to go on with the fight, but almost immediately he was knocked over by a musket ball.'

Wightman's recital of the butchery was very moving if only for the quiet unemotional way he gave it, and there were gasps from the female element among the spectators. Wightman waited patiently.

'Please go on.'

'The smoke in the battery was so thick, I couldn't see an arm's length around me. I saw a small group of Lancers and Lord Cardigan some way ahead. Then I saw Mr Maxse who shouted to me not to ride over him. He pointed to Lord Cardigan and told me to rally on him. But a Cossack came at me and sent his lance through my thigh. I went for him bull-headed and he bolted. I drove my lance into his back and unhorsed him in front of two of the Russian guns. People were trying to rally in groups, and I tried to rally on Lord George Paget's orderly, who was supporting a wounded officer and slashing at the Russians with his free arm. I then joined a friend of mine, Private Mustard, and we decided we had done enough for honour and turned to ride back through the guns.'

Wightman paused. 'But my horse was riddled with bullets by this time,' he went on, 'and I'd been struck again on the forehead and shoulder. As my horse fell, I scrambled out and a Cossack came at me and stabbed me several times in the neck, shoulder and back and under the ribs. As I got to my feet and tried to draw my sword, his lance then went through my hand. I blinded him by throwing gravel in his face and escaped, but I was in no state to resist and I was taken prisoner. I came round to find myself being carried on the back of a man who, though I didn't know it then, was dying of his wounds. When the Russians came, an officer said we must have been drunk to do what we did. Private Kirk of Ours exploded. "By God," he said, "if we'd so much as smelt the barrel we'd have taken half Russia by now." Sergeant-Major Fowler checked him for his impertinence to the officer. Sergeant-Major Fowler had been run through the back with a lance and he was already dying.'

Lucan allowed the murmuring to disappear before putting the next question. 'As the Brigade first moved off, what was your position with regard to Lord Cardigan?'

'I was directly behind him, sir.'

'Did you see Captain Nolan move forward and try to turn the brigade?'

Wightman frowned. 'I saw him move forward and then swing towards the right, sir. But that happened after he was hit. He was struck in the chest and his body seemed to curl up. I wondered, in fact, how it remained in the saddle.'

'We have had a witness here, Wightman, who disputes that. And Mr Kinglake, the historian, claims to have a diagram drawn for him by an officer who saw the charge – an unknown officer, I should point out. this diagram purports to indicate that Captain Nolan crossed in front of the brigade to direct it to the right. Is that what he did?'

Wightman flushed. 'Sir, I was right behind His Lordship. I knew him well and I'd recognise him anywhere from his stiffish style of riding. I even knew his horse, Ronald, because my father had been his riding master and had broken it in for him. Captain Nolan never tried to direct the charge to the right. He was going straight, sir, down the valley, as we all were, and he was shouting to us to come on until he was hit. Then, as he was wounded, he clutched at himself with his left hand, sir. Automatically. And because he was still holding the reins, sir, it was that which caused the horse to swerve.'

'But it didn't swerve before?'

'No, sir.' Wightman was adamant. 'Never, sir.'

As Lucan paused, Souto's clerk, Pizzey, slipped into court and handed Souto a packet. 'General Bosquet's reply, sir,' he said. 'The messenger's just returned from Paris. The other replies that have come are also included. Most of them took note of my request for a speedy return.'

Souto nodded, and Pizzey bent closer. 'Our man's here, sir,' he said. Souto nodded, touched Lucan's arm and whispered to him.

Lucan listened and looked at Pizzey. 'Here?' he whispered. 'Outside.'

Lucan gave one of his mirthless smiles. 'Thank you. We can proceed.' He looked up at Wightman. 'Do you know a Private Lees, Wightman?' he asked.

Wightman nodded. 'I *did*. In the 17th. As we rode down the valley he was my right hand man. My left hand man was Peter Marsh and beyond him was Private Dudley. Private Dudley was a bit afraid, I think, sir. He was a hard-swearing man and going on a bit. Marsh told him that to swear when he might be knocked into eternity the next minute wasn't the thing to do.'

'How would you describe Private Lees?'

'He was a grand old soldier, sir. Enlisted 1846 and served in India. His time was nearly up.'

'Would it surprise you to know he is here today?'

Wightman looked startled, then pleased. 'Yes, sir,' he said. 'It would. I thought he was dead. It was beginning to get hot and it was becoming impossible to hold the horses back. I think we all thought that the quicker we could get through the grapeshot and musketry the better chance we'd have. Even Lord Cardigan was having to extend his horse to avoid being ridden down.'

Wightman stopped, as if he felt he was saying too much. Lucan waved him on.

'I saw several men and horses go down, sir. It left gaps. Trumpeter Brown had been wounded. Captain Webb had had his shin smashed. Cornet Cleveland had had his horse hit and the lines were opening to go round them as they fell, then closing again to make the line compact. The officers kept shouting "Close up, close up." The line must have looked like a concertina, sir.'

'And Private Lees?'

'I thought he was caught by a shell burst. I heard the crash and saw the flame and the dust, and thought it had hit him. He managed to touch my arm, and smile at me – a sad smile, sir, on his old face – then he said "Domino, chum" and fell from the saddle.'

'Did you ever see him again?'

'He wasn't with the prisoners down the valley. And I didn't see him when I was released after the war finished. He wasn't with the regiment, but, of course, he might have got back and been taken to Scutari.'

'Where, God help him,' Lucan said, 'he would be lucky to survive.'

Wightman eyed him blandly. 'So I heard, sir.'

'Did you know him well?'

'Oh, yes, sir. We were only two squadrons and everybody knew everybody else.'

'What horse was he riding?'

Wightman looked puzzled. 'Daisy, sir. A grey mare.'

'Not a black? Or a chestnut?'

'No, sir, a grey. After he disappeared she kept alongside me for some distance, but she'd been hit in the belly, sir, and was beginning to tread on her own entrails as she galloped and finally she gave a shriek and dropped out of sight.'

'And you thought Private Lees was dead?'

'I did, sir. And if he isn't I can only say how pleased I am to hear it. Round shot, grape, shell and musketry were mowing us down in whole groups at the time.'

Lucan paused and looked at Eyland. 'At this juncture, sir,' he said, 'I would like to recall one of the earlier witnesses.'

'Now?' Eyland looked surprised. 'You already have your witness.'

'I have another, sir. I warned the court I would probably wish to recall a witness and the court granted me that favour. I now wish to do so.'

'You can't question two witnesses at once.'

'I don't wish to, sir. I wish what the French call a confrontation. I wish them to face each other, that is all. The second witness will not be required to speak.' He paused. 'Not yet,' he added ominously.

'Very well. You may introduce your witness. Who is it to be?'

'Private Lees, sir. He is waiting outside now.'

'Let him appear.'

The door opened and the court orderly barked in a voice that made Souto wince. 'The witness, Private Lees, sir.'

The witness with the scarred face seemed reluctant to appear and was prodded forward unwillingly. Wightman stared at him, frowning, then he turned to Lucan.

'Lees, sir? Private Lees?'

'That's who he says he is. Take a good look at him, Wightman. You know him well. Is that your right-hand man?'

278

Wightman stared at the witness, frowning with concentration. 'Well, my lord,' he said slowly, 'I can't say for sure. The light's not on his face, and that scar – I didn't know he'd been hit about the face. But – I think, my lord, he looks younger than I remember him.'

'I think he *is* younger, Wightman,' Lucan said. 'Thank you for your help. You may go. Call William Pennington.

Pennington was a tall young man with good features and a smaller moustache than most. Even in civilian clothes and without the cherry trousers and blue braided tunic and pelisse of the 11th Hussars, he was a striking figure.

'William Pennington?'

'Yes, my lord.'

'You rode in the charge?'

'I did, sir, and very proud to have done so.'

'But you have now purchased your discharge?'

'That is so, sir.'

Like Wightman's, Pennington's voice was calm and brisk, but it was also strong and well-modulated.

'You sound an educated man, Pennington,' Lucan said.

'My father was the principal of one of the most respected private schools in London, sir. He made sure I went through the mill.'

'Yet you joined the army?'

'After adventure, sir.' Pennington smiled. 'I got more than I bargained for. However, I have managed to buy myself out. My father's helped.'

'Didn't you like the army?'

'It was rough, sir. But a lot of what you hear about it comes from old hands trying to frighten the recruits. I was very happy.'

'Except between 11 a.m. and 11.20 a.m. on the morning of 25 October 1854.'

Pennington smiled again. He was a young man with a lot of charm and he knew how to use it. 'Not just then, sir. But I had a lot on my mind and didn't have much time to think about it. From the moment I heard the Advance sounded, I had no hope of life. My heart was like a lump of stone inside my chest.'

'So was mine,' Lucan grunted. 'You were wounded?'

'Yes, sir. I had a good mount which had managed to keep her condition all through the campaign but after about a mile down the valley she was hit in the hind leg and became useless. She stopped and, as the brigade went on, I felt very much alone. A bullet went through my right leg and another tilted my busby over my right ear, then my poor mare went down with a crash. When I got to my feet I could see disarmed men being speared by groups of Russian lancers, so I started to hobble back to our lines. Someone found me a riderless horse and after that I rode back, keeping well to the left so I could keep the Cossacks on the side of my sword arm. I was so pleased to reach safety, as I dropped to the ground I kissed that horse on the nose. She carried me well.'

There was a long silence as the court digested Pennington's evidence. Like Wightman's it had been given without boasting but with a great deal of pride.

'Has this witness,' Harboursford pointed out, 'told us anything that has any bearing on the responsibility for the charge?'

'No, indeed he has not,' Lucan agreed. 'But there are other things which he *will* be able to tell us.' He looked at Pennington. 'Now that you have left the army, Pennington, what are you doing?'

'I am on the stage, sir.'

'That's an unusual ambition.'

'Not with me, sir. I've always been keen and Mr MacReady, the actor, who retired a year or two ago, is a friend of the family and he told me I could make a go of it.'

Eyland frowned. 'Is this anything to do with what we're enquiring into, my lord?' he asked.

'I think you will see it is, sir, in a moment.' Lucan turned to Pennington. 'With your interest in the theatre, do you know a great deal about it?'

'Yes, sir. I also go whenever I can, sir. I see whatever I can manage.'

'So you'll be well acquainted with many of the actors in London? Great and not so great?'

'Yes, sir. And many other places, too.'

'Have the witness, Lees, rise again, please.'

The scarred-faced man was prodded upright and Pennington stared at him in that calm, confident manner of his.

'Would you, by any chance, Pennington, know the man who is now standing in the courtroom?'

Pennington gave a little laugh. 'Of course, my lord. I know him well. That's Barnaby O'Halloran. His real name's Jack Orchard. Used to play straight roles. But he could never keep off the booze and one night he got into a fight in Whitechapel after a performance of *The Road to Ruin*, and was cut about the face with a broken bottle. So he had to grow a beard. Ever since then, he's had to play heavies, and not many of those. He was in *The Spectre* and *The Murder At The Old Inn*. But there aren't many parts for him really. Not with that scar. At the moment he's in *Her Father's Face* at Pester's.'

Lucan's smile was thin. 'Thank you, Pennington,' he said. 'I trust you'll do well in your chosen profession.'

Chapter Seven

There was a long silence in court, during which heads bobbed about as people whispered to each other. Lord Fitzsimon and Major-General Porter-Hobbs conferred closely with the president, while the other judges murmured together and Harboursford bent to talk to the Judge-Advocate. In the end, he decided to ask no questions and Pennington was allowed to disappear.

Lucan smiled. 'Now, gentlemen,' he said, 'with the court's permission, I will call on the man whom you have just seen identified to be re-examined, the man you were told was Private Lees of the 17th, but who turned out to be Barnaby O'Halloran or, more correctly, Jack Orchard, an actor.'

Unwillingly, the actor took his place before the court and Lucan leaned forward.

'You are here against your will this time, are you not?'

The actor scowled. 'Yes, I am.'

'You had to be brought here, didn't you?'

'Yes.'

'Where from?'

There was no answer.

'I'll tell the court. You were found at Dover, trying to board a cross-Channel ferry. Am I right?'

'Yes.'

'Where were you going?'

Orchard lifted his head in a gesture of defiance. 'Where *do* you go on a cross-Channel ferry?'

'Indeed, where? To France. Or even further afield. Yet, Mr Orchard,' Lucan leaned forward, 'if I'm not mistaken, when you gave your evidence you stated that you were short of money and that your pension was very small. So how did you come to find the fare to cross the Channel?'

'I was given it.'

'Who by?'

'A friend.'

'Why?'

'I'd done him a favour.'

'Indeed you had, and in a moment we'll learn what that favour was.' Lucan fished among his papers and produced a large sheet of paper which he held up. It was a theatre playbill. 'Will the witness take a look at this playbill which I hold in my hand?' he asked. 'It concerns, sir, a performance of *A String of Pearls* (*or the story of Sweeney Todd, the Demon Barber of Fleet Street*). This is a play which is currently in the repertoire of Thomas Rowan's players, at the moment appearing at Pester's Theatre, Balham, but, at the time of this bill, was on at Caspar's Theatre, Hoxton. I will read it to the court.' Lucan looked at Eyland. 'I'll not trouble the court with the whole list of the cast, sir. Just the first few. Sir William Brandon, a judge, represented by Mr C Williams; Colonel Jeffery, of the Indian Army, by Mr J Reynolds; Johanna, his daughter, Miss Colwell; Sweeney Todd, the Barber of Fleet Street, Mr Mark Howard; Dr Aminadab Lupin, a wolf in sheep's clothing, Mr Barnaby O'Halloran —'

'My lord —' Harboursford tried to protest but Lucan refused to be stopped.

'Please be patient, gentlemen. Following the performance of *A String of Pearls*,' the playbill was held up again, 'I see we have a song by Master Howard and then a dance by a Miss Johnson. Then we have a performance of another drama – or if you wish, a melodrama. I'll not go into this too deeply, except to read the names of those who took part:

283

Miss Robotham, Mesdames Robbets and Kemp; and Messrs Robbets, Pennett, Reeves, Lewis, Douglass, Widdicombe – and O'Halloran. Notice, sir, that same name. O'Halloran – and notice, sir, the date. 24 October 1854. Mr Babington's Private Lees, gentlemen, is none other than Barnaby O'Halloran, an actor, as I think we have proved, and, since he was appearing in two plays at Caspar's Theatre, Hoxton, on 24 October 1854, he could hardly have been riding with the Light Brigade down the North Valley at Balaclava the following day and seen what Captain Nolan was up to. This whole business of what Captain Nolan did is a mish-mash of misunderstanding or imagination – as, I suggest, gentlemen, is Mr Kinglake's verdict on what happened. There is no proof whatsoever that Nolan was trying to turn the brigade. Private Lees, who claimed to see it, has been proved to be an imposter and Mr Kinglake's so-called "witness" has still not been named. Let's find out more about our friend "Private Lees" who is not Private Lees. As has been said, he is Jack Orchard, once a bandsman in the 13th Light Dragoons who deserted in October 1852, and took the name of Barnaby O'Halloran. He was next seen in the orchestra pit of a music hall in Sheffield and then in a travelling menagerie. He finally became an actor and until a day or so ago was appearing in *Her Father's Face* at Pester's Theatre. Is that so?'

There was a buzz round the court.

'The witness will answer,' Eyland said.

The witness was silent then he lifted his head. 'Yes, I am. It wasn't my fault. It was —'

Lucan held up his hand. 'And the money you received to take you across the Channel was to take you away from the jurisdiction of this court. It was suspected that your identity might be discovered, so it was decided you should disappear for a while.'

'Yes.'

'Who gave you the money?'

284

'A friend.'

'Was it Mr Spencer Valentine, a solicitor?'

'Yes.'

'On behalf of whom?'

'He said it was a Mr Babington.'

'I think you knew that already, didn't you? You were not only seen on the stage of Pester's Theatre, you were also seen entering a public house, the Shades Vaults, in Sick Heart Yard, nearby, and were observed deep in conversation not only with Mr Spencer, but also with Mr Babington. Am I right?'

'Yes.'

'And this favour you did for Mr Valentine – or Mr Babington, it doesn't matter much which – was that using the name and number of a soldier killed in the charge and wearing a Crimean medal, doubtless loaned for the occasion for a half a guinea by some impoverished soldier, you would pose as a survivor of the charge and give false evidence that would clear the name of Captain Nolan from responsibility for the disaster.'

'They paid me twenty guineas.'

'What was behind this plot? Do you know?'

'There was some talk about a legacy to the family. From an old friend of Captain Nolan's who held him in some esteem and wished to do right by his family when he was killed. I think Mr Babington had been collecting it.'

'I think so, too.' Lucan looked at Eyland. 'I would like, sir, to call Mr Babington to ask him a few questions.'

Eyland nodded agreement. 'I think you should, my lord. I would like to hear the answers.' He glanced about the court. 'Is he here?'

'He is outside, sir. He has been brought here.'

Quirk, the barrister who had been appearing for the Nolan family, rose slowly. 'Gentlemen,' he said, 'I would like to assure the court at this juncture that I have had no part in these proceedings. Indeed, I have never heard of them until this minute. I have never been a party to underhand methods of any kind, either in court or out, and, in the circumstances, so that I cannot be accused of being a party to a fraud, I would like to withdraw from the case at once.'

Eyland nodded. 'I think your attitude is admirable, Mr Quirk.'

Quirk gathered his papers and rose. At the door he met Babington. Quirk gave the solicitor a glare and swept past. Prodded forward, Babington had an uneasy look as he sat down in the witness's chair. On Souto's suggestion, Lucan left him there, saying nothing, for a long time to enable the court to get a good look at him. Babington shifted uneasily.

Eventually Lucan turned to face him. 'You are Archibald William Babington?'

'I am.'

'And your interest in the case?'

'I am representing the Nolan family. It was feared that there would be some attempt to shift the blame for the Light Brigade's disaster on to Captain Nolan.'

Lucan nodded. 'I see. Would you describe Captain Nolan? As fully as possible.'

'He was a brilliant rider, trainer of horses and instructor of riders. He had written two books on the subject. He had a great knowledge of war.'

'And his background?'

'Entirely military. He came from an old and distinguished military family. His father served with great distinction.'

'My lord, we've already heard this,' Harboursford protested.

'I beg you, sir,' Lucan said. 'Hear it again. From *this* gentleman.'

Babington continued. 'After service in the Austrian army, Captain Nolan was persuaded to return to England by high-ranking officers from the Horse Guards, one of them said to be His Highness, the Duke of Cambridge. His father was a distinguished Irish officer who was vice-consul in Milan where he met his wife, the captain's mother, a beautiful Italian lady of noble birth.'

286

'And his military experience?'

'Vast.'

As Lucan held up a sheet of paper, Eyland sighed. 'I have here a group of documents, gentlemen,' Lucan said. 'One is signed by Mr Willings McArthur, a notary, who was very familiar with Captain Nolan's background because he acted for his father on many occasions. The second is signed by a Mr J W Cazaly, secretary to Mr William Taylor Money, British Consul-General in Milan. The third is signed by Sir Thomas Sorell, Consul at Oporto, who was appointed to succeed on Mr Money's death as Consul-General for the Lombardo-Venetian Kingdom and the Austrian Ports on the Adriatic.'

'You have been very thorough, my lord.' Eyland's sarcasm was not disguised but Lucan quite failed to notice it.

'I always am,' he said. 'I'll read the major points of the letters to the court.'

He rattled the papers triumphantly. 'First, Captain Nolan's grandfather,' he said. 'He was a common trooper in the 13th Light Dragoons and died of fever in the West Indies. Captain Nolan's father, the orphaned son of that trooper, was granted a commission in a foot regiment through the generosity of his father's commanding officer. So much for the old and distinguished military family. The father's service was entirely on garrison duties and he never saw action. After leaving the army at the age of forty-six, he turned up in Milan on half-pay, acting as unpaid assistant to the Consul; a post, as far as it is possible to see, he acquired through pushiness rather than selection. His wife, Captain Nolan's mother, that "beautiful and noble Italian lady," was, in fact, a widowed Englishwoman, Mrs Elizabeth Harleston Ruddach, and she came from Holborn. I have the family trees.'

'None of this is Captain Nolan's fault,' Eyland said gently.

'No, sir. But it seems his father had a great ability to delude himself and perhaps Captain Nolan suffered from the same problem.'

Lucan passèd the depositions and family histories to the court and picked up another.

'I have here another deposition, signed by Colonel William Key, who was his friend. But, though he was his friend, Colonel Key has been honest. He says he feels that, on military matters, Captain Nolan was headstrong and impatient, even sometimes arrogant and intolerant, especially where senior officers were concerned.' Lucan paused. 'His military experience has been set down here. He had *no* experience of battle whatsoever before the Crimea. Although he served in India from 1843 until 1851, he never saw action because, during the decade that saw the hardest fighting ever to take place in India, the 15th Hussars in which he was serving were never on active service. Those were stirring times, gentlemen, but Captain Nolan missed them all. Colonel Key is quite honest about Captain Nolan's military knowledge. "It was pure theory," he says.' Lucan handed over the sheet of paper and turned to Babington. 'Does the witness wish to dispute these facts?' he asked.

The witness clearly did not. He was sitting hunched-up, his face red, his eyes on the floor.

'Let it also be known, gentlemen,' Lucan continued, 'that *our* Captain Nolan, the Captain Nolan of the Crimea, was *not* asked to return from Austria to England by senior officers in the British Army but returned of his own accord because he preferred to serve in the army of his own country. All these stories about his background and experience are pure legend and, since everyone we have heard in this court seems to be aware of them, it's clear he never denied them. He was living a lie, gentlemen – a small one, if you like, because everyone wishes to better himself – but a lie nevertheless. He was claimed, chiefly, it seems, by his father, to be an expert and of good family when he was nothing of the sort and he allowed that assumption to continue.'

'It would be very normal in a proud man,' Eyland observed mildly.

'Indeed, sir. But it was a fraud nevertheless.' Lucan stared at Babington giving the court time to digest what he had said. 'Is it true,' he went on, 'that you approached Mr Serjeant Souto, my adviser, informing him that you possessed letters purporting to support the Nolan family's claim, which would aid the prosecution and endanger my case? From General Bosquet, General Scarlett, Sir George Brown, Colonel Beatson, General Bacon, Colonel Shewell, Prince Radziwill and others, including officers and men who rode in the charge, among them – I name them – Private Spring and Corporal Morley.'

Babington frowned. 'I did have occasion to talk to the gentleman you mention.'

'About those letters which you offered to suppress in return for money?'

'No.'

'I think yes. But the letters are all forgeries, are they not?'

'No, sir.' Babington looked sheepish.

'I have General Scarlett's word here – in a letter to me,' the letter was duly flourished, 'that he has written no such letter. Sir George Brown says the same. Prince Radziwill, I understand, is in St Petersburg, and could not possibly have been in contact. General Bosquet writes from Paris denying any letter. General Bacon,' Lucan gestured irritably, 'an old enemy of mine and, therefore, in this context, of no consequence whatsoever. Other officers and men you claim to have produced letters have written denying writing any such letters. As for Private Spring, of the 11th Hussars, who rode in the charge, he was found to be a deserter from the 17th Lancers, and when he was returned to that regiment and punished I had to confirm it. I imagine he does not like me. Corporal Morley,' Lucan gave a grim smile, 'he considers he should have been given a medal. He thinks, in fact, he should be given the Victoria Cross and he has pestered me considerably to that end. Though like Private Spring, he is undoubtedly a brave man, he did no more than many others but he seems a little obsessed by his desire for glory.'

Eyland took the letters with a bored look but, as Souto knew, there was no getting away from what they showed.

Lucan looked at Babington. 'Why did you forge these letters?' he asked. 'Why did you try to pervert the course of justice? Because you were in need of money and, suspecting that the legacy that had gone to the Nolan family, on which you had been feeding for two years, was likely to come to an end with the evidence that would be brought out in this court, you were determined to acquire money in other ways? You were willing, were you not, to have myself, an innocent man, pilloried so that the legacy should not finish?'

'It's not true!'

'No? Let us take a look at it. Is it true, sir, that Colonel William Key, an officer of great distinction and wealth, who has recently returned to this country, had offered on Captain Nolan's death a pension to his family of £700 a year?'

Babington's words could hardly be heard. 'He was a great admirer and friend of Captain Nolan and wished to see the family supported.'

'But Colonel Key is also a good soldier and, when he learned of the interpretation of Captain Nolan's behaviour at Balaclava, which was considered by many to have caused the destruction of the Light Cavalry and the deaths of many brave young men, he had second thoughts and said that the pension should be continued only in the event of Captain Nolan being proved to be not guilty of arrogance and error. Is that true?'

'Yes.'

'As it happens, Colonel Key has generously decided that the pension shall continue, whatever emerges in this court, but you did not know that until now and I suggest you thought that Captain Nolan's reputation might not leave this court unscathed, and therefore took pains to ensure that he was presented in the best possible light because he had been a sound source of income for you. Who was administering this pension? You?'

Babington scowled. 'Yes.'

'I understand you will no longer. To achieve your ends, did you therefore get the support of Mr Spencer Valentine, the solicitor, pointing out that a decision against Captain Nolan would also not be to the advantage of the Beaufort family because it would inevitably harm the reputation of Lord Raglan? Since Mr Valentine was drawing money from the Beaufort and Raglan families for what he claimed to be a watching brief for them – a profitable one, too, I might add – did he agree to provide money to fund this plan of yours?'

'I believe he did.'

'You believe? Don't you know?'

Sir Godfrey Goudge, for the Beaufort family, sprang to his feet. 'I can say quite categorically, gentlemen, that those funds *were* given but later regretted. The Beaufort family have no wish to profit from unreliable testimony.'

As Goudge spoke, Lord Cardigan, who had been listening to the exchanges with growing discomfiture, suddenly snatched a sheet of paper and a pen from the table and started to scribble. Leaning across, he handed the note to Souto, who glanced at it and handed it to Lucan.

Lucan glanced at it and spoke to the court. 'I have a note here, gentlemen, from the Earl of Cardigan who admits that he also employed Mr Spencer Valentine at various times on his own behalf. But,' Lucan glanced at Cardigan and for the first time there was a glimmer of rapport between them, 'he insists it was never for any distortion of the truth and I accept that.' He paused and stared hard at Cardigan who rose, bowed to the Court and stalked out, a long-legged, pop-eyed, over-whiskered, slightly ridiculous figure.

Lucan watched him go then turned back to Eyland. 'I think, sir,' he finished, 'that I must leave it to you to decide what must be done with these men, Babington, Valentine and Lees, whose object clearly was to pervert justice.'

Eyland nodded and summoned the court orderly. 'Let these gentlemen be detained,' he said. 'And inform the police. The Judge-Advocate will decide what is to be done with them.' He looked up. 'Is that all, my lord?'

'I have one more witness, sir. He will not take up much of the court's time. I would like to call Sergeant Robert Henderson, of the 12th Hussars.'

Eyland looked puzzled. 'The 12th Hussars were not involved in the Light Brigade's action. What can he add in explanation?'

He was obviously growing tired of the whole sorry business and looked as if he would be glad to be shot of it. Lucan was not put off in the slightest.

Henderson was a handsome man of some education and breeding who said he had been left destitute by his father's death and obliged to join the cavalry.

'You knew Captain Nolan?' Lucan asked.

'Yes, sir, I did. Very well. I met him during the time I was stationed at Maidstone Barracks, during the 1840s. He was a gentleman of good temper and great kindness and disposition. I often fenced with him and in a long and varied experience I have never seen anyone with such an amiable temper and kindness of manner. He won us all over. He was a thorough soldier and a finished gentleman, and as a horseman he was a perfect enthusiast and a great expert.'

Lucan seemed a little put out by the lavishness of the praise. 'What was his view of the British cavalry?' he asked abruptly.

Henderson hesitated. 'He rated them second to none and, under the right leadership, capable of miracles.'

'Did you serve in the Crimea?' Lucan asked.

'Towards the end, sir. I exchanged into the 12th from the 15th Hussars, in which I was serving when at Maidstone. We went out as reinforcements and reached the Crimea in the spring of 1855.'

'Did you discuss the charge with any of the survivors?' Eyland asked.

'Many times, sir, and I was assured by them that there was no question of Lord Lucan misconceiving his orders.'

'In spite of your intense admiration for Captain Nolan,' Lucan said, 'did you come to the conclusion, despite any evidence to the contrary, that he insisted on an advance not towards the Causeway Heights but against the guns at the end of the Valley?'

'I did, sir.'

'You have said you considered him an expert. So why do you think he was led, as you feel certain he was, to direct the Light Brigade so wrongly on its fatal ride? Because he lost control? It has been suggested that he was excited and mis-construed his orders. Do *you* think that to be so?'

Henderson frowned, weighing his answer. 'I don't know about being excited or out of control, sir,' he said. 'Certainly he could become excited. But that isn't the reason. I hold the view I do because of what he used to say to me at Maidstone. I often heard him express his conviction that cavalry could accomplish anything when it had scope to act. On one occasion, sir, I remember him putting a hypothetical case of cavalry charging in a plain. He drew a rough sketch of what he meant on the wall of the Quartermaster's store. It showed guns to right and left and ahead, all supported by cavalry and infantry.'

'Do you recognise the position?'

'Yes, sir. Very clearly. While in the Crimea I visited the field of Balaclava. As nearly as possible, what Captain Nolan drew on the wall represented the positions of the Russian artillery and the British light cavalry there.'

'But this drawing was made some years before Balaclava?'

'Yes, sir.'

'And what was Captain Nolan's view of the result?'

'He assumed the certain capture of the guns. His death prevented him ever being undeceived in this world.'

Chapter Eight

Lucan was just on the point of rising to begin his closing speech when Eyland looked at his watch and stopped him.

'One moment, my lord,' he said. 'Is your speech to be a long one?'

'Of course, sir,' Lucan snapped. 'I have much to say.'

'I thought you might have,' Eyland said dryly. 'In that case, I would not wish to interrupt it. The court will therefore rise for lunch and you may begin your speech on our return. I understand that the prosecution does not intend to draw out the proceedings so that should give us time to hear the summing up by the Deputy Judge-Advocate and enable us to reach our verdict. Does that suit you, sir?'

It obviously did not. Lucan looked as if he were prepared to go on all night if necessary but he had no choice but to agree. Souto stretched gratefully. He was tired and had long since grown weary of the troubles of the Light Brigade and Lord Lucan.

Dabbing at his damp face with his handkerchief, he studied the judges as they left their places and headed for the door, obviously eager for some cooler air. Eyland's face was blank, but Souto noticed Sir Alexander Crowley was arguing fiercely in a whisper with Lord Fitzsimon, and Major-General Porter-Hobbs, purple in the face, had his head close to that of Major-General Hooe. The other judges were also murmuring together as they left the room, Colonel Craufurd with Colonel Yapp, Colonel Rowntree with Colonel Minchin. It was impossible to tell how they would vote when they had to reach their verdict.

As Souto left the building, lost among the brilliant uniforms, he was met in the corridor by Lieutenant Morden, and they hurried to the line of cabs to choose one that would take them to the Pestle and Mortar for luncheon.

'I didn't expect you here today,' Souto said.

'I rode in the charge, sir,' Morden reminded him. 'I wished to hear the verdict.'

Souto smiled. 'I'm pleased to see you, of course,' he said. 'Lord Lucan can be a bit of a bore with his self-righteousness.'

In his hand, Morden held a newspaper. 'Special edition,' he said. 'Just picked it up.'

'Oh?' Souto looked surprised. 'About the case?'

'No, sir. Graver news than that, I fear.'

The newspaper, a small half-size edition, had unexpected headlines. 'News from India,' they said. 'Mutiny of Indian Troops at Meerut. General Conflagration Expected. Mr Russell To Go For The Times. Sir Colin Campbell Called To War Office.'

Souto stared at the paper for a moment or two. 'So it's come,' he said slowly. 'That cloud in the sky of India that Lord Canning said was no bigger than a man's hand has finally turned into a whirlwind.'

Morden gestured at the headlines at the other side of the page that dealt with the court martial. 'They got it in just in time,' he commented. 'It's always been agreed that if troops were needed in India, they would come from the Crimean veterans. The witnesses will be recalled to their regiments. Another month and they wouldn't have been able to hold the court martial.'

'Lucan had it that Campbell would command if troops were to be sent,' Souto said. 'It seems he was right. But I suppose it was inevitable. Campbell was one of the few who came out of the Crimea with an unsullied reputation. Will you be going?'

Morden shrugged. 'I don't know, sir. The 17th Lancers are sure to, though. It's their turn for overseas.' He frowned. 'Is it nearly over?' he asked.

'Nearly. After Lucan there will be a discussion on the legal position and the Deputy Judge-Advocate will review the evidence and draw attention to the points of conflict. There will be quotes from learned judges and books like *The Law of the Constitution*, comparisons will be made with other judgements, and then the judges will make their decision.'

As they reached the Pestle and Mortar, Souto handed his hat to a girl in mob cap and apron, Morden following with their gloves and sticks. Making their way to the dining room, they sat down at a table in a corner away from everyone else where they could talk without being heard. Souto ordered drinks and, as they lifted their glasses, Morden looked up.

'How do you think it went today?' he asked.

Souto shrugged. 'The evidence of the last witness was very telling. And, coming last, will be remembered when a lot of what's gone before will be forgotten. Lucan will make his plea and it will be a good one, I'm sure. He doesn't dispute the facts of the charge, only the orders he received, which he claims were hastily conceived and more hastily written so that they were quite unclear. The suggestion Raglan made that the two orders should be read together is totally unacceptable, of course. And whether they were issued because Raglan wished the Russians driven off the Causeway or because he wanted to save his guns is quite immaterial. However, if Cardigan's behaviour throughout the campaign hadn't made Raglan worry so much for his cavalry, it might never have happened.'

'I think he was right to worry, though,' Morden said. 'There weren't many of us. On the other hand, Lucan was right to ignore the jeers and keep his eye on the defence of Balaclava. It was terribly isolated.' He sipped his drink thoughtfully. 'There was just too much in his way with

Cardigan's itch for glory, and Nolan's wish to see the cavalry in action.'

Souto shrugged. 'It was an unenviable situation,' he admitted. 'Lucan was never popular with Raglan because he was too abrasive and all along he had to deal with that lunatic, Cardigan. There's a lot of blame which could be laid at a variety of doors but we also mustn't forget the clash of personalities. Lucan, Cardigan, Raglan, Nolan. It was almost as if the Lord had arranged for those four to come together in the greatest clash of personalities since the beginning of time. Lucan must have seemed an incompetent nincompoop to Nolan, and that morning of Balaclava Nolán doubtless seemed an ambitious young prig to Lucan. I have to admit that he *must* have been rather a self-satisfied young man.'

'The Duke of Wellington had no time for young staff officers who made a point of showing themselves off,' Morden agreed. 'Or for those who spread idle gossip about their superior officers. He said he had to put an end to them before they put an end to him.'

As the waiter appeared they ordered their meal, then sat for a moment, both of them deep in thought. Souto's mind was still on the evidence he had heard when Morden broke in on his considerations.

'Lucan's record as a soldier wasn't bad, you know,' he said slowly. 'And the charge *he* initiated, the Heavies', came off splendidly. Even the one Raglan initiated, the Light's, disastrous as it was, was a magnificent affair. Despite the talk, there was nothing really wrong with the cavalry, after all. The courage and discipline were visible to everybody and if Lucan had been allowed to use his initiative, they might have done wonders. As it was, I suppose, they were destroyed by the over-caution of the very man who was trying to conserve them. That, and the eagerness of Nolan. Had they clashed before?'

'Curiously,' Souto said, 'Lucan swears he had never noticed Nolan until that morning.'

'I'm surprised,' Morden frowned, 'because he was hard to miss, the way he went on. I think in his anxiety to see his beliefs put into action he lost control. Poor old Lucan – beset on one side by a Commander-in-Chief terrified of losing his cavalry, and on the other by a brigadier and an "expert" *determined* to lose it.'

The waiter appeared with a tray and they began to eat. But their minds were still busy and eventually between mouthfuls Morden started again. He gave an apologetic smile.

'I suspect,' he said, 'that when I'm an old man with grand-children, I'll still be trying to decide whose fault it was. Despite all that's been said, all that's been written, all the evidence that's been given.' He stared at his food for a moment. 'But, whichever way it goes, there's no getting away from the one fact that Raglan forgot. He was five hundred feet above the action and could see everything, while Lucan, like the rest of us on the plain, could see nothing. And he had no opportunity to get his instructions clear. The order said "immediate", "rapidly" and "to the front." He could hardly waste time sending a messenger all the way up to the Sapouné Ridge to clarify things. He had to rely on Nolan, and Nolan directed him wrongly.'

'You know,' Souto paused, deep in contemplation for a moment, 'I suspect now that Raglan's first thought after the charge was not to accuse Lucan, whom he knew to be clever and cautious, but to feel that Cardigan had made an ass of himself again, as he had so often done before. Which is why he attacked him first, and it was only when Cardigan proved his innocence that he turned on Lucan. In the end, too, I think that Raglan knew that *he* – Raglan – was to blame. After all, it's a well-known maxim that if things go wrong you lay about you right and left to convince everybody it's not your fault. Perhaps that's why he went for Cardigan and Lucan in the first place – and in a way that was completely out of character.'

There was another long silence between the two men that seemed like an oasis among the clatter of dishes and the cries of white-aproned waiters. For a while they stared at their plates, then Morden looked up.

'What will happen, sir?' he asked.

Souto gestured. 'Who knows? Of one thing I am certain. The army will not have enjoyed having its dirty washing done in public. If it finds Lucan not guilty despite his un-pleasantness, and Raglan, despite his saintliness, to have been a failure, it will not be entirely because it's convinced, but because it doesn't like the politicians it claims always let it down and it will use it as a stick to beat those who ran the war.'

'Will Lucan win?'

Souto nodded. 'Without a doubt,' he said. 'In fact, I doubt if they'll even bother to question him. Quirk backing out made that certain. To say the blunder was caused by the quarrel between him and Cardigan is nonsense because for once they appear to have put their dislike for each other aside and there was no dispute. In fact, they seem to have been the only two people out of everybody who was in-volved who showed any degree of sense that day.' He smiled. 'And there's been a great change of heart since Lucan returned from the Crimea. Once he was blamed for everything. Now he's seen as a badly-used man.'

'What's your view?'

Souto paused. 'The charge was *never* his fault,' he said firmly. 'But, you know, I've heard it said that an indifferent polite officer often gets more done than a good rude one. Perhaps if he'd been less abrasive he might have come out of the affair with a crown of glowing laurels.'

'But he'll be found not guilty?'

'I think so. He might even eventually get his baton.' Souto's smile came again. 'As a sort of compensation. But only when he's too old to be no longer a nuisance. Whatever happens, though, he'll never be employed again. He offends too many.'

Morden was silent for a long time, as though something were worrying him. Eventually he looked up. 'Could Nolan have done it deliberately?' he asked. 'To prove what everybody was beginning to demand that he prove – that he *was* an expert and that he really did know what he was talking about. People were growing awfully tired of his going on about the cavalry. They were beginning to laugh at him. Could what have happened have been the result of hurt pride? Could he have been trying to show he was right? Could he have deliberately directed the cavalry to the guns down the valley, certain they could capture them as he always said they could? And, as he spurred forward, could he have been urging them into the wild charge he believed was the proper way to do it? If it had come off, it would have meant a swift advance in rank. The man who was the cause of the cavalry driving the Russians off the field would have gone a long way?'

'Could he?' Souto smiled. 'I doubt it. Generals have a habit of claiming the laurels for themselves. Many a battle must have been won by some astute or courageous young officer, but I wager that officer would be quickly removed if he claimed *he* had won the victory.' Souto's smile came again. 'If it *had* come off, I think Nolan would have remained exactly where he was before, and Raglan, Lucan and Cardigan would have quarrelled over who had won the battle just as much as they did about who lost it.'

EPILOGUE

The verdict of the Lucan court martial is an assumption, of course, because, since there was no court martial, there could be no verdict. But some indication of what it might have been had there been one can be gained from what happened afterwards.

Souto was right. While Cardigan's glory faded, Lucan's slowly increased and he was eventually promoted to full general, and in 1869 became Colonel of the 1st Life Guards. In 1887 his position in the House of Lords had changed to that of a respected elder and on the occasion of Queen Victoria's Jubilee, he was created a field-marshal. He died, alert and active to the end, in 1888, and his coffin was borne on a gun carriage by the Chestnut Troop of the Royal Horse Artillery and escorted by a hundred non-commissioned officers and men of the Life Guards. Among the crowd who watched were many survivors who had ridden at Balaclava.

As for the others, Templeton was right about the Duke of Cambridge, who clung to the office of Commander-in-Chief for almost forty years. Many of the soldiers died during the Mutiny in India where they were sent. It was said that it was the heat of the sun on the silver plate in his skull that did for Morris. A few others, as was the custom for old soldiers in those days, died in poverty.

As for ex-Private Pennington, as he had always hoped, he became a famous actor who was called 'Gladstone's favourite tragedian.' Yet, to the end of his days, whenever he was introduced to distinguished members of his audiences, he always made less of his ability on the stage than of the fact that he had ridden with the Light Brigade on their desperate mile-and-a-half.

However, a few of the officers reached high rank and, since the cavalry contained a large number of men of education, some of the ordinary troopers were given commissions. One became Mayor of Wednesbury. And there were still enough of them alive in 1911 to provide a small parade at the coronation of George V.